Sir Francis C. Burnand

**Happy Thoughts**

Sir Francis C. Burnand

**Happy Thoughts**

ISBN/EAN: 9783337406615

Printed in Europe, USA, Canada, Australia, Japan

Cover: Foto ©Andreas Hilbeck / pixelio.de

More available books at **www.hansebooks.com**

# HAPPY THOUGHTS.

# Happy Thoughts

## By F. C. BURNAND

AUTHOR OF "VERY MUCH ABROAD," "RATHER AT SEA,"
"QUITE AT HOME," ETC.

WITH

Illustrations from "Punch."

LONDON

BRADBURY, AGNEW, & CO. LD., BOUVERIE STREET

1890

# CONTENTS.

# HAPPY THOUGHTS.

## CHAPTER I.

Life in the Country.

OW delightful it must be to live in the country. On such a day as this, 85° in the shade, one would have all the windows looking on to the lawn open during dinner, luncheon, and breakfast. Go out and throw bread to gold-fish in a pond. There must be gold-fish. In the hottest part of the day lie out on the grass with a book, or go to sleep *sub tegmine fagi.* Or pull oneself in a boat, very gently, to a shady cool nook, beneath the boughs of a drooping tree, and there lie down, read, and smoke the soothing pipe.

*Happy Thought.*—Croquet when it is cooler : or feed the gold-fish. The more I think of it, the more certain I am that no country-house is perfect without gold-fish. A visit to the farm, in the early morn, or in the evening. How sweet to have a favourite pig, or a goose, or geese, or a cow, a favourite cow, which would feed out of your hand, and lay eggs—I

B

mean, give milk every morning for breakfast.    What a charming picture !    Then how picturesque is the elegant swan upon the peaceful lake.    How cool appear the carp and the pike, and how lazily will even the little ducks waddle down to their accustomed pond.    And how interesting, *now*, to watch the gold-fish.    I have thought of it again, and conclude that there *must* be gold-fish. And at night, calm, serene, and peaceful.    The moon—the tranquil moon—sheds her gentle beams upon the scene.

[*Happy Thought.*—" Shedding a beam ; " try it in a poem.]

One can open one's bedroom window, and sniff the dying fragrancy of the honeysuckle still lingering on the scarce moving breeze.    Oh ! delightful thoughts ; on this the hottest day of June in London.    Yes ! to the country ! away !    To the gold-fish.

*Happy Thought.*—" An old Elizabethan House far away in the country to let, at a low rent, furnished, for the summer months. Pond, farm, &c."    *Pond !* and gold-fish ?

*A Decision.*—Mine, by all that's ancient and rustic, on this hottest day in June !    I take it that I shall like it.

*Happy Thought* for epigram, Like it, take it.

*Note.*—I am there.    All is ready for me.

And there *are* gold-fish in a small pond !
There is a cow : and a pig-stye with pigs.
And a farmyard with cocks and hens.
There are peacocks, too.

*Happy Thought.*—Farewell business, work, and hot days in London.

     *       *       *       *

*Another Happy Thought.*—I shall take down a fly-rod, and some biscuits for the gold-fish.    *   *   *   *    I am there.

*Note.*—As hot as it was in London.    Hotter ; 95° in the shade, that is, in what they *call* the shade.    All the windows open of course, looking on to the lawn.    Cooler in-doors than out, except when one has to jump up and throw books at wasps, which happens at intervals of five minutes, varied by every one—every one means my mother, my maiden aunt, her companion, Miss Jinsey, and a country friend—taking up poker, shovel, tongs, paper-knife, or anti-macassar against a hornet. Hot work. I thought there were no wasps in June. Country friend staying with us says, "Oh, ain't there!" and gives me particulars to the following effect :—

*Every wasp that flies about in the early summer is a Queen Wasp ; she is double the size of other Wasps, and has twice the sting.*

*Happy Thought.*—If we had two of the windows looking on the lawn closed, we might abate the nuisance.

*Note.*—In doing this, we shut in a Queen Wasp. It was knocked down with an anti-macassar, and is supposed to be either in that useful piece of crochet-work, or on the floor, crawling about. We are all sitting with our feet on the sofas or chairs, and the anti-macassar has been thrown out of window. Country friend rather thinks, by its size, that it was a hornet, and tells us that when he knew the Elizabethan House in old Soandso's time, it was "quite celebrated for hornets." I ask him why he hadn't mentioned this when I was taking the house, partly by his recommendation. He says, "O what's it matter? Who cares about a hornet?" I reply, "Yes, of course, that's true : but still they *are* nasty things," and he then gives me the following particulars :—

*At this time of the year every Hornet is a Queen Hornet.*
*They have treble the sting of an ordinary Hornet.*
*Three Hornets will kill a horse.*
*Hornets sting after they are dead.*
*One once killed a man,*

(name unknown), but not quite sure that it wasn't in this very place, *i.e.*, the grounds of the Elizabethan House. Here we have all the windows shut.

*Happy Thought.*—If your windows are shut you can always, in the country, lie down out of doors. On the grass, and read, and smoke. Of course this doesn't apply to my mother, my maiden aunt, and Miss Jinsey. Country friend and self place seats for them.

*Note.*—It is difficult to get into a comfortable position on the grass. One so easily becomes cramped. It is difficult, if there is the slightest breeze, to read a newspaper, or to keep a place in a book. You can't read lying on your back. If you lie on your left

B 2

side, you've pins and needles in your left arm; if on your right, in your right arm. Sleep is the only remedy; that you may do, on your back, if you can only get your head comfortably placed. A great point is gained when you determine that you *are* comfortable. A buzzing—I am disturbed by a wasp : settled down again. More wasps—no, hornet !—Queen hornet ! All rise to receive her : she is gone. We settle ourselves again. Bumble-bees, or Humble-bees, we now notice, are not afraid of coming quite close to your ears. Humble-bees are *supposed* not to sting. There are plenty of ants about : "Plenty," says our country friend, "regular good place for ants." He adds that these reddish-black ants are peculiar to this part of the country (meaning my Elizabethan House and grounds) and *do* bite like winking. We all get up ; it is a balance of comfort.

*Indoors.*—Wasps and hornets, if they can get in : shut windows and heat.

*Out-of-doors.*—Wasps, hornets, bumbles and humbles, ants, and many other curious insects, including odd flies with long bodies : but, fresh air.

*Happy Thought.*—The Lake—not the pond where the gold-fish are, but the lake. At this suggestion my aunt retires ; so does Miss Jinsey. My mother will remain where she is and watch us. It'll be delicious : once in the shade. How elegant and peaceful the white swans look as they sit basking and winking in the noon-day sun.

The swans are between me and the boat. I can't get at it without disturbing the Swans. I wish I had some bread to throw to them, or the biscuits for the gold-fish.

They hiss savagely on my approach. They do not move but hiss. I never knew this before. If they move at all, they seem to evince a disposition to run at one. Country friend says, "Oh, yes, savage fellows—Swans," and gives me these particulars :—

*A blow from a Swan's wing will break a man's leg.*

*A Swan once pulled a boy out of a boat, and held him under water till he was nearly drowned.*

*Swans are always vicious, unless they know you.*

*Even when they know you, they are uncertain-tempered.*

Hot work getting into the boat. Blazing sun. Row quickly to get into shade. Hotter than ever after rowing quickly. Some difficulty in getting underneath the trees. What strength there is in a small branch if it comes suddenly against you! I had no

"A Rat! A Rat!"—*Shakespeare.*

idea that it would knock one right back in the boat with one's head against the rudder. Country friend says, "Oh, didn't I know that?" and picks my hat out of the water.

*Happy Thought.*—This promises comfort. Now for a pipe: tobacco will keep off the little flies and insects. Unfortunately the fuzees have fallen into the water. A nuisance ; and we've left our books on the bank. Still, with the exception of the very small flies, which, I fancy, bite—("Bite !" my country friend would think they could bite, rather : they *do*, too)—we might be very comfortable.

*Another Happy Thought.*—The flies have left off. This is peaceful and delicious, and——

A splash ! What was it ? Country friend points out to me a great big rat close to the boat. Good heavens ! He shows me another on the bank. Should they jump into our boat ! Let us pull off at once. Where to ? Anywhere where there are no rats. Friend says it would be a difficult thing to find out that place on the lake. Then there are many rats here ? "Many !"—he informs me that "it," meaning the lake in the grounds of the Elizabethan House, "is celebrated for rats." Nothing I detest so much. We will row to shore.

*Note.*—In hot weather in the country it is difficult to know when to dine.

*Happy Thought.*—Dine in the Heat of the Day. Two o'clock. My aunt agrees ; so does Miss Jinsey. My mother is doubtful on the point.

*Note.*—Early dinner, sure to produce indigestion : and the windows must be closed on account of the wasps and hornets. And what are you to do afterwards ? I answer, feed the gold-fish. Friend says, " Pooh, bother the gold-fish."

*Another Happy Thought.*—Dine at four.

*Query by Every One.*—Then when are we to lunch ? Poser. But why not a biscuit, and then you can feed the gold-fish ?

*Happy Thought.*—Dine at six, no wasps then, and windows open.

*Objection* (by my aunt, seconded by Miss Jinsey).—But you lose the cool of the evening out-of-doors.

*Happy Thought.*—Split the difference, and say five. Then, what is one to do (is the objection by my mother) from two till five ? I don't know—feed the gold-fish. Five is settled.

## CHAPTER II.

IN THE COUNTRY—THOUGHTS ON FLIES—BATS—PET ANIMALS—ON GHOSTS—ON RATS—ON GEESE—GAME COCKS—THE FERRET.

"Tea out of doors."

**V**ERY *Happy Thought.* —We are still in our Elizabethan House. Everyone languid or irritable, or both, from the heat.

*Happy Thought at* 7.30 P.M.—We'll have tea out of doors. On a rustic table: sit on rustic chairs, made of twisted wood with knots in it. Theatrical friend from town says, "like the opening of an opera — chorus — happy Peasants." I like a fellow from town to enliven us. Tea soon gets cold out of doors. [*Mem.* Get some other sort of rustic chairs; all very well for ladies; no comfort for men in twisted wood with knots in it.] Lots of little creatures appear in the air: not gnats?

*Happy Thought.*—Let's stroll up that walk and smell the delicious Honeysuckle. * * * Curious! something's biting one's hands and neck. Country friend says, "Ah, then it'll be a fine day to-morrow; these little stinging flies always come out when it's going to be a fine day to-morrow." He gives me the following facts:—

*Small flies in the evening bite any one who's fresh to the country.*
*They quite disfigured one man once by biting him.*
*They are not poisonous.*

They are all about the honeysuckle and the bushes.

Noticed the bats for the first time. Country friend tells me "it" (the Elizabethan House and grounds) is famous for bats. You can catch 'em with a net. I say " Indeed, can you really?" and we go in-doors. Hate bats : friend gives me a few facts as to bats.

*Bats in some parts of the country will settle in your hair.* (N.B. Never go out without a cap at night.)

*Bats can bite ferociously when they like.* " They're nasty things," he adds, " to tackle." (N.B. Never tackle a bat.)

*Happy Thought Indoors.*—To-morrow visit the farm ; see the cow and the pigs. " How jolly it would be "—I say to my aunt, who agrees with me, substituting "pleasant" for "jolly," in which amended form Miss Jinsey expresses *her* opinion—"how jolly it would be to have a pet cow, and pet pigs, and pet ducks, and everything to feed out of your hand, and come up when you call." The ladies say, " Charming ! and a dear little pet lamb." Country friend says, " Dirty little beasts, pet lambs." Everybody says, " he's got no heart." I suggest that one might train the gold-fish. Friend says, " How?" I say, " Anyhow —with biscuit." The conversation turns on training animals generally, and we conclude that all it wants is "an eye." We then talk about Van Amburgh.

*Conclusion.*—Any animal can be trained by the eye.

*Happy Thought.*—Early to bed, and up with the lark. Charming old Elizabethan House with old passages and old oak. Conversation turns upon ghosts. No one believes in ghosts. Are there any here ? Country friend tells us about a haunted house in the neighbourhood. He'll show it us. [N.B. It's very stupid to talk about these sort of things, because it frightens the ladies.]

11.30.—Bed-time ; windows open ; no moon. The idea of believing in ghosts ! If one *did*, this is just the sort of place where they might come ; I like lots of light at night. There's something on the wall ; a shadow. I don't know what fear is, but my nerves are a little unstrung by the heat ; or, perhaps, as it has been ninety in the shade, my imagination is heated. No : *it's a bat !*

Let me see, a bat is a nasty thing to tackle. If I shut the windows he can't get out ; if I leave 'em open other bats may come in. There is another—no, a moth. Hate moths; I can't sleep with a bat in the room. I've heard they suck the breath of infants (or cats do that?).

*Happy Thought.*—Called in my country friend. I said, "Such fun! here's a bat." As if I enjoyed it.

*Another Happy Thought.*—I stand just outside the door to look in and direct him while he's catching the bat. Country friend says "he's a curious specimen : very rare :" I hope so, sincerely. Shut the windows : bed, \* \* \* Queer noises : scrambling and thumping. Not bats again : it must be in the room. Mice? hate mice. *It can't be rats!* \* \* \* There's no doubt about it, rats : detest rats. Suppose one should jump on my bed! Country friend, whom I ask next day, says, "Oh, didn't I know? 'It'" (the old Elizabethan House) "is almost eaten up with rats." He gives me the following facts :—

*Swarms of rats are in the wainscots.* "Good gracious!" from my mother.

*They can't come out.* General satisfaction.

*They do come out in the scullery.* Maiden aunt tells Miss Jinsey to ring the bell and order scullery-door to be kept shut.

*On the top of the cellar-steps they've been seen as large as rabbits.* (N.B. Avoid top of cellar-stairs.)

*They come in the winter into a house, stop for the spring and early summer, and go out again at harvest time.* (N.B. Wish it was harvest time.)

*Their bite is poisonous.*

*A few rats will kill a man.*

*Happy Thought.*—Fresh eggs for breakfast, early in the morning. Charming! Sleep interfered with by bats, rats, and moths, but a regular country breakfast is *the* thing to set one up. Fresh eggs! \* \* \* Very sorry, no eggs : footman says that under-gardener tells him the rats have sucked all the eggs and killed ten chickens.

*Happy Thought.*—Send for Ratcatcher at once. Friend and self say, "What fun! and have a rat hunt!" Country friend adds, "Take care they don't get up your trousers." Miss Jinsey makes some remark about "petticoats," but is stopped by my aunt.

*Happy Thought.*—I shall enjoy the sport. Anticipate good fun.

*Happy Thought, on the lawn, looking at the Gold-fish.*—How horribly hot it must be in London. Go and lounge over the peaceful farm. I never knew that pigs got savage and ran at one. Country friend says, "You ought never to bolt from a cow, or she's sure to run after you." I explain that I had no intention of bolting until she did run after me. Farm labourer says, "he had two minds about telling us the beast was vicious when he saw us gentlemen going in." What idiots farm labourers are : very hot running. Country friend gives me this fact about geese,

*Geese will bite your shins dreadfully if they get hold of you.*

It seems to me that the Peaceful Farm is full of savage animals. We go to the Hen-house : the fowls, at all events, won't hurt me. Country friend says, "He's not so sure of that," and gives me this fact :

*Game Cocks can't be depended on.*
*They'll fly at you, and peck your eyes as soon as look at you.*

The Ratcatcher has come. I shall see the Ratting from a window. * * * Ratcatcher has lost his ferret; he thinks it *must* have run into the house.

*Happy Thought.*—Have my bed-room door shut *at once*. My mother, my aunt, and Miss Jinsey have all locked themselves up in their bed-rooms until that "horrid man," the Ratcatcher, has gone.

The Ratcatcher manages to kill three rats, which I believe he brought with him, and charges us for the loss of his ferret.

For a week afterwards the ferret is always being expected to reappear. My aunt and Miss Jinsey look under all the chairs and sofas three times a day. My mother never ventures about alone.

*Happy Thought.*—Search my bed well every night. Awful thing if the ferret were hidden underneath the clothes. After ten days we are obliged to leave. Unhealthy to stop, ferret and rats having fought it out, and died together in the wainscot.

*Happy Thought.*—Took Elizabethan House by the week. Leave immediately. Wonder how next tenant will like it.

*Happy Thought.*—I have now hit upon a very happy thought.

## CHAPTER III.

COMMENCEMENT OF MY GREAT WORK — BY THE RIVER — THE
SOLITARY IN THE PUNT—BARGES—EARWIGS—THE RETREAT--
ON DIBBLING AND SNIGGLING.

The Solitary in the Punt.

**B**EING in need of quiet, in order to commence my great work on "Typical Developments," I have found a charming retreat on the banks of the Thames, somewhere about Twickenham, or Teddington, or Richmond, or Kingston, and all that part.

Capital fishing here. In punts, with a man, and worms: average sport, one tittlebat in ten hours.

*First Happy Day.*—Charming; perfect quiet. See a man in punt, fishing. Ask him how long he had been there? He says, "Three hours." Caught anything? "Nothing." He is quite cheerful. Full of happy thoughts, and commence my *Typical Developments.* In the evening catch an earwig; not a bit frightened of him. *The pincers in an earwig's tail don't bite.*

To bed early. Leave the man fishing; his man with the bait asleep. Been there all day? "Yes." Caught anything? "Nothing." Quite contented.

*Second Happy Day.*—Up early. Same man in punt, still fishing; new man with bait. Ask him how long he has been there? "All night." Caught anything? "Nothing." Not at all irritable. * * * Kill two earwigs in my bath. Sit in my parlour to write.

Before me is my little lawn : at the foot of the lawn runs the river.

9 A.M.—I commence my *Typical Developments*, and note the fact, keeping by me this journal of observation in case anything turns up. Something has turned up : an earwig. Distracting for a moment, but now defunct. All is peace. I walk down the lawn. Caught anything? "Nothing." His voice is, I fancy, getting weaker. I am meditating, and my soul is rising to sublime heights. * * * * A Barge is passing slowly, towed by horses against a strong stream, while the happy bargeman trudges cheerily along ; and other happy bargemen, with their wives and children, loll lazily on deck. (The fishing punt has suddenly disappeared.) Ah ! how easily may we float against the stream of life, if we are towed ! How sweet it is to——a Barge has stuck on the shallows.

*Scientific Note.*—How distinctly water conveys sound. I can hear every word that happy bargeman on the opposite shore says, as if I were at his elbow. He is using language of a fearful description to his horses. The other bargeman has lifted himself up (he was on his back kicking his legs in the air on deck) to remonstrate. His remonstrances are couched in still stronger language, and include the man and the beasts. Woman (his wife I should say) interferes with a view to peacemaking. Her soothing words are more forcible than those of the two men, and include them both with the beasts. The children have also joined in, and are abusing the bargeman (their father, as I gather) on shore. My gardener tells me they'll probably stick here till the tide turns. I ask him if it often happens? He tells me "Oh ! it's a great place for barges." My sister and two ladies in the drawing-room (also facing the lawn) have closed their windows. *Typical Developments* shall have a chapter on the "Ideal Barge-man." To write is impossible at present. A request has been forwarded to me from the drawing-room to the effect that I would step in and kill an earwig or two. I step in and kill five. Ladies in hysterics. The punt has reappeared : he only put in for more bait. Caught anything? "Nothing." Had a bite? "Once, I think." He is calm, but not in any way triumphant.

*Evening.*—Tide turned. Barge gone. They swore till the last moment. From my lawn I attempted to reason with them. I called them "my good men," and tried to cajole them. Their immediate reply was of an evasive character. I again attempted to reason with them. Out of their next reply I distinguished only one word which was not positively an oath. Even as it stood, apart from its context, it wasn't a nice word, and my negociations came to an end. Went back to my parlour and killed earwigs.

*Night.*—Man in punt still fishing. He informs me that he doesn't think this a very good place for sport. Caught anything? "Nothing." He is going somewhere else. I find that I can write at night. No noise. I discover for the first time that I've got a neighbour who looks at the Moon and Jupiter every night through a large telescope. He asks me would I like to step in and see Jupiter? * * * * I have stepped in and seen Jupiter (who gave us some difficulty in getting himself into a focus) until my head aches. He has a machine for stopping the earth's motion while we look at Jupiter. It is very convenient, as you can't get a good look at Jupiter while the earth is going round.

*Happy Thought.* — To call my astronomical acquaintance "Joshua." I do. He doesn't like it. No writing to-night. During my absence, five moths, attracted by the gas-light, and at least a hundred small green flies, have perished miserably on my MS. paper and books. * * Screams from the ladies' bed-room. Off. * * * * Maid servant up!!! Lights!! "Would I mind stepping in and killing an earwig?" Bed. I open my window and gaze on the placid stream. Why, there's a punt; and a man in it: fishing. He has returned. Caught anything? "Nothing." Good night. "Good night."

*Third Happy Day.*—Five earwigs in bath, drowned. Fine day for *Typical Developments.* Man and punt gone; at least I don't see them. Commenced Chapter 1st. * * * Dear me! Music on the water. A large barge with a pleasure party. They're danc-ing the *Lancers.* The gardener says, in reply to my question about the frequent recurrence of these merry-makings, "Oh, yes, it's a great place for pleasure parties and moosic. They comes up

in summer about three or four at a time ; all a playin' of different
toons. Quite gay like. The *Maria Jane* brings up parties every
day with a band." The *Maria Jane* is the name of the pleasure
barge. Bah ! I will overcome this nervousness. I will abstract
myself from passing barges and music, and concentrate myself
upon—tiddledy tiddledy rum ti tum—that's the bowing figure in
the *Lancers*—hang the bowing figure !—Let me concentrate myself upon—with a tiddledy tiddledy rum ti tum. It's difficult to
remember the *Lancers*. The barge has passed. Now for *Typical
Developments.*—Message from my aunt, " Would I step in and kill
an earwig in the work-box ?" * * * A steamer ! I didn't know
steamers were allowed here. " Oh yes," the gardener says, " it's
a great place for steamers. They brings up school children for
feasts." They *do* with a vengeance ; the children are shouting
and holloaing, their masters and mistresses are issuing orders for
landing ; thank goodness, on the opposite bank. They've got a
band, too. " No," the gardener explains, " it's not *their* band I
hear, that belongs to the Benefit Societies' Club, as has just come
up in the other steamer behind." The *other* steamer ! They're
dancing the *Lancers*, too. I *must* concentrate myself ; let me see,
where was I ? *Typical Developments.* Chap. 1. Tiddledy tiddledy
rum ti tum, with my tiddledy tiddledy rum tum tum and
my tiddledy tiddledy, that's the bowing figure, now they're
bowing—and finish, yes, tiddledy tiddledy rum ti tum. The
*Lancers* is rather fun * * Good heavens ! I find myself
unconsciously practising steps and doing a figure. I *must* concentrate myself.

*Afternoon.*—Barges and swearing. Pleasure boat with band,
and party dancing *Lancers*, for the fourth time. Return of all
the boats, steamers and barges ; they stop opposite, out of a mistaken complimentary feeling on their part, and play (for a change)
the *Lancers*, Tiddledy tiddledy rum ti tum. Becoming a little
wild, I dance by myself on the lawn. The maid comes out.
"Would I step in and kill an earwig ?" With pleasure—bowing
figure—and my tiddledy iddledy rum ti tum.

*Night.*—The turmoil has all passed. I walk down the lawn and
gaze on the calmly flowing river. Is it possible ? There is the
punt and the man, fishing. He'd been a little higher up. Caught

anything? "Nothing." Gardener informs me that people often come out for a week's fishing. I suppose he's come out for a week's fishing. Neighbour over the hedge asks me, "Would I like to have a look at Jupiter?" I say I won't trouble him. He says no trouble, just get the focus, stop the earth's motion, and there you are. He *does* get the focus, stops the earth's motion with his instrument, and, consequently, there I am. I leave my *Typical Developments*, Chap. 1. * * * Looking through the telescope makes one's head ache. We *did* have some brandy-and-water. Shan't stop up so late again. Cocks begin to crow here at midnight. It's quite light at midnight. I can't concentrate myself like the man in the punt. Caught anything? "Nothing." Good night. "Good night."

*Fourth and Fifth Happy Days.—Typical Developments*, Chap. 1. Man in punt disappeared. *Lancers*, tiddledy iddledy rum ti tum from 11 A.M. till 2 P.M. School feasts 2 till 5. Earwigs to be killed every other half hour. Cheering from Odd Fellows and Mutual Benevolent Societies. Barges at all hours and strong language. Festive people on opposite shore howling and fighting up till past midnight. Gardener says, "Oh! yes, it's a great place for all that sort of thing." Disturbed in the evening by Jupiter, Saturn, and the Moon, which have got something remarkable the matter with them. Accounted for, perhaps, by the machine for checking the earth's motion being a little out of order.

*Happy Thought.*—I have found a more charming "Retreat" on the banks of the Thames, *i.e.*, to retreat altogether. Have heard of an old Feudal Castle to be let. Shall go there. Shan't take my mother, nor my aunt, and, of course, not Miss Jinsey.

*Happy Thought.*—To be alone. Moat and remote; put that into *Typical Developments*, Chap. 1. We have packed up everything. I open my note-book of memoranda to see if I've left anything behind. I walk down the lawn to see if I've left anything behind there. Yes! there he is. The man in the punt, still fishing. He says he's been a little lower down. Any sport? "None." Caught anything here? "Nothing." Good bye. "Good bye." And so I go away and leave *him* behind.

Surprising! I couldn't get that man in a punt out of my

head, so I found in my note-book a few mems about fishing. It is there recorded as a—

*Happy Thought.*—That I would stop at a small house near a running stream for a few days, on my road to the Feudal Castle, which is, I hear, to let. There is a meadow between my lodging and the river. It is a fishing village, and the natives generally wear high boots, so as to be ready to go into the water in pursuit of their favourite amusement and business at any hour. I believe they sleep in their boots.

*First Morning, after breakfast.*—Put on my landlord's big boots and walk in the meadow. Man in a small boat fishing; ask him civilly what he's doing. He answers, without taking his eye off his hook, and being disturbed, he answers gruffly, " Dibbling for chub."

I watch him dibbling. Dibbling appears to consist in sitting still in a boat and holding a rod with the line not touching the water. A fish to be caught by dibbling must be a fool, as he has to come four inches nearly out of the water in order to get at the bait. Luxurious fish they must be too ! epicures of fish, for the bait is a bumble, or humble, bee. The moral effect on a Dibbler is to make him uncommonly sulky. All the villagers dibble, and are all more or less sulky.

*End of First Hour of watching the man dibbling for chub.*— Man never spoke ; no fish. He is still dibbling.

*End of Second Hour.*—I have been watching him ; one chub came to the surface. He wasn't to be dibbled ; man still dibbling.

*End of Third Hour.*—I fancy I've been asleep ; the man faded away from me gradually. I am awake, and he is still dibbling for chub.

*End of Fourth Hour.*—I begin to feel hungry. I ask him if he's going to leave off for luncheon ; he shakes his head once and goes on dibbling. Much dibbling would soon fill Hanwell.

*Fifth Hour.*—I have had luncheon and sherry ; I come down the meadow in the landlord's boots. Man still dibbling; no chub. I think I will amuse him with a joke, which I have prepared at luncheon. I say, jocosely, " What the *dibble* are you doing ? " He answers, without taking his eye away from his line,

" I'll punch your 'ed, if you ain't quiet." I try to explain that it was only a joke, and beg him not to be angry. He says, " I'll let you know if I'm angry or not ;" but he goes on dibbling, and I say no more.

*Eighth Hour.*—I have been asleep again ; it is getting damp. Man still dibbling. I ask him politely if there is any chance of catching a chub to-day. He says, "Not while you sit there chattering." Whereupon I rise (which is more than the fish do) and wish him a very good night. At ten o'clock I notice him in the clear moonlight still dibbling. Up and down the stream there are dibblers. To-morrow I shall dibble.

*To-morrow.*—I am divided between two suggestions. A man interested in me as far as letting his boat out goes, says, "Go out a dibbling for chub ?" The landlord, disinterested, says, "Sniggle." I ask, "Sniggle for chub ?" He pities me, and answers, "No. sniggle for eels." So I am divided ; dibbling for chub, or sniggling for eels : that is the question. The man with a boat settles it, like a Solomon. "Dibble," says he, "by day : sniggle," says he, "by night." That's his notion of life. It gives me an idea for a song. The fisherman's chant :—

> Oh ! the Fisherman is a happy wight !
> He dibbles by day, and he sniggles by night.
> He trolls for fish, and he trolls his lay—
> He sniggles by night, and he dibbles by day.
>> Oh, who so merry as he !
>> On the river or the sea !
>>> Sniggling
>>> Wriggling
>> Eels, and higgling
>> Over the price
>> Of a nice
>>> Slice
>> Of fish, twice
>> As much as it ought to be.

Let me request Sir Arthur Sullivan to put a little old English music to this, and if he'll bring a piano on board the gallant punt, I'll sing it for him, anywhere he likes to mention, on the river Thames.

Oh ! the Fisherman is a happy man ;
He dibbles and sniggles, and fills his can !
With a sharpen'd hook and a sharper eye,
He sniggles and dibbles for what comes by.
    Oh, who so merry as he !
    On the river or the sea !
      Dibbling
      Nibbling
    Chub, and quibbling
    Over the price
    Of a nice
      Slice
    Of fish, twice
    As much as it ought to be.

They tell me chub are good eating, when caught by dibbling.
The village children are all fed upon it ; in fact, I guessed as
much, from noting their chubby faces. (N.B. Nobody, here, sees
a joke. I try some jokes on the landlord. I tried the song on
the landlord ; he liked it very much, and demanded it three times.
N.B. I've since found out that he's a trifle deaf in *one* ear, and the
other has got no notion of tune. He was under the impression
that I had been singing *God Save the Queen.*)

*Third Day.*—In bed : having been out all yesterday dibbling,
and all night sniggling. Caught nothing, except (the landlord
knows this joke and always laughs at it) a violent cold. I have
no books, and no papers. I shall compose my epitaph :—

    " *Here lies a Sniggler and a Dibbler.*
    *Hooked it at last.*"

Then a few lines on a Shaksperian model might come in—

    To sniggle or to dibble, that's the question !
    Whether to bait a hook with worm or bumble,
    Or take up arms of any sea, some trouble
    To fish, and then home send 'em. To fly—to whip—
    To moor and tie my boat up by the end
    To any wooden post, or natural rock
    We may be near to, on a Preservation
    Devoutly to be fished. To fly—to whip—
    To whip ! perchance two bream !—and there's the chub !

The Doctor has just come in to say my head must be kept cool. He allows me to write this note, and then I must take a soporific. Farewell, a long farewell, to all my dibbling and sniggling! Good night.

*Postscriptum.*—I re-open my dairy (that's rather funny, because I mean "diary") to say that I've been able to go out in the garden in a Bath chair. I asked what I could do to amuse myself for an hour in the Bath chair. The landlord said "Dabble for trout." What extraordinary lives these people lead! The Boots was out all last night sniggling. Whether he was successful or not, I do not know, as he was discharged on his return.

*Happy Thought.*—What would a Boots go out sniggling with? Boot-hooks. Doctor says my head must be kept cool.

## CHAPTER IV.

At the Station.

APPY THOUGHT.— To take that old Feudal Castle, which is to be let for one month, to see how I like it. I have written about it, and the answer is " two months with the shooting." I may certainly note it down as a happy thought that I have agreed to the terms, including the shooting. The next thing is a gun. I must ask what sort of guns are used now. That'll do in a week or two; I think I'll get a Whitworth or a Needle.

*Happy Thought.*—To pack up at once and leave the dibbling and sniggling country. * * [Besides my portmanteaus I carry a rug, an umbrella, a fishing-rod, a stick, a great coat, and a writing-case.] * * Having done so, I am overtaken, on my road, by the discharged Boots with a Telegram, (I find I had forgotten to tip the Boots), to say that the present family are going to stop in the Feudal Castle for a fortnight longer ; so I must defer my tenancy. I don't think I can return and dibble. A happy thought just at this time occurs to a friend, whom I meet at the Popham Road Station. He says, "Come down with me to Boodels," the name of his little place in the country, "and we'll have some fun." I reply, "With pleasure, what fun ?" He answers, "Oh, lots of things : drag the pond." I see that he is enthusiastic upon the subject, so I rub my hands, clap them together, and cry, "Capital

—the very thing : nothing I should enjoy more—by all means, drag the pond." We will be off by this train. My friend, who appears much troubled at the loss of a watch-key, here asks " What's the *exact* time ?" I put down my rod, my umbrella, rug, great-coat, and writing-case, unbutton my frock-coat, and tell him " 2·15." Just as I'm doing this he sees the station clock, and begs pardon for having troubled me. I say, " Oh, no matter," and button up my frock-coat again.

\*   \*   \*   \*   \*   \*

(N.B. As I find that at the end of a day it is difficult to keep my diary of " Happy Thoughts " satisfactorily, I now take down jottings as I go along. My friends think that I am collecting materials for my great work on " Typical Developments," which I commenced in Twickenhamshire. I smile, and say " Ah !")

Meet Old Merrival, whom I haven't seen for ever so long Merrival says, " Hallo ! *you* here !"—as if, in the ordinary course of things, he had expected to meet somebody else. I answer candidly, though without much point, " Yes, here I am !" He says, " Well, and how have you been this long time ?"—by which he means an interval of ten years. I give him a condensed report, and reply, " Oh pretty well, thanks !" and ask him how *he's* been, in a tone which might convey the notion that I shouldn't be surprised at hearing that he had had the measles, scarlet fever, hooping-cough, chicken-pox, and a series of minor illnesses. He answers carelessly, looking out of the window, " Oh, much the same as ever ; " and I haven't an idea what he means. After a pause, during which Old Merrival regards with curiosity my friend from Boodels, who is fast asleep, with his leg over the arm of the seat, looking like the letter " V " in a quaint vignette, I hit upon a

*Happy Thought.*—I ask after his brother Tommy, who went into the Army.

My friend says, " Haven't you heard ?" I reply " No," pleasantly, expecting to find Tommy made a Lieutenant-General. It turns out that the mention of Tommy is unpleasant : he has not been heard of since he went out to hunt alligators in a bush. I wish I'd not been so confoundedly inquisitive. A damp has fallen on our spirits.

Old Merrival presently attempts a change in the conversation by inquiring where I'm going. I tell him "Boodels." He says, "Oh! where they had the fever so bad at the beginning of the year." I inform him that "I don't think *that's* Boodels." He says, "Oh, I'm wrong. Boodels is where all those burglaries took place. By the way," he adds, musingly, "they've never caught the fellows." I pretend to attribute no importance to the news, but I don't like it. I tell him, in order to show him that Boodels is not entirely given up to burglary, that "we're going to have some fun there." He says as I did, "What fun?" I reply, as if that *was* something like a joke, "Drag the pond." He doesn't seem to take much account of this, and rather snubs my notion of pleasure by remarking, inquiringly, "Slightly slow work, isn't it?" I reply, sticking up for it, "Oh, no! capital fun." The train stops at Hincham, and he gets out. He says, from the platform, "Very glad to have seen you again," I return, "so am I him." He adds, as a happy thought, just as the train is moving, "If you're coming by this way at any time, look us up, will you?" I answer that I'll be *sure* to do so, and wonder how he'd like me to look him up at 1 A.M. He nods, and adds, "Don't forget!" I say (with my head out of the window), "I won't." He turns away, and shows his ticket to the station-master, with whom I see him, the next second, in conversation, and then we leave each other for, perhaps, another ten years. This idea tending to melancholy, I shake off the remembrance of Merrival, and begin to doze. Hereupon, my friend Boodels wakes up, and says, "Hallo! where are we, eh?" being under the impression that we've passed the station. He informs me that he has been asleep. He wants now to know the *exact* time. I rouse myself with much trouble, and tell him, adding, that I am now going to follow his example, and doze. He says, "You can't; we're just there." Whereupon I shake myself, fold up my rug, exchange my travelling cap for my hat, take down with considerable difficulty my umbrella, stick, and fishing-rod, from the net above, strap up my writing-case, stuff my newspapers inconveniently into my great-coat pocket—

*Happy Thought.*—I must learn the art of folding a newspaper into a portable form——

—button up my frock-coat, and, having forgotten what time I said it was just now, unbutton it to look at my watch, re-button

it, place my writing-case, umbrella, fishing-rod, and so forth, on
the seat, in order to put on my gloves, take all the newspapers out
of my great-coat pockets, with a view to finding my gloves, which,
however, are in the breast-pocket of my frock-coat, where I had
put them in mistake for my pocket-handkerchief, button my coat
for the third time, put on my gloves, take my writing-case and
rug, fishing-rod, and umbrella, in my hands again, my great-coat

Setting the exact time at Boodels.

over my arm, and sit as if meditating a sudden spring out of the
carriage-window on the first opportunity, when Boodels (of
Boodels) who has suddenly found his watch-key, wants to know
"the *exact* time." I pretend to guess it. He says, "No! *do* look,
as I want to set my watch." I lay down, for the third time, my
rod, umbrella, stick, writing-case, rug, and great-coat, and
unbutton my frock-coat, also for the third time, take out my

watch, and tell him "3·30," with perhaps a little irritability of manner. He doesn't say "Thank you!" but sets to work winding up his watch. By the time I have my umbrella, great-coat, rod, writing-case, rug, and stick in my hands, and on my arms, for the fourth time (it seems the fiftieth), he inquires, "Did I say 3·30 or 3.36?" I reply, "3·30; but that *now* it may be 3·35." He puts his watch to his ear, looks at it, appears satisfied, and pockets it. The train stops opposite a small platform. Low, flat country all round. "Boodels?" I ask. No; it's where they take the tickets.

Take the tickets? Oh, that entails laying down my umbrella, stick, writing-case, fishing-rod, and rug for the fifth time, unbuttoning my coat, and feeling for the ticket. Ultimately, after much anxiety, I find it, with my latch-key, which appear, both together, to have made a hole for themselves in my waistcoat pocket, and gone on a burrowing excursion into the lining. Thank goodness, I get rid of the ticket at last. Not at all: the man only snips it with a pair of champagne-wire clippers, and goes on. It appears that we are half-an-hour from Boodels. I won't put my ticket into my waistcoat pocket again, because of the nuisance of unbuttoning, &c. The question is, for such a short time, is it worth while to undo one's rug, exchange hat for travelling cap, take off one's gloves, unbutton one's coat for the sixth time, and be comfortable? I get as far as taking off my gloves, when my friend says, "It's no good doing that, we're just there." So it is. We are before our time. Boodels at last; and what the deuce I've done with my ticket, since it was snipped, I'm hanged if I know. Friend says, "You put it into your waistcoat pocket again." I am positive I did not. I unbutton my coat for the seventh time and don't find it. My friend is more positive than ever that it's in my waistcoat pocket. I unbutton again for the eighth time, and find it with my watch. How it got there I don't know, as I assure the guard and my friend, "I *never* by *any chance* put a ticket in my watch-pocket."

*Happy Thought.*—To have a separate pocket made for tickets. But where?

*Happy Thought.*—To have separate pockets made for everything.

*Happy Thought.*—That here we are at Boodels. His groom not
here. He wants to know the *exact* time. I refer him (being
buttoned up myself) to his own watch. He says, " It's stopped
again, he can't make it out." I have just put down my fishing-
rod, umbrella, writing-case, and rug, on the platform, and am

I give him the exact time.

unbuttoning my coat, when friend says, " Oh, don't bother, here's
the station-master will tell us," who does so, and I button up
my coat for the eighth time.

The groom arrives, with pony trap. The groom says while
we're driving that the pond can't be dragged before the day after

to-morrow. My friend is satisfied. So am I. So's the groom.
I say to the groom, affably, who is sitting with his arms folded
regarding the country superciliously, "It's good fun dragging a
pond, eh?" He answers shortly, "Yes, Sir," as if he thought I
was taking a liberty in addressing him.

*Happy Thought.*—Always ingratiate yourself with servants :
talk to grooms about horses, if you can. Here we are at Boodels.
It turns out on arriving at the House, that the time at Boodels is
different from either London time or railway time, and, therefore,
just as I am going upstairs to my room, my friend asks me for the
*exact* time. I place my rug, umbrella, coat, fishing-rod, stick, and
writing-case, on the hall table for the tenth and last time, and tell
him 4·30. Whereupon he goes off and sets the big clock in the
hall, the musical clock on the stairs, the little clock in the dining-
room, the time-pieces in the bed-rooms, while the butler disappears,
and is heard telling the cook all about it, when a whirling noise
comes from the pantry and the kitchen. The Groom goes off to
set the clock over the stable door; the Gardener walks down to
the sundial; the Footman returns looking at his own watch. I
follow him up-stairs to my room. Before he is out of the room I
find myself asking *him* the time, and referring to my own watch.
He should say (diffidently) that it's "*about* twenty minutes to
five." I correct him, and give him the *exact* time. He withdraws
thankfully, and I remain standing opposite the window, medita-
tively, with my watch in my hand, ready to give anyone the exact
time. * * * * Knock at the door. "Dinner is at half-past six
to-day." Very well, thank you. "Could I give Master the exact
time, as his watch 'ave stop again."

*Happy Thought.*—I send him the watch bodily; and calmly
commence dressing for my first dinner at Boodels.

## CHAPTER V.

CHEZ BOODELS OF BOODELS—LITERARY AND SCIENTIFIC EVENING—
FIRST APPEARANCE OF MILBURD—BOODELS' POETRY.

Boodels' Butler.

**D**INED with Boodels (of Boodels) alone. Nothing so conducive to Happy Thoughts as a good dinner. Had it. Boodels (to whom I have imparted the fact of my being engaged upon my grand work entitled *Typical Developments*) says, "Well, old boy, I'm glad to have an evening together. We'll have a regular literary and scientific conversation. Hey?" I say, "By all means!" and we adjourn, it being a little chilly outside, to the study. Boodels (of Boodels) is a bachelor, and enjoys literary ease. He says that I shall be perfectly quiet here, no one shall disturb me, and that I can get on with my work on Typical Whatshisnames (being corrected, he says yes, he means "Developments") as fast as I like. He adds, that there'll be lots of fun besides. I find he means dragging the pond. I say, out of compliment to him, that I am looking forward to this; and he seems pleased. He lights a cigar, and we then enjoy literary conversation—that is, I read to him my manuscript materials for my work. Just as I am commencing, he asks me for the *exact* time, as at nine o'clock he has a friend coming in. I tell him it's past that now, whereupon he says, "Perhaps he won't come : it's only Milburd, who lives in the next place ; he won't disturb us," and finishes by asking me to "go on, old fellow !" I go on, accordingly.

*Happy Thought.*—It's a rare thing to find any one possessed of the faculty of appreciation. Boodels has it. Boodels is a very good fellow. I don't know any one for whom I would do more than I would for Boodels. There are very few to whom I'd read my manuscript materials for *Typical Developments*—very few ; but I don't mind reading them to Boodels. It isn't every one to whom I'd say, "Now, my dear fellow, pray tell me any fault that strikes you : do." But I say it to Boodels, because Boodels is not a fool.

9H. 5M. P.M.—*Note.* I shall time myself in reading this first chapter. Now. "*Typical Developments*, Book I., Chap. 1. In the earliest——" Boodels stops me. I have asked him to stop me whenever anything strikes him. Something has struck him. "Why do I call it *Typical Developments ?*" Why ? Well, because,—in fact,—I explain, that opens up a large question. He will see, I inform him, as I go on. He says, "Oh, I only asked." I thank him for asking, and tell him that that's exactly what I want him to do. He replies, "Yes, he thought I liked that." I say, "Yes, I do." The lamp wants trimming, and Boodels rings for the butler. There is silence for a few moments, because one can't read aloud while a butler is trimming a lamp. The butler says, "he thinks that'll do now, Sir." Boodels says, "Yes, that'll do." I say, "Oh, yes, that'll do capitally" (N.B. Always be on good terms with the butler), and the butler having retired, I recommence. "*Typi*——"

*Happy Thought.*—Must time the reading. Let's see. 9·20 P.M. "*Typical Developments*, Book I., Chap. 1. In the earliest——" (correct this with pencil to "very earliest"). "In the very earliest——" Boodels pushes a cigar towards me without speaking. No, thank you, not while reading. "In the very earliest ——" I don't know : yes, I will just light a cigar. Let's see the *exact* time—9·27. Now we begin fairly.

"In the very earliest and darkest ages of our ancient earth——"

*Happy Thought.*—Stop to alter "ancient" to "old" with a pencil. Read it to Boodels. "Ages of our *old* earth." How does he like it ? He is dubious. If he doesn't like it, why not say so ? Well, he thinks he *doesn't* like it. "Ancient"'s better ? I ask. On the whole, yes, he thinks, "ancient"'s better.

*Happy Thought.*—Alter "old" to "ancient" with a pencil. I

respect Boodels because he speaks his mind; if he doesn't like a thing he says so. "Won't I," he asks, "have a pen and ink?" No, thanks! I'd better. Well, then, I will. If I'd known that this would have entailed ringing for the butler, who had to fill the ink-stand and find a pen, I'd have been perfectly satisfied as I was with the pencil.

"Now, then, old fellow, fire away!" says Boodels, who is lighting another cigar. Mine is out. "Better light it," says Boodels, "it's more sociable." Well, then, I will. No matches. Bell. Butler: who explains that he told James, the footman, to see that the box was filled every Thursday. Bell. Footman: corroborates butler, but says, "Anne must have taken them away by mistake when she cleared." Explanation satisfactory. Matches are produced. Butler remains (officiously—who the deuce wants to have his cigar lighted by a butler?) to light the cigars. Butler leaves us. "Fine weeds these, hey?" says Boodels. They are. "Fire away, old boy, will you?" says Boodels, as if *I'd* been making the interruptions.

*Exact* time, 9·50. Boodels doesn't think Milburd will drop in at this time. "However, if he does," he explains again, "he needn't disturb *us*." He *needn't*, but it's very probable that, if he comes, he will. "Fire away, old fellow! it's getting late."

9·57.—I am firing away. "In the very earliest and darkest ages of our ancient earth, before even the Grand Primæval forests ——" Boodels interrupts me, and says that comes from Long-fellow. I protest. He says, "No, no, you're right: I was thinking of something else. Go on." I go on—— "the Grand Primæval forests could boast the promise of an incipient bud——" Boodels (who is a little too captious sometimes) wants to know "what I mean by 'forests boast the promise?' Why 'boast?'" I tell him he'll see as we go on. He returns, "All right: fire away!"

I shirk "boast," and continue—— "an incipient bud, there existed in the inexhaustible self-inexhausting Possible, innumerable types——" Here Boodels suggests what a capital idea it would be for me to give a Public Reading. Safe to do. Take enormously.

*Happy Thought.*—To give a Public Reading. Of what? I can't help asking, though. "Wouldn't it, p'raps, be a little slow?" Boodels, on consideration, says, "Yes, it might be, without a piano; but, of course, I'd have a piano; and a panorama; or, he's got it,

wigs!" "Wigs," he thinks, would make the thing go first-rate.
"I might, he fancies, give it here, in the large room at the inn,
and see how it went." I object, "Oh, no, that wouldn't do."
Boodels is serious. "He can't see—why not?" Well, because——.
"Well, never mind; fire away, old boy." I fire away. *Exact*
time, 10.15. "—hausting Possible, innumerable types." I've
got it. "—innumerable types, of which the first generating
ideas having a bearing upon——" Here Milburd drops in. With
an eyeglass and a pipe. He's afraid he disturbs us. "Not in the
least," from Boodels. "Oh no, not at all; not the slightest," from
*me*. What'll he take? Well, nothing, thank you; he's only just
dined. "Tea?" Are we going to have tea? "Always have tea
now," says Boodels. "You'll have tea" (to *me*). Of course, just
the thing? "And we'll read afterwards, eh." Bell. Butler.
Orders. Boodels explains to Milburd that I was reading my work
on "Typical Developments" to him. Milburd says, "O yes, very
nice. Yes," as if it was jam, and goes on to observe that "he'd
only come round to know about dragging the pond." Bell. Butler.
Butler uncertain as to to-morrow's arrangements. Footman with
tea. Difficulties with window-shutters between foomant and
butler. Complicated by the assistance of Boodels. Further complications arising from Milburd "lending a hand." Departure of
butler and footman. We sit down. Milburd's afraid he's disturbed us; would I go on with the "*Biblical Elephants.*" (This
fellow's a fool. Biblical elephants! Idiot.) I correct him. He
laughs stupidly, and says it would have been funny if it had been
elephants. Boodels says, "Yes, it would." (N.B. I am astonished
at Boodels.) I remark, that, I fear my paper won't much interest
him (meaning the man with eyeglass, Milburd). He replies,
"Oh, yes, it will. Jolly. He likes being read to like winking."
He seems a hearty fellow, after all. Shall I begin where I left off?
or from the beginning? Milburd replies, "Let's have all we can
for the money; the beginning." Very well. "In the very
earliest and darkest ages of"——. Milburd begs my pardon one
moment. Has Boodels heard that the niggers are at the Inn to-
morrow, the Christy's, or something, with an entertainment. He
tells us the word "darkest" in my MS. had put it into his head.
He begs pardon, will I go on, as he must be off soon. "—ages of
our ancient earth, before even——" Butler, without being called,

with footman to clear away. Then footman alone with the
chamber candles.

Eleven o'clock. "*Not* eleven?" says Milburd. Boodels had no

The Appeal to the Hall Clock.

idea it was so late. "Past eleven, Sir," observes the butler.
Boodels refers to me for the *exact* time. I say "11·10." Milburd,
through his eyeglass, "makes it," he says, "11·15." The footman,
at the door, appeals to the hall clock, which 'as struck just as he

came in. We all go to the hall. Milburd says, "Ah, he makes it
11·17." We all make it our own time, and Milburd says he 'sposes
he'll hear in the morning about dragging the pond. P'raps he'll
drop in. Not into the pond. "Ha! ha!" (Hate a fellow who
laughs at his own jokes.) Good night! good night! "Nuisance
to be interrupted," says Boodels, going up-stairs. "I'm very much
interested in it. Good night!"

*Happy Thought.*—I'll go to my room, and read it over to myself
with a view to corrections. Now     *     *     *     *

11·35.—A knock at my door. Boodels in a dressing-gown.
"Come to hear some more *Typical Developments?*" I ask, smiling.
No. With some diffidence he produces a manuscript, and tells me
he wants my opinion on a little thing of his own—a—in fact—
poem, which he thinks of sending to the *Piccadillytanty Magazine.*
Of course, I shall be delighted. Didn't know he wrote? "Oh, yes,
often." It isn't long, I suppose? "Oh no—merely thrown off."

12.—Middle of his reading. (N.B. I never *can* follow poetry
when I hear it read to me for the first time.)

12·15.—Still reading. (*Note.* That last line rather pretty.)
Still reading. I've lost the thread.

12·45.—Still reading. I've asked him "to read those last few
lines over again," in order to show that I am interested.

1 A.M.—Still reading. He is my host.

1·20.—Still reading. I say something feebly about that's not
being quite so good as the last. I make this note, too. I don't
know what I'm saying.

2.—I think he's begun another. I don't recollect him finishing
the other.

3.—He says reproachfully, "Why, you're asleep!" I reply,
"No, no! merely just closing my eyes." He wants to know which
I like the best. It appears he's read *ten* of his little compositions.
I say, "I don't quite know; I think the third's the best," and get
into bed. He observes, "Ah, you can't judge all at once; you
must hear them again. Good night, old boy!" And the *exact*
time is 3.20. Oh, my head!

## CHAPTER VI.

STILL CHEZ BOODELS—THE DOGS—PROCEEDING WITH TYPICAL
DEVELOPMENTS—ON INDISTINCT NOTES.

Boodels' idea of Fun.

T BOODELS. *The morning after the literary conversation already recorded.* Second day at Boodels. 6·30 A.M. *exact* time.—It's wonderful to me how Boodels (of Boodels) manages to get up at half-past six in the morning, after going to bed at 3·20. He *does* do it, with a horn, too, which he comes to my bedside and blows (*his* idea of hearty fun!) and with dogs, which he brings into one's room. I didn't see the animals last night; now I do. I don't like them—at least, in my bedroom. There's one Skye, a black-and-tan, a pug, and an undecided terrier. He explains that two of 'em always sleep in his room, and he then makes them jump on my bed.

*Happy Thought.*—Always lock your bedroom door, on account of sleep-walkers. I recollect a story of a monk stabbing a mattress, and somebody going mad afterwards, which shows how necessary it is to lock the door of your cell. At all events, it keeps out any one with a horn, and dogs.

6.35.—Boodels says (while dogs are scampering about), "Lovely morning, old boy," and pulls up my blinds. I like to find out it's a lovely morning for myself, and pull up my own blinds, or else I get a headache. The undecided terrier and the pug are growling at what they can see of me above the counterpane. I try (playfully, of course, because Boodels is my host) to kick them off, but they only snap at my toes. Boodels says, "They think they're

D

rats. Ah, they're as sensible as Christians, when they know you."
They don't know me, however, and go on taking my toes for rats.

6·35 to 6·45.—Boodels says, "We'll have a little air, eh?" and
opens both windows. He says, "There, that's better." I reply,
"Yes, that's better," and turn on my side, trying to imagine, by
shutting my eyes, that Boodels, with dogs, is not in the room.

*Happy Thought (made in my note-book suddenly under the clothes.
Always have note-book under my pillow, while collecting materials.)*
" Poodles " rhymes to " Boodels."

He then says, examining his horn, "This is how they get you
up in Switzerland;" and then he blows it, by way of illustration.
He says, "That wouldn't come in badly in an entertainment,
would it?" He suggests that it would come in capitally when I
give a public reading. At this point, the voice of James, the
footman, summons the dogs below. Rush—scamper—rush—
avalanche of dogs heard tumbling down-stairs.

Boodels says, "James always feeds 'em." I reply, sleepily,
"Very kind." Boodels says, "What?" I answer, rather louder,
that "it's very kind," and keep my eyes shut. Boodels won't
take a hint. He goes on—"Look at this horn! ain't it a rum
'un?" and I am obliged to open my eyes again. I ask him, feebly,
"where he got it?" Boodels says, "What?" (I begin to think
he's deaf.) And I have to repeat, "Where did you get it?" He
then begins a story about a fellow in Switzerland, who, &c., which
I lose about the middle, and am recalled to consciousness by his
shaking the pillow, and saying, "Hi! Hi! You're asleep!" I
explain, as if hurt by the insinuation, "No, only thinking."
Whereupon Boodels says, "Ought to *think* about getting up."
[This is what *he* calls being happy at a repartee. I find he rather
prides himself on this.] " Breakfast in half-an-hour?" I say,
"Yes, in half-an-hour," lazily. He is silent for a minute. I doze.
He then says, "What?" And I repeat, more lazily, to show him
I've no idea of getting up yet awhile, "Yes, in half-an-hour."
Boodels goes away. I doze. He reappears, to ask me some
question which begins, "Oh, do you think that——" But he
changes his mind, and says, "Ah, well, it doesn't matter!" adding,
in a tone of remonstrance, "You're not getting up!" and disappears again, leaving, as I afterwards found, the door open.

doze * * * * Something in my room. I look, inquiringly,
over the side of the bed. A bulldog, alone! White, with bandy
legs, a black muzzle, and showing his teeth: what a fancier, I

Something in my room . . . . . A Bull-dog, alone!

believe, would call a beauty. Don't know how to treat bulldogs.
Wish Boodels would shut the door when he goes out. I look at
the dog. The dog doesn't stir, but twitches his nostrils up and
down. I *never* saw a dog do that before. I say to myself, in order

to inspirit myself, " He can't make me out." I really don't like to get up while he's there.

*Happy Thought.*—To keep my eye on him, sternly. He keeps his eye more sternly on me. Failure.

*Happy Thought.*—To pat the bed-clothes and say " Poor old boy, then ! Did um, a poor old fellow, then ! a leetle mannikin, then ; a poo' little chappy man, then "—and other endearing expressions : his eye still on me unflinchingly. Then in a laudatory tone, " He was a fine dog then, he was ! " and encouragingly, " Old boy, then ! old fellow ! " His eye is mistrustful ; bull-dogs never growl when they're going to fly at you : he doesn't growl.

*Happy Thought.*—If you hit a bulldog over the front legs, he's done. If not, I suppose you're done. [This for my chapter, in *Typical Developments*, on " Nature's Defences."] If you wound a lion in his fore paw, he'll come up to you. On second thought, p'raps, he'd come up to you if you didn't. Bulldogs always spring at your throat. If in bed, you can avoid that by getting under the clothes.

*Happy Thought.*—One ought always to have a bell by the bed in case of robbers, and a pistol.

7.45. The dog has been here for a quarter of an hour and I can't get up. Willks, the butler, appears with my clothes and hot water. The dog welcomes him—so do I, gratefully. He says, " Got Grip up here with you, Sir ? He don't *h*offen make friends with strangers." I say, without explanation, " Fine dog, that," as if I'd had him brought to my room to be admired. Willks, the butler, informs me that " Master wouldn't take forty pounds for that dog, Sir ; " and I say, with surprise, " Wouldn't he ? " Butler repeats, " No, Sir, not forty pounds—he's been offered thirty." Whereupon, finding I've been on a wrong tack (N.B. Never be on a wrong tack with the butler), I observe, knowingly, as if I was making a bargain, " Ah, I should have thought about thirty—not more, though." Butler says, " Yes, Sir, Master could get that," and I answer positively, " Oh, yes, of course," which impresses the butler with the notion that I'd give it myself any day of the week. Think the butler likes me better after this : because if I'd give thirty pounds for a dog, what would I give to a Butler ?

I calculate upon getting ten minutes more in bed. " What's

the exact time?" The butler has a watch, and is ready. "8.10."
"*Exact?*" "Exact." "Then" (by way of a further delay)
"bring my clothes, please." They are here. "Oh, well," (last
attempt,) "my boots." Been here some time. Then I *must* get
up, that's all. That *is* all, and I get up. Breakfast. Milburd
has sent in to know if we drag the pond to-day. Boodels consults
Willks. "What does *he* say, eh?" Willks consults the footman,
and the footman says the gardener has been to see a man in the
village about it, and it can't be managed to-day. All the dogs are
at our breakfast, whining for bits, and scratching at my trousers
to attract attention.

*Happy Thought.*—Politic to feed strange dogs. Specially the
bulldog.

Terrier still vicious. Boodels says, "Oh, he'll soon know you."
I hope he will: I hate a dog who follows you, and *then* flies at
your legs. Boodels says, "Well, if we don't drag the pond, you'd
like to get on with your work, eh?" With *Typical Developments?*
Certainly: very much. Boodels is fond of literature, and says
that I can go to my room, and shan't be disturbed all day. I
observe, I should like to get to work at once. Just 9.30: capital
time. I show him that I can do a good deal to Chapter One
between 9.30 and 1. He is glad to hear it; and I tell him that
if he likes, I'll read what I've done to him in the evening. He
says "he should like that." I say "I won't, if it bores you." He
answers, "Bore me! I should be delighted!" I tell him I like
reading out aloud to an appreciative friend, because he can give
advice. He says, "Yes," rather quickly, and proposes one turn,
just as far as the pond, before I sit down to work. I think I
ought to get to work: but how far is the pond? "Not a hundred
yards, or so." Very well; just *one* turn, and then in. "With a
cigar?" Well, p'raps, a *very* mild cigar. We are at the garden door.

9.40.—Excellent time. Still at the garden door. The butler
and the footman have been looking for Boodels' little stick with a
notch in it. Boodels says "It's very extraordinary they *can't*
leave that stick alone." That being found (in Boodels' bed-room,
by the way), we want the matches. Butler thought they were in
the study. Footman (who is followed everywhere by all the dogs
while clearing away) recollects seeing them there last night.

Thinks Anne, the housemaid, must have taken them. Will ask her. Boodels says, "It's very extraordinary they *can't* leave the matches alone." Anne, from a distance—voice only heard—says "she ain't touched them ever since they were put back last night." Being appealed to before the footman and butler, I say, "I think I recollect them in the study,"—trying to corroborate everybody. Subsequently, Willks finds them in Boodels' bedroom.

10.—Now, then, for *one* turn, and then in to work hard at my MS. Willks asks Boodels, "Will he speak to the cook about dinner?" "Oh, yes," Boodels answers, "or you won't get any dinner." This to me, good-humouredly. I laugh (stupid joke, really), and say, "Well, make haste!" While he's away, I think of the first sentence I'll write when I get in, so as not to waste time. " In the very earliest and darkest ages of our ancient earth——" when Boodels comes back quickly, to know if I like turbot. Yes, I don't care. Because there's a man come with turbot. "One can't get," he explains, "fish regularly in the country." I answer, "Oh, anything." He says "I'd better come and see the turbot. He's no judge." I protest, "No more am I." But he thinks, at all events, I'd better see 'em. I assent, "Very well." He says, "What?" (He must be deaf sometimes.) I explain that I only said "Very well." We go to the turbot man. The cook is already there. We are joined by the butler. The footman looks in. Boodels asks *him* "if he thinks they're good." He replies, "Yes, Sir, looks very nice," and refers to the butler. The butler is a little uncertain at first, but decides for the turbot. I say, "Yes, I think very nice." The housemaid, passing by, stops for a moment with her broom, and says nothing. Cook feels them, and weighs them in her hand. We are all silent, meditating. Turbot settled on. When I get back to the hall, it is 10.45. Boodels says, "Now one turn to the pond, and back, just to freshen you up." I say, "Very well, and then I *must* get to work."

*Happy Thought.*—While walking I needn't waste time : make notes.

N.B. For the benefit of note-takers, I insert this. Always make your notes as full as possible ; if not, much trouble is caused. Thus, with my notes, when I came in—

*First Valuable Note in Book.*—"*Snails—why—who*"—What the dickens was it I thought about snails? Snails, let me see. Quarter of an hour lost over this : give it up. Try next valuable note—"*Ogygia—seen—Philip—but wasn't.*" Ogygia: what was it made me think of that? Philip! I recollect saying something about Philip, very good, to Boodels. He laughed : that was the thing, he said, ought to be in some magazine. Can't remember it. Try next valuable note : "*Floreate hues — Firkins — why not ?*" Can't make it out.

*Happy Thought.*—Always to make full notes in future.

## CHAPTER VII.

### ON POCKET BOOKS—PROGRESS OF TYPICAL DEVELOPMENTS—INTERRUPTIONS.

Come in !

HAPPY THOUGHT. —I find that, generally speaking, materials for the lives of remarkable men are found in their pocketbooks. Shall use pocket books in future. By the way, Milburd spoils Boodels. I regret it, but he does. Boodels used to sit for hours either listening to me reading my manuscripts to him, or enjoying my conversation. Now he doesn't, and has taken to personal remarks, which he calls repartee (hate it), and he and Milburd play at *Clown and Pantaloon* in the passage. It's really waste of life and talents. * * * Talking of that let me get to work.

11 o'clock, A.M.—By the *exact* time, which I have just given Boodels from the top of the stairs. Ought to have begun at nine. Good room for writing my *Typical Developments* in. View of a lawn. No noise. Boodels said I should be undisturbed, and quite alone. I like that in Boodels : he *is* considerate, when he sees you are in earnest. Delightful morning : just enough breeze to cause a sigh through the trees. N.B. Mustn't forget "breeze" and "trees" when I write a serenade. [Mentioned this idea, subsequently, on a lovely moonlight night, to Milburd, who immediately made a hideous grimace, and said, "Yah ! yah ! yah ! Ho !" with a sort of steam-engine whistle, "Niggar ! are you dar ? Bolly golly black man, boo !" and then he and Boodels both laughed. What at ? I pitied them. Boodels is really losing all sense of poetry. Milburd said that my saying "sere-nade" had suggested the Ethiopian Serenaders to him.]

\*       \*       \*       \*       \*       \*       \*

To work. *Typical Developments,* Book I., Volume I., Section 1, Chapter 1, Paragraph 1. "In the very earliest and darkest ages of our ancient earth, before even the Grand Primæval forests could boast the promise of an incipient bud, there existed in the inexhaustible self-inexhausting Possible, innumerable types, of which the first generating ideas having a bearing upon the forms of the Future, were at that moment in too embryotic a condition for beneficial production." Good. I think that's *good*—very good. I'm getting into the swing. My ideas flow. Paragraph, No. 2. Now. "Man at once possible and impossi——" Knock at the door : nuisance : pretend not to hear it. "And im-possi——" Knock. "Come in," I say, very pleasantly. It is Willks, the butler, diffidently. "Oh, Sir, Master thinks he left his cigar-case here." I haven't seen it, and I don't rise to look. The butler says, "No, he don't see it," begs pardon, and retires. I hear Boodels on the landing, saying, "It's very odd they *can't* leave my cigar-case alone !" The slightest interruption gets you out of the swing of ideas. I must try back again. "Man at once possible and——" Knock at the door. "Come in." Boodels put his head in, and sings, "Who's dat a knocking at de door ?" as if that placed the interruption in a more sociable point of view. It only reminds me of that idiot Milburd. I think Milburd copies

Boodels, or Boodels Milburd. Whichever it is, I hate an imitation. However, he explains that "he wouldn't disturb me
without knocking first," as if he'd have disturbed me more by not
knocking. I look as pleasant as possible ; "he wants my advice,"
he says. I am flattered ; though if he didn't come to me, his old
friend, for advice in a difficult matter, to whom should he go ?
Not Milburd. He commences by asking, "How are you getting
on, eh ?" and I answer, "Oh, pretty well," when Willks returns
with the cigar-case, which has, it appears, been (as usual) found
in Boodels' bedroom. As Boodels after this seems inclined to
wander, I bring him back to the point by asking "what he was
going to say to me ?" Boodels waits a minute, looking out of
window, and then says, "What ?" (He *is* getting deaf. If he
gets very deaf, I shall go away.) I repeat my question. He
replies, "Oh, yes ; look here. Do you think I ought to give the
man who came about dragging the pond a shilling, or not ?" I
try to interest myself in the question. "Well," I say, dubiously,
"What's he done ?" "Well," explains Boodels, "he hasn't
exactly done much ; but he's been up to the pond, and examined
it, and so forth, you know." I say, decisively, to show that I'm a
man of business, "Oh, yes, give him a shilling," and take up my
pen again, by way of a hint to Boodels. "It's rather too much
to give him, eh, for merely looking at a pond ?" objects Boodels.
I return, settling to write again, "Oh, no !" as if I generally gave
double that sum. "What ?" says Boodels. (He *must* be deaf.)
I explain that I only said, "Oh, no." "'Oh, no !' What ?" he
asks, rather testily. I think he's in a nasty temper : you never
know a man well till you stay with him.

*Happy Thought* that. I lay down my pen. "Well," I explain,
mildly, because it's no use having a row with Boodels about this confounded pond, " I mean if the man has come to—to— or if he merely
—why—that is, if the fellow——" I own I am wandering. Boodels
notices it, and says, with some tinge of annoyance in his tone, " I
came to ask your advice ; I really thought you might have attended
to me for one minute. You can't be so busy as all that." I feel
hurt. Some people are easily moved to tears. A little more,
and I should be moved to tears. As he is going out of the door
(he's hurt, too), he turns back, somewhat mollified, and asks me,

"I say, if I give him a shilling, to-morrow, when he comes with the net, it will do, eh ? "   I say enthusiastically, "Yes, that'll do—the very thing ! " which only elicits from Boodels a "What?" and I have to repeat, encouragingly, " Yes, that's the idea !   A shilling to-morrow—capital ! "   Boodels leaves me, and as he does so I feel a sort of pity for Boodels, I don't know why, and then become sensible of a beast of a fly on my neck.  Bother !  Missed him !  By the way, when you *do* miss a fly, can't you hurt your ear tremendously !  It's a buzzing fly.  I'll get a book, and smash him. * * *  I have got a book, but I haven't smashed him ; at least, I don't think so. * * * I hate uncertainty as to whether you've killed an insect, or not. They turn up afterwards with three legs and one wing—a sort of Chelsea pensioner of an insect—in uncomfortable places.  Think I had him there.  No.  Had the ink, though.  That'll be a nuisance. Ink always hangs about the side of your little finger, and smears itself all about your papers after you think it's all been dried up with care.  Bless it, inked my light trousers conspicuously.  Inked my wristband.  Inked everything within reach.  Brute of a fly ! * * *

Paragraph, No. 2.   "Man at once possible and impossible "— let me see—"man at once poss—" knock at the door; I wish I could abstract myself.   Knock again: appearance of Boodels' head.   "Only me, Sambo ! " says Boodels.  (What a fool Boodels is getting; but I laugh, because he's my host; I shouldn't if it was that donkey Milburd.   For my part I don't believe that black people go about grinning out "yah, yah," and asking each other iddles and " gibbing 'em up " like Boodels and Milburd do ; or else where are the Missionaries ?)

*Happy Thought* that.   Boodels comes in and says kindly and seriously, " I wouldn't disturb you, old boy, without first knocking, 'cos I know how busy you are."   I thank him, and say it doesn't matter.   " It's very near luncheon time," says Boodels.   Good heavens !  and I've only written six lines.   It appears that he came up to tell me this, and to ask if I'd like to lunch later, say at two. By all means.   " What ? " asks Boodels.  (How provoking it is to hear a fellow always saying "what?")   I explain that I only said, " Yes, by all means," and add inadvertently " as the old Duke of Cambridge used to say in Church."   " Oh, what's that ? " inquires Boodels, and I have to tell him the story, beginning "Oh, it was only that the old Duke once," &c., and it doesn't come out well after all ; besides, when I finish, it appears that Boodels knew it, only he thought it was something else.

*Happy Thought.*—To get up a few stories to tell well. Makes you popular in country houses. I find that everyone knows this one about the old Duke of Cambridge. Willks the butler announces Mr. Milburd and another gentleman down-stairs, just when Boodels had begun to recollect a story. Lucky, very. " Who is the other gentleman ? " He didn't catch the name, but Mr. Milburd has come to see about the pond. Boodels wondering " who the other fellow is," leaves, reminding me, " lunch at two." Thank goodness, for the next hour, if there is an hour,—no, three-quarters—I shall be at peace.

Let me get into the swing again : now then. Read over first few lines. * * * * Good. Now : Paragraph 2. "Man at once possible and impossible, was by his original destination—" Odd sound, now, as if people were creeping about on tip-toe outside my door. It is impossible to write when you've a nervous feeling of people hovering about you. Let me abstract myself. " Man at once possible—" Knock at the door. " Come in." A tall gentleman appears in a shooting suit, with very long light beard, reddish moustachios and a slouching white hat in his hand. With him, Boodels. I have never seen the tall gentleman before : I rise. Boodels apologises : " I told Captain," name I don't catch, " that we musn't disturb you, but he said as he's going away almost immediately " (by the way, he was here the whole afternoon and then missed his train) " he'd like to——" Here Boodels looks at the Captain, and that gentleman evidently feeling that his opportunity has been thrust upon him rather too suddenly, pulls at his moustache, and says with a short, jerky, nervous laugh, " Ya-ya, ya-as, ya, ya," not unlike that Milburd's boasted negro delineations, only that it's natural. " You-ar-don't r-remember me ? " No, I don't remember him. I try to, feeling that I ought to remember him. I smile and shake my head. I haven't even the faintest recollection. He is somewhat taken aback by this non-recognition ; I don't wonder at it, seeing that I hear, afterwards, how when he thought I was miles away, he had exclaimed on hearing my name, " Know him ! I should think so. Ah, I *should* like to see him again." He looks at me, almost imploringly. Boodels looks anyhow, and the tall man says, half defiantly, " My name's Cawker." His face bothered me, but his face *and* his name together have knocked me over.

Feeling that something hearty is expected of me, I say, radiantly, " Oh, of course, Cawker! How are you?" In fact, I am very nearly overdoing it upon the spot, and calling him Old

"You-ar-dun't r-remember me?" said the Captain.

Cawker. We shake hands heartily, and I suppose, to myself, that, in the course of conversation, he'll let out where the dickens I've seen him before. Cawker laughs very nervously. " Ya-a-a—haven't-a-a—seen you far "—(he puts *a* for *o* very often, I notice, but this doesn't recall him to my memory)—"far an age." Then he laughs, and so does Boodels. Why? I answer, steadily, " No, not since——" and I leave him to fill up the blank, which he does, unsatisfactorily, with a laugh. There we stop. After a while, Captain Cawker, who has been staring at my papers, says cleverly, "Writing something, eh?" and laughs. I reply that I am writing something, "Yes." He answers, "Ah, ya-a-as—not much in my line, writing." I say, "No? Indeed?" flatteringly, to give him the idea that he might do it if he liked. Boodels comes to the rescue. It appears Cawker and I were schoolfellows. Ah, I know now. He used to be hated, and called "Snobby" Cawker, but I don't remind him of this. "You're so altered," I tell him. "Ya-a-a-as," he returns, conceitedly, stroking his red moustache, "Ya-a-a-as. *You're* not. I recollect him," (here he turns to Boodels, and talks of me) "at school." Here I begin to be interested. "He was a little, short, pudgy, fat fellow, all suetty." I am obliged to laugh; but when he's gone, I'll tell Boodels that we used to call him "Snobby" Cawker at school. I wish I hadn't said he was altered.

Boodels cuts in. "Well, come along, we musn't delay you." Cawker (who is a Captain, too! Snobby Cawker a Captain? how the Army must be going down!) says, "Ya-as—leave him to his writing, ya-a-as," and laughs. I feel as if I could give up writing there and then, and be transported for merely one kick at Cawker. Boodels wants Cawker to come and take a turn before lunch.

*Happy Thought.*—As I haven't been able to get on with *Typical Developments* this morning, I'll pretend to go to bed early, and work to-night. And as I only came here to see a little life, that is, I mean, see the pond dragged, if it isn't dragged the day after to-morrow, I go. Luncheon bell.

## CHAPTER VIII.

CHEZ BOODELS—AFTER-DINNER SIESTA—A PRIVATE READING—A
NIGHT WITH THE DOGS—REPARTEEISM—LEAVING BOODELS.

Leaving Boodels.

N THIS evening I will retire to my room early, to work at *Typical Developments*, Book I., Volume I., Section 1, Chapter 1, Paragraph 2. I feel that if I don't do it now, while I am in the vein, I never shall.

9.30 P.M.—We are alone, Boodels (of Boodels) and I, in the study. I shall leave Boodels, unless he drags the pond to-morrow, because that's what I came down for. Boodels praises Milburd in his absence, as if he was disparaging *me*. I don't like the tone. Shall leave Boodels unless he drags the pond to-morrow.

I am now sitting with my note-book in my hand, so as not to waste my time, watching Boodels. Boodels is apparently going to sleep in his arm-chair. Good. When Boodels is asleep, I shall retire very quietly to my room. It's a bad habit, that of Boodels', sleeping after dinner. He is only dozing; if I move, he'll wake. I'll pretend to read; but I'll watch. I am going to think, so as not to waste time. Can't fix my thoughts. Something flits through my brain about Mesopotamia,—then fire-irons,—then cockles,—then——

\*        \*        \*        \*        \*        \*        \*

*I've* been asleep. Boodels has gone.

11 P.M.—Another evening passed, and no *Typical Developments* done. Willks, the butler, appears with my bed candle, and says

that his master is smoking a cigar, up-stairs. I'll just say "good night" to him, and then to work—to work in the silent night—at *Typical Developments*, Volume I., Book I., Section 1, Chapter 1, Paragraph 2.

I find Boodels on a sofa, with all his dogs. They jump up, and bark at me; all, except the bulldog, who creeps round me, smelling my calves.

This noise makes Boodels quite lively. He says, "Oh, don't go to bed yet." I plead "work." He says, "Bring it in here." Shan't I disturb him? "Not in the least: he'd like it; wants to hear how I'm getting on." I like Boodels when you've got him alone; he's himself then. Evil Milburds corrupt good Boodels. I think of this while I fetch my MS. My paper is spread out: pens, ink, all ready.

My last sentence where I left off commences, "Man at once possible and impossible——" I stick there. Boodels is petting the dogs, and it distracts me. Seeing that it has this effect, Boodels considerately tells the dogs to lie down, and then he smokes solemnly. Somehow, this distracts me more than ever. I feel a strong desire to talk. I must get myself into the swing. Would Boodels mind my reading aloud just to get myself into the swing? "No; he'd like it immensely."

*Happy Thought.*—Always try to interest your host.

I tell him that I consider him as representing a section of the public, and I should like to have his opinion. "Candidly?" he asks. "Candidly," I answer, "as a friend." He says, "Very well; fire away." I fire away. I read what I've done. * * * * Well, how does he like it? "Candidly?" he asks. Yes, of course. Well, then, he *doesn't* like it at all. He doesn't set up for a judge, he admits. I should think not. Boodels a judge of this sort of thing? Good heavens! I tell him that I don't think he understands it. He answers, rather tetchily, "Very likely not." I ask what passage he finds fault with? He answers that "he dislikes the idea." I say, "Hang it! dislike the idea! That's confoundedly illogical." He replies, that "he's not a logician; and if he'd known I would have got so angry on hearing an honest opinion, why——" "Angry! No, dash it! I'm not angry; because there's nothing I like to hear better than an honest opinion; but I mean to say that if he dislikes this of mine, why, he wouldn't care about Buckle's *History of Civilisation*, or Darwin's 'Book'" (I forget the name, so I call it "book"), "or Hume, or old Jeremy Bentham" (I like saying "old Jeremy," it sounds familiar), "or the ancient metaphysical writers" (I think this will shake him a little), "or, in fact, any of those fellows." I didn't want to say "fellows," feeling that it rather lowered the tone of my argument. Boodels rejoins, sharply, "Good heavens! you don't mean to say you put yourself on a par with Darwin, and Buckle, and Bentham!" I don't say I do. He says, "What?" I repeat, loudly, "I don't say I do." He takes me up—he is very nasty to-night, "Do, indeed! I should think not." He adds, "that he doesn't know what I mean by *Typical Developments*, and he supposes that I don't either." I repress myself—he is my host —and luckily recollecting a repartee of Sheridan's, or some one's, which I've used successfully on several occasions, I say, with quiet satire, "My dear fellow, I can't find you books and brains, too." Having said it, it strikes me that I hadn't got the repartee quite right. Boodels returns, "Find brains for *me!* You must have sufficient difficulty in providing *yourself* with that article." [N.B. On calm consideration, this is such an evident reply that I don't think I could have got *my* repartee right. If I did say it right, why didn't some one make that reply to Sheridan?

*Happy Thought.*—The wits of whom we hear so much were not such very sharp fellows, after all. For *Typical Developments*, Chapter XIII., when I get to it.]

Silence. Can't see the answer to Boodels' repartee. There must be one. Boodels takes his candle to go to bed. We shake hands. He's a good fellow, after all, only he oughtn't to talk about what he doesn't understand. I regret, to myself, while shaking hands, that I can't think of an answer to Boodels' repartee. Something about "*his* not having any brains" would do it, but I can't see my way. He makes a discovery. We've been talking so much, he's quite forgotten to ring for Willks to take the dogs away. All servants in bed now. The pug always sleeps in his (Boodels') room, but the bulldog and the terrier ought to be out-side. I propose letting 'em out. It appears we can't without disturbing the entire household in order to get the keys.

A happy thought, as *he* calls it, strikes Boodels. "He will take the pug and the terrier to his *room,* and I shall take the bulldog and the skye to mine." He says, "it's better than disturbing the whole household." I don't think so, but, under the circumstances, won't make an objection. I hope the bulldog will settle the matter for himself, by refusing to follow me. This difficulty is obviated by Boodels carrying him. Boodels wishes me "good night," and retires with his pug and the terrier.

12·30—I am alone. The bulldog and the skye have not moved from the door. The skye is sniffing, and the bull is watching me, mistrustfully. I'll take no notice of them, but put on my dressing-gown, and sit down to write. While brushing my hair, I wish, for the fourth time, that I'd thought of an answer to Boodels' repartee about brains.

Now, for an hour's quiet work. * * * * Both dogs have taken to sniffing, or whining, alternately. This'll drive me distracted. I don't like to turn them out in the passage, Boodels is so particular about his dogs. P'rhaps they'll tire themselves out. Let me write. "Man at once possible and impossible, took his origin from the pulverisation of hitherto conflicting natural particles. Man was developed, slowly, among the ruins of a mammoth world, to rule the brute creation, to make the tawny lion bend before his iron will, to——" That infernal bulldog has got on the bed; just on the part where the sheet is turned down—in fact, where I get in. He is disposing himself for sleep. If the bulldog sleeps there, I don't. I'll wait till he's asleep, and shake him off suddenly. I'll bide my time. Let me see. "Man——to rule——to make the tawny lion bend before his iron will, to—subdue, by the mesmeric authority of his intelligent eye, the stupendous elephant, the" (leave a blank for a good epithet here), "rhinoceros, the untamed denizen of the Primæval Jungle, the——" The bulldog is asleep. I approach the bed on tiptoe. He knows it, the beast; and growls, without taking the trouble to open his eyes! I retire to my chair. How am I to get into bed?

*Happy Thought.*—To open the door. Hang Boodels, I can't help it if he likes it or not; they must go into the passage. I shall leave this to-morrow.* * * * The scheme has succeeded—they've gone. In the distance I hear them scratching at Boodels' door and whining. To bed.

E

*Happy Thought.*—Turn the key first. * * * Savage knock : Boodels in a rage : why the deuce can't I keep the dogs. Row : I won't open the door. Wish for the fifth time that I could think of an answer to his repartee about brains : it would have just come in now. I shall certainly go to-morrow : Boodels is rude.

*Next Morning.*—First post : two letters. In consequence of my not deciding to take the Old Feudal Castle with the shooting, the landlord has let it, and the shooting, separately, to my friend Childers and a party. I know Childers, but not the party : will write to him. A Feudal Castle must be so calm and retired. And then the moat and the bastions ! charming. The other letter is from Mrs. Plyte Fraser. An invitation to Furze Lodge. "We shall be so *delighted* to see you, and I dare say you will be able to pick up some *character* here : our neighbourhood *abounds* in *curiosities.*" Clever woman. After all, one must have female society. To see much of Boodels and Milburd, Cawker and dogs, has a very deteriorating effect on one's mind. I'll accept Mrs. Fraser's note, at once : in fact, telegraph, and go to-day.

*Happy Thought.*—Tip the butler : he's really been very civil, so has the footman. So has everyone ; tip everyone. Difficult thing to do neatly. One ought to make some pretence about it : say, for instance, to the butler, "Here's half a sovereign for you to buy ribbons," or shoes, or neckties, or something. I have tipped them —awkwardly, I'm aware : they took it condescendingly. Boodels is sulky to-day ; Milburd looks in to know about dragging the pond ; Boodels doesn't know. I should like to try Sheridan's repartee on Milburd, and see what *he* says. The Fly has come. Boodels doesn't say he'll be glad to see me again. Milburd makes an ass of himself by pretending to embrace me and then cry bitterly.

*Happy Thought.*—Never ask a friend's opinion on one's original MS. Leads to difficulties.

*Happy Thought in Railway Carriage.*—I've thought of the answer to Boodels' repartee. When he said that about "my not being able to find him in brains," I ought to have said, " Brains ! don't talk of what you know nothing about." That would have done him ; I wish I was quicker at thinking of these things. I must practise repartee.

*Happy Thought.*—Having nothing to do in the carriage, I'll begin practising repartee with myself, in my note-book.

Let's suppose cases. 1*st Hypothesis.* Some one says to me " What a fool you are !" Now, what's the repartee for that ? I

"If I'd come out there," he said, "he'd show me if he was a fool!"

don't know what I should say exactly. There must be an answer to it of some sort. To return " Not such a fool as *you* are," sounds rather weak ; at least it isn't the brilliant style of repartee that I want to have at my fingers' ends. I'll try it on somebody presently, and see what he says. Better try it on a boy ; some sharp lad, not too big.

E 2

Suppose another. *2nd Hypothesis.* Some one says to me, "Why you've got no more brains than a cat." What should I reply to that. Something about "cat:" I don't quite see what, but that's the line of thought for the repartee to that. Odd, how slow I am at this sort of thing : I *must* practise.

*Happy Thought.*—As I can't see any little boy, I'll try "What a fool you are" on some sharp-looking railway porter, just as we're moving away from the next station. * * * Now * * * I have tried it : I thought we were moving on, but we were only taking on fresh carriages or something, and came back to the same place. The man, a herculean porter, was at my window again in a second, very angry. "If I'd come out there" (he meant on the platform) "he'd show me if he was a fool or not." He got quite a crowd round the door. I couldn't give him a shilling because everyone was looking. The Station-master came up for my name and address. I tried to explain that it was merely a sort of witticism, but the policeman, with the Station-master, said it was wilfully provoking an assault. The porter wouldn't take an apology. I have left my card. This doesn't help me with repartees : I must think 'em out for myself.

*London Terminus.*—To another station on my road to Mrs. Fraser's. Repartee with cabman about fare. Cabman had the best of it in strong language. He finished up by crying out, at the top of his voice, "Call yourself a man! Why, I'm blanked if I ain't seen a better man than you made out of blanky tea-leaves!" There was a shout of laughter from every one at this, and he drove off before I could get up a repartee. There must be one to this. I'll get a good one, and be ready with it. Why not a *Dictionary of Repartees?* Handy pocket-volume size. Think over it. Off by train again.

## CHAPTER IX.

FROM THE LONDON TERMINUS TO CHOPFORD STATION AND FARTHER
THAN THAT.

Desultory reading

CHOPFORD is the station for Furze Lodge or Cottage, or Furze Heath Lodge or Cottage. I've lost the address, but recollect that whatever else it is or isn't it's certainly *Furze* something or other.

*Happy Thought.*—To buy a little book for addresses only, and keep it in my pocket. Or have a pocket made for it. That reminds me I was going to have a special pocket made for railway tickets.

Luggage to be labelled "Chopford" immediately. Porter says it's no good labelling it immediately, as the train doesn't go for two hours. It appears that only the very slowest trains, which have nothing better to do, stop at Chopford. But I say, "There's one at twelve." "*Was* one at twelve," he corrects me, adding that "if he'd known as I was going by the Chopford train when I was talking to the cabman, he'd a told me as there warn't time to spare." It was trying; that confounded repartee lost me the train. A policeman says, affably, "Late, Sir! Very unfortunate, Sir. There's a nice refreshment-room for waitin' in, Sir," and he offers to conduct me thither. I know what he means. He wants a glass of beer. I hate such sycophancy. I reply, sternly, "No. I don't want the infernal refreshment-room. I want the train." A Hansom cabman (impudent fellows those Hansom cabmen, because they're so high up), says, jocosely, "Have a ride, Sir? it'll cool your temper." I should like to have had something ready for that. That's what I want—ready wit. I must get some ready. Good subject, by the way, for a chapter in *Typical Developments*, Book VI., Vol. III., Ch. 10, Par. 1, when I come to it; heading, " Ready Wit. Its Origin. In Use among the Ancients. Examples in Animal, Vegetable, and Mineral Life."

*Happy Thought.*—Might compile a small Handbook of Repartees for Travellers. 'Twould make a most useful pocket companion, with marginal references to *Typical Developments*.

*Happy Thought.*—Kill two books with one pen.

*Happy Thought.*—I'll have plenty of marginal references in my book. I like them. I'll arrange this Handbook of Repartees alphabetically. Thus, A : What comes under A ? Armourer. Well, there you are, repartee for an armourer. Also (so as to be quite fair), repartee to be said *to* an armourer. B. What's B ? Baker. Butcher. Repartee for baker or *to* baker ; ditto for butcher or *to* butcher. C stands for cook. Capital little manual for cooks and housekeepers in conversation with tradesmen. There might be permutations and combinations with bakers and butchers and cooks. This opens up a large subject. Will try a little book specially for notes on repartees : to put in my pocket. Might have a pocket made on purpose for it : also for railway tickets, and addresses.

Nearly two hours to wait at the Terminus. My life seems to be cast among railway officials. Dull work waiting : no man with a note-book can be dull : I am, though. I might as well have remained at Boodels as waste my time here. Perhaps, if I had stopped, he'd have dragged the pond. On second thoughts, it was better to come away when I did. Never stop too long at a friend's, or they won't regret your leaving. I dare say Boodels misses me. Don't know, though ; dare say he doesn't. I think he'd miss me if it wasn't for Milburd : Milburd's an ass. Time goes very slowly at a station.

*Happy Thought on seeing the Book-stall.*—One can pick up a great deal of knowledge from desultory reading. Take out the last new books as if you were going to buy them ; read a page here and there. You can get an idea of most of them in ten minutes ; at least, enough for ordinary conversation. For instance, when Mrs. Fraser, who reads everything (well-informed woman,

Mrs. Fraser), says to me "Have you read *Felix Holt ?*" I am able to reply, " Well, I've not had time to go right through it," having, in point of fact, read not more than three pages in the first volume, in consequence of the stall-keeper's becoming rather annoyed at my taking down ten books one after another without buying. I shan't tell Mrs. Fraser this. Some one at dinner will suppose that " Of course, you've read Sir Samuel Baker's book," and I am enabled to reply, " Well, um, not *all* of it," as if I'd only got one chapter more to finish. This is an age of cheap literature. Mine is, perhaps, the cheapest form of acquiring superficial knowledge.

*Happy Thought.*—Go and see a train off. They won't let me on to the platform, without a ticket. * * * Been doing nothing for the last quarter of an hour.

*Happy Thought.*—Go and see a train come in : might pick up character. Can't : too much noise. Back to book-stall. Man objects to my taking any more volumes down, and suggests his terms of subscription. I have not pacified him by the purchase of a penny paper. Dull work even with a note-book.

*Happy Thought.*—I don't know much about locomotives. Will go and talk to a stoker. I walk up (having eluded the official, at the wicket, on the pretence of seeing a friend off by this train) to an engine. On it are two dirty men : I don't know which is the stoker. Say, the dirtier.

*Happy Thought.*—To open the conversation by making some remark about steam. I say to him, " It's a wonderful invention." One grins at me, and the other winks, knowingly. Odd, this levity in stokers ; that is, if they're both stokers. Whistle—shriek : they are off. The train passes me. I feel inclined to wave my hand to the passengers. A funny man in the second-class nods familiarly to me and says, " How's the Missus, and the shop, eh?" Guards on platform laugh : I've nothing to say. A repartee ought to have flashed out of my mouth, like an electric spark : but it didn't. Gone—I am lonely again. The Guards are telling other Guards what the second-class man said to me : they enjoy it—I don't. Wish I was at Boodels. * * * Been doing nothing for another quarter of an hour. Other trains starting and arriving.

*Happy Thought.*—Take some luncheon. Inspecting the refreshment counter I note pork pies whole, pork pies in halves, flies, pork pies in quarters, with parsley, Bath buns, plain buns, more flies, ham sandwiches, two bluebottles, acidulated drops (what sort of passengers refresh themselves with acidulated drops?) cuts of chicken and sprigs of parsley, flies, salad in little plates, pickled something in the fish line, cakes with currants, crowds of flies. Indecision. * * * Wasted another quarter of an hour. Young

The Refreshment Counter at the London Terminus.

women behind the counter sewing, and stopping to giggle. More indecision.

*Happy Thought.*—Ask for Abernethy biscuit: this leads to a request for ginger-beer.

Both together lead me to wish that I hadn't asked for either. I should think they keep their ginger-beer near an oven. * * * Another quarter of an hour gone. I wish I'd stopped at Boodels. At all events, being here insures me against all hurry and bustle when my train *does* start. It suddenly occurs to me that I've never been inside St. Paul's or Westminster Abbey. There's another three-quarters of an hour good. Which shall I go to? One ought to see these things. * * * P'raps I'd better leave it for another day. Indecision. The comfort is, that here I am in plenty of time for my Chopford train. * * * Another quarter of an hour gone. Horrid ginger-beer that was. * * * I suddenly find that it's just ten minutes to two, when my Chopford train starts. Hurry. Get my luggage. As much rushing about as if I'd only just arrived, and was late. Porter fetches somebody else's luggage out of the Parcels' Room. Rush to the train. In the carriage with five other people. Guard looks in. "All here for Pennington and Tutcombe?"

*Happy Thought.*—To correct him, rather funnily, by saying, "I am 'all here' for Chopford." His reply is startling—"The Chopford train's on the other side." I am conscious of not coming out of the carriage well. I wish I hadn't been funny at first; or wish I could have kept it up when getting out, so that the people might miss me when I'd gone! One ought to have good things ready for these occasions. Must get some up.

At last fairly off for Chopford. After all it's just as well I didn't sleep at Boodels. Horrid ginger-beer that was. Boodels used to give us capital luncheons. I rather enjoyed myself at Boodels. It's impossible to make notes in a train. On referring to some I made the other day, all the letters appear to be "w"'s and "y"'s straggling about. I'll get my MSS. out of my desk and look over them. "Man at once possible and impossible," Vol. I., Book I., Section 1, Ch. 1, Paragraph No. 2. * * * I'm tired: never *can* sleep in a train * * * Am awoke by somebody getting in. He begs pardon for disturbing me. I say, "Oh, not at all." Shriek —whistle: on we go. "Beautiful country this," observes my companion: I assent.

*Happy Thought.*—Ask where we are. He replies, "This is all the Chopford country." Lucky I awoke. "The next station is Chopford?" I inquire. "Oh, no," he answers, "where we stopped just now. I got in at Chopford."

Confound it, I wished to goodness I'd stopped at Boodels.

## CHAPTER X.

SLUMBOROUGH FOR CHOPFORD—RAILWAY SUGGESTIONS—OFFICIALS—
CARRIAGE FOR FURZE LODGE—A LIVE DUKE.

A Shaker.

Y LOT, as I have before remarked, seems to be cast among railway officials. I am obliged to get out at Slumborough, and I have to go back to Chopford, which we passed while I was asleep.

*Memorandum for suggestion to Railway Authorities.* —At any station if the guards see a passenger asleep, they ought to wake him. Or, there might be, —a very Happy Thought this,—there might be a set of officials, called Shakers, attached to every train, whose duty, whenever it stopped, should be to go into all the carriages, shake any one they might find asleep, and ask him where he's going ?

*Happy and Poetical Thought.*—Female shakers might wake the gentlemen, and win gloves. No shaker to be eligible over six-and-twenty.

It's an out-of-the-way place, is Slumborough station. No one to talk to. Let me observe. There's a porter, who is always whistling ; an impulsive Station-master, who won't be stopped to be spoken to, he's so busy ; a potato-garden, a small neat cottage, three broken helpless looking trucks, the commencement of an unfinished line, with the ends of its rails turning upwards towards the sky, as if that had been their destination. I may note down as a

*Happy Thought.*—That this is a sort of Tower of Babel line. When this idea comes to be developed, Vol. IV., Book VIII., Chap. 1, *Typical Developments*, it will be very poetical. Odd, how full of poetry I am to-day. This is the second poetical thought I've had within the last half hour.

*Happy Thought.*—Ask the porter, in order to get at statistics, " How many trains pass here in a day ? " He stops his whistle, about four bars from the end of the tune, I should say, and answers, " If you look at the time-table, it's all up there," and then he starts a fresh tune. An express passes, and I wonder if there's any one I know in it. The porter takes another turn at the truck, and then strolls into the potato-garden, and kicks the potatoes. P'raps this is the process of gardening in this part of the country. (" Agriculture," *Typical Developments*, Vol. III., Book VI.) I should like to talk to the Station-master. I go inside. Office shut up. Behind the partition I hear the scratching of a pen, and rustling of paper. He is then, probably, hard at work. While I am thinking this, the door in the partition opens, and he comes out briskly. I say to him, " Can you tell me——" He replies, impulsively, " Yes, there's the time-table," and goes out on to the platform. In a minute he is back again, as brisk as ever. I address him, " Will the train——" He replies, with his hand on the brass knob of his door. " Office open five minutes before train comes," and disappears. More scratching of pen and rustling of paper within. There is a large clock with an impressive tick. I compare my watch with it, and, though I arrive at no conclusion on the subject, feel satisfied at having done something.

*In the Waiting Room.*—Dreary. Wonder if Boodels' butler packed up my sponge ? Hate uncertainty in these matters, but don't like to unpack in the station. I'll go into the office, and see if my portmanteau is there. No. Where? Of course taken out at Chopford. I shall see it there, at least, I hope so. The pigeon-hole suddenly opens, and the Station-master appears. Now's the time for conversation, and picking up character and materials. I have several questions to ask him. I say, " I want to know first ——" He catches me up impulsively, " First, where for ? " " Chopford," I answer, and before I can explain the accident which has brought me to Slumborough, he has dashed at a blue ticket, thumped it in one machine, banged it in another, and has produced it cut, printed, double-stamped, and all complete for authorising me to go to Chopford. "One and a penny," says he. I explain that "I don't want it, because——" He listens to nothing more, but sits down at his desk, pounces upon a large book, which he opens and shoves aside, then seizes a pen, and begins adding up something on one sheet of paper, and putting down the result on another. While he is engaged in this, I see the telegraphic needles working. He is too absorbed to notice it. 'Twill be only kindness on my part to direct his attention to it. I say, "Do you know, Sir——" He is up in an instant, with a pen behind his ear. He evidently doesn't recognise me. "Eh, First? where for?" I can't help saying, "Yes, Chopford—but——" when he dashes, as before, at the stamping machines, and produces, like a conjuring trick, another ticket for Chopford. That's two tickets for Chopford, and a third I've got in my pocket. I tell him I don't want it, and am adding, "I don't know if you observed the telegraph needles——" when he sits down, evidently in a temper, growling something about "if you want to play the fool, go somewhere else." I'd say something sharp if he wasn't at work, but I never like disturbing a man at work. Stop, I might ask him, it wouldn't take a second, how far it is from Chopford to Furze. I approach the pigeon-hole; I say, mildly, "If you would oblige me, Sir, for one second——" He is up again more impulsively than ever. "One, Second. Thought you said, One First," and before I can point out his mistake he has banged, thumped, and produced for the third time a ticket to Chopford, only now he says, "Tenpence," that being the reduction on Second class. I am really afraid of making him very violent, so I buy the ticket. What a sad thing to have such a temper, and be a station-master!

*The Train arrives.*—Hurrah! For Chopford at last. Now do the Frasers live at Furze Lodge or Cottage?

*Chopford Station.*—Get out. Official receives my ticket. Very nearly getting into a difficulty with him, as I have tendered my Second class ticket from Slumborough to Chopford, and he saw me get out of the First class carriage. * * * What an agony it puts one in not to be able to find the proper ticket. * * * Right at last. I've often said I must have a regular pocket made for tickets, and so I must. Luggage here. No name on it, but labelled Chopford. I am going to Furze Lodge, I tell him : because if it *isn't* Furze Lodge and *is* Furze Cottage he'll correct me. The official is most civil. "Furze Lodge, oh, of course." The Frasers are evidently well known, and highly respected. "The carriage for Furze Lodge is waiting, Sir, to take you. Here's the footman." He takes me up to a tall menial in a handsome livery and a cockade. (I note that the Frasers are going it.) The menial touches his hat, on the station-master introducing me politely as "the gentleman for Furze." A porter puts my luggage into the carriage, and I put myself in after it. The coachman touches his hat on seeing me, the footman bangs the door, the station-master salutes me, the porter interests himself in my welfare to inquire " if I've got everything," which simply means sixpence for himself. (*Note for travelling.* Always carry threepenny bits.)

My spirits rise. Such a carriage. Damask lining : softest cushions. I suppose Fraser is a Deputy-Lieutenant or something, or else why should the servants wear cockades ? It can't be to impose upon the country people. No, Fraser's above that. He is not a snob.

We enter Furze gates. Pretty little lodge at the gate. Old woman comes out and bobs a curtsey to me. Nice old woman. I bow to her and smile. For a moment I imagine myself the Prince of Wales. It must be very tiring to go on bowing and smiling : but gratifying. Deer in the park. Old timber.

*Happy Thought.*—I must get up my sketching again, and practise trees. Splendid oaks. Chestnuts. Cows. Two labourers : or peasants. What's the difference between labourer and peasant ? One's real, and the other poetical. (Query this in Vol. IV., *Typical Developments.*) They touch their hats respectfully to me. I return, graciously. Feel like George the Fourth in that picture of him on the sofa. More gates. What a delicious place Fraser has. Knowing him and his wife only in town, where they take lodgings for a month in the season, I had no idea he was so wealthy. (N.B. Never judge a man by his merely taking lodgings in London for the season.)

THE CROQUET PARTY.

An artistically-planted flower garden. A lawn, like a soft green carpet without a wrinkle in it, laid out for Croquet exclusively. On it is a Croquet party. They are in fancy costumes; from which I gather it is a Croquet Club. Charming. I *shall* enjoy this. Mrs. Plyte Fraser, too, is such a nice person. All clever people here, I'll be bound, or they wouldn't do this sort of thing; because there is originality about it. Delightful; simply delightful! I think I see Fraser and Mrs. Fraser among the party. I wave my hand. I feel exhilarated. I shout, "How are you, how are you?" Meaning Fraser, who of course can't answer at that distance, but will take the inquiry for what it's meant. I like being hearty with people.

Here we are at the door of Furze Lodge. A grey-headed butler descends, solemnly : he is like a clergyman, indeed for the matter of that, an archbishop. Livery opens the carriage door. The archbishop stands on the steps as if about to impart a benediction. I should like to kneel to him.

*Happy Thought.*—If I do get up my sketching, I'll draw a picture of *Hospitality in the Olden Time. Arrival of Pilgrims at the Archbishop's.*

More livery servants. Fraser must be *very* rich. (I have time to make a note or two while they are engaged with my luggage.) The butler tells the servants "The Blue Room," and I think of *Fatima* and *Baron Abomelique.* (N.B. Another subject for a sketch.) I see my packages being carried up the grand old oaken staircase adorned with portraits of Fraser's ancestors, all with very white hands and pointed finger tips. This is just *the* place I like. Beautiful!!! I address the butler for the first time, having given my hat, coat and umbrella to a livery, who has disappeared with them. In an off-hand manner, in order to show that I am accustomed to all this grandeur, and am quite one of the family, I ask him, "Are they in?" He replies, benignly, "I was to show you to the study, Sir, directly you came." I answer, "Oh, very well," and then inquire, also in an off-hand manner, "Who's in the Croquet ground?" The butler calmly replies, "There's Lord Adolphus, Sir, and Lady Adela, they only came down this morning; there's Mr. Aylmer, Captain Doodley, Miss Ascutt, Colonel Lyne, Lady Tulkorne and Miss Græme, and the family, Sir. His Grace hasn't been able to go out, Sir, for three days." I had no idea the Frasers did this sort of thing. What a letter I shall write to old Boodels about the place. He'll be precious glad to get me back again to Boodels, thinking I'll introduce him to the Frasers. But I won't; or perhaps I will, and astonish him. That vulgar fellow Milburd, wouldn't get on here. I note this while in a library, where the butler has left me, while he prepares his master for my coming. From what the butler says I fancy poor Fraser has got the gout. "The gout," the reverend domestic has casually observed, "*does* make an invalid very irritable." He returns and motions me towards a door artfully concealed from view by sham bookshelves. I enter, prepared to say, "Well, old boy, I'm sorry to see you like this," when the butler announces me softly, so softly that I cannot hear what he says, to the invalid, who is in a large comfortable chair, swathed in flannels. The room is partially darkened, and I see that noisy heartiness is out of the question.

I go up to him. "Well, doctor," says he, groaningly, "glad you've come." Fancy of his to call me doctor, I suppose. What a change : Fraser's voice is quite altered.

*Happy Thought.*—To reply, "Well, I hope I shall be a good doctor to you, old fellow. Cheer you up a bit."

He turns round sharply and almost fiercely. "Who the ——?" * * *

It isn't Fraser ; and I've never seen his face before in my life.

*       *       *       *       *       *       *

I have been shown out. There is a very simple explanation, and this is it. The Frasers Live at Furze Cottage, but at Furze *Lodge* resides his Grace the Duke of Slumborough, who is now suffering from a complicated gout, and to whom I have just been presented. * * *

His Grace, being irritable, won't listen to apologies. The butler, who is the *major domo* of the establishment, receives his dismissal on the spot. * * * I don't exactly know what to do. The butler is still in the study with his Grace, and I am in the library. As all the doors, I now observe, are concealed by sham bookshelves, the general effect is that there are no doors at all. When I do get out, how shall I obtain my luggage from the Blue Room ? How can I face the butler ? No more Archbishop's benediction. Subject for sketch, *Archbishop Cursing Pilgrims :* companion picture to the other. Very uncomfortable. How can I defend my presence in the library to the Duchess if she comes ? Dreadful ! I must (as I have said often before) get an address book, and write them all down. When I get out of this infernal hole I will. I thought the Frasers couldn't live here. * * *

*Happy Thought.*—Out at last. Son of the family found me. Introduces himself; Lord Heath. Has heard of the mistake. My luggage is all down and put into a pony chaise. Will I take anything before I go ? Mr. Fraser's cottage is not far from here, he says, a pretty place. In fact, it is on his father's estate. His father, the Duke, has been ill for some time ; it makes him very irritable. Yes. Hope I'll enjoy myself at Furze Cottage. Good-bye. I am driven off by a groom in a small pony carriage, which is just large enough to hold us and my luggage. I am conscious of the eyes of the Croquet party. I don't wave my hand this time. The pony is very slow. Lord Heath has joined his friends. I hear them laughing. I feel savage with the aristocracy generally. I could be a Democrat, if it wasn't for the groom by my side, who is inclined to treat me flippantly. Silence and Thought. We drive out of the Lodge Gate. The old woman doesn't curtsey. Sycophant !

## CHAPTER XI.

NOTES WRITTEN DOWN SOON AFTER MY ARRIVAL AT FRASER'S—I
MEET SOME YOUNG LADIES—CROQUET—CHILDREN.

Ogling the Nurserymaid.

GROOM who took me in the pony carriage was not quite certain which *was* Furze Cottage. After going up a considerable hill, we came to a door which seemed to appear suddenly out of a plantation. There was nothing outside to indicate that it belonged to the Frasers or anybody else. Here I find notes made on the spot.

Pretty place, if Fraser's or any one's. Honeysuckles, creepers, and crawlers all over the wall.

*Happy Thought.*—Must learn the names of plants. *Typical Developments,* Vol. VII., to be entirely devoted to Floriculture.

See a small window: a child appears at it. I call out to him, is this Mr. Fraser's? Whereupon he makes faces at me. Little idiot. I repeat my question, and he repeats his faces. I threaten him, when he suddenly disappears, having, as I hope, tumbled off a chair. If this is the Frasers', they have children, or at all events, *one* child, who makes faces at visitors. I don't like this.

Why the groom, on seeing the child, should say, "Oh, yes, this is Furze Cottage," I don't know: on looking again at the window I catch sight of a comely nurserymaid, and from certain indications on her countenance I am inclined to think that the groom is upon, at all events, winking terms with the domestic. The groom gets out to ring the bell while I hold the reins. I am glad when he has rung, and is at the pony's head.

*Happy Thought.*—Must practise my driving.

A youngish butler opens the door, he lacks the stateliness of the archbishop at Furze Lodge, but he is dapper and genial; and a butler should be genial. Wishing to do things well for the sake of the Frasers, and with a view to reading the Duke's groom the useful lesson that a menial mustn't despise any one who may happen to be shown out of a nobleman's house, I give him half-a-crown. I watch the effect upon him. None, visibly. Turning suddenly, a few seconds afterwards, I am confident I saw him with the half-crown in his right eye, pretending to ogle the nurserymaid at the window. Analysing this act subsequently, (with a view to materials for chapter on "Human Nature,") I find in it ingratitude, immorality, and tomfoolery. [*Query.* Why *Tom*-foolery? Why not Henry-foolery or John-foolery? Must think over this, and startle the world when I've found it out.]

*Happy Thought.*—That groom's a Lothario. Who was Lothario? Useful thing to get a history of him. Everybody is hearty at Fraser's. The butler and the footman are hearty. They get out my luggage heartily. They hang up my hat, on a peg in the hall, heartily. The butler putting down my hat-box "thinks that that's all," heartily. The footman thinks yes, that that *is* all, very heartily. They smile at one another and breathe, heartily. I begin to feel hearty myself. The load of the aristocracy is off me, now that the Duke's groom (much worse than the Duke himself as oppressing me, until I saw him with my coin in his right eye) is gone. I notice that there are about ten pairs of little shoes, and hoops, and hoop-sticks in the hall. The Frasers have evidently a large family. Didn't know this before. Mrs. Plyte Fraser comes in from the garden. She talks in italics, most heartily. "*So* glad to see me: *so* delighted: *so* sorry if I hadn't come: should *never* have forgiven me: *never*. You'll have a cup of tea? We're *just* come in to have tea: and a *chat*: so *long* since we've had a chat." Mrs. Fraser then gives some directions about Master Adolphus coming down to dinner, and the others to

F 2

dessert. Very large family, I'm afraid. Asking for Fraser, I am told he is arranging a bin. I like Mrs. Plyte Fraser. She is thoroughly appreciative. She is fond of literature, specially of the higher walks in which I am engaged, and she interests herself in what interests me. I shall get her to give me an opinion on the first Chapter of *Typical Developments.* A clever woman's opinion is worth a great deal ; and then, of course, she represents a class. Now my mistake in appealing at all to Boodels was, that he didn't represent anybody.

Odd question for Mrs. Fraser to put to me, almost directly we are in the drawing-room, "So you're not married yet?" I laugh, and reply, "No, I'm not married yet," having, in fact, no other answer ready. She returns, knowingly, "Well, we'll see what we can do for you?" I smile, but I don't quite like this style of conversation. Analysing it, subsequently, for materials for chapter on "Human Nature," I find in it frivolity and curiosity. I take this opportunity, while we're sipping our tea, of informing Mrs. Fraser how hard at work I am on *Typical Developments.* She says, "Oh, she should like to see it *so* much ! I *must* read it to her ;" and adds, slyly, "I'm sure it's romantic ; I do like anything *really* romantic."

She is so enthusiastic on the subject that I don't feel inclined to explain that it has nothing to do with romance, but say dubiously, as if I hadn't quite made up my mind about it, "Well, no, not perhaps exactly romantic, that is in the sense you mean." She was at me in a moment, she is so quick, "Romantic in another sense? I don't quite understand." Being unable to put it in a clearer light, I say, smiling mysteriously, "You shall see," which pacifies her for the time.

*Happy Thought.*—I'll throw in a little romantic touch here and there, before I read it to her. Perhaps it would improve it : on consideration, I don't quite see how.

Here three young ladies join us. The Misses Symperson and Miss Florelly. I wish Mrs. Fraser wouldn't introduce me as "a gentleman of whose literary fame you've often heard, I've no doubt." It is so awkward when people don't know anything about you. This was the case with the Sympersons and Miss Florelly : rather stupid girls, except the second Miss Symperson. There's a something about her which attracts me. Why? When Mrs. Fraser makes the introductory speech above recorded, I laugh and say, "Oh, no, no, no," as if their ignorance of me was just pardonable and that's all.

*Happy Thought.*—I must get something published at once, because, then, when you are introduced, as above, you can refer to some work or other that every one knows something about. But if you're introduced as a gentleman of great literary fame, and on being asked what you've written are obliged to reply "nothing," it makes one look so foolish. I don't say "nothing," I qualify it; I reply, "I have *published* nothing, though I have *written* a great deal," and then I depreciate publication as merely a gratification of personal vanity.

[*Happy Thought.*—Wonder if Mr. Bradshaw is introduced as the author of the celebrated Railway Guide?]

This was what I said to Miss Harding, who is another young lady at the Frasers', supposed to be very clever and very sharp, and asked, I find, on *my* account. Miss Harding replies, "Gratification of personal vanity! then Milton, Ben Jonson, Shakspeare, Bacon, Chaucer, simply gratified their vanity? for they all published. You surely can't mean that?" I do not mean that, or at least I didn't expect to be taken up so quickly, and wish to goodness she wouldn't talk so loud, as Mrs. Fraser and every one in the room is listening. I feel that I am placed on my mettle; by a girl only eighteen, too! I reply, "No, *they* were not vain,—and when I said that publication was a gratification of vanity, I did not suppose for one minute you would understand it literally." Every one, I see, is satisfied with this answer: she is not. "If not literally," she returns, "how do you mean it—metaphorically?" I reply, seeing that everybody is waiting for me to crush her, "Well, you see, you must analyse the motives which prompt a man of high cultivation and lofty soul-stirring aspirations to"——here Plyte Fraser himself comes in, from the wine-cellar. He dusts himself and shakes hands with me apologetically, "Glad to see you—don't let me interrupt you." I say, "No, no, not at all." "Ah!" says he to Miss Harding, "you get him to sing to you '*The Little Pig Jumped over the Wall.*' It's capital—he does the squeak, and everything." Miss Harding raises her eyebrows, and I protest I don't sing *now*—that I've given it up. Plyte Fraser insists: "You'll give it us this evening—squeak and all—and we'll have the children down to hear it." Here he slaps me gently on the back. He's stopped too long in the wine-cellar ; a little tasting is a dangerous thing. I must take the first opportunity I can of explaining to Fraser that I am not a buffoon.

Mrs. Fraser and the other ladies are in the garden. One of the boy Frasers, nine years old, is there. I don't know how many children they have : on inspection, I don't think this is the one who made faces at me from the window. We join them. At any other time I should have disdained croquet, but a man who does the pig and the squeak (confound Fraser's memory !) cannot affect to be above simple lawn sport like croquet. Miss Florelly says to me sweetly during the game, "Oh, I *do* hope you'll sing that song about the pig. Mr. Fraser says you wrote it yourself. It's wonderful to me how you can think of such clever things." Here's a reputation : not as the author of *Typical Developments*, but the writer of "*The Little Pig Jumped*," who sings it, and does the squeak himself ! When shall I be known in my true character ? When will my lofty aspirations be recognised ? I think all this in a corner of the croquet-ground, and I find myself frowning horribly.

Here I am called upon to push a ball through a hoop : I fail. The boy Fraser says, "You can't play as well as I can," and is told not to be rude. Miss Harding not only laughs at me, but hits me (I mean my ball) to the other end of the ground. The boy Fraser then alters his remark, "You can't play as well as Miss Harding, you can't." I say, with a dash of sentiment, wishing to be friends with her, "You've sent me a long way off, Miss Harding," and she replies, curtly, "Yes, terrible, isn't it ?" The boy Fraser, whom I begin to detest, says, "You can't run as fast as I can." I nod to him pleasantly to propitiate the boy, but he only asks, "What do you mean by that ?" and imitates me. I have to run across the ground : I am conscious of not appearing to advantage when running. I wish that croquet had never been invented : I feel that I am scowling again : it strains me to smile. Now at Boodels one wasn't bothered to play at croquet with women and children. I must explain to Mrs. Fraser that I want to have as much time as possible to myself for writing, and I can't be playing croquet all day. Fraser himself doesn't play, and I'm the

The boy Fraser refuses to assist me, and says, "Pick 'em up yourself."

only man here. He looks into the ground for one minute, and says, "Hullo, getting on all right?" I reply, smilingly, "Oh, yes, all right," and he disappears into the cellar again, I believe,

as the next time I see him is in the hall, with a couple of cob-
webby bottles in his hands.  Bell : thank heaven : dinner time.
The worst of being the only man with five ladies is that one has to
pick up all the croquet balls, put the mallets back in the box,
draw the stumps, and carry the whole lot of things into the
house.  The boy Fraser refuses to assist me, and says, " Pick 'em
up yourself."  Nice child, this !  I should like to pinch him, or
box his ears ; but I'm afraid, he'd make such a noise.

*Happy Thought while Dressing for Dinner.*—To tell Fraser
quietly that I don't care about croquet, and then he'll get me out
of it another time.

Hope there's not a party at dinner.  Hope he's forgotten all
about asking me to sing " *The Little Pig.*" * * * Lost a stud.
Can't find it anywhere.  This *is* annoying.  Hate going down
hot and uncomfortable to dinner.  Ring bell.  Footman after
some delay answers it.  He brings up hot water (which I've
had before) and announces that dinner will be ready in five
minutes.  We both look for the stud.  He thinks his master has
a set, though he don't generally wear 'em.  While he is gone, I
find that the stud is missing which fastens my collar.  Ring the
bell again.  This causes another bell to ring.  Hate giving
trouble in a strange house.  Little boy Fraser comes to the door
as the butler enters with more hot water.  The horrid boy makes
remarks on my dress.  I tell the domestic my difficulty.  Master
doesn't wear studs, it appears.  The boy Fraser is overhauling the
things on my table.  I ask him to leave my comb alone, and he
goes to the brushes.  The footman (with more hot water, not
knowing the butler was there), says the Maid would pin it on, if
that would do ?  That *must* do.  The boy Fraser is putting hair
oil on my clean pocket-handkerchief.  He thinks it's *scent.*
Another minute and the Maid appears.  Shall she sew on a
button ?  " Is there time ? " I ask.  " Well, she'll try," she
answers, and goes for the button.  I implore the boy Fraser, who
is now trying on my boots, to go away.  He won't.  The dinner-
bell rings.  Now I'm keeping them waiting.  Boy Fraser informs
me that he's coming down to dessert.  Maid returns.  What a
time sewing takes.  Painful attitude it is to stand in, with your
head in the air, and trying all the while to see what a mischievous

child is doing with your watch. Done at last. White tie won't come right. Dash it, let it come wrong. Rush down to the drawing-room. Obliged to leave horrid boy in my room. I stop on the stairs. Forgotten my watch. Run up again. Rescue it from boy who was going to examine the works with the aid of my gold pin. Luckily one of his nurses appears. I leave them to fight it out, and rush down-stairs again. At drawing-room door, standing on mat to button my waistcoat, which, in my hurry, I had left undone. Door opens. Every one is coming out.

*Happy Thought.*—Always be careful to finish dressing before one makes a public appearance. Apologies from Master and Mistress of the house. Large party ; all paired, except myself and a youth from school, about fourteen years old, in jackets. I don't know him at all, but he wants to be sportive, and says, " I s'pose you'll take me in." I snub him. I think the servants are laughing at something he's doing. Hate boys of this age. It was a smaller one than this who made faces at me from the window.

*Dinner.*—Seated : next to the Lady of the House. Miss Harding on the other side. I mentally note as not at all a happy thought, that if there's anything to carve I shall have to do it. I hope the old gentleman on the other side of Mrs. Fraser will offer first. She introduces us across. He is an American general. On being told by Mrs. Fraser of my literary fame, he only says, " Oh ! indeed," and appears surprised. I wish she wouldn't say anything about it. I have my pocket-book ready for short-hand notes, as he'll be full of information. Dinner goes on.

## CHAPTER XII.

DINNER PARTY AT FRASER'S—THE GENERAL.—I OBLIGE THE COMPANY
WITH A SONG.

"When In doubt play the lobster sauce."

AT DINNER. In con
sequence of having to
listen to several whis-
pered observations on the
company present from Mrs.
Plyte Fraser, who tells me
who every one is, and how
clever they all are, I find
myself left alone, eating fish.
I make three picks at my fish
and finish. The butler and
footman are both in the
room, but neither will catch
my eye, and I can't get my
plate removed. The coach-
man, who comes in to wait
occasionally, and is very hot
and uncomfortable all the
time, *does* catch my eye, and

sees me pointing to my plate. He looks in a frightened manner
at me, as though begging me not to ask *him* to do anything on
his own account. He is evidently debating with himself whether
he oughtn't to tell the butler that I'm making signs. I should
say that this coachman is snubbed by the others. His rule for
waiting appears to be, when in doubt play the lobster sauce;
which he hands with everything.

Mrs. Fraser whispers to me to draw the American General out.
"He was in the war," she says, behind her fan. I say, "Oh,
indeed!" and commence the process of drawing out. It's a difficult
art. The first question is everything. I ask him, diffidently,
"How he liked the war?" Before he can reply, Mrs. Fraser
informs the company, as if she were exhibiting the military hero,
"Ah! General Duncannon was in all the great engagements——"

The General shuts his eyes and nods towards a salt-cellar. "He knew," she continues, still exhibiting him, "all the leading men there——" The General looks round the table cautiously to see, perhaps, if anybody else did,—"and he was in the very centre of the battle, where he received a dreadful sabre wound, at—at—" she looks for assistance to the General, who seems rather more staggered than he probably did in the battle, and Plyte Fraser, from the top of the table, supplies, "Bull's Run." "Bull's Run," repeats Mrs. Fraser to the General, as if challenging him to contradict it if he dares. "General Duncannon's property," she goes on, still lecturing on him as a kind of mechanical wax-work figure, "was all—all—all—dear me, what's the word I want?" She turns to me abruptly. I don't know. The General doesn't know. Perhaps he never had any property. Everybody being appealed to, separately, "has the word on the tip of his tongue!" "You," says Mrs. Fraser to me, "of course have quite a storehouse of words. I never can imagine an author without a perfect magazine of words. It must be *so* delightful *always* to be able to say what you want, you know. Now what is the word I'm waiting for? You know when a man has all his property taken by Government—taken away—not '*compromised*'—no—dear me——" All eyes are upon me. Of course I know. Boldly but with a nervous feeling that I'm not quite right yet, I say, "Sequestered," and lean back in my chair, somewhat hot.

*Happy Thought.*—Sequestered.

Mrs. Fraser adopts it. "Sequestered by Government." Miss Harding goes into a fit of laughing. I see the mistake, so does Mrs. Fraser, so does every one. Every one laughs. They all think it's my joke, and Mrs. Fraser taps me on the hand with her fan, and explains to the General "*sequestered*, you know, for *sequestrated*." Every one laughs again, except Miss Harding, who, Mrs. Fraser keeps whispering to me, is "such a clever girl, so well read. Draw her out." She won't be drawn out any more than the General. The party, I subsequently find, has been asked expressly to meet *me*, and the Frasers do their best to give everything a literary turn. Odd; I don't feel a bit brilliant this evening. Very disappointing this must be to the guests. I can't even talk to Miss Harding. In consequence of what is expected of me, I can't stoop to talk about the weather, or what any one's "been doing to-day." After the haunch of venison I am going to begin to Miss Harding about "the Human Mind in its several aspects," when she says, "I thought you authors were full of conversation and sparkling wit." It's rather rude of her, but Mrs. Fraser shouldn't lead her to expect so much. I can only say, "Did you?" As an afterthought I ask "Why?"

She replies, "Well, one reads of the meetings of such men as Sheridan, Burke, Grattan, Dr. Johnson, and they seem to have said witty things every moment." I feel that I am called upon to defend the literary character for *esprit* in the present day. I reply, "Well you see," deliberately, "it's so different now, it's in fact more——" I am interrupted by a gentleman, on the other side, in a white waistcoat and iron-grey whiskers, "No wits now-a-days," he says. "Why, I recollect Coleridge, Count D'Orsay, Scott, Southey, and Tommy Moore, with old Maginn, Sir, at one table. Then, Sir, there was poor Hook, and Mathews, and Yates. I'm talking of a time before you were born or thought of——" He says this as if he'd done something clever in being born when he was, and as if I'd made an entire mistake in choosing my time for an existence. Every one is attending to the gentleman in the white waistcoat, who defies contradiction, because all his stories are of a time before any one at the table "was born or thought of." It's very annoying that there should ever have been such a period.

*Happy Thought.*—In Chap. 10, Book IX. of *Typical Developments,* "The Vanity of Existence." From literature he gets to the Drama. He seems to remember every actor. According to him, no one ever did anything in literature or art, without asking *his* advice. His name is Brounton, and he speaks of himself in the third person as Harry. I try to speak to Miss Harding, but she is listening to a story from Brounton about "Old Mathews." "You didn't know old Mathews," he says to Fraser, who humbly admits he didn't. "Ah, I recollect, before he ever thought of giving his entertainment, his coming to me and saying, 'Harry, my boy '—he always called me Harry—'Harry, my boy ' says he, 'I'd give a hundred pounds to be able to sing and speak like you.' 'I wish I could lend it you, Matty,' I said to him—I used to call him Matty—'but Harry Brounton wouldn't part with his musical ear for' "—— Here a diversion is created by the entrance of the children. I see the one who made faces at me from the window. Ugly boy. The child who would bother me when I was dressing is between Mrs. Fraser and myself. I give him grapes and fruit to propitiate him : great point to make friends with juveniles. He whispers to me presently, " You don't know what me and Conny's done." I say, cheerfully, " No, I can't guess." He whispers, " We've been playing at going out of town with your box." I should like to pinch him. He continues, whispering, " I say, it's in your room, you know : we got such a lot of things in it." I don't like to tell Mrs. Fraser, who says, " There, Dolly, don't be troublesome." I am distracted. The boy on the side of Mrs. Fraser (he was the nuisance in the croquet ground), says, pointing at me, " Oh, he's got such a funny hat," and is immediately silenced. I should like to hear more about this hat. I ask Dolly, who whispers, " the nurse took it away from him, 'cos she said that he'd hurt himself." The little Frasers have evidently been smashing my *gibus*. The ladies rise, and the children go with them. " You won't stop long," says Mrs. Fraser, persuasively. " No, no," answers Fraser. " Because I've allowed the children to sit up on purpose," continues Mrs. Fraser, looking at me. " All right," returns Fraser ; " we'll just have one glass of wine and then we'll come into the drawing-room, and "—smiling upon me—" he'll give us ' *The Little Pig Jumped*,' with the squeak and all."

I find that all the guests have been asked expressly to hear me sing this : I also find that there are a great many people coming in the evening for the same special purpose. I haven't done it for years. Fraser seems to think that any man who writes is merely a buffoon. I only wonder that he doesn't ask me to dance a saraband for the amusement of his friends. I *am* astonished at Mrs. Fraser. I tell Fraser I've forgotten the song. He won't hear of it : he says, " You'll remember it as you go on." I say, I can't get on without a good accompaniment. He returns that the Elder Miss Symperson plays admirably. Every one says, " Oh, you must sing." The American General, who speaks for the first time, now says, " He's come ten miles to hear it." Brounton supposes " I don't recollect Old Mathews *at Home ?* " I don't, and he has me at a disadvantage.

He goes on to ask me if I accompany myself ? No, I don't.

"Ah!" says he, "I recollect Theodore Hook sitting down to the piano and dashing off a song and an accompaniment impromptu. You don't improvise?" he asks me. I am obliged to own frankly that I do not, but in the tone of one who could if he liked. "Ah," he goes on, "you should hear the Italian Improvisatori! Ever been to Italy?" No, I haven't: he has, and again I am at a disadvantage. "Ah," he exclaims, "that is something like improvisation: such fire and humour—more than in the French.

The children who have sat up on purpose to hear "The Little Pig Jumped!"

Of course you know all Béranger's songs by heart?" Before I have time to say that I know a few, he is off again. "Ah! the French comic songs are so light and sparkling. No English comic song can touch them—and then, where are your singers?" I wish to goodness he'd not been asked to hear "*The Little Pig.*" Going out of the dining-room, Fraser says to me, "Capital fellow, Brounton, isn't he: so amusing." If I don't admit it Fraser will think me envious and ill-natured; so I say heartily, "Brounton! very amusing fellow—great fun," and we are in the drawing-room.

Here I find all the people who have been invited in the evening. I should like to be taken ill. The children are at me at

once. " Ma says you're to sing." Little brutes ! The elder Miss
Symperson, who will be happy to play for me, is seated near the
piano. She is half a head taller than I am, and peculiarly elegant
and ladylike. My last chance is trying to frighten her out of
accompanying me. I tell her the tune is difficult to catch. Will
I hum it to her ? I hum it to her. In humming it is difficult to
choose any words but "rum tum tum," and *very* difficult to
convey a right notion of the tune. Two children standing by the
piano give their version of it. I say, "hush" to them and lose
the tune. Miss Symperson does catch it, and chooses a key for
me. Fraser, thinking the song is beginning, says, "Silence," and
interrupts Brounton in a loud story about his remembering "Old
Mathews singing a song about a pig—he was inimitable, Mathews
was "—when I have to explain that we're not ready to begin yet.
The conversation is resumed : Mrs. Fraser seats herself on an
ottoman with her two very youngest children, who are fidgety,
near the piano ; the two others insist on standing just in front of
me by the piano. Miss Harding takes a small chair quite close
to me ; by her sits a Captain someone, who has come in the evening with his sister. I feel that she despises buffoonery, but if the
Pig-song is to be anything at all, it must be done with a good
deal of facial expression. The Captain is evidently joking with
her at my expense. Don't know him, but hate him : because it's
very ungentlemanly and unfair to laugh at you, just when you're
going to sing a comic song. I tell Fraser, apologetically, that I
really am afraid I shall break down. Brounton says, "Never
mind—improvise." Miss Symperson says, "Shall I begin?" I
answer, " If you please," and she plays what she thinks is the air.
I am obliged to stop her, and say that it's not quite correct.
This makes a hitch to begin with. Brounton says something
about a tuning-fork, and every one laughs except the Captain,
who is talking in a low tone to Miss Harding. Mrs. Fraser's
youngest child on her lap says, "Ma, why—doo—de "—— Hush !
Miss Symperson, in not a particularly good temper, plays it
again. More like a march than a comic song, but I don't like to
tell her so. I begin—

> "A little pig lived on the best of straw,
> Straw—hee-haw—and Shandiddlelaw."

And the idea flashes across my mind what an ass I'm making of myself. At the "hee-haw," the pianist has to do six notes up and down, like a donkey braying. This is one of the points of the song. Miss Symperson doesn't do it. I hear, afterwards, that she thought it vulgar, and omitted it purposely. I go on—

> "Lillibullero, lillibullero, lillibullero,
>        Shandiddlelan,
>    My daddy's a bonny wee man."

I feel it is idiotic. Miss Symperson plays a bar too much. She didn't know I finished there. I beg she won't apologise. Next verse—

> "This little pig's mother she was the old sow,
>    Ow, ow, ow, and Shandiddleow."

I feel it's more idiotic than ever. Here I see Miss Harding exchanging glances with the Captain, and Mrs. Fraser with several ladies; they raise their eyebrows and look grim. I suddenly recollect I've got some rather broad verses coming. The idea also occurs to me for the first time that when Fraser *did* hear me sing it, years ago, it was amongst a party of bachelors after supper. I go on with lillibullero, and have half a mind to give it up altogether :—

> "The Farmer's wife went out for a walk,
>    Walk, ork, ork, and shandiddle lork,
>    'I fancy,' says she, 'a slice of good pork.'"

This I used to do, I remember, with a wink and making a face like a Clown. I risk it. I feel I don't do it with spirit, and nobody laughs. I see Brounton whisper behind his hand to the American General, and I am sure that he's "seen old Mathews do this very thing," or something of that sort. Getting desperate, I make more hideous faces in the Lillibullero chorus. Miss Harding looks down; the ladies regard one another curiously—I believe they think I've had too much wine; the ugly boy, by the piano begins to imitate my faces, and the youngest in arms bursts into a violent fit of tears. Miss Symperson stops. The child won't be comforted. Mrs. Fraser tells the wretched little brat that

"the gentleman won't make any more ugly faces, he won't."
And turning to me, asks me to sing without the grimaces : "They
can't," she argues, "be a necessity ;" and Fraser reminds me
reprovingly, that when I sang it before, I didn't make those faces.
I have half a mind to ask him (being rather nettled) what faces I
*did* make ? The result is, however, to set the two boys off
making faces at their little sisters, for which they are very nearly
being ordered off to bed instantly. Miss Symperson asks me
"Shall I go on !" I say, despondently, "yes, if you please, we
may as well."

> "The Farmer's wife was fond of a freak,
>  Eak, eak, eak, and shandiddleleak,
>  And she made the little pig squeak, squeak, squeak."

Here used to follow the imitation. I think it better not to do
it now, and am proceeding with the next verse, when Fraser says,
" Hallo ! I say, do the squeak." I tell him I can't, I don't feel up
to it. He says, "Oh, *do* try." I hear Miss Harding say, "Oh,
do try." The Captain, too, remarks (I see his eye), "He hopes
I'll try," and Brounton hopes the same thing, and then tells something about Hook (probably) behind his hand to the General. I
say, "Very well," and yield. I begin squeaking : I shut my eyes
and squeak : I open them and squeak. I try it four times, but
am obliged to own publicly "that there is no fun in it unless
you're in cue for it." No one seems in cue for it. The children
begin squeaking, and are packed off to bed. People begin to resume
the conversation. I say to Fraser I don't think there's any use in
going on with the song? He answers, "Oh, yes, do—do by all
means." But as he is not by any means enthusiastic about it, I
thank Miss Symperson, who acknowledges it very stiffly and
coldly, and cuts me for the remainder of the evening. Brounton
comes up and tells me loudly, "That he remembers old Mathews
doing that song, or something exactly like it, years ago ; it was
admirable." Miss Florelly asks me quietly, "if I'd written many
songs." I disown the authorship of the pig. The Captain sings
a sentimental ballad about " *Meet me where the Flow'ret droops* "
to Miss Harding's accompaniment, and every one is charmed.

*Happy Thought.*— Bed-time. I'll never sing again as long as I
live.

G

*In my Room.*—My shirts, brushes, combs, ties, opera-hat, fire-irons, boots, collars, sponges, and everything, have been thrown anyhow into my portmanteau. Who the——

Oh, I recollect: this is what that horrid little wretch meant, when he told me at dessert, that he and his sister had been playing at packing-up in my room.

I wish I was back at Boodels'. I daresay they're dragging the pond, and enjoying themselves. I don't think I shall stop here any longer.

---

# CHAPTER XIII.

STILL AT FRASER'S—PROGRESS OF THE GREAT WORK—I THINK OF THE YOUNGER MISS SYMPERSON—NIGHT THOUGHTS—INTERVIEW WITH A COUNTRY POLICEMAN.

"You just come down."

HAPPY THOUGHT.—To stop here as long as I can. I don't get on with *Typical Developments.* Have hardly made a note for three days, except about the Sympersons: they live in the neighbourhood. Mrs. Fraser likes the Younger Miss Symperson, Miss Fridoline, very much. I have had to escort her a good deal: she can talk sensibly. I have consulted her on several subjects in *Typical Developments.* She understands me, and is not a mere fritterling. No one has asked me again to sing The Little Pig," and Mrs. Fraser is now more impressed with the serious and deeper-toned side of my character. I reproached old

**Fraser** with making me appear a buffoon. He owned his mistake, and said I was not a buffoon : we are as good friends as ever. In fact, to humour him, I offered to sing "*The Little Pig*" the other night when no one was here, feeling in the vein. They were delighted at the proposal, but feared it would wake the children : so I didn't.

The above is a brief *résumé* for the last few days up to to-night.

*Happy Thought.*—I've not left my present address anywhere, so business can't call me away. I am in the humour for the pen. Now : the moon is shining : the sweet autumn moon. I think of Fridoline Symperson.

*Happy Thought : Midnight.*—If I open my window I shall see the Sympersons' carriage pass here on their road home : *she* will be inside, and how it will delight her to see me watching for her. Not in my dressing-gown, though : my dark shooting-coat. I sit down to *Typical Developments.* Can't do it. I feel poetical : inspired. My pen. A poem—I feel it ; coming. I will dash it off—

"Ah ! fairest ! whose dear eyes——"

"Dear eyes" suddenly strikes me as too nautical. Odd thing inspiration is : it's almost oozing away now. I will fix it :—

"Ah, fairest, whose blest form,
Calm as pale Dian's orb——"

**Wheels :** I am at the window with a palpitating heart. No—yes—no ! A cart, a wanderer's cart ; a houseless pedlar, maybe. Whoever he is, he's very intoxicated, and calls me "Old Cocky-wax," which gets a laugh from another miserable creature, invisible. This is not the Sympersons. * * * *

"Ah, fairest Fridoline, whose——"

I don't think I ought to introduce her name into the first line. Strange : inspiration has ceased.

*Happy Thought.*—Will write her a song. To the window, I say rapturously, "Oh, Moon," but nothing comes of it, except that my eyes begin to water. How quiet and still. Not a soul stirring : not even a patrol. One o'clock : why this house might be broken into, over and over again, without a patrol. Carriage-wheels! louder, louder, louder,—less loud—faint, fainter, fainter—it has taken a turning--not the Sympersons. * * * I look at myself in the glass: I am pale. Am I going to be ill? * * * Yes, I shall be ill: given up. Fridoline will rush into the room. I shall then confess my concealed passion; so will she. I expire in her arms, or am about to expire, when the crisis passes, and I suddenly get quite well: then we are married. Happy thoughts, all the above. There are tears in my eyes: I call myself a fool. A minute afterwards I find myself shaking my head, pointlessly at the moon.

*Happy Thought.*—To write a novel on this subject. Might make notes for it now.

*Half-past One.*—No patrol—how very dangerous: I shall certainly call Fraser's attention to this. * * * Yes, Mrs. Fraser asked me when I first arrived, "If I was still a bachelor?" *She* likes Fridoline Symperson, and talks to me of her. How happy the Frasers are: ah, how delightful to retire— * * * Wheels? no. * * * to retire into married literary ease. Little secluded cottage, honeysuckles up the trellis, sort of church-porch before the door, myself writing at a window opening on to a beautiful lawn, my wife sitting knitting on a small stool. I write a bit, then read it to her; she smiles and encourages me. I write another paragraph, and then read that to her; she smiles and encourages me again. So we go on: reading, writing, smiling, and encouraging. Then, in my old age, when my name shall be known everywhere in connection with *Typical Developments,* I shall sit in the porch, grey hair falling on to my shoulders, my hands patting the little children's heads, while I strew fresh flowers every morning, before breakfast, over a little white stone in the churchyard, whereon is inscribed but two words, in old English characters, "MY FRIDOLINE." I see it all: tears dim my eyes: I'm feverish.

*Two o'clock,* A.M.—Odd that there should be no police. I *will* mention it in the morning.

I wonder with whom she is dancing? Is she dancing with that fellow, Talboots? I wish I had spoken to her yesterday, when I walked twice past their house, waiting for an opportunity to go in. I saw her in the garden, and only bowed ; agony.

*Happy Thought.*—Call to-morrow, and ask how she is after the party.

She told me she wished she hadn't got to go. Has she told any one else the same thing? Or is it because I am not going to be there. I wonder if she has one passing thought for me. Yes, I believe in sympathy ; in that strange electrical bond of union which binds two hearts together. There will be fools who talk nonsense to her ; she hates that vapid frivolity. To-morrow I *will* call on her. The Frasers won't mind it ; Mrs. Fraser understands me. I'm afraid it will look too pointed, though. I wish I had gone in yesterday when I saw her in the garden. I went there on purpose, yet I only bowed and walked on. Fool! thrice sodden fool! * * * All this sort of thing is very bad for calm writing.

*Three o'clock.*—No wheels. There, I've sat here for three hours and not seen a sign of a watchman or a policeman. I shall certainly call Fraser's attention to the absence of the patrol. He will complain to the inspector. The air is getting chilly. * * * How a sneeze relieves one's head. I can smile now : what at? I don't know. The roll of wheels—the spanking trot of fast horses—lights—it is the Sympersons' carriage? They mustn't see me at the window : I withdraw on one side. * * * It has passed : what an ass I was not to stand at the window, and wave, or perhaps kiss, my hand. I dare say she was looking out ; she *might* have been? I wish it would come over again. There's a ledge in front of my window, by stepping up there, I can see them turning into their own gates : I do it. The candle gutters out. I am on the leads. Ah, Fridoline! dear Fridoline! No, the gates must have been open, as they've driven in, and vanished. Ah, Fridoline! my sweetest dreams . . . . Somebody moving below ; in the road. A voice, "Hallo!" Probably another drunken creature (degrading vice of the country!). I will get in again, and not encourage him in his coarseness. A light shines about me vividly. What is it? From below. The same rough voice says, "Hallo! what are you up to there?" It is the patrol. I say quietly from the leads, "S-s-s-h, it's all right." He won't believe it, and says he'll soon *make* it all right. I tell him I'm stopping in the house. He wants to know "What I'm doing up there, then?" I answer, "Nothing." "I thought so," he says. "You just come down." He adds, "Or else he'll very soon know the reason why," threateningly. I assure him that he's wrong. He is getting very angry, and tells me, "He'll soon let me know if he's wrong or not." I own to him candidly that appearances *are* against me, but that I came out there to look after the Sympersons' carriage. I wish him to understand that it's only a joke. These country police are so officious; always in the way.

*Happy Thought.*—To throw him sixpence. He is indignant. I implore him not to be a fool. He now loses his temper entirely, and says, "He'll soon let me know who's the fool." I tell him, in as soft a whisper as can be audible from the leads, to call in the morning and I'll settle it. I point out to him (hearing a window opening somewhere) that he's disturbing the house. He says, "he means to," the idiot! and rings the gate-bell violently. I get into my room and close the window. I hear Mrs. Fraser screaming "Is it fire?" Fraser growling, the children crying, and the servants moving about below.

*Happy Thought.*—If I explain, I shall look such a fool, and Fraser will be in such a rage. Will tell him when it's all blown over.

*Happy Thought.*—Jump into bed. Fraser, butler, footman, with pokers, tongs, and shovels, enter in a tumult. In the distance I hear the maids and Mrs. Fraser all more or less hysterical.

*Happy Thought.*—I ask, "What's the matter?" They all say, in a muddle, "Man—broke in—p'liceman saw him." I haven't seen him: no. Patrol, from outside, says he hasn't come back again. One of the maids shrieks, and they all rush out, thinking some one's caught sight of him on the stairs. I try to pacify them: I tell Mrs. Fraser, in the distance, on account of the costume, that it must have been the patrol's fancy. I begin to wish I'd explained everything at first. The butler, who now returns from conversing with the policeman, describes the burglar as dressed in a short sort of dark coat, and details the substance of my remarks to him (the policeman) from the leads. "He said as he was a-lookin' after Mister Symperson's carriage." Fraser at once convicts the burglar as a liar, "Because," as he informs me, "the

Sympersons' carriage hasn't been out this evening, in consequence of their not going to the ball."

3·30. Everyone announces the impossibility of going to bed again. The coachman can't make out why the dog didn't bark. With the groom he searches the grounds. Everyone goes about searching everywhere, and coming upon each other suddenly round sharp corners ; frightening one another, as if it was a game. Fraser pops out of his room every other five minutes on some false alarm, to ask me " if I heard anything then ?" or to say, nervously, " Who's there ?" when the answer generally is, " It's only me, Sir," from the butler or the footman, who appear to be running away from Fraser, or catching each other, like blindman's buff. An *al fresco* game of the same kind is being played in the grounds by the groom, the coachman, and the policeman. The prevailing idea among the females is, that there is a man in the store-cupboard : the strictest search will not convince them to the contrary.

The butler spends the remainder of the night on the plate-chest, with a poker in his hand. The footman sits at the top of the servants' stairs, and alarms the entire household, for a second time, by falling asleep, and tumbling down half-a-dozen steps. After this he is all brown paper, vinegar and groans ; but heroically at his post, at the bottom of the stairs where he fell, with a poker. Everyone seems to have got a poker.

*Happy Thought.*—Shan't say anything about inattention of police, or they'll find I was at my window. Oh, Fridoline ! Bed —sleep.

## CHAPTER XIV.

AT FRASER'S—I HAVE A TÉTE-À-TÊTE WITH FRIDOLINE AND LOSE AN
OPPORTUNITY—A STRANGE ANNOUNCEMENT.

A téte-à téte.

THERE is no one up : except the servants. Fraser is in the wine-cellar, as usual ; some samples having just arrived from town, and two cases. Miss Fridoline calls, while I am at work on *Typical Developments.* I can see her arrive from my room. She is talking to the footman, who, from his rubbing his left shoulder very often, is evidently telling her about his having fallen downstairs, and last night's affair generally.

*Happy Thought.*—To let her see me at my window.

I wonder if she *did* see me. I ought to have looked at her. She's gone in. I really must work. Ch. 4, Vol. I., "On the Varieties of Inanimate Nature." I sit down to write. Hearing a door slam, I jump up again. It is not Miss Fridoline. To work. "Philosophers, in every age, have directed their attention to the——" A rustling in the passage by my door. I look out quietly. It is the housemaid, who, not having got over her fright of last night, screams on seeing me. The household, being generally nervous this morning, is immediately disturbed. The matter is explained unsatisfactorily, because Mrs. Fraser begs I'll be more quiet, and I return, rather annoyed (it *is* annoying to be misunderstood), to *Typical Developments.* "Philosophers, in every age, have directed their attention to the possibilities of the power inherent in mere particles. The

calm mind of inductive science, undisturbed by——" It *is* Miss
Fridoline. I hear her saying, "Yes, Mrs. Fraser, I'll get them for
you." She passes my door, and descends the staircase. Shall I?
I will. *Typical Developments* can wait.

*Happy Thought.*—Brush my hair, and settle my tie.

We meet in the hall. She is going to the hot-house to get some
grapes for "poor Mrs. Fraser." I say, "I'm going in that direction, myself," and then look at her with a smile intended to be full
of meaning. On repeating, afterwards, the same smile to myself
in the looking-glass, the meaning doesn't appear sufficiently distinct
and definite. But then it is difficult to look tenderly at oneself in
a looking-glass.

*Happy Thought.*—Try the effect in the glass, before, not afterwards, another time.

We are walking along the gravel path, about two feet apart
from one another.

She is humming a tune. I feel that all my conversational
powers have entirely deserted me. She says, "I'm sure it's boring
you very much to walk with me. I really can go alone, I assure
you." I feel taken aback by the remark : somehow, with all my
knowledge of human nature, it isn't what I had expected her to
say. I should like to come out with something now which would
clinch matters. I reply, "Oh no, I'm not bored," which, I feel,
implies that I am only saying so out of politeness. After this, it
seems that my power of speech has entirely deserted me. If I
talked at all, I should like it to be on very serious subjects. It
strikes me that if there was a third person here, I could be
brilliant. We enter another path. Miss Fridoline remarks,
laughingly, that I don't talk. Again I have no answer ready. I
can't make out where my answers have gone to. I am sure she
knows what my feelings are towards her, and she oughtn't to
laugh. I'm afraid, after all, she is frivolous. I ask her "What
we shall talk about?" She says, "Oh, you must start a subject."
Something, I don't know what, suggests, as a subject, "Beetles."
I can't put it down as a happy thought.

*Happy Thought.*—The art of talking to anyone with whom you
are secretly in love, is included in the power of making repartees.

She is evidently getting tired of me. She wants to know if I haven't any stories to tell her. No, I haven't. "Dear me!" she returns, "I thought you would be such an amusing companion. I thought you'd have a fund of anecdotes." So I have: somewhere. I defend myself by saying, "I didn't come out to tell anecdotes." I am obliged to laugh after this speech, as I am conscious of its having a certain amount of surliness in its tone. "Didn't you?" is her reply. "You don't expect *me* to do it." I feel I am becoming cross: I tell her that "I don't want any one to do it." A little more, and we shall quarrel. She suggests, "Well, you can sing me a comic song then? I'm sure you must know numbers of songs." This is an allusion to "*The Little Pig Squeaked.*" I don't like it. The idea of walking about with the girl whom you secretly love, and doing nothing but sing comic songs to her! I brood over this, and am silent. I make up my mind to lead up to the subject nearest my heart, on the next opportunity. We turn up another gravel path. She observes that she's "afraid I'm not well." Is this an opportunity? No: I'll wait for a better. I tell her that I'm not very well this morning, in order to excite her compassion. "Then," she says, "don't fatigue yourself to walk with me." The time has come I pump up my voice with difficulty, through a very hot throat. When it does come out, it sounds as if I'd been eating a pound of nuts, with the husks on, and was talking under a blanket. I say, "I can't feel fatigued," here I clear my throat, but am still under the blanket, "while walking with you." And I clear my throat again.

*Happy Thought.*—Not to clear your throat in the middle of a speech. Ineffective.

She apparently hasn't heard my observation, as she remarks, immediately, "What a beautiful place this is!" I answer, coming a little way out of the blanket, but hotter than ever, "You didn't hear what I said?" She asks, "What, just now?" I answer "Yes." Her reply is, "that she *did* hear it: but why?" I don't know "Why."

*Happy Thought.*—Always have some fixed attitude for one's hands. To pocket them looks careless when you're talking to some one you really like.

I try to explain " why." I say, pointedly, with my wide-awake well shading my eyes, " I don't think you understand me." I am getting to the point. She returns, that "she didn't know there was anything particular to understand." Not seeing my way to an explanation, I say, " Oh ! " in a tone of disappointment. She suggests that we had better make haste to get to the grape-house, as poor Mrs. Fraser is waiting. I say nothing, but quicken my pace despairingly. She commences another topic. " What a very nice person Mrs. Fraser is ! " Not caring to talk about Mrs. Fraser, I feel inclined to depreciate her. I say, sourly, " ' Nice ! ' I hate that phrase." Well, then, Miss Fridoline will substitute "so agreeable and kind, and so lively ; " adding, " I like lively people." I am aware this is a cut at me. Feeling hurt, I can't help saying, " I'm afraid I'm not lively." She returns, " No ; you do not seem very lively this morning."

*Happy Thought.*—Never give anybody an opening to make a cutting remark.

" One cannot always be lively," I answer, bitterly, "and playing the fool. Women, I suppose, are fond of that sort of thing." "Thank you," says Miss Symperson, " I didn't know I was fond of playing the fool." " I didn't say that," I explain. " I give you credit, Miss Fridoline, for appreciating thoughts of a more serious character." I should like to talk to her about my *Typical Developments.* While I am thinking how I shall begin, she asks me, " Are you generally so dull ? " I see the opportunity. I answer, " No, not always ; but——" (here I made the plunge) " with *you* I can't help it." She interrupts me, " Oh, then, with anyone else you'd be lively and cheerful ? That's a nice compliment."

*Happy Thought.*—Never come out without a pocket-hand kerchief. When you're talking with anyone you really care about, it's a very difficult thing to use a pocket-handkerchief with anything like grace. You can't say, " I love you ! " with your nose hidden. I find it ; but wait for an opportunity. If we come to a narrow path, where I can walk behind her, I'll use it then.

We turn a corner, and come suddenly upon the children. " Dear little things ! " cries Miss Fridoline. She takes the baby from the nurse. I look on, morosely. The ugly boy is there making faces at me. I think I could strangle them all. Miss Fridoline shows me the baby, and asks me if it isn't a pretty little darling? I smile on it, and say, "Charming!"

*Happy Thought.*—Always take care what one says of children before the nurses. They may tell Mrs. Fraser. One of the children, a sharp little girl, who ranks between the ugly boy and his younger brother, begs to be allowed to walk with " Friddy." Nurse says, "She'll be a nuisance to Miss Fridoline," who replies, " Oh, no—not at all ; *do* let her come ; I'll take care of her." I agree with the nurse, but keep it to myself, and say, gratuitously, " I always get on well with children." The child says, "Come on, Friddy." How I should like to call her "Friddy !" Away we walk towards the hothouse—she, I, and the sharp little girl. The sharp little girl begins pleasantly. She says to Fridoline, "I say, Friddy, we don't want *him* with us, do we?" meaning *me*. I should like to box her ears. I say, "Oh, yes, you *do*, though," and smile. She continues, " Oh, you're a great stupid, you are ; we don't want *you*." Miss Fridoline laughs. I laugh, too ; such a laugh ! I tell the child, hoping to stop her sharpness, "You mustn't be rude." Whereupon she cries out, " You're Mister Pigsqueaker, you are ; that's what we all call you, Mister Pigsqueaker !"

Miss Fridoline is laughing : the child is encouraged, and goes on, crying out, "Wee, wee, wee, Mister Piggysqueaker !" I should like to duck her in a pond. Miss Fridoline says, "Hush, Edith !" but not with authority ; and the child, who can't be very sharp, as she's only got this one idea of fun, goes on in a sort of variation on the theme, " Piggy, wiggy, squeaker, Mister Piggy-wiggysqueaker." She is beneath notice ; I will address my conversation, over her head and intelligence, to Miss Fridoline. I begin, "Do you believe in sympathies springing up between two beings for the first time?" Miss Fridoline pauses to reflect. I have touched the chord. The odious little brat cries out to me, " I say, when are you going away?" I tell her, condescendingly, that I do not know, and ask her if she wouldn't be very sorry to lose me? Her reply is not in keeping with my assertion that I get on very well with children : it is, " No, I shall be very glad. You're a Mister Piggysqueaker." The child has picked this name up from somebody else. Perhaps from the nurses ; perhaps from

Mrs. Fraser.    Perhaps the whole household calls me Mister Piggysqueaker.   It's impossible to make love in this character.   I almost wish I'd never come down.   That was the beauty of Boodels' place : there were no horrid children about ; and one couldn't fall in love with Milburd.

.In the Hothouse.    Miss Fridoline offers me a Peach.

*In the Hothouse.*—The gardener gives us some beautiful peaches. Miss Fridoline offers me one.   I accept it from her, and begin to ·eat it.   The infernal child says, " Oh, what a mouth ! "   I wonder if my mouth *is* so very large.   Children often speak the truth, unintentionally. I must be careful how I open it when laughing. I take the opportunity afforded by the necessity of wiping my hands, to use my pocket-handkerchief. The child gets hold of the other end, and tries to pull it away from me. Miss Fridoline does not reprove her. Tenderness is out of the question. I loiter behind with the gardener, and hear him talk about mushrooms. I could almost weep on his shoulder. I suppose I must look unhappy, as he observes, "He thought that peach as I was eating warn't a very ripe 'un." He takes me to the mushroom-house. It is damp and tomby. I feel that I have nothing to live for, and should like to stop here, among the mushrooms.

*Epitaph.* "Here lies Mr. Piggysqueaker, among the Mushrooms." The gardener is waiting for me, with the key in his hand. I come out. Miss Fridoline and the abominable child have disappeared. I return to the house. I will leave this place to-morrow. I ask where Mr. Fraser is. I want male society. He is in the cellar arranging a bin. He always is, during the day-time, in the cellar. To my work: I have been wasting my time. I will go to-morrow morning. I sit down to work. The butler enters. He looks very serious. "A policeman," he informs me, "wants to see me." A policeman! It can't be that window affair, last night. "Show him in."

## CHAPTER XV.

I RECEIVE A SUMMONS—A CONSULTATION—I LEAVE FURZE
COTTAGE ON IMPORTANT BUSINESS.

Fraser arranging his Bins.

A POLICEMAN to see me : show him in. Hitherto a policeman has been considered by me as a bugbear for children, and a terror to the lower orders. He is shown in, and is evidently not at his ease. I try to think of historical examples of anybody receiving the officers of justice in a dignified manner. I ask him, blandly, "Well, policeman, what's the matter?" He replies, "This here," and hands me this printed paper :—

"WHEREAS you have this day been charged upon oath before the undersigned, one of the Magistrates of the Police Court of the town of Dornton, sitting at the Town Hall of Dornton, in the county of Dampshire, and within the Boddington Police District, for that you, on the 16th day of September instant, at the parish of Little Boddington, in the county of Dampshire, and within the said district, did unlawfully assault and threaten and beat one George Cornelius Pennefather, whereby the said George Cornelius Pennefather goes in fear for his life.

"These are therefore to command you, in her Majesty's name, to be and appear before me, on the 1st of October next, at 11 o'clock in the forenoon, at the Police Court aforesaid, or before such other magistrate of the said Police Court as may then be there, to answer to the said charge, and to be further dealt with according to law.

"Given under my hand and seal," &c., &c.

"MORGAN JAMES BULLYER."

Good Heavens! Where's Dornton? Where's Boddington?

Who on earth is George Cornelius Pennefather? I tell the official, then and there, that I never beat, or assaulted, or threatened, anyone. He says, "He ain't got nothing to do with it; it's forwarded from the other county district." He adds, as a formula, that "anythink as I say now is safe to be used agen me at my trial," and goes out with the butler. "In Her Majesty's name!" I wish I was a Magistrate.

*Happy Thought.*—Refer to my diary. It was on that day, I find, that I tried to get the repartee out of the railway porter, and there was a disturbance in the Station. I suppose the porter's name is Pennefather. Why, I'd forgotten all about it: Pennefather hadn't, though. He's been going about in fear for his life ever since: Pennefather must be a fool. "To be further dealt with according to law." Don't understand it. I'll run down to see what Fraser says to it.

*Happy Thought.*—N.B. Anyhow, consult a solicitor.

Fraser's in the cellar, arranging his bins, as usual. From the top of the stairs I shout, "I say, Fraser!" and then his voice comes up suddenly from the cellar, "Hallo!" like a ventriloquist's. I say to him, still from the top of the cellar steps, "What shall I do in this case?" He answers, "Is there another up there?" being under the impression that I am alluding to wine.

I explain, coming down five steps to do so, and Fraser listens while putting away some curious old Madeira. When I've finished, I ask him what I shall do? He replies immediately, "Dine at six, sharp." "Yes," I say, "and after dinner I'll go up by the last train to town, and see my solicitor in the morning."

Fraser agrees with me, and as I come up the stairs, Captain Talboots and a Mr. Minchin, who was at the party the other night, come to make a call of ceremony. Mrs. Fraser can't receive them, being still unwell, so I call down to Fraser, and announce them. He replies, from below, just like the ventriloquist's man in a cellar, "All right, I'll come up directly." I tell Talboots about the summons. He is bellicose, and says, "If he was me, hang'd if he'd pay any attention to it. Bless'd if he wouldn't go and punch the infernal Magistrate's head." I point out to him that this would hardly clear me of a charge of assault.

*Happy Thought.*—Note, while I think of it. I *will* take

H

lessons in boxing : capital exercise. Gives you such a quick good eye : and such a bad eye occasionally. See about it, after my solicitor.

Minchin, who is a young barrister, wants to hear the case in full. Fraser joins us, and listens, with Talboots, like a couple of jurymen. Minchin appears in several characters, during my story ; but first, as the judge, with his hands in his pockets, his legs apart, and his head very much on one side like a raven. I feel while I am telling it, that I am making an excellent case for the porter. In attempting to be unprejudiced I catch myself knocking over my own defence and strengthening Pennefather's position. On finishing, I don't seem to have put matters in a very brilliant light, as far as I'm concerned. Fraser and Talboots look to Minchin. Minchin, in the character of prosecutor's counsel, examines me, as if on my oath. On the whole, I begin to wish I hadn't mentioned anything about it to Minchin.

*Happy Thought.*—In recounting your own grievances never try to be unprejudiced. No one gives you credit for candour.

"Now," says Minchin, for the prosecution this time, "Did you, or did you not, strike this railway official?" I hesitate, and Minchin repeats the question emphatically. I answer, "No, I did not *strike* him." Minchin repeats, as if to show Fraser and Talboots what a clever chap he was to get that admission from me. "No, you did not strike him," and then goes on, evidently enjoying it, "And now, Sir, let me ask you, did you or did you not *touch* him?" I admit I did. Minchin is calmly triumphant, repeating, "You did," whereat Fraser and Talboots, in their impersonation of jurymen, shake their heads. Minchin continues, "Did you or did you not call this railway official a fool?" I can't help it, I'm obliged to admit that I did. Jury dead against me. Minchin now as the judge, having evidently abandoned any idea of appearance as counsel for the defence, sums up carefully. Somehow or another Minchin's opinion suddenly appears most valuable to me, and I listen anxiously.

Minchin says—"You touched him ; lightly or heavily, no matter ; the fact stands that you touched him. If you had no weapon in your hand, yet you touched him. The porter was an unarmed man ; *you* own that you had an umbrella, and you are not sure that you did not touch him with *that.*" I shake my head. " Be that as it may, you touched him, and that touch was an incitement to him to riot. It is no defence to say, 'I touched him gently on the shoulder.' The question is, whether you *could* have touched him roughly in the position you were placed in, that is, from the window of the railway carriage ? But the law deals with intentions, and judges of the intentions both by words and

Captain Talboots and Fridoline practising a Duet.

deeds. Now, you accompanied this blow "—(I deprecate the use of " blow," and he substitutes " touch," as if it really didn't make any difference)—" You accompanied this blow, or touch, with the opprobrious epithet of ' Fool.' Now the law having regard to the liberty of the subject, and being no respecter of persons, will not allow any man to go about, touching, or blowing, his fellow citizens, lightly or heavily, and calling them fools. No," con- tinues Minchin, discarding the Judge, and appearing finally as a private friend, " I'm afraid it's a nasty case." I own I think so too. I put it thus, "If he says I did, and I can't say I didn't, what defence am I to make?" I don't see. Minchin considers: Fraser is perplexed. Captain Talboots says, with a laugh, "Oh, you sing '*The Little Pig Squeaked*' to the Magistrate, and he'll let you off." His levity is ill-timed. They smile out of compliment, but the joke is a failure. Minchin says, "Well, he must be off." Talboots says, "He must be off, too." Talboots has nothing new to suggest; he can only repeat, "Punch the Magistrate's head."

*Happy Thought.*—They *are* off.

*Dinner.* 6. Melancholy. Fraser thinks it good taste to joke about "the prisoner sat down to his usual meal, of which he partook heartily." On my telling him how much I have enjoyed my stay here, hoping that he'd re-invite me (Oh, Fridoline!), he replies, jocosely, "The prisoner expressed himself sincerely grateful to Mr. Jonas, the Governor of Newgate, for all his kindness." My train goes at nine; at half-past eight I hear music in the drawing-room. I find out that it's Miss Fridoline, who's been dining up-stairs with Mrs. Fraser. A fly at the door. Captain Talboots arrives with his cornet-à-piston: he and Miss Fridoline are going to practise a duet. He offers me *his* fly to take me to the station: I am obliged to accept it.

I go in, drearily, to wish Miss Fridoline good-bye. She says, "Oh, are you going so soon?" I have no reply ready, except "Yes, I'm going now." Whereupon she returns my adieu with the addition of wishing me a pleasant journey. As I am stepping into my fly, I hear the piano and cornopean in a duet, "*Yes, we together*," from *Norma*. If I could run back, burst into the room, jump on Talboots' back, and cram his cornopean down his throat, I would do it. *He* might summon me, if he liked, I should soon become used to *that*. Drive on: he drives on. Furze Cottage is a thing of the past.

*Happy Thought, or rather Unhappy Thought.*—An opportunity missed. When Fridoline said to me, "Are you going away so soon?" I ought to have returned impressively, "Soon! I am glad to hear that since I have been here, the time has flown so fast. It will appear like an age to me before I see you again. For," and here I should have taken her hand, and if neither Talboots, nor Fraser, nor the butler were looking, I might have kissed it fervently, saying, as I relinquished it, "Fridoline, I love you!" Then, unable to utter anything more, I should have got into my fly comfortably, and she would have staggered to the sofa, put one hand on the back and another on her heart, like the lady in Millais' picture of "Broken Vows." *Happy Thought.* Suggest this to an artist. View of me stepping into a fly in the distance. I wish I could have those minutes over again. I wonder if I should really do what I think I should. I should like to drive back and try it. No—it can't be.

*Happy Thought.*—To prepare oneself for occasions of this sort. I'll suppose cases as I go up in the train.

*Nine o'clock.* Off to London : *Addio*, Fridoline and Furze.


## CHAPTER XVI.

STILL ON URGENT PRIVATE AFFAIRS—A JUVENILE SOLICITOR—I DINE WITH MILBURD AND SPEND A CONVIVIAL EVENING—NEXT MORN- ING—THE BIRDS—LONDON STREETS—AN INVITATION—THEATRE —A MUSIC HALL—A LUNCHEON—A SERMON.

Boots is satisfied.

OING *up in the Train by Night.*—I intend to call on my Solicitor about this assault affair directly I get to town. Think I'd better dismiss all thoughts of it from my mind. Will read paper. Can't. Light in carriage so bad. At the first station I want to get out to complain to Guard. Can't : carriage locked. Passenger gets in with his own key, and brings with him a private railway lamp : most useful. Other passengers get in : all got keys and lamps. If we go on like this we shall bring our own cushions. Last man *did* get in with a cushion. The next thing will be to bring your own carriage.

*Happy Thought.*—To buy a railway lamp.

Can't sleep, on account of the blaze of light in my eyes from lamp opposite. Arrive in town late. Go to Solicitor's. Shut up. To hotel. Get up early to-morrow. I see that I'm chalked up on a black board. 89. 7·30. The Boots is satisfied : another Boots coming by accidentally is satisfied. Waiter assures me, on my inquiring anxiously, that if I gave the Boots my instructions, it would be all right.

Difficult to get to sleep. Noise, after quiet of country, terrific.

*Happy Thought.*—Central hotels bad for going to sleep in. Do for men of business, though, who want to be up early in the morning. Bed.

*Morning.*—Not called : had to ring the bell to tell them to call me. Boots says he didn't know I wanted to be called, didn't see it on the black board. A different Boots. I refer him to the other Boots for confirmation, in fact to the other pair of Boots. He doesn't know them : he alludes to them disdainfully, as the Night Porters.

*Happy Thought.*—Small Hotel's best : where the Boots and Night Porters are on friendly terms. Do it next time.

I'm very late. They bring me number ninety's boots ; and number seventy-five's breakfast, which I don't like. More delay. Off at last to Lincoln's Inn Fields. To Seel's, my Solicitor's.

On the door is a brass plate with Mr. Seel above, and Mr. Percival Seel below. Who Mr. Percival is I do not know ; probably Seel's son just come into the business. I knock and ring.

The clerk is a small boy with a large forehead, ready for all the law that's coming into it one of these days, curly hair which won't lie down under any pressure of pomatum, and large eyes, which wander all over me.

On being asked if Mr. Seel is within, he replies, " No, he's *not,*" in an uncertain sort of manner, which leads me to suppose that he *is.* I give him my card. He looks at it, and then at me, as if unable to trace any connection between my name and my appearance.

*Happy Thought.*—I note that to be brought up in a lawyer's

office makes boys suspicious. He evidently doesn't believe either me or my card.

Boy says, "He's *not* in : " but he adds, "you can see Mr. Percival, if you like." He speaks of them as if they were a show. I ask who Mr. Percival is, and he replies that he's Mr. Seel, Junior, which he evidently thinks is a more dignified form of description than calling him Mr. Seel's son. I consider. Well, yes, I *will* see

Mr. Seel's clerk evidently doesn't believe either me or my card.

Mr. Seel, Junior. I am shown suddenly into Mr. Seel, Junior's room. Mr. Seel, Junior, is very much junior to Mr. Seel, Senior.

He offers me a seat timidly. He says, awkwardly, that he believes my business is with his father. I say yes, but I suppose he'll do as well. He evidently detects some hesitation in my tone, as he answers boldly, and, to my thinking, defiantly (as though if his father *did* come in *he* didn't care), that, "Oh, yes, it would be precisely the same thing."

I tell him it's a very simple case, whereat I fancy he seems more

at his ease.  I suppose he can advise me.  He replies, " Oh yes, of
course."  But he doesn't inspire me with confidence.  I tell him,
to re-assure him, I've known his father some years, which seems
to make him uncomfortable.  I tell my story very carefully.
When I've finished, he asks me to tell it again.  I do.  At his
special request, I tell it once more, with (I can't help it) variations,
which puzzle him.  I ask him what I shall do?  He appears confused, and thinks; at last, he says, " Well, you see, I've only
lately come into the office, and——" (here he laughs nervously)
" I can't exactly advise you—without—without—um——" (here
he loses his theme, but recovers himself) " without, in fact, consulting my father."  Then I'd better see his father?  " Yes," he
says, diffidently, " if you please."  I say I will, whereat he is
much relieved, and, so to speak, breathes again.  I must see his
father to-night—most important—at eleven.  I suggest, at all
events, that, having spent one hour with him in painstaking
narration, Mr. Percival may put the case before his father.  I don't
believe he has understood a word of what I've been saying, as he
replies, " No, you'd much better do it yourself."

*Happy Thought.*—What a dreadful thing it would be to have an
idiot Solicitor !

Eleven to-night, punctually !  Eleven.  Special appointment.
I note it down.  Good-bye.

*Happy Thought.*—Nothing to do in London.  Dismiss all
thoughts of Pennefather's assault from my mind.  How shall I
amuse myself?  Go to Charing Cross.  Stand for ten minutes
waiting to cross the road.  Don't know why I should cross at all,
having no object in reaching the other side, except to come back
again.  I came up to be very busy with my Solicitor, and here I
am with nothing to do.  I stroll into Bow Street.

*Happy Thought.*—Visit the Police Court, and get up the forms
and ceremonies, so that when I have to appear, if I ever have,
before a Magistrate, I may know when it's my turn to speak, and
when to be silent.  Go into what I take to be the Police Court.
Am asked what I want by two policemen.  They are civil, but
suspicious.  I won't go in : I will dismiss all these thoughts from
my mind.  I find myself continually dismissing these thoughts.

Drop into my Club. Letter waiting for me from Childers at the Feudal Castle. Will I come down when I like : only telegraph. I will, when this business is over. This business——no, I said I would dismiss these thoughts from my mind, and I will. But I must answer him. Not necessarily. I can wait until I know if I am free to . . . Dismiss thoughts again for the third time within ten minutes.

In St. James's Street. Somebody slaps me on the back and says "Hallo! What brings *you* to town?" It is Milburd. I dislike Milburd at Boodels', but when you meet him in town, and can't get any one else to talk to, he's not a bad fellow. I wish he wouldn't think slapping on the back a sign of heartiness. He tells me afterwards that he considers "slapping a fellow suddenly on the back when he doesn't know who the deuce it is," a first-rate practical joke. I don't think it first-rate. "Well," he puts it, "not bad." I state my general objection to all practical jokes. He agrees with me, excepting slapping on the back. I give in on this point, not liking to be obstinate, and suffer for it, as he's always, being with me for two hours in the day, trying to take me by surprise. I tell him my case. He sympathises. He is not a bad fellow when you know him. He says, "Look here," I avoid his slap, and he goes on somewhat disappointed, "come and dine with me this evening. Dismiss all thoughts of your trial," I don't like his way of speaking of it, but his idea is the same as mine about dismissing the thoughts, "and spend a quiet evening. I'll give you dinner at my Club." I tell him that I'm not in the humour for a dinner-party. He informs me that it's no dinner-party, only Byrton of the Fusileers. I repeat, "Oh, only Byrton of the Fusileers," as if his presence was nothing at all ; though I've never seen him in my life. Milburd says, "Yes, that's all : say 6·30 Bradshaw."

*Happy Thought.*—Always note down engagements. I am noting this. Milburd (he is an ass sometimes) says, "Good-bye, old boy," and slaps me on the shoulder. I am inclined to be annoyed, but he laughs, and cries out, "Another practical joke, eh?" so I can't be angry. Besides, he *has* asked me to dinner.

He comes back for one minute, to ask me "if I think that bon-neting a fellow, knocking a hat right over his eyes, is a good practical joke, eh?" I treat the notion with contempt, as beneath such a man as Milburd. I think this is the best way of stopping him, by representing such conduct as *unworthy* of him, or if I don't, he might crush mine in: he's just the sort of fellow to do it. "Full of animal spirits," his friends say. It's a nuisance if you're not full of animal spirits at the same time. Go to my hotel. Unpack writing materials. Try to do something in *Typical Developments* about "Spirits of Animals." Think of Fridoline. Think if this matter ends happily . . . Dismiss all thoughts of this sort from my mind. Doze. Hot water. Dress to go to Milburd's Club.

He introduces me to Byrton of the Fusileers. He is friends with me in five minutes, and is telling us in a half-whisper, with his head well forward towards the soup-tureen, something "which of course," he knows, "won't go beyond this table."

Byrton can tell us curious circumstances about every one. If we talk of the Great Mogul, he is ready with a curious circumstance about him, of course *entre nous!* Milburd and I are perpetually swearing ourselves to secrecy all through the dinner. Trying to note down (privately outside the door) one of his remarkable anecdotes, names excepted, I find myself making rather a muddle of his confidences.

*Happy Thought.*—Capital wine, Moselle: sparkling. Not so strong as champagne.

We dispute this point, and try champagne. I note down the name of the wine-merchant. Byrton tells us something rather curious about *him*. It is decided that we shall return to the Moselle. I must keep my head clear, having to see my Solicitor at eleven. Milburn says, "Oh, don't think about that, *now*. We will have some more Moselle, or champagne." [On referring to my notes in the morning, which I made as opportunities occurred outside the door, I find the names of several wine-merchants put down as "Mr. Moselle" and "Mr. Champagne Sparkling," and I don't know quite what I meant.] The dinner goes on. So does the Moselle.

*Happy Thought.*—Ask for Moselle at my Club. Ask Milburd and Byrton to dine with me. [Referring to notes in the morning can't make out date.]

They accept. We accept to dine also with Byrton : don't know when. The room is getting hot. The next bottle of Champagne wants more icing. Capital wine Champagne : so's Moselle. We are all telling good stories in confidence, hoping they'll go no farther than that table, like Byrton. I am telling good stories : and it seems to me that we are all talking together, or else some one is speaking very loud. Liqueurs. I say, must go S'lic'tor. Not time yet. Dismiss thoughts. Fine Port.

*Happy Thought.*—Lay-in-stock-port. We're talking Theol'gy. Byrton is telling us something cur'ous 'bout Arch'shop Cranbury. I say it's not Cranbury. Milburd agrees—me. What's it then ? Byrton wants—know. " Arch'shop," I tell him, " of Crantier-brarry." Smoking room. Don't like going up-stairs. Come down 'gain. Time go S'lic'tor. Cab.

*Happ Thought in Cab.*—'Stake t'king port a'f'er Mamselle : mean M'selle. Think I've had 'nough. Sh' like biscuit : and water. Very soon at S'lic'tor's. Very. Seel Sen'r in. Come talk : ser'ous mat'r : 'sault. Seel wantsknow pericklers. I've f'gott'n p'ricklers : ask P'en'fath'r. He thinks I'd bet'r call morn'g. Very hot in 's room. While tell'ng p'ricklers refer'n notes . . . . sleepy . . . .

*Hotel.*—Think it's 'tel. S'lic'tor still here : somehow. Can't make him un'stand. Stupid. * * * * So's the waiter * * * * Stupid . . . . won't un'stand. * * * very sleepy. * * The weather * * odd weather * * trouble undressin'.

*Happ Thght.*—Go to bed in my boots. * * * *

Don't know how I got to bed last night. Odd that I should forget to wind up my watch. I find from my notes of the previous evening, that I *did* go to see my Solicitor. Can't tell from them, as they're so indistinctly written, whether he advised me. I think he advised me to go to bed. Don't feel at all well to-day. It's the weather : and when the weather is unhealthy, it doesn't do to mix Champagne, Sherry, Moselle, and Port. Horrid weather. Might write a short chapter in Vol. VI. of *Typical Developments,* " On Influences."

I am rather hazy as to what I did to my Solicitor last night. I hope I didn't hurt him. I have got some sort of notion that I

wanted him to dance. However, he's a man of the world, and
knows that, if it's at all unhealthy weather, or if you are a little
out of order, or not quite the thing, one so easily gets upset by a
single glass of wine, and then you become excited in conversation,
and do some stupid things which in cold blood you would not do.
Of course, in cold blood one would not dance with one's Solicitor.

*Happy Thought.*—Better call on him, and make it all right.
Bring him some game from the country. Sort of little attention
he'd like.

*Happy Thought.*—Buy the game as I go along. Grouse. Without telling him a positive untruth, I will give him to understand
that I shot them myself.

*With* Mr. Seel, Senior.—He hears my story. No allusion to
last night, except on my part. *He* appears to have forgotten it
entirely. I wonder if he'd been dining, too. I've got a great
mind to ask him whether he wanted to dance with me, or I with
him. I won't. He says he'll settle this assault case and Pennefather into the bargain. Finding that this is an easy matter, I
suggest retaliation. Can't I bring an action against the Company?
He asks, what for? I tell him that I suppose he knows this better
than I do. I'm to hear from him in a couple of days; this is
Saturday—say Monday evening. Conversation. I tell him where
I've been. He asks me if I've had any shooting yet? I say,
"No." Remembering the birds in the passage, I add, "Nothing
to speak of." On leaving, I present him with the grouse. He
remarks, that he didn't understand me to say I'd been to the
moors. I tell him that I haven't; and he replies, "Oh, indeed!"
and smiles.

*Happy Thought.*—The study of law engenders a habit of suspicion. But I ought to have asked, when I bought the game,
where these sort of things are shot. I thought all birds got into
turnip-fields: and turnip-fields are everywhere. Seel asks me if
the birds are very shy this year. I answer, in an offhand manner,
"No, not *very* shy: at least, I didn't find 'em so," as if they made
an exception in my case, as, indeed, they might have done if I'd
had a gun. I must take up shooting and hunting, this winter.
Can't help thinking of Fridoline. I should like to appear before

her one morning in a red coat, buckskin breeches, and brown tops, and wave my hand to her as I gallop away on my bright chestnut.

*Happy Thought.*—Buy a horse for the winter : not too high.

Nothing to do in London. Walk about. Inspect small streets near Leicester Square. Useful to know London. One street smells as if all the inhabitants were preparing to dine off onions. Walk about. Think I'll get my hair cut. Stop, to look at a wheel turning round in a shop-window. Feel myself fascinated by it. Small crowd looking on. Everyone apparently fascinated. Wonder what the other people see in it. Ask a respectable elderly person what it's for. He doesn't know. I ask another. He laughs, and doesn't know. Now, I'll go and get my hair cut. Walk on. See another crowd round another window. Wait until I can work myself to the front. In the shop-window is a small jet of water, which takes up a little gilt ball with it as it rises. Everyone appears pleased. Nobody offers to go in and buy it. Having seen it for four minutes, I experience no sort of inclination towards walking into the shop to purchase it. Strange, after seeing this, I feel depressed. Stop to look at a man with a bird-whistle.

*Happy Thought.*—Get my hair cut. Meet Chesterton. Haven't seen Chesterton for years. He has lately become a clergyman. Quite lately. His manner is subdued and gentle, and I should think he intends it to be winning. He asks me, sorrowfully, to lunch with him to-morrow (Sunday). I accept. He informs me that two friends of his, whom I know, are coming—Huxley and Wright. They are coming to hear him preach his first sermon, in the afternoon, after luncheon. He must leave me now, he says, having to write his discourse. He smiles sadly and seems to glide away. Too late to have my hair cut to-day. Something to do for Monday.

*Saturday Evening.*—Dinner alone at the Club. Don't know anybody. Read newspaper : that is, try to. Find myself reading the same lines over and over again. Afterwards, I write to my Solicitor, and ask how he's getting on. Don't know what to do with myself. Will go to the theatre. Come in at the end of a farce. Comic man in red check trousers is saying, "So, after all,

Maria, it was not you." Roars of laughter. Allusion to a bracelet. More laughter. Wonder what it was about. Ask a gentleman sitting next me. He informs me that it's just over. I say I know that, but he is sulky, and goes out as the curtain comes down. I don't think he treads upon my toes by accident. Wish 1 hadn't come. In the lobby I meet Milburd. Capital man to fall in with in town. Knows everybody.

As a piece of news he tells me that "Old Boodels is going to drag the pond next Monday. What do I say to coming down." I reply, "yes, by all means, but," not to make myself too cheap, "I'm afraid I've got an engagement." I own I can manage to put it off. I don't tell him that it's only to have my hair cut, which I forgot to-day. Capital. Not having a bill, I ask him to point out any celebrities. He asks me do I know Phelps. I do by reputation. Odd, until Milburd showed him to me, I had always thought he was a tragedian, and here he is with a red nose and a red wig, dancing a sort of double shuffle, and singing something about being "a magnificent brick, my boys, my boys, for I" —meaning himself Mr. Phelps—"I'm a magnificent brick!" As Milburd has heard it all before, and as I've not long to stay in town, I ask him to take me somewhere. We go to a Music Hall. Miss Emily Montacute is obliging the company with another song. She has a weak voice, but does a great deal with her right eye, and her hand. The audience, who are taking refreshments and tobacco, join in the choruses enthusiastically, being principally incited thereto by the chairman, who applauds everything by hammering upon the table, and announces, after every song, good or bad, encored or not encored, that Mister, or Miss, or Mrs., as the case may be, "will sing again." He amuses me. No one else does.

The chairman recognises Milburd on his entering and condescends to wink at him as he passes to his seat. Immediately after this he raps sharply, as though to recall himself to a sense of his dignified position. A man comes on in an absurd dress with a tall hat, and sings something about "his, or her, being a cruel deceiver, with his (the singer's) diddlecum doddlecum doddlecum doodlecum didlecum day." The tune is catching, and I find myself humming it. Milburd, who doesn't at all understand the depth of my character, suggests that I should turn my *Typical*

*Developments* into a Comic Song, and do it at a Music Hall, with a good chorus. He says, "Look here, capital idea, chorus, 'with my Typical Typical Typical Typical toodlecum ti.'" I smile, but do not encourage him. We leave: I with a headache. Before parting I inform him of my engagement to-morrow with the Rev. Edward Chesterton. It appears that Milburd knows him. I tell him that it's on the occasion of his first sermon. Milburd cries out, "What a lark! I'll come"—and then sings, "with my Typical Typical Typical toodlecum"—but here I stop him, and say, not priggishly, that it's not a thing to joke about. To which he replies, "No, this here ain't a Comic Song, am it?" We part good friends (with the exception that I don't like his going on singing with my Typical toodlecum, which is all very well for once and away; but palls upon you very soon. Though on the whole I wish I'd not told him about Chesterton.

*Happy Thought.*—Go to bed.

*Sunday.*—Luncheon with Chesterton. Rather heavy, being *his* dinner. Huxley and Wright are old College friends of his. Their reminiscences are hardly fitted to the occasion, being of Beefsteak Club dinners, wild drives to Newmarket, Loo parties, and one great one about bonneting the porter of Chesterton's College. Chesterton is evidently uncomfortable. After luncheon, which finishes about 2·30, they smoke. Chesterton leaves us for half an hour, begging we'll make ourselves at home. Milburd drops in and soon makes *himself* at home. I try to draw their attention to serious topics. Milburd, who will make a jest of everything, calls them "Serious Toothpicks;" and the two others, who are becoming stupid and sleepy, laugh at him. The Rev. Chesterton returns. "Will we come now?" he asks sadly, as if he was taking us all to instant execution, with benefit of clergy. We will. He is delighted, he says, to see Milburd. Will he too come and hear his poor efforts? Milburd answers that he means to encore him if it's very good. Poor Chesterton smiles with melancholy sweetness. He evidently means to be winning.

*Happy Thought.*—To get a comfortable seat in the corner of the pew. Away from Milburd.

*Four o'clock.*—Note book. Milburd is seated next to me. The three very decorous. Chesterton is in the pulpit. I miss the text because Milburd will make such a noise blowing his nose, and the two others cough.  People settling themselves.  I think Chesterton is nervous.  He looks towards us, and Milburd jogs me with his elbow.  I frown.  Sermon proceeding.  Small boy in front of me keeps looking round.  Frown at him.  Shake my head reprovingly. Boy laughs.  His mother angry.  Boy cries, and points at me. Chesterton sees it but goes on : is annoyed.  Milburd snores.  I am afraid of pinching him.  Huxley, who is in the right-hand corner, has succumbed to drowsiness, and is suddenly awoke by his head coming sharply against the back of the pew.  Wright, who has been opening and shutting his eyes for the last five minutes, gives way at last and falls against Milburd.  They are falling against one another like cards that won't stand upright.  I wish I could appear as if they didn't belong to my party.  Boy is looking round at us and grinning.  His mother, I fancy, must be deeply interested in the discourse, as she doesn't take any notice of him.  I try to avoid his eye.

*Happy Thought.*—I will close my eyes to prevent distractions, and listen critically to Chesterton's sermon.  I note down a good passage. * * * * I am roused by the general movement of the congregation, and Milburd whispering to me, "Oh, how you have been snoring !"

We meet Chesterton coming out of the vestry and greet him with "Excellent! first-rate! just the right length!"  He seems pleased.  Wright wants him to publish it.  So does Huxley. Milburd turns to me and suggests that I might throw in a chorus "With my typical, typical, typical," &c., which notion I repudiate.

*Happy Thought.*—Don't think I shall go down with Milburd to drag the pond at Boodels.  Doesn't do to see too much of Milburd. Shan't be at home when he calls, and if Seel sends to say Assault cause settled, I shall run down at once to the Feudal Castle.

*Happy Thought.*—Hair cut on Monday.  No dragging ponds.

## CHAPTER XVII.

MONDAY IN MY HOTEL—OUT OF IT AT THE HAIRCUTTER'S—THE
TELEGRAM—OFF TO BOVOR—I ARRIVE AT BECKENHURST.

The Beckenhurst Station-master.

DULL : no news from Solicitor. Send up porter with note to Seel to ask how's the matter going on. Lonely place a hotel when you don't know anybody.

*Happy Thought.*—Go to the bar and ask for letters.

*Happy Thought.*—To ask for letters at a hotel gives you some importance. No letters : didn't expect any. Porter returns : Seel not in. No answer : provoking. Go and write a Chapter for Vol. VIII. *Typical Developments,* on "Loneliness in Crowds." Think the idea's been done before : will ask some one. Won't write just now.

*Happy Thought.*—Go and have my hair cut.

Man who cuts it wishes to know insinuatingly, whether I use their Bohemian Balsam. I don't like hurting his feelings, but am obliged to say that I do not. He can recommend it strongly, he says, and wishes to "put up a pot for me." I say no, not to-day. I feel that I am in his hands, and if he presses it very much, I'm done. He supposes, as a matter of course, that I am never without their Chloride of Caranthus. I answer, in an off-hand way, that I haven't used any of it lately, though I don't add that I've never heard of it before. Shall he put me up a couple of bottles ? I take time to consider : as if this was a difficult matter to decide. I answer after a few minutes. "Well—no—not to-

I

day," whereupon he proposes sending it to me in any part of the country.

*Happy Thought.*—To tell him that I don't like the Chloride of Caranthus: that will settle it. I tell him: it doesn't settle it. He is astonished to hear this from me, and says, "Indeed! dear me!" quite pityingly. I wonder if he's taken in. He tries to flatter me by pretending that he recollects how I like my hair cut. "Not very short, I think," he says. Humbug! I've never been here before. He tells me that some gentlemen *do* prefer the Gelatinium; perhaps, he inquires, that is *my* case, perhaps I prefer the Gelatinium. On my saying, dubiously, "No," he proposes putting up a bottle of each to try.

*Happy Thought.*—Always be decided in speaking to a hairdresser. Say boldly that you don't use any of these things, or that you don't want anything at present.

I casually praise a brush whirled about my head by machinery, and he offers to put that up for me, machinery and all, I suppose. Nothing easier, he explains. Will I have my head washed? I answer, "Yes," adding inadvertently, "I have not had that done for some weeks." He seizes upon the admission, and deduces from it that I have none of their Savonian Bruilliantine. I have not. He says decidedly that he will put me up a couple of bottles. He is actually going to give the order when I call out, "No, I won't." A little more and I should lose my temper altogether. He's afraid that I don't use their Gelissiton Sphixiad for my whiskers and moustache. He says this in a tone implying that I may expect them to drop off at once if I don't adopt his remedy. I despise myself for getting cross with a hair-dresser; but one is entirely in his power. You can't jump up and run away with the apron sort of thing round your neck. He is very officious in assisting me with my coat and waistcoat: his hands are greasy, but I don't like to hurt his feelings. Won't I have any soaps, brushes, combs? can't he put up any little thing for me? toilette bottles? Eau-de-cologne, scents? Then he concludes with "Nothing more to-day?" Whereupon I reply, as blandly as I can, "No, thank you, nothing more to-day." He bows me out.

*Happy Thought.*—Won't go *there* again. Ought to go to a

dentist's. Shan't. It hurts; and I might be laid up with a swelled face.

Back to hotel. Send message up to Solicitor. Ask for letters again. None. Porter returns. No answer from Solicitor. Odd. Think I'll write to Fraser. In his letter send a passage to Miss Fridoline. Can't send her "my love." "Kind regards" is what you would send to an elderly lady. I'll put it generally, thus: "Remember me to all at Furze." Send up to Solicitor's, for the third time to-day. Think I'll take a walk. As I go out, ask for letters. None. I appear surprised and puzzled. Don't think the Manageress is taken in. Solicitor sends answer :—"All right. You can go away. Send me your address, in case of an accident. Pennefather withdraws."

I am in high spirits. Hang Pennefather!

*Happy Thought.*—Go down to Bovor Castle at once. Change of scene. Telegraph—"Coming down. Last train. Dine in town. No answer."

Splendid invention, telegraphing. So easily done. I send a line : in an hour's time Childers will get it : will order a trap to meet me by last train : prepare supper, fire, bed for me : an everything will be ready for my arrival.

*Dine at my Hotel.*—Notice character. Patronising head-waiter, who keeps on catching my eye. Officious waiter, who will insist upon bringing every course before I want it, and receiving everything before I've quite done. One man dining alone smiles on everyone, as if he'd be ready to drink or eat with anyone at a moment's notice. Another bestows his umbrella carefully away in a corner at his elbow, as though there was some chance of its raining during dinner-time, in which case he would be prepared. A third calls the waiters by their Christian names, and gets served quicker than any one ; whereat others (myself included) are scowling. The head-waiter whispers to him the best cuts, and keeps him alive to the arrival of the hottest joint. There is another unfortunate man, who sits down at the same time as myself, and apparently asks for everything they haven't got, and is only beginning his fish as I am finishing my dinner. Cab to Station.

*Happy Thought.*—When I return to town, to learn boxing. To give an impertinent cabman one on the nose, or in the eye, would beat repartees all to nothing. As it is, I have to give him six-pence over his fare to avoid a row.

Ticket for Beckenhurst. Nearest station for Bovor Castle. No sleeping this time.

Bright night. Carriage shaky. Hope my luggage is all right. It suddenly flashes across me that I don't remember packing up my sponge. Wish I could get at my portmanteau, and see. No good, by the way, if I could.

*Beckenhurst.*—Luckily some one in the carriage tells me it's Beckenhurst, or I should have missed it. Get out. Very cold. I've got two portmanteaus, a bag, a writing-desk and a dressing-case. I tell this to the guard, who whistles, and the train is off. I find my luggage on the platform. Station-master asks for my ticket. I give it him. Porter asks me where I'm going to? I say "Bovor Castle," with a feeling that there's something wrong. On the contrary, all right. Station-master says, politely, "Oh, you're the gentleman who telegraphed from town to say he'd be down by last train." I am, I reply, graciously. Station-master runs off to look after two or three other tickets.

To telegraph was a Happy Thought indeed. The telegram (I say to myself) has arrived : old Childers has evidently sent a trap for me, prepared supper, and all I've to do is to drive to Bovor as quickly as possible, and enjoy myself. Good fellow, old Childers. The train is half-an-hour late, but that doesn't matter, as the telegram has arrived. Station-master returns. I am curious to know how quickly that telegraphic message travelled. "When," I ask him, in the greatest good humour, "did you get it here?" "Well," replies the Station-master, "the fact is, the line was a little out of order." "Ah, I see, it didn't come as quickly as usual ; well, at all events, it came." "Oh, yes," continues the Station-master, slowly, "it came ; but they sent it to Brighton first." "To Brighton!" I exclaim. "Why?" The Station-master says he doesn't know why to Brighton, as they needn't have done *that*. "Well," I ask, "when did you get it, then?" [I think to myself it *is* a wonderful thing this telegraphing : here a message goes by mistake fifty or sixty miles out of the way, and it makes hardly any difference after all. Wonderful!] He answers, "Well, Sir, it didn't come till very late." I begin to be nervous. "But," I inquired, "you sent it on to Mr. Childers, at Bovor?" "Well, no, I didn't," he replies. "Not!" I exclaim. "But, good heavens! here I've come from London on purpose to—to—to—to go to Bovor—" I am aware of the climax not being powerful, but proceed, angrily, "—and had settled everything—and—

Beckenhurst.—We start for Bovor Castle.

hang it—I telegraphed on purpose that there might be no inconvenience. Why on earth didn't you send it on?"

"Well, Sir," says the Station-master, deprecatingly, "it wouldn't have been any use, as you'd have been there before the telegram." "What!" I exclaim. He explains, "The message only arrived ten minutes before you came down." He adds that his porter walking wouldn't get to Bovor, which is four miles off, as soon as I should driving, and therefore he didn't send it: he then begins to recapitulate the circumstances of the line being wrong, message going to Brighton, when I cut him short. "I shall complain of this," I say, wishing to frighten him. He isn't a bit frightened, and agrees with me. He says, "Yes, there ought to be a complaint about it." "To whom?" I ask, producing my pocket-book. Well, to the London Telegraph Office, he thinks. It shall be done. I make a great note, "*To the Manager of the Telegraph Office—To Complain—Brighton*," and return the memorandum to my pocket.

What's the time? Eleven. Why, they'll all be in bed. The Station-master thinks it not improbable. Shall I go over there? The porter can get me a fly: in five minutes. He does so: in a quarter of an hour. "If," I ask the Station-master, who has sat down to work, and has quite forgotten me, "I *do* go to Bovor, and can't get into the Castle, I suppose I can get a bed in the village?" "What village?" he asks. Well, I mean in Bovor village. "Oh," he says, "there's no Bovor village, there's only the Castle; it's a good four miles from here." "Well, then, I must return to Beckenhurst, if I want a bed." "Yes, that's it," he says, adding, "there's a fairish inn at Beckenhurst."

Shall I stop at Beckenhurst, and go on in the morning? I am undecided. The fly arrives. The porter decides me by placing my luggage in the boot. It isn't a fly at all, it is a sort of dog-cart, and I have to sit next to the driver. It is very cold. It is very dark, after coming out of the Station. Brightish night. We start for Bovor Castle.

## CHAPTER XVIII.

EN ROUTE FOR THE CASTLE—THOUGHTS ON THE STARS—
A COMMUNICATIVE DRIVER.

GET into the gig, and leave the Station. Very cold. At first starting it seems a brightish night. Getting away from the Station (where the gas is on, which is all the difference), it is pitch dark.

*Happy Thought.*—I think of the word "pitch," and hold on by the rail at the side of my seat. Feels unsafe. Always feel unsafe when being driven.

*Happy Thought.*—What must others feel when I'm driving them?

An after-dinner drive by moonlight.

Recollect I once did drive some one through a lane, in Devonshire, in the dark. I say "some one": I now forget who he was, as I never saw him again. Drove him and everyone up against a wall, which I thought was the continuation of the road. Recollect driving once again in Devonshire, after dinner, by moonlight. We walked the horse, so as to be particularly careful. Drove him up a bank, which I thought wasn't a bank, and upset everybody, with a boot full of rabbits which we'd shot, and three guns. Didn't drive again in Devonshire, except once more in broad daylight, when I tried to turn a corner very neatly. I recollect, on that occasion, one fellow went into a green mud pond, and was laid up for three weeks, and the other fellow disappeared over a hedge, and said he wasn't hurt much. The driver always falls easier than the others: at least, I did.

I wish I hadn't recollected all these things.

*Happy Thought.*—Unfasten the apron, so as to be ready.

Talk to the man in order to give him confidence, and not to let him think I'm afraid. I observe to him, "It's very dark." *He* observes, "No, it ain't," which doesn't promise well for a sustained conversation. I *think* we're turning a corner, by the feeling of being at some sort of an angle with the hand-rail, but I can't see. Whatever it is, we're safe again, and (I think) on a straight road.

The horse stumbles. I suggest he'd better "hold him up." Hate careless driving, specially in the dark. Man, who is well wrapped up, replies from behind a high coat-collar and comforter, and from beneath a hat (which three things are all I can see of him), "He's all right." Man is sulky : perhaps been called out of bed to drive me to Bovor Castle, and doesn't like it. I shouldn't.

*Happy Thought.*—Be kindly towards him. Hint at the possibility of his having a warm drink on the road, if he'll only drive carefully.

*Happier Thought.*—To give it him at the end of the journey, not at the beginning. He might get excited.

In a dark, narrow lane. I say, as pleasantly as possible, "Nasty place, this ; can't pass many things here," by which I mean to convey that if any other vehicle was meeting us, one of the two would be in the ditch. He admits, with reserve, "No, there ain't much room." He doesn't seem to know what he should do if another vehicle comes. I wonder (to myself) if I could jump into the hedge. Something is coming. No. Yes. No. Horse stumbles again. I laugh, and, not liking to give advice to a professional driver, say, "He wants a little holding up, eh ?" Man replies, gruffly, "No, he don't." From his tone I gather that he won't take advice. Stars are appearing, as it seems to me.

*Happy Thought.*—Looking at the stars (it *is* clearer now), I remember how African travellers in the deserts, or jungles, or prairies, or somewhere where nobody is, except occasional lions and tigers, guide themselves by the stars. Wonder how they do it. M. du Chaillu in his book says he did it. I suppose it requires a thorough knowledge of the Heavenly Bodies. At present the only Heavenly Body I know is the Great Bear; which, by the way, is about as much like a bear as—as—say a poker. [That's where I fail, in simile.] If I looked at the Great Bear, I wonder where I should get to at last. In other directions, too, you see other stars and lights. This would be very puzzling. Sailors steer by the stars. It must be very difficult to find which way to turn at sea. First turning to the left, we'll say, for instance, takes you to America. Well, that can't be easy to find at any time—specially at night. At least, I've always thought so, looking at it from Brighton.

These thoughts distract me from my present danger. I don't know that there is any danger, but I feel as if there was. Horse stumbles. Man informs me that " We're going down a rather steep hill." Odd, I don't know it. But why doesn't he " hold him up?" I ask. He replies, " He doesn't want any holding up." He says, " he knows the horse well enough." So do I by this time : a beast. Driving on. Another corner. The driver is rather rash at corners, but steady in the straight road. I feel I should like to say to him, " Don't try to drive so dashingly." But perhaps it will only irritate him.

I want to pull his right rein when he's going round a left-hand corner. Perhaps I make matters worse by interference.

Shall be glad when this is over.

" Where," I ask, " is the Castle?" He answers, " Oh, that ain't here : this is Beckenhurst, this is." " Well," I say, " we've come two miles, and the Station was Beckenhurst." He corrects me, with, evidently, the clear knowledge of a native, " No, that's Beckenhurst *Station :* this is Beckenhurst village."

" What, *all* this?" I ask, alluding to the distance we've already travelled. He informs me, with his whip pointing straight forward, and then from left to right, at the hedges, " Yes, all this : Bovor's a matter of four mile from here."

I tell him that they said it was only four miles from Beckenhurst Station : which notion seems to amuse him behind his collar and comforter, and under his hat.

*Happy Thought.*—These country people never know what distance is : therefore, he may be wrong. Yes, but wrong which way? Is it more or less than four miles? I ought to have asked at the Station how much a mile the fly charges here. This is just one of those occasions when I want presence of mind. I think of these things, just like my repartees and similes, a quarter of an hour after I ought to have said them.

*Happy Thought.*—To pretend I know the road : then he won't impose on me. I *do* recollect having been in this neighbourhood, or at all events in Kent, when I was a child. I observe, with decision, "Oh, it's not more than four miles." It doesn't seem to make very much difference to him, so perhaps they charge here by the hour. I don't like to ask him to drive fast ; and yet if he dawdles for the sake of running up a bill, I shan't get to Bovor Castle, until, perhaps, one o'clock in the morning, when every one's fast asleep.

*Unhappy Thought.*—Supposing I can't get in ? Because, hang it, as my telegram has not arrived, they don't expect me. If I do get in, p'raps they won't have got a bed. House full, perhaps. I put this case to the driver, and add, "I suppose (as a matter of course) that I can easily get a bed at the Hotel." He asks, gruffly, "What Hotel ?" I say, "Why, at Bovor." This amuses him under his wrapper, as before, and he observes, presently, "There ain't no Hotel." I think he's stickling for names, and putting too fine a point (so to speak) upon it ; so I explain that when I say *Hotel,* I mean village Inn. He answers me, displaying some little petulance, "There ain't no village :" adding, as a con sequence, "and there ain't no Inn." "No Inn !" I exclaim. I hardly like asking after this if there *is* a Castle. Supposing it should be only a practical joke of Childers ? Impossible.

"If the worst comes to the worst," I say, "I can get a bed at the hotel at Beckenhurst, then ?" He is doubtful about this, as they're sure to be closed, being so late.

*Happy Thought.*—This flyman comes from some stables : the stables belong to an Inn, of course. I put this to him, thus, that "if the worst *does* come to the worst, I can get a bed at *his* Inn." He extinguishes all hope in this quarter by telling me that "his master only lets out horses and flys."

I hope to goodness Childers will be up. He used to be a great fellow in town for sitting up late. Perhaps in the country he goes to bed early.,

*Happy Thought.*—Dismiss anxiety, and obtain information about the country from the driver.

I ask him about the crops. He doesn't know much about crops. "Any floods?" I inquire. He's not heard of any.

*Happy Thought.*—Get some statistics from him about Cattle Plague. I ask him "if he's had much Cattle Plague here." He is angry and returns that "he hasn't had no Cattle Plague." He

Arrival at Bovor Castle.

thinks I'm laughing at him. These country people are very tetchy. I tell him politely, that I don't mean that *he's* had the Cattle Plague (though he's ass enough for anything, but I don't *say* this), but I want to know has it been bad here. "He hasn't heard as it has."

Perhaps he's got some information about the antiquities of the county. No he hasn't. "Bovor Castle's very old," I suggest, to draw him out. He "supposes as it is." I ask "How old?" He don't know; but it's been there ever so long. "Is he acquainted with Mr. Childers?" "No, he ain't."

He won't be drawn out. It is lighter now. The moon shines.

Delightful night to arrive at an old Feudal Castle. I imagine to myself a grand entrance : Gothic or Norman arches : [*Happy Thought.* Get up my architecture] a fine old bridge, a large massive gate, with an iron rod at the side, which moves a deep-toned bell on the arrival of a guest. Or, perhaps, a horn hung up outside, wherewith to summon the warder. Shall read *Ivanhoe* again. We go down hill.

We are in a lane full of ruts : there is no doubt about that. He informs me "We're just there." It is past twelve o'clock.

I can't see the Castle ; perhaps it will burst upon me presently in the full light of the pale romantic moon. It doesn't, however, and my driver pulls up at an old wooden five-barred gate leading into a field.

"Here's Bovor Castle," says he, as we stop short ; and he looks over his comforter at me as much as to say, "And what are you going to do now?"

I don't know. I only see a common gate leading into a sloshy field.

"Can't we get nearer to the Castle than this?" I ask, not seeing the Castle at all anywhere.

It appears we can't, as the Castle is in a sort of hollow. It is surrounded by a moat, and there's no getting up to it driving, nor even on foot, if the drawbridge is up.

*Happy Thought.*—To write a chapter in *Typical Developments* on the idiotcy and thoughtlessness of our Norman ancestors. I wonder if they ever arrived late at night and couldn't get in. I will descend.

*Happy Thought.*—To doubt the honesty of this country driver. If I descend, he may drive off with my luggage ; and I shall never see him again. In fact, as he has been behind his wrapper, coat-collar, and underneath his hat, I haven't seen him *yet*, and couldn't swear to him in a Court of Law.

*Happy Thought.*—To make *him* get down and drag my luggage out, while I stand at the horse's head. Good. But what's next? Here's my portmanteau, box, desk, bag, hat-box, rugs, dressing-case, and how am I to get up, or down, to Bovor Castle?

*Happy Thought.*—He shall take them on, and I'll remain with the horse. He doesn't like the idea, and mistrusts my stopping with his gig and horse.  These apparently simple bumpkins are full of low cunning.  Capital subject for a chapter in *Typical Developments*.  He opens the gate, and carries my portmanteau across the field.  Following him with my eyes, I gradually become aware of a building in the distance, across apparently two fields, by moonlight.  Not my idea, at present, of Bovor Castle.

If Childers is not up, and I have to carry all these things back, and then drive about Kent during the night looking for a bed, it will be pleasant.

*Happy Thought.*—Childers *shall* get up.  What a surprise for him!

Luggage still being carried.  Half-past midnight.

# CHAPTER XIX.

BOVOR CASTLE—THE DRAWBRIDGE—THE RECEPTION—SUPPER—THE HAUNTED ROOM.

Bovor Castle.—The Drawbridge.

WHAT inconvenient places these old castles are!  This Bovor Castle is in a splendid state of preservation: one of the few, I believe, with a drawbridge.  The drawbridge, when I arrive, is up for the night.  I wish Childers was up for the night.  No bell.  No knocker.  No horn.  Nothing.

*Happy Thought.* — Tell the flyman to shout.

He says if he shouts it will frighten the horse.  I *must* shout, and he must run back and tie his horse up: then return and shout.  In his absence I walk along the side of the moat, to see if there's any way of crossing without the bridge. None.

It's very solemn and grey in the moonlight, and mysterious and dark out of it. I feel as if I'd come to release Mary, Queen of Scots. I see a punt moored to the opposite bank : Mary, Queen of Scots, again.

I see the places where they used to pour hot lead out on to the people below.

Hope Childers isn't hiding, and going to have any practical jokes.

Flyman returns. I tell him to shout.

*Happy Thought.*—A man can't shout with any energy in cold blood. The shouting of a hireling cannot be so hearty as that of the person interested.

I tell him to shout louder. He asks, "what name he shall shout?" I tell him "Childers." He begins, "Hi, Childers! *Chil-ders!*" I don't like hearing him behave so familiarly, but won't stop him, in order to insert the "Mister," or perhaps he won't shout any more. I fancy he takes a secret pleasure in calling the present owner of the Castle "Childers."

He says he can't do it any louder. Absurd! A flyman, and can't shout!

I begin, "Childers!" I take a turn of two minutes. There's no echo ; no effect of any sort, except a growing sense of hopeless desolation. The flyman is sitting on a portmanteau, and beginning to doze. "*Chil-*ders! Chil-*ders! Childers!*"

I can't believe they're all asleep. They hear me, and won't get up. It's cruel. "Chil-ders, hi!! Hi!!!" He may not be at home. Somebody must hear.

*Happy Thought.*—Make the flyman shout *with* me.

Duet—"Childers! Hi! Hi! Chil-ders! Hi!" I don't like leaving off for a minute, but we are obliged to do so for want of breath, the hireling giving in first.

*Happy Thought.*—Throw a stone at a window. Glazier less expensive than driving to a hotel.

We look for a stone. Flyman says *he* should like to break a window or two. I tell him there's no necessity for that. Can't find a stone. Can't throw grass.

Shout once more. Wish we'd not left off shouting, to look for stones; as, if we had roused them, they'll all have gone to sleep again.

Wish I was in London—in bed. Wish I'd asked for an answer to my telegram. Wish all this while I shout.

A light behind a red curtain at a window. A voice, which comes in as a pleasant relief to ours, says, "Hallo!" A stupid thing to say, by the way. I shout, "Hallo, Childers!" He answers, "Who's that?" That settles the question: it *is* Childers. I tell him that *I* am here. He exclaims, "*You!* By Jove, all right!" and disappears, light and all. I wonder if he's glad to see me! I wonder what he's saying now?

The flyman suddenly becomes more respectful, I fancy; he had evidently begun to think that I didn't know any one at Bovor Castle.

Noise on the other side of the gate. Unbarring.

Childers is there in a dressing-gown, with a lantern, like Guy Fawkes. He cries out, "Stop a minute, and I'll let down the drawbridge," as if I was going to attempt crossing over without it.

It is down: he works it with one hand. He says, "Oh yes, it was no good calling the maid to do it. They're all in bed." Flyman crosses with the luggage. I pay him, standing under the portcullis: he grumbles, and I pay him again. I stop to admire the romantic scene. Childers says, "Yes, deuced cold, though. See it better to-morrow morning." He closes the gate, and leaves the drawbridge down. He tells me he was asleep when I arrived.

*Happy Thought.*—Praise the place as much as possible to put him in a good humour. Wish I could recollect if he's got a family or not, I'd ask after them. Ought to recollect all these sort of things before calling on anybody. Safe question to ask him, "All well at home!" only it sounds as if *he* had just arrived, not I. His reply is, "All quite well," and I wonder to myself whether there is a Mrs. Childers. I've only known Childers as a bachelor in town. I don't recollect his mentioning Mrs. Childers *then*.

We cross a court-yard, which reminds me of being in a small college, and coming home late. In fact I can't help expecting to see plenty of lights, and hear jovial voices. Neither.

He asks me, doubtfully, if I won't take any supper. I say, "No, my dear fellow; don't let me put you to any trouble." By which I want him to understand that I'm very hungry, and had expected to find chickens, champagne, and salad awaiting my arrival. He replies, "Oh, no trouble in the least. As you don't want any, you'd like to go to bed at once."

I say, "Yes, at once!"

*Happy Thought.*—Never travel without biscuits. Makes you independent. So do matches and soap.

A noise in the passage. Two men come in loudly. One who, I should say, sleeps in his spectacles, has evidently had his trousers, slippers, and shooting-coat close by his bedside. The other has only been able to lay hold of the two first articles. They rush in, shake me by the hand heartily, and say "How d'ye do, old fellow?" I respond as energetically, "How d'ye do? How are you?"

*Happy Thought.*—I have certainly never seen either of them before. They are asleep, I think.

They insist on shaking hands again. They then look at one another and laugh. I laugh. Childers laughs. We all laugh. We then sit down, and there is a pause.

*Happy Thought.*—I say, cheerfully, "Well, I've kept my promise. Here I am."

The short man in spectacles laughs as if he were going to make an observation, but doesn't. The taller man smiles thoughtfully at the candle. I am almost positive they are asleep. Childers observes, "That he didn't expect me so late," but adds, "that he's deuced pleased to see me." The short man in spectacles leans forward to shake hands with me again, and laughs. The taller has evidently expended all his energy at first, and is fast asleep upright in his chair. More noise; another man enters in a sort of barbarian costume, consisting of knickerbockers, a railway rug, and a Scotch cap. He says, "He thought the orchard was being robbed:—he'd loaded his gun, and looked out."

*Happy Thought.*—Narrow escape, this!

Seeing me, he says, cheerfully, "How d'ye do?" I respond equally cheerfully, and we all laugh again, including the tall man, who wakes up to do it, and then resumes his dozing.

I suppose they don't introduce people at Bovor. Wonder if they're brothers or cousins, or only friends. Must take care what I say.

First night at Bovor Castle.—Childers's friends.

Short man in spectacles inquires for something to drink. Childers, addressing him as "Bobby," tells him he *can't* want anything at *that* hour. It appears, however, that he *can*, and does. The taller man also wakes up at the mention of something to drink; and the barbarian, who has now lighted a pipe at the solitary candle, is struck with the idea, as a good one.

They all know where everything is to be found. Bobby says he wouldn't mind something to eat. Tall man, becoming more wakeful every minute, suggests "cheese," and, as an after-thought, "bread." The barbarian, taking a kindly view of my case, asks me to join him in a pipe, and wait till Childers brings in some cold pie. This (with the exception of the pipe) is thoughtful. I take to the barbarian.

*Happy Thought.*—Note for *Typical Developments.* The short cut to a man's heart is through the stomach.

Every one is gone to get something. There is an air of hospitality about them all that I like. But I can't make out whether they are all Childerses, or friends, or cousins. Each one seems to be the host.

Childers returns alone, with a cold pie and a plate.

*Happy Thought.*—To ask him, now he's alone, who the other fellows are. He is surprised. "What, don't I know them?" No. Oh, then he'll tell me. The short one, in spectacles, is Bob Englefield, the dramatist. Don't I know him?

*Happy Thought.*—Say (in order not to offend him), "I've heard the name somewhere."

"The tall one," he continues, "is a very rising fellow—Jack Stenton." I ask, "Rising? in what way?" Childers replies: "Oh, in every way: philosophy, and that sort of thing." Then adds, as if this wasn't enough to determine his character, "Writes for several reviews."

*Happy Thought.*—Best thing to say is, "Does he, indeed?" which I say accordingly.

The Barbarian in the rug is Poss Felmyr. "Old Poss is writing a novel down here," he tells me. All I can say is, "Is he, indeed?" again.

I remark that they've all got familiar Christian names—Bobby, Jack, Mat (Childers is "Mat," I find), and Poss.

"Why Poss?" Nobody knows: they've always called him so.

*Happy Thought.*—I like these sort of names. They're terms of affection among men. I never had a name of this sort. I wish these fellows would call *me* "Poss," or something. I like this style of thing : no women ; all *men*, clever, brilliant, literary, and artistic.

I give out this sentiment over the pie :

Childers says, "Oh, my wife's here." I say, "Oh, indeed!" and try to explain away my remark by saying, "Ah! that's a different thing."

They smoke, eat, and drink all at once.

I make a good supper off pie, cheese, and cold brandy-and-water.

The next question which occurs to the party is, "Where shall we put him?" meaning me.

I say, politely, anywhere. Hope (to myself sincerely) that it will be a comfortable room.

Bobby jumps up, and says, "He's got it."

We regard him inquiringly.

He looks round at us and says, "How about the Haunted Room?"

I repeat (I am aware, feebly), "The Haunted Room?" and smile. Of course, I don't believe in ghosts. Pooh!

## CHAPTER XX.

BOVOR—THE HAUNTED ROOM—ROUGHING IT.

The Old Woman's Ghost.

"F COURSE I don't mind a haunted room?" Of course not.

I announce, as a curious fact, that I never was in one. Somebody says, "No? really!" as if I was quite an exception to the general rule.

*Happy Thought.*—Try to test them by saying, "You've not seen a ghost?"

They admit they've not; "but, perhaps," Childers says, "he'll be more polite to visitors." Have I had all I want? Childers wants to know. Yes. We retire from the dining-room in procession, Bobby first, Childers last, myself just before Childers.

It *is* a very old house. Tiles on the floor in some parts. Can't see the advantage of tiles: perhaps they thought they were going to build roofs, and changed their minds.

We pass through a large hall with a splendid old fire-place. Enormous chimney. [Note for *Typical Developments.* Look up authorities about the Mediæval Sweep.] There is an oak screen at one end.

My candle (they know their way about without any), though not particularly brilliant, puts everything else in the shade.

I can't help exclaiming, having an eye for the picturesque, "Charming, delightful old place!"

Childers replies, "Yes. Wants doing up."

"Doing up!" I exclaim. "Oh, no."

"Ah," says he, "you don't know it. Rats and damp. Come along to bed."

Somebody says "Hallo!" from above. It startles me. Whether it is the shadows or the candle, or the family boots all in a row, I don't know, but I am nervous. Childers points Bobby's face out to me, high up, looking out of a little window in the screen. I daresay an ancestor put it down as a "Happy Thought" to have a window in the screen. Idiot!

I stumble up the glorious old oak stairs. My candle only shows me the next step each time. The shadows which I make by moving the light about look exactly like rats. These stairs twist so. Ancestors could never have walked straight.

*Happy Thought.*—Winding staircases originated by inebriated architects.

*Happy Thought.*—To ask if there are any black beetles.

No. None. Except in the hall through which we've just passed. I stumble up three more stairs and some loose tiles. Did ancestors have carpets?

*Happy Thought.*—Look out in some Useful Knowledge Dictionary. "Carpets. When introduced into England. By whom?"

*Happy Thought.*—Probably by the Turks. Rhubarb and carpets might have come over together. Turkey in both instances.

We are on an old landing. I ask, jocularly, whose ghost it's supposed to be that haunts my room?

Childers doesn't know. Jack Stenton (the rising philosopher) does. He informs us, "Old woman burnt."

I say, "Oh?" inquiringly. "Old woman burnt, eh?" and meditate on it. I don't know what I think about it. But I *do* think. We all stop to think.

"Let's get in," I suggest. They say, "Let's do so."

Childers stops on a stair to say, he hopes I'm prepared to rough it a little, as he didn't expect me.

I tell him I like roughing it. Wonder (to myself) what *his* idea of roughing it is. I knew a man whose idea of roughing it in the country was to have a villa in a park, a French cook and a valet. He used to tell me he would be perfectly content with homely fare; his idea of homely fare was *potage à la reine*, mullet, ortolans and woodcocks. Hope Childers calls *this* roughing it. Childers stops suddenly, and looks at Bob Englefield, the dramatist in spectacles. A notion has struck him. He says, "I don't know how we'll make you a bed, though." This promises to result in roughing it.

I am ready with a manly reply, "Oh, I can sleep anywhere."

*Happy Thought.*—To qualify this by adding, "for *one* night."

Bob Englefield, who has a ready invention, says, "Oh, I've got a rug."

Stenton, the reviewer, who appears more thoughtful, perhaps because he's sleepier than the others, says, in a deep voice, "sheets."

*Happy Thought.*—Lessen the roughing it process as much as possible. Say, decidedly, "Yes, sheets."

Childers doesn't know where the sheets are.

Poss Felmyr asks, "How about a pillow?"

With the same view as before, I second this inquiry.

Bob Englefield has it. "The sofa cushion."

Carried *nem. con.*, and I brighten up.

Bob Englefield has it again. "There are two sheets in his room for him to-morrow."

I say, "Don't bother on my account," politely. Childers replies, cheerily, "Oh, we'll dodge it somehow," and I look forward to roughing it. We are obliged to bring all my luggage up, as I can't recollect in which thing my sponge is.

*Happy Thought* (*noted down while resting with carpet-bag on stairs*).—How easily a man becomes accustomed to hardships. When I return home I'll take to visiting prisons and workhouses in disguise, like Mrs. Fry and the Casual gentleman who wrote the workhouse articles. Splendid subjects for *Typical Developments*, "Human Miseries," Vol. XI.

Some one (the novelist, I think) says he'll lend me a towel. Each one will give something, like the three witches in *Macbeth*. They all say, "Here's a lark!" and run off to collect the materials. Childers gets the sofa cushion, and we make for my room. Luggage on a landing.

*In my Room.*—This is, I am informed, the Haunted Chamber

where the old woman was burnt. Odd; as I remark there is no fire-place. Bob Englefield, Jack Stenton, and Old Poss are making my bed. It is one of those iron unfolding things which is intended for a chair and a bed.

The Haunted Room.—Making the Bed.

Childers apologises for its being a little cranky, and Old Poss tells me I must take care when I am lying down to lean more on the left than the right side, or it will give way.

They enjoy making the bed. I fancy they laugh because they think it'll be uncomfortable. It appears none of them have ever done such a thing before. Poss Felmyr says he recollects making apple-pie beds at school. I'll examine mine when they're gone.

*Happy Thought.*—Every man ought to be able to sew his own buttons on, and make beds, if necessary. If I ever have a family they shall learn all these things.

The bed is made, and, as they are all immensely pleased, I thank them, and they retire, hoping I'll find it all right, and adding that "If the Ghost comes, I'd better throw the sofa cushion at her."

I *do* hope that there are not going to be any practical jokes. I recollect hearing of a man becoming an idiot when a practical joke about a ghost was played on him.

*Happy Thought.*— To wind up my watch while I think of it.

Childers walks to the window.

"I'm afraid," he says, apologetically, "that the window doesn't fasten very well."

I say, "Oh, never mind," implying that there's no necessity to send for a plumber and glazier at this time of night on my account.

"But," he explains, "it's a tumble-down old place."

I tell him I like this sort of thing amazingly. He expresses himself glad to hear it.

"Am I quite comfortable?" is his last inquiry.

I look round at the truckle bed, at my bag, at the towels, and reply that I am, cheerily. I have a misgiving that I shall want something when he's gone.

*Happy Thought.*—To ask where the bell is.

There's no bell : what fellows our ancestors were ! [When were bells invented, and by whom first used in private castles. *Typical Developments*, Book X., Vol. XII.]

The servants sleep on the other side of the castle, where the children are. [*Note.* Childers' children : ask after them.]

"If I want anything, I can call to the other fellows," I suggest.

"Yes, you can," Childers admits, jocularly, "but," he adds, "they won't hear you." It *is* an oddly-built place; everyone appears to be sleeping in "another passage," with a staircase all to himself.

I make the best of it, and say, cheerfully, "Oh, I shan't want anything till morning."

"Then, that's all right," returns Childers. He comes back to tell me that if I want a bath in the morning, Englefield's got it.

I thank him. When he's gone I remember that I don't know where Englefield's room is. He comes back once more to tell me that the door doesn't fasten very well. He wishes he could give me a better room. "My dear fellow," I say, "Capital—excellent —*the* very thing I like. So quaint," I add.

"Well," he says, "it *is* a quaint little place : better than a great uncomfortable modern room."

I don't answer this. Somehow I don't like his praising the room. He ought to have left *that* to the visitor. Childers wants tact. He hopes I shall sleep comfortably, and laughingly trusts I won't see any ghosts.

I reply, I'll tell him all about the ghost in the morning. I remember (as he says good night) a story of this sort in Washington Irving, I think, where a man jested about telling them in the morning about a ghost and *was* haunted. I think his hair turned white, and he saw a picture roll its eyes, and the top of the bed came down : I forget exactly ; but it's not the sort of thing to remember just as you're going to bed in a strange place. He is gone, and I quite forgot to ask him about Englefield's bath. How my presence of mind deserts me !

*Happy Thought.*—Brush my hair.

Very dull and lonely here. My face in the glass looks spectral ; not like it does in other glasses. I feel as if some one was going to look over my shoulder. Shake this off. Make notes. Analyse my nervousness for a chapter in *Typical Developments*.

Oak panels. No fire-place. Wind is getting up.

*Happy Thought.*—Early wind getting up as I'm going to bed.

Joke this. Laugh to myself. Look in the glass. In the glass I appear like a dull photograph. Window blown open. No blind. As Childers says, it does *not* fasten well : as a matter of fact.

Wind getting up more than ever. Rain, too. Casement windows begin to rattle.

*Happy Thought.*—Fasten the window-latch with my rug-strap. Done.

Rats in the wall, I think. Can't come out. Manage to latch my door. Very cold and damp feeling. Think of Fridoline Symperson. Fancy some one's coming in. A sense of desertion and loneliness comes over me. Note it down, and, having done so, feel it less. Horrid candle, and no snuffers.

*Happy Thought.*—Put my note-book and candle by bedside on my portmanteau, and jump into bed quickly. Do it.

Truckle-bed gives. They've managed to make the bed so that I get more blanket than sheet. The sheet seems to be chiefly round the pillow. Try to pull it down. Worse. Leave bad alone. Will read in bed. Remember some one saying it's dangerous. Suddenly think of the old woman burnt; p'raps from reading in bed. Casement rattles. Rug-strap won't hold. * * * * Window blown open. Shall I get out, and shut it? Think over this.

No; more healthy to let the air in, as there's no fire-place. * * * Let me give myself up to romance. This is a feudal castle. * * * This is a feudal castle. * * * I don't get beyond this idea. Feudal castle. Feudal castle. Barons. Childers' children. * * * See Mrs. Childers to-morrow. * * * Wonder what she's like? Wind * * * Violent gusts * * * Candle out. Long wick and sparks all over the place. Old woman burnt.

## CHAPTER XXI.

BOVOR IN THE EARLY MORNING—MEDIÆVAL NOTIONS—BREAKFAST —A PUZZLE—WORK AT BOVOR—THE WEATHER—PROSPECTS— LUNCHEON.

The amorous Baker.

APPY THOUGHT. — No ghost after all : and they call this a haunted room. I don't believe in the old woman who was burnt to death here, unless (as a Happy Thought) they burnt her ghost into the bargain. Note for Vol. XI. of *Typical Developments,* " On Popular Superstitions."

Always wake early in the country, and always expect a nice bright morning in the country. Looking at the weather from my bed, I should say it drizzles. I don't hear anybody getting up. My clothes and boots have not been taken : it must be very early, or very late. My watch is on the table—can't see it from here. It *must* be very early—I'll lie in bed and think. * * * Odd : I was quite awake a minute ago. * * * I'll take my note-book and arrange some work for the day. * * * Put note-book on pillow. * * * Write down heading *Notes for Typical Developments,* Vol. IX. * * * which is all I find on the page when I wake up again with a galvanic start. Noise in courtyard below ; jump out ; it *must* be late now.

Frost and damp on the glass : window open : it looks on to the court-yard. Here, in mediæval times assembled pilgrims, retainers, falconers, barons, knights, ladies, mitred abbots, pages, dogs in leashes, and good-looking young men coming of age on the steps.

" By my halidome! gadso!" quoth the shorter of the two knights, over whose fair head some twenty-five summers had shed their something or other, I forget what now.

Ah, I wish I'd lived then. On thinking over it, why? Chiefly I think because they said " By my halidome," and "zooks" and " the merry maskins," and, generally, because it was "the olden time." Ours will be the olden time one of these days. Perhaps this very room will be exhibited as the place where the author of *Typical Developments* slept. I wish this would happen while I'm alive, though : how it would surprise my relations.

*Happy Thought.*—Surprise my relations.

I will. Get on with *Typical Developments* as quickly as possible. I feel *now* that I *can* do it. I will dress at once : no more delay. I wish to goodness I could get my clothes brushed ; and boots.

*Happy Thought.*—Picture of Norman Baron preparing for the chase. Hang it, where's the bath?

Look out of window : drizzle over. Dull : housemaid kneeling in a crinoline cleaning steps of portcullis archway. Who cleaned the steps in mediæval times? Look up subject : Housemaids, when first introduced. A bumpkin of a boy stands under the archway, cleaning boots. He leaves off, to draw up the portcullis, being thereto summoned by the baker with the rolls, and I hear a voice say, Muffins, outside.

*Happy Thought.*—Muffins. Buttered.

I say, " Hallo!" All three below puzzled : perhaps they can't see me. Put my head out : boy laughs—so does the baker. The maid still kneeling, sits on her heels, and smiles too. I think (from this distance) she sniffs : cold morning. I say, " I want my boots cleaned, please." The baker, who evidently doesn't wish to be mixed up with the matter at all, looks at the boy. The boy replies, " Yes, Sir," takes the bearings of my room, cleverly deducing the locality of my body from putting this and that together. *This* being the head, and *that* the window.

He shuffles towards a side doorway in the quadrangle. The baker says something of an amatory character to the housemaid, at least, so I imagine, from her tossing her head in an " Ah,-yes,-I-dare-say " sort of style, as she resumes her work, while the gay young baker walks across the quadrangle, disappearing, after one look back at the housemaid, at a small side door. Demoralising life a baker's or a butcher's, if he has to call at many houses every day. Might call them butterfly tradesmen, sipping the sweets from every——come in. Boot boy. He will also take my clothes.

Bovor Castle in the early morning.—"I want my boots cleaned, please."

Mary, he explains, however, brushes *them*. Will he be good enough to ask Mr. Englefield if he'll let me have the bath? He will be good enough, and goes.

*Happy Thought.*—" Conferring on the boy the order of the bath." I'll say this at breakfast. Must manage to introduce it neatly.

Sheridan used to arrange a lot of good things before he went out to dinner (I don't know if he said any good things at breakfast) and led up to them. Note it down, or I shall forget it. If you don't note it down, it's a nuisance to bother yourself all day with trying to recollect what that good thing was you thought of in the morning. Knock: come in. Boy and bath, with Mr. Englefield's compliments. Dressing. * * * Dress anyhow in the country. Can't: ladies.

*Happy Thoughts while Dressing.*—One ought to have a secretary in one's room to write things down while one is dressing. I hum tunes when brushing my hair, which are really very good, if some one could only catch them and fix them on paper at the moment. I wonder how many composers are lost to the world through this. I'm certain I could do an oratorio. Hum one, I mean: I can't write it, or play it. Oratorios are not effective with one finger on the piano. I find, that, on trying to pick out on the piano any original composition, I lose the tune before I can hit upon the notes. Also find that what I thought was original, some one has heard before. I think I might have been a composer if I'd never heard any body else's tunes. As to arranging a piece for an orchestra, that would be easy enough, as I can imitate most instruments with my mouth, which would show any practical musician what effect I want, and then he'd do it.

Boy comes for Englefield's bath. I ask, "Is anyone down?" and am told, "Oh, yes, Sir; Mrs. Childers is breakfastin'."

I wish they'd ring a bell, or send up to one's room. Now, for Mrs. Childers.

Awkward stairs—find my way—came through this hall last night. There's the screen—here's the door. No. Suddenly find myself in the courtyard. See warm-looking room in right corner of quadrangle: see breakfast-table: a lady eating, and a man's back, seated, and by the movement of his elbows, eating.

They see me: I must look unconcerned, as if I was up and taking the air, without any idea that breakfast is going on. The window is opened by Stenton, the rising philosopher, who says, "Good morning." I ask him "How he is?" and he replies, "Come in at this door, here—breakfast is quite ready."

The philosopher is dressed in knickerbockers and a shooting

coat, and has his hair cut like a Vandyke child. This strikes me as original. I like the idea. Now, I shall see what Mrs. Childers is like. Walk in briskly and smilingly. Be agreeable. Show her that though I do write on deep and serious subjects, yet there is a lighter and brighter side to my nature.

*In the Breakfast Room.*—There are two ladies, one is making the tea, the other the chocolate and coffee. It is a round table, so there is no top or bottom. Which is Mrs. Childers? Childers is not down. The philosopher, Stenton, has to introduce me to them, which he does in a stupid fashion of his own, by merely mentioning *my* name to them, and not theirs to me. Which is Mrs. Childers? They are both blondes, and very nearly of an age. Will I have tea? I will, thanks. Muffin? with hesitation—yes, thanks. Oh (chocolate-lady hands them), pray don't: oh, thanks, thanks. Oh (to tea-lady, who hands tea), thanks. Will I have some fish or some broiled ham? Mustn't be too long considering: I say in a hurry, "Ham, please"—meant fish. Oh, thanks, thanks. To the philosopher for the butter, to the chocolate-lady for the mustard, and to the tea-lady for the pepper, Thanks, thanks, thanks. Then to the three collectively for everything, "Oh, thanks." I should like to say something brilliant now at *once*, but, here I am, flustered by a muffin.

*Happy Thought while eating Muffin.*—They're twins: sisters. Still, this doesn't tell me which is Mrs. Childers, and I want to ask after the children.

"Am I looking for anything?" No: thanks. I am, though, but can't make out what it is; that's where my want of presence of mind bothers me. Oh, it's a small knife: on sideboard. "Oh, don't move," (to everyone) "thanks, thanks." *Note.* Must get out of this habit of saying "thanks": it's nervousness, not gratitude. Besides, "Thank you" is more graceful. Will I have any more tea? If you please. Finding that this wish of mine involves ringing a bell, fresh hot water, and trouble generally, I say, "No—no—please don't: I'd *rather* have chocolate. Thanks. I *prefer*, I assure you, I prefer chocolate." Tea-lady smiles, and says, "I'm sorry there is no chocolate." It turns out to be cocoa. I meant (I say) cocoa: all the same—cocoa and chocolate. Thanks. Philosopher Stenton says, "No, it isn't—quite different." I don't want a discussion before ladies, so I merely observe, smilingly, that it doesn't matter. Thanks. I think I've ingratiated myself so far with whichever is Mrs. Childers.

Tea-lady observes, "Mat will want some tea directly he comes down."

*Happy Thought.*—Mat is Childers—this is Mrs. Childers. I say, relying upon this, "This is a very quaint old place, Mrs. Childers." Having said it, I think it was a little rude ; ought to have thought of that before speaking : that's just like me—me to the ground, in fact. The ladies smile, the philosopher smiles, so do I, but am uncomfortable. I won't try names again, or remarks on where your host lives : it *is* rude.

Childers appears : he calls tea-lady Nelly, which makes me think I was right, until he addresses the chocolate-lady as Ally— which unsettles me. I can't keep up conversation without names. Besides, I want to ask after the children. Englefield arrives, very lively, and nodding at me, and is called Bobby by everyone. Poss Felmyr (they all call him Poss, and he calls the ladies Ally and Nelly, so there's no rule) comes down shivering, and rubbing his hands ; he nods at me encouragingly ; they all nod at me, as they come in, encouragingly, as much as to say, "Don't be frightened —it's all right." I find myself, I don't why, nodding back in the same style, as much as to assure them, "Yes, here I am, all right, not a bit frightened," but I'm sure I shouldn't be doing this if I only knew which was Mrs. Childers. It's like being ignorant of a language. They are all Bob, Mat, Ally, Nelly, Poss, and Jack, to one another. They can't be *all* Childerses of various kinds and relationships.

The philosopher solves the difficulty : he asks Mat "How Mrs. Childers is this morning ?" To which Childers replies, "Pretty well," and that " she's coming down."

Perhaps, then, Ally and Nelly are two Miss Childerses. I won't hazard this in conversation, though. They might be any of the other fellows' sisters, as they are all Christian names to one another. Breakfast finished, but all waiting for Mrs. Childers. Children with nurses in the courtyard.

Childers, in character of papa, looks out of window. Fair- haired child, very pretty, runs up.

"What a fine boy," I remark, to please Childers.

There is a smile. "Girl," Childers explains. At that moment I dislike the child. [Analysing this feeling for *Typical Developments* subsequently, I ascertain it to be the result of humbled pride. I had said the girl was a boy, and he was a girl. Chapter on "Insight into Character."]

Nurses call children off, "like a huntsman and dogs." I say this to Childers, by way of a sharp simile, which will be appreciated by clever men. I fancy I'm saying rude things this morning. I wish Mrs. Childers would appear, and I should be on safe ground again.

The door opens : it is Mrs. Childers. Elderly lady—old enough to be Mat's mother. I talk to her at once about her children. She smiles graciously : all smile. Bob Englefield bursts out into a guffaw, and says he can't help it. Mat Childers explains—"not his wife, his mother."

Bob Englefield shouts out, "Oh, haven't you got a chance for a compliment." I laugh foolishly, I feel it's foolishly, and say, "Yes, I have." But the only thing I can think of is something about "A man not being able to marry his grandmother," which I don't say, thank goodness. But where *is* my repartee ? That's where I fail. What ought I to have said ? A quarter of an hour after, I shall think of it : provoking. However, I now find that the tea-lady is *the* Mrs. Childers.

*Happy Thought.*—Difficulty of relationship settled. Get particulars from Stenton.

Getting Stenton, the philosopher, alone by the window, I find it all out. Mrs. Childers is Childers's mother, yes, of course. I say "Yes, of course," as if I'd known it for years. Nelly is Mrs. Matthew Childers. "Yes," I say, "and the other is her sister." I am wrong. Ally is no relation : Ally is Mrs. Felmyr. Oh, now I see it all : Poss Felmyr is Mrs. Felmyr's husband. Stenton further explains : Bob Englefield is Poss Felmyr's brother-in-law, and Nelly is his, Stenton's, the philosopher's sister. She was a Miss Stenton, and the other was a Miss Englefield, and that Mrs. Felmyr is a very old friend of Mrs. Mat, and Mrs. Childers has known her from a child, and he and Bob were children together, and so was Mat and Old Poss, who has been brought up abroad, "and so they get on," he says, continuing what *he* calls his expla-

L

nation, "very well together, more like brothers and sisters." "And mothers," I suggest, thinking of Childers's mother. Childers coming up at this moment seems grave ; perhaps he thinks I was sneering at his mother. I wouldn't sneer at a mother for anything.

*Happy Thought.*—Not to say anything about it now : ask him quietly afterwards if he thought I was insulting his mother, and then explain that I wasn't. Good fellow, Mat.

"What would I like to do?" they want to know. Anything, I return. The ladies have gone to their household duties. Bob Englefield is busy this morning, hard at work at a five-act drama. He won't tell me what it is about. Stenton informs me that it's about Anne Boleyn and Henry the Eighth : scene laid here, in Bovor Castle. Stenton is also hard at work : an article for a weekly review. Childers whispers to me *The Saturday.* Stenton is evidently a superior man. May I ask what he is writing for that periodical. He smiles mysteriously : shakes his head, and says, "Oh, no, no, Mat's joking." I see by his manner that he *does* write for the *S. R.* Will ask him all about it afterwards. Mat tells me apart that Stenton's doing an article on "Henry the Eighth and Mediævalism,"—in fact, about Bovor.

*Happy Thought.*—Write for the *Saturday Review :* they needn't put it in, but I can smile and shake my head. I wonder if the contributors to that paper know one another by sight? or by any masonic signs? If they do I should be found out. I wish I could find out Stenton.

Poss Felmyr says, looking at his watch, that he had no idea it was so late, and must get to work. What work? His novel. May I ask what's the story. He can't say : send me a copy when published. Englefield tells me, apart, that it's to be called *Bovor*, and is about Henry the Eighth and Cardinal Wiseman—he means Wolsey.

Mat Childers must get to work too. What, *he* at work? I say with surprise. All laugh except Childers, who, I think, doesn't seem pleased at my remark. Poss Felmyr takes me aside immediately afterwards and asked me didn't I know that Mat was engaged on a grand historical picture for next year's Academy. I didn't, I wish I had : in fact, I didn't know he painted. What?

didn't I hear last season about the row and the A.R.A.'s? It won't do to go on being ignorant of these sort of things, so I say, "Oh, *that*," as if he'd brought it all, vividly, to my recollection now.

*Happy Thought.*—Get an almanack or something, and see who's President of the Academy. Ought to know these things.

It seems that Mat is an injured man, academically speaking. I will condole with him, if he likes it. What is the subject of his picture? I ask him. Historical, he says. There are none of them willing to enter fully into their subjects. Felmyr takes me aside and informs me that Mat is painting *Boror Castle in the Olden Time*, and is portraying Anne Boleyn playing on the dulcimer to Henry the Eighth.

Being asked what I'm going to do, I reply, as they're all so busy, I've got plenty of work to do, and commence giving a brief outline of *Typical Developments*, its scope, subject, and object. This is to impress them, and to show them that I am not a mere idle lounger, but an artist, one of themselves. They are not much interested in my work.

*Happy Thought.*—The future: I'll astonish them. One day they'll be cringing to me for a copy of *Typical Developments*.

Mat wants to know, if, before I go to work, I'd like to see the Castle. I should, but don't let me take him away from his work. Not in the least: they'll *all* show me over. We take umbrellas (it is raining) and look at the moat. The moat is swollen and has risen. If it goes on like this, says Mat, the baker will have to come in a punt. The water will be over the drawbridge and into the Castle. They show me the piggery; there are no pigs. And the orchard; no apples, to speak of. They show me a fine old room with painted panneled ceiling and side gallery. Englefield, who, Mat informs me, is an authority on these matters, says that this was the old Chapel. We (none of us) think it could have been the chapel, because of the fire-place. Then, says Englefield, positively, it was the Refectory. Refectories, says Mat Childers, were only in monasteries. I chime in, "Yes, only in monasteries." Englefield is positive that it *must* have been the chapel or the refectory, or, after some consideration, the armoury. "But," objects Poss, "they wouldn't have had that sort of window." Englefield says, "Why not?" which is treated as an absurd question; whereupon he suggests that it's the Hall. "No," says Stenton, "the other's the Hall." They all agree with Stenton, "Oh, yes, the other's the Hall." I say, "Yes, I think the other's the Hall," meaning the place I came through last night, where Bob Englefield looked through a window in the screen at me. Englefield, after looking at the chamber for a minute longer, says with certainty, "This was two rooms once," and we leave him there regarding the chamber sorrowfully.

Mat then takes us up winding stone stairs to top of tower. I think, while going up, what's the best way of coming down again without feeling giddy; sideways, like a horse down-hill. On the roof. I always thought castle roofs were flat, and that warders with Carbonels (am not sure of the word, so won't say it) walked up and down. This castle roof is like any roof on an ordinary second-rate London house; very disappointing. In fact, but for the name of the thing, it is simply being "on the leads." There is no view, as Bovor lies in a valley, and is hemmed in by hills. If they were snow mountains it would be grand, but they're only spongy-looking green hills. There are no gargoyles to discharge the rain. I want to know which is a bastion? Englefield, who is an authority on all these subjects, as he is getting them up for his historical drama, doesn't know what a bastion is, but shows me a gable. I want to know where the Donjon Keep is? It appears it hasn't got one. What a castle! Englefield, however, says that it's one of the few in England that have a barbican. "Don't I know what a barbican is?" "Well, we can't see it from here, but it's a—sort of—it's difficult," he says, "to describe exactly, but surely I *must* know what a barbican is." I answer, "Of course, I've seen one often enough; but I don't *exactly* know what it is." With this answer he seems satisfied, as he merely returns, "Oh, of course you do," and volunteers no further explanation about the barbican.

*Happy Thought.*—There's a Barbican in London, somewhere. Where? Wonder if I've seen it? If not, go and see it.

"Some of the passages, here," says Englefield, as we descend, "are beautifully corbelled." I am getting tired; I hate sight-seeing and having knowledge thrust on me, so I merely reply, " Yes, beautiful," and nearly fall down the winding stairs. Bob Englefield, on the drawbridge, shows me what he calls a first-rate idea for a scene. Troops pouring out from under the Norman arch, enemy coming down on them from the heights ; the fair Thingummy, Alice, Anyone, he says, a prisoner, waving her hand from the turret, while the tyrant is below ready to dispatch her. " Good that," he says, appealing to me, " and original, eh ?" I say, " Yes, very original." But on consideration I suggest to him diffidently, " Isn't it a little like *Blue Beard ?*" He says, " Oh, if you turn everything into ridicule—why——." I think he's annoyed. We meet Mat, Jack Stenton, and Poss. They've none of them been to work yet ; they all say they *must* go, at once, as it's getting so late. Mat asks Englefield if he's shown me the machicolated battlements. Bob says no, rather sulkily. Odd, he can't get over *Blue Beard.* I say I don't care about machicolated battlements. Well, we'll leave them till to-morrow. By all means—till to-morrow. They say they are going to work in earnest now, till luncheon time. One hour.

*Happy Thought.*—Write some letters. Ask when the post goes out ?

Childers says, "Oh, not till night," that is, he explains, not the regular post. From which I gather that there is an irregular post which goes out in the day. I am right : the irregular post is the butcher. He comes from Beckenhurst, and, to oblige us, will post any letters before 2 P.M. at Beckenhurst. The only thing against the butcher is, that he's rather uncertain on account of his pockets. If my letter is not very important I'd better send it by the usual post. If it *was* very important I certainly shouldn't intrust it to the butcher. There's no sort of necessity for my letter to go by an early post, but the fact that there is only a late one seems to cause me a great deal of inconvenience. Why ? Analyse this feeling for Vol. XII., *Typical Developments,* Sec. 2, Par. 3.

We meet at luncheon time : it is still raining. The ladies regret that we're running into winter, because there's no more croquet. Mrs. Mat Childers says if the rain continues, the feudal castle will be swamped. Mrs. Felmyr says, she'll be glad to get back to town ; it's so damp. Poss Felmyr says, " Pooh ! they came down to rough it." Childers sides with him. There's a row threatening : awkward for a visitor. Mrs. Childers asks me if I think it's fair to keep her down in this dismal place all the season, and only to return to town when nobody's there ? I feel that Childers's happiness in private life will materially depend upon my answer, but I can't help agreeing with Mrs. Childers. If I knew her better I wouldn't, as I hold with Mat's view of the case—picturesque feudal castle, rustic scenery, *versus* town house and right-angled streets. I shall explain to Childers afterwards that I only said it to please his wife. [When I *do* tell him afterwards, he says, testily, that " he can't understand how a man can be such a humbug," having evidently had a scene with Mrs. Childers in consequence of my observation.]

Poss wants to know if I'd take a walk in the rain. For exercise, I will. Stenton stops at home to do something with some photographs he's been taking. When he's not writing for a review, he's always going in and out of the back kitchen with wooden frames, glasses, and slips of damp paper. When there's a sun he holds glasses up to it. He shows me views of Bovor, and portraits on damp glass, with a backing of coat-sleeve. He says I can't see them now. He's right. When in the back kitchen, which is a dark place, one may just catch a glimpse of him stirring up wet photographs in a large red pie-dish. [His pictures are always "getting on," or "coming out very well," but they don't come out of the pie-dish, at least while I'm here.] He offers to take one of me.

*Happy Thought.*—To be taken with MS. of *Typical Developments* in my hand.

*Happy Thought.*—To get an expression on my face which shall be neither a scowl nor a grin. To be taken to-morrow. Walk now—in the rain.

*Happy Thought.*—When difficulty occurs between husband and wife (as between Mat and Mrs. Childers to-day), and they make me referee by implication, to invent an anecdote indirectly bearing upon the case, and tell it. It gives all three breathing time.

## CHAPTER XXII.

### AT BOVOR—PLAY A GREAT GAME OF WHIST.

Scoring honours.

**E**VENING after dinner. On the moat in a punt with Englefield. Dark night: cold: damp: romantic, but for this. Englefield says, abruptly, "Capital point." I ask here, what? He replies, "Two fellows, one the Villain, the other Injured Innocence, in punt: real water easily done on the stage. Villain suddenly knocks Injured Innocence into the water: he sinks: is caught in the weeds below: never rises again. Or, on second thought, isn't drowned, but turns up somehow in the last Act." I own it a good idea, and propose going in-doors, as I see Mrs. Childers making tea.

*In-doors.*—Stenton, the philosopher, says, "Tea is an incentive. So much tea is found in every man's brain." Poss says it ought to be a caution to anybody not to use hot water to his face, or he might turn his head into a tea-pot. I'm sorry Poss turns this interesting theme into ridicule, as I like hearing Stenton's conversation. He has a deep bass voice which is very impressive. There is a pause. Considering that we are all more or less clever here, it is wonderful how dull we are. I suppose that the truth is we avoid merely frivolous and common-place topics. Englefield, who is a nuisance sometimes, suddenly looks at me, and asks me "to say something funny." I'm glad they know nothing of the Pig-squeaking song.

I smile on him pityingly. Childers says, "Come, you're last from town, haven't you got any good stories?" This poses me:

I know fellows who could recollect a hundred. I know fellows, merely superficial shallow men, who are never silent, who have a story or a joke for everything. I consider, "Let me see:" I try to think of one. The beginnings of twenty stories occur to me, mistily. Also the commencement of riddles as far as "Why is a ——," or "When is a ——." I've got some noted down in my pocket-book, if I could only get out of the room and refer to it quietly, in the passage. I can't take it out before everybody; that's the worst of an artificial memory.

*Happy Thought.*—To read two pages of Macmillan's *Jest Book* every morning while dressing, committing at least one story to memory.

Childers proposes "Whist." I never feel certain of myself at whist : I point to the fact that they are four without me. Poss Felmyr says if I'll sit down, he'll cut in presently. "I play ?" I reply, "Yes, a little." I am Stenton's partner : Englefield and Childers are against us. Sixpenny points, shilling on the rub. Stenton says to me, "You'll score." Scoring always puzzles me. I know it's done with half-a-crown, a shilling, a sixpence, and a silver candlestick. Sometimes one bit of money is under the candlestick, sometimes two.

*Happy Thought.*—To watch Englefield scoring : soon pick it up again.

*First Rubber.*—Stenton deals : Childers is first hand, I'm second. Hearts trumps : the Queen. It's wonderful how quick they are in arranging their cards. After I've sorted all mine carefully, I find a trump among the clubs. Having placed him in his position on the right of my hand, I find a stupid Three of Clubs among the spades : settled *him*. Lastly, a King of Diamonds upside down, which seems to entirely disconcert me; put *him* right. Englefield says, "Come, be quick:" Stenton tells me "Not to hurry myself." I say I'm quite ready, and wonder to myself what Childers will lead.

Childers leads the Queen of Clubs. I consider for a moment what is the duty of second hand; the word "finessing" occurs to me here. I can't recollect if putting on a three of the same suit is finessing : put on the three, and look at my partner to see how he likes it. He is watching the table. Englefield lets it go, my partner lets it go—the trick is Childers's. I feel that someho it's lost through my fault. His lead again : spades. This takes me so by surprise that I have to re-arrange my hand, as the spades have got into a lump. I have two spades, an ace and a five. Let me see, "If I play the five I"——I can't see the consequence. "If I play the ace it *must* win unless it's trumped." Stenton says in a deep voice, "Play away." The three look from one to the other. Being flustered, I play the ace : the trick is mine. I wish it wasn't, as I have to lead : I'd give something if I might consult Poss, who is behind me, or my partner. All the cards look ready for playing, yet I don't like to disturb them. Let me think what's been played already. Stenton asks me, "If I'd like to look at the last trick." As this will give *me* time, and *them* the idea that I am following out my own peculiar tactics, I embrace the offer. Childers displays the last trick : I look at it. I say, "Thank you," and he shuts it up again. Immediately afterwards I can't recollect what the cards were in that trick : if I did, it wouldn't help me. They are becoming impatient.

About this time somebody's Queen of Diamonds is taken. I wasn't watching how the trick went, but I am almost certain it was fatal to the Queen of Diamonds : that's to say, if it *was* the Queen of Diamonds ; but I don't like to ask. The next trick, which is something in spades, trumped by Englefield, I pass as of not much importance. Stenton growls, "Didn't I see that he'd got no more spades in his hand." No, I own, I didn't. Stenton, who is not an encouraging partner, grunts to himself. In a subsequent round, I having lost a trick by leading spades, Stenton calls out, "Why didn't you see they were trumping spades ?" I defend myself ; I say I *did* see him, Englefield, trump *one* spade, but I thought that he hadn't any more trumps. I say this as if I'd been reckoning the cards as they've been played.

*Happy Thought.*—Try to reckon them, and play by system next rubber.

I keep my trumps back till the last ; they'll come out and astonish them. They *do* come out, and astonish *me*. Being taken by surprise, I put on my king when I ought to have played the knave, and both surrender to the ace and queen. I say, "Dear me, how odd !" I think I hear Stenton saying sarcastically in an undertone, "Oh, yes ; confoundedly odd." I try to explain, and he interrupts me at the end of the last deal but two by saying testily, "It's no use talking, if you attend, we may just save the odd."

*Happy Thought.*—Save the odd.

**A quiet Rubber at Whist.**

My friend the Queen of Diamonds, who, I thought, had been played, and taken by some one or other at a very early period of the game, suddenly re-appears out of my partner's hand, as if she was part of a conjuring trick. Second hand can't follow suit and can't trump. I think I see what he intends me to do here. I've a trump and a small club. "When in doubt," I recollect the infallible rule, "play a trump." I don't think anyone expected this trump. Good play.

*Happy Thought.*—Trump. I look up diffidently; my partner laughs, so do the others. My partner's is not a pleasant laugh. I can't help asking, "Why? isn't that right? it's ours." "Oh, yes," says my partner, sarcastically, "it *is* ours." "Only," explains little Bob Englefield, "you've trumped your partner's best card."

I try again to explain that by *my* computation the Queen of Diamonds had been played a long time ago. My partner won't listen to reason. He replies, "You might have *seen* that it wasn't." I return, "Well, it couldn't be helped, we'll win the game yet." This I add to encourage him, though, if it depends on *me*, I honestly (to myself) don't think we shall.

*Happy Thought.*—After all, we *do* get the odd trick. Stenton ought to be in a better humour, but he isn't ; he says "The odd ! we ought to have been three." Englefield asks me how Honours are? I don't know. Stenton says, " Why you (meaning me) had two in your own hand." "Oh, yes, I had." I'd forgotten it. " Honours easy," says Stenton to me. I agree with him. Now I've got to score with this confounded shilling, sixpence, half-a-crown, and a candlestick.

*Happy Thought.*—Ask Bob Englefield how *he* scores generally.

He replies, " Oh, the usual way," and as he doesn't illustrate his meaning, his reply is of no use to me whatever. How can I find out without showing them that I don't know how?

*Happy Thought* (*while* Childers *deals*).—Pretend to forget to score till next time. Englefield will have to do it, perhaps, next time, then watch Englefield. Just as I'm arranging my cards from right to left——

*Happy Thought.*—To alternate the colours black and red, beginning this time with black (right) as spades are trumps. Also to arrange them in their rank and order of precedence. Ace on the right, if I've got one—yes—king next, queen next—and the hand begins to look very pretty. I can quite imagine Whist being a fascinating game—Stenton reminds me that I've forgotten to mark " one up."

*Happy Thought.*—Put sixpence by itself on my left hand. Stenton asks what's that for?

*Happy Thought.*—To say it's the way I *always* mark.

Stenton says, "Oh, go on." I look round to see what we're waiting for, and Englefield answers me, "Go on, it's you; you're first hand." I beg their pardon. I must play some card or other and finish arranging my hand during the round. Anything will do to begin with. Here's a Two of Spades, a little one, on my left hand; throw him out.

"Hallo!" cries Englefield, second hand, "Trumps are coming out early." I quite forgot spades were trumps; that comes of that horrid little card being on the left instead of the right.

*Happy Thought.*—Not to show my mistake : nod at Englefield, and intimate that "He'll see what's coming."

So, by the way, will my partner. In a polite moment I accept another cup of tea. I don't wan't it, and have to put it by the half-crown, shilling, and candlestick on the whist-table, where I'm afraid of knocking it over, and am obliged to let it get quite cold, as I have to attend to the game.

Happening to be taking a spoonful, with my eyes anxiously on the cards, when my turn comes, Stenton says, "*Do* play, never mind your tea." Whist brutalises Stenton : what a pity !

*Happy Thought.*—Send this game, as a problem, to a Sporting Paper.

*Happy Thought.*—Why not write generally for Sporting papers ?

Stenton says, "*Do* play !" I do.

*Happy Thought.*—Write a treatise on Whist, so as to teach my-self the game.

We finish a second game, and Stenton says, "We win a single." This I am to score : having some vague idea on the subject, I hide my half-crown under the candlestick. When our adversaries subsequently win a double, and there is some dispute about what we've done before, I forget my half-crown under the candlestick, until asked rather angrily by Stenton if I didn't mark the single, when I am reminded by Poss Felmyr that I secreted the half-crown. This I produce triumphantly as a proof of a single.

*Happy Thought.*—Buy *Hoyle's Laws of Whist.* Every one ought to know how to mark up a single and a double.

I get very tired of whist after the second round of the third game. Wish I could feel faint, so that Poss Felmyr might take my place ; or have a violent fit of sneezing which would compel me to leave the room.

*Happy Thought.*—If you give your mind to it, you can sneeze sometimes. I talk about draughts and sneezing, while Englefield deals. Englefield says, *à propos* of sneezing, that he knew a man who always caught a severe cold whenever he ate a walnut. If a fact : curious.

## CHAPTER XXIII.

Old Mrs. Childers.

OLD Mrs. Childers has woke up (she has been dozing by the fire with her knitting on the ground) and begins "to take notice," as they say of babies. She *will* talk to me : I can't attend to her and trumps at the same time. I think she says that she supposes I've a great deal of practice in whist-playing at the Clubs. I say, " Yes ; I mean, beg her pardon, no," and Stenton asks me, before taking up the trick, if I haven't got a heart, that being the suit I had to follow. I reply, "No,"
and my answer appears to disturb the game. On hearts coming

up three hands afterwards, I find a two of that suit, which being sticky had clung to a Knave of Diamonds.

*Happy Thought.*—"Heart clinging to Diamonds;" love yielding to the influence of wealth; or by the way, *vice versâ*, but good idea, somehow. Won't say it out, or they'll discover my revoke.

*Happy Thought.*—Keep the two until the end of the game, and throw it down among the rubbish at the end. I suppose the last cards which players always dash down don't count, and mine will go with them unobserved.

*Happy Thought.*—One act of duplicity necessitates another, just as one card will not stand upright by itself without another to support it. [Put this into "Moral Inversions," forming heading of Chapter 10, Book VI., Vol. XII. of *Typical Developments.* Must note this down to-night.]

The game is finishing. Luckily, our opponents have it all their own way, and suddenly, much to my surprise and relief they show their hands and win, we only having made one trick.

*Happy Thought.*—Poss Felmyr takes my place.

On reckoning up I find that somehow or other I've lost half-a-crown more than I expected. You can lose a good deal at six-penny points. Stenton, who hears this remark made to Mrs. Childers, observes, "Depends how you play." I do not retort, as I am fearful about the subject of revoking coming up. *Moral Query.* Was what I did with my Two of Hearts dishonesty or nervousness? Wouldn't it lead to cheating, to false dice, and ultimately to the Old Bailey? I put these questions to myself while eating a delicate piece of bread-and-butter handed to me by Mrs. Felmyr. I smile and thank her, even while these thoughts are in my bosom. Ah, Bob Englefield has no such stage for his dramas as the human bosom, no curtain that hides half as much from the spectators as a single-breasted waistcoat. More tea, thank you, yes.

*Happy Thought.*—Single-breasted waistcoat! Ah, who is single-breasted? Is that the fashion! [Note all this down in cipher in my book, "Moral Inversion" chapter, *Typical Developments.*]

I pick up old Mrs. Childers's knitting. I take this opportunity of saying, jocosely, that I suppose that's what ladies call "dropping a stitch." No one hears it, except the old lady, who doesn't understand it. I shall repeat this another day when they're not playing cards, or talking together, as the ladies are.

"Heart clinging to Diamonds."

*Happy Thought.*—To tell it as one of Sheridan's good things. Then they'll laugh.

Old Mrs. Childers says she thinks the moat's rising, and that the baker will have to come over in the punt. Childers, at the table, says, "Nonsense, mother." She appeals to me as to whether it isn't damp, and whether the rain won't make the moat rise? And do I think, from what I've seen of it, that the punt is safe for the baker? Yes, I do think so. She observes that I'm too young to have rheumatism, or suffer from cold in the ears. I don't know why I should feel offended at the old lady's remark, but I do. I feel inclined to say (rudely, if she wasn't so old) that I'm not too young, and have had the rheumatics : the latter proudly. She dares say I don't remember the flood there was in Leicestershire in 1812 ! No, I don't : "Was it bad?" I ask—not that I care, but I like to be respectful to old ladies. "Ah !" she replies, shaking her head slowly at the fire, as if it was *its* fault. I get nothing more out of her.

Mrs. Childers is working something for the children. Mrs. Poss asks about a peculiar sort of trimming for her dress. Mrs. Childers stops to explain, and point her remarks with the scissors. They are deep in congenial subjects, and don't mind me. No more does old Mrs. Childers, who has dropped her knitting, and is asleep again, quite upright, in her chair.

*Happy Thought.*—To ask the ladies to play on the piano.

It will disturb the game, Mrs. Childers thinks. Two of the players seem of the same opinion, but they're losing, I discover. The two others are smiling, and would like a tune to enliven them. Childers calls out "Mother !" loudly, which makes the old lady wake with a start, and on finding that the moat has not risen and that the baker hasn't come in the punt ("which she was dreaming of, curious enough," she says), she begs Mat not to call like that again, and I pick up her knitting for her. She thanks me, and asks if I recollect the great floods in Leicestershire in 1812? I reply, as I did before, That I don't. It leads to no information. Wonder how old she is?

She rises, and thinks, my dears, that it is time for Bedfordshire, which is her little joke ; she gives it us every night at exactly the same time, and in exactly the same manner. It always commands a laugh. The ladies didn't know it was so late, and put up their work, hoping I'll excuse them not playing this evening. They're afraid I've found it very dull.

*Happy Thought.*—To say "More dull when you're away." Just stopped in time, and turned it off with a laugh and a good-night. I must have looked as if I was going to say something, as Mrs.

Poss says, "What?" and I reply, "Oh, nothing," vaguely, and *she* laughs, and I laugh, and Mrs. Childers laughs, and says good-night, laughing, and old Mrs. Childers smiles and repeats her joke about Bedfordshire, which she evidently thinks we are all still laughing at, and this makes us all laugh again, and Stenton and Englefield, who, having lost, are fondly clinging to the whist-table, laugh as well, and saying good-night becomes quite a hysterically comic piece of work, so much so that I wonder we don't all sit down in our chairs, or on the carpet (old Mrs. Childers on the carpet!) and have convulsions: and all this because I *didn't* say what I was going to say. They didn't laugh when I *did* make a really good joke this evening.

The ladies have gone. "Now," says Childers, "how about pipes and grogs." Carried *nem. con.* Englefield proposes we stop whist and play Bolerum. What is Bolerum? Doesn't anyone know? Childers knows, it appears; he and Englefield will show it us: and to begin with, he and Englefield (this, they say, will simplify matters) will keep the bank.

The game, they explain, is very simple: so it appears. In fact its simplicity hardly seems to be its great charm to those who do not happen to be the bank. The players back their sixpences against the bank, and the bank wins. Childers calls it "a pretty game."

"One, two, three, four—bank wins," cries Englefield; "pay up!" And we give him sixpence a-piece.

"One, two, three, four, five—bank again," cries Childers: "tizzies round," by which he means that we are again to subscribe sixpence a-piece. Poss says, after five times of this, that he doesn't see it. Stenton, the philosopher, taking a mathematical view of it, attempts to show how many chances there are in the players' favour, but ends in demonstrating clearly that it is at least a hundred to one on the bank each time. This argument occupies a quarter of an hour, and three pieces of note paper, which Stenton covers with algebraic signs. Childers still sticks to it, that "It's a pretty game." We admit that it is very pretty, but we get up from the table. What game shall we play? We decide (and sixpences are at the bottom of our decision), "None."

"Quite cold," observes Stenton. We gather in front of the fire.

M

Poss suddenly wonders that I've not yet seen the ghost in my room. Childers says "Ah," and then we all stare at the fire, wondering at nothing : silence.

Childers turns quietly to Englefield and inquires, " If he knows Jimmy Flewter ? " Englefield does. Childers asks " If he heard about his row with Menzies ? " Englefield, with his pipe in his mouth, and embracing his knee, nods assent. " It's settled," says Childers, and stares at the fire again. " Foolish of him," observes Poss. " Very," says Stenton, in his deep bass. It would be rude to ask who Flewter is, but this sort of conversation is very irritating.

Childers anticipates me by saying, " You don't know Jimmy Flewter ? " I do not, but signify I am ready to hear anything to his advantage or disadvantage for the sake of conversation.

" Ah, then," returns Childers, "you wouldn't enjoy the story."

" Must know the man," puts in Stenton, "to enjoy the story." Poss assents, and smiles as if at a reminiscence. They all chuckle to themselves. I wish I had a story to chuckle over to *myself.* Wish I knew Flewter.

" Seen my lord, to-day ? " asks Englefield of Childers. Wonder who " My lord " is.

" No, comes to-morrow," is the answer.

" Paint ? " asks Poss. " Sketch," answers Childers.

" Odd fish," observes Bob Englefield, putting on his spectacles to wind up his watch. " Very," says Poss. We knock out our ashes, and finishing our grog, go to bed.

*Happy Thought.*—Shall find out who " My lord " is to-morrow. Hang Flewter ! Rain, violent : no ghost. Room seems darker. Window troublesome. Think of Fridoline. Wish it was Valentine's day, I'd send her a sonnet. Too sleepy to think of it now. * * * * Jimmy Flewter. * * * *

Another rainy day. They are all at work : Childers at his picture, Stenton at his articles, and stirring up his dish of photographs ; Poss Felmyr at his novel, Bob Englefield at his drama.

*Happy Thought.*—Work at my handbook of repartees : quite forgotten it for a long time. Childers tells me that the room in which I am writing was Anne Boleyn's boudoir. He leaves me to meditate upon this. What reflections do not occur to one's

mind ? * * * What reflections *do* ? * * * "This," I remind
myself, "was Anne Boleyn's boudoir. Here," I say to myself,
standing by the window, "she looked out of the window." I feel
a gentle melancholy stealing over me. "In this cupboard," here
I stand by a small cupboard in the oak panel, "she perhaps kept
her—her——" I open it and find a piece of string, a screw, and
a broken saucer—these things suggest nothing particular, so I
alter my sentence to "Here she kept something or other." How
difficult to be enthusiastic : you can't force it. I know men who,
if they were shut up in this room, would overflow with poetry.
Why don't I? I don't know. Why is it that the only thought
that forcibly presents itself to me is, "Why didn't she have a fire-
place here ?"

*Happy Thought.*—Feel just in the humour to write repartees.
According to my original notes, take them alphabetically. It
will be a useful volume, I am convinced, to a large number of
people. To make a beginning, I arrange my paper. Now—

ABBOT. *What to say to an Abbot.*—
By the way we must start with the hypothesis, in every case,
of the person having made some observation to you demanding a
repartee. The way to arrange this clearly would be thus :—

*Name of person.*—Hyp. *What he says to you.* Rep. *What you'll
say to him.*

Very well then.
ABBOT. Hyp. Here's the difficulty, what *would* an abbot say to
you ?
Englefield looks in for a minute to ask me how I'm getting on
generally, and I consult him. I ask him what I can put down an
Abbot as saying ? He replies that I'm wrong in beginning with
Abbot, as *Abbé*, alphabetically, comes before Abbot.

*Happy Thought.*—Do French repartees. Make a separate book
of it. Very useful to tourists. Or why not translate them into
*all* languages ? Easily done with a dictionary and grammar ; and
friends from a distance would assist.

*Happy Thought.*—And why not illustrate it ? Capital. Englefield says this *is* a good idea. Abbé offers an opportunity for a
French repartee. See how it works. We must have a hypo-

thesis. For instance, Englefield points out that the Abbé *must* first be rude.

I explain that according to my developed idea, it will be between a French Abbé and an Englishman, or a Frenchman, or a German, or a Spaniard, or an Ojibeway, as the case might be.

Wonder what the Ojibeway would say? Englefield suggests, "he'd tomahawk the Abbé."

Let us suppose an out-of-the-way case. "The essence of surprise is wit," I remind Englefield. I wonder if this is an original idea of mine. On thinking it over I find I mean, "The essence of wit is surprise," however, it doesn't matter, as Bob Englefield answers, "Yes." "*Hypothetical case :*—An English tourist comes to an abbey in France. The Abbé won't admit him. The Abbé is rude, and says out of the window, '*Allez au diable, vous gros Anglais, vous !*' The repartee is ready to hand, '*Vous en êtes un autre.*'" This would shut up the Abbé completely.

In England there is, I think, only one Abbot, who lives in Leicestershire, and people would hardly go out of their way for the sake of making repartees to him. Besides, I believe he is a Trappist, and bound by vows not to speak to anybody. As it would lead to complications to draw up separate directions for " Repartees to be repartee'd to persons who won't speak to you," I shall not consider his and any similar cases. Now what's the next word, alphabetically? There's nobody beginning with Abe. Except Abel. But that's out of the question. Take Academician. "*Hypothesis :* Academician says to you, 'What a conceited donkey you are.'" Then you'd say as a repartee, "This Academician does but estimate the character of any other individual than himself, by the knowledge he already appears to possess of his own." I read this with emphasis to Englefield, who considers it, he says, "crushing, certainly, but too Johnsonian." I ask Stenton his opinion. He replies that " If any fellow said it to *him*, he'd knock his head off." I attempt to turn the conversation by wondering how it would sound in Spanish. Poss Felmyr, who has been in Spain, observes that if I said such a thing to a Spaniard, he'd have a stiletto into me like one o'clock.

These criticisms are rather against the publication of my book of repartees. When you come to proceed with it, it offers many difficulties. For instance, what to say to an Accountant, to an

Acrobat, to an Aëronaut, to an Armourer, and so on through the letter A, because so much depends upon what they've said to you. But, in a general way, I shall arrange it like a conversation book, and my readers must take their chance.

*Happy Thought.*—Send it to my publishers.

*Notes for the Book.*—

In B we have Repartee to a Baker, a Beadle, a Buccaneer.

C. To a Corn-cutter, and a Coal-whipper.

D. What to say to a Dragoon, to a Dragoman, &c. E is awkward. F includes Funny Fellow, and Fool, and Footman. Also a Fakeer; though I don't see the reply to a Fakeer.

I shall leave it for to-day.

*Happy Thought.*—Why not say the same thing to every one? If it's a good one, 'twould tell equally well on an Abbot, a Buccaneer, or a Footman.

Going through the hall I meet a common-looking dirty man, with a sort of portfolio under his arm, and carrying a box. One of the travelling pedlars who go about the country, and into any houses they find open, on pretence of selling something. I ask him what he wants here? He answers that he wants nothing. Then I tell him he'd better go. He observes that I am perhaps unaware to whom I am speaking.

*Happy Thought.*—Under letter P, Repartee to a Pedlar. Can't think of one now. I show him the door.

The Butcher brings a letter for me. It is from old Johnny Byng, who wants me to come to his bachelor establishment, and keep Christmas with him before he goes to France: if I will, I am to come at once, or he shall ask the Swiltons. Don't like the Swiltons; at least, I mean, if we were at Byng's together; he always gives Mr. and Mrs. Swilton the best room, and is always so confidential with Swilton; and then Mrs. Swilton, becoming *the* lady in the bachelor's house, is so confoundedly patronising to me. In fact, it is staying at the Swiltons', not Byng's. So I shall go at once, and prevent the Swiltons.

I announce this at luncheon. They are all so sorry I am going. Mr. Childers says, "You haven't been out in the punt to catch jack in the moat!" "You haven't sat for your photo-graph," says Stenton. "We were to have had a good walk together," cries Englefield. "You mustn't go," says Poss. Mrs. Poss sweetly hopes there's no necessity for my leaving them. Mrs. Childers observes, "it's awkward too, as she'd promised Lord Starling to bring their guest with them to-morrow to dinner." "Very kind of her," I say, though I don't like being "brought" in this manner.

The "brought friend" is coldly welcome for the evening, and they never speak to him afterwards. Still I shouldn't mind knowing Lord Starling. Mrs. Childers tells me, "Oh, you'd be *charmed* with them. Lady Starling is such a good, kind person." "Not at all stuck up," puts in Mrs Poss. "Ah," says Mrs. Childers, "you haven't known 'em so long as we have," by which she meant to say to Mrs. Poss, "Don't *you* talk about the aristo-cracy : it was through *us* you knew anything about them."

Childers, foreseeing unpleasantness, interposes with, "My Lord was here this morning. I thought he would be." "Oh, Mat," says Mrs. Childers, "I *hope* you asked his Lordship in to lunch." "I did," returns Mat, "but he wouldn't come." I feel glad of this ; and so I'm sure does Mrs. Poss, who is only in her morning dress. She says, however, taking a small radish, "I suppose the Duchess expects him." A Duchess ! I should like to stay over this party, and *then* go to old Johnny Byng's. I'd astonish Byng.

"I think," I say for the sake of conversation, "I know Lord Starling." [Analysing the feeling that prompts this observation, I found it would come under the head of *Natural Attraction to Magnates.*] Mrs. Childers regards me with interest. "Funny little chap," says Childers. "He was here to sketch this morn-ing. He'd his old paint-box, which belonged to his great grand-mother, and a remarkably antique portfolio." "A box and a portfolio ?" I repeat, as it occurs to me that I've seen something of the kind within the last hour. "Yes," says Stenton, in his bass voice, the deeper for his having just lunched, "and such a slouch wideawake and old greasy coat." "And ragged gaiters," adds Englefield. "Looks," says Poss, "like the Wandering Jew : a wandering Jew pedlar." "Yes," returns Childers, who is at the window, "he's only just now going off in his dog-cart." I join Childers.

" Is that Lord Starling ?" I ask.

" Yes," answers Childers. "You wouldn't think, to look at him, that he is the owner of this Castle and all the property about here."

I shouldn't, and what is more, I hadn't ; for the gentleman in the dog-cart is the Pedlar to whom I made my practical repartee of showing the door. His own door !

*Happy Thought.*—Go to Byng's.

Still raining.

*Happy Thought.*—I've stopped here, but the rain hasn't. I shall say this as Sheridan's, or Dean Swift's.

The butcher orders a fly from Beckenhurst, and the fly fetches me from Bovor. Old Mrs. Childers regrets my departure, but says, to cheer me, that she dares say they'll all be driven home by the moat rising.

*Happy Thought.*—I shall be driven home by the fly.

*Happy Thought.*—Say this. They laughed.

*Happy Thought.*—Send it to *Punch.* Say so. Englefield suggests, "Why not write for *Punch ?*" Stenton, the philosopher, says, " Yes, write for *Punch* regularly, and they'll send it you regularly." (Stupid joke, after *mine.*) Poss Felmyr shakes hands warmly and apologises for the rain.

Mrs. Poss says good-bye, and I feel that I almost sneak out of the drawing-room. I wish I could say something by which they'd remember me. The ladies (I see them from outside) have composed themselves before the fire, and are intent on their books. I came into this place like a lion, I leave it like a lamb. Artistically speaking, a conversationalist ought to come in like a lamb and go out like a lion. When Childers and the others have carried my luggage to the gate, I beg they won't trouble themselves. They say it doesn't matter, as it doesn't now.

*In the Fly.*—I look out of window. They have all disappeared, as if they were tired of me : no waving of hands, no cheers. In old feudal days there'd have been some hearty stirrup-cup ceremonies. Dreary : windows of fly up. See nothing : cold, raw, damp. Christmas-time coming on fast. I should like to send

Fridoline Symperson a present, just to hint the state of my
affections.  What can I send?  Christmas-time only suggests
turkeys and sausages.  Get out my MSS. and make notes.  * * *
By the time I have found my MSS., which had been scrunched up
by the maid in among the boots, I find we are at Beckenhurst.
Ticket to town : Station-master smiling, asks me if I ever did
anything about that telegram ?  I recollect now I'd threatened to

The Stirrup-Cup in the old feudal days.

write to the *Times.*  I reply, " Ah, they'll hear about it *yet,*" as if
my vengeance had only been dozing.

*London.*—Ought at this season of the year to take some Christmas present down to old Byng.  Besides, it's his birthday.  He'll be
just as glad to see me without it.  (*I* shouldn't, on *my* birthday.)
There's not going to be any party of ladies or he wouldn't have
asked me ; but we shall spend a quiet Christmas-time together,
with cosy chats over the past : yes, we're very old friends.   How-

ever, I'll just walk through the streets, and have a look at the shops. The difficulty is, I can't tell what Byng would like.

*The Haymarket.*—A pony runs away, traces broken. Crossing-sweeper knocked down.

*Happy Thought.*—Step into a shop.

Shopman says, "Spirited little animal that, Sir." I return carelessly, "Yes, nice little fellow ; might easily have been stopped, if they'd had any sense." I am quitting the shop feeling that I have perfectly requited the shopkeeper for the temporary refuge by giving him my opinion on the subject, when I feel a tremendous slap on the back, and a voice, which I do not at once recognise, says, "Hallo, old boy ! practical joke, eh ?" It is Milburd.

He is buying the hottest pickles he can find (it is an Italian warehouse we are in) to take down to Byng as a birthday present. We are both going to the same place. Together? Together : he will call for me.

*Happy Thought.* —This diminishes cab-fare. I won't have any change, that shall be *my* practical joke on him.

*A Night in Town.*—Milburd and I go to the theatre. Milburd has got a voice like a Centaur. (I think I mean Stentor. N.B. Who was Stentor? look him out.) People are annoyed. He begins by taking seats which turn out not to belong to him, and then the people come in and there's a row in the dress circle.

*Happy Thought.*—Step quickly into the lobby. Milburd coming out, angrily says, "he'd have knocked the fellow's head off for two pins." I try to pacify him. I say, "What's the use of getting into a row. It never does any good." I feel it wouldn't as far as I'm concerned. Milburd insists that the pair of us would have licked the lot, and wants to catch them coming out. I say "No !" decidedly, to this. I'd rather not catch them coming out. He goes on to observe that "he should like to punch his head." I agree with him there : I should *like* to.

*Happy Thought (for the twentieth time).*—Learn boxing.

*Happy Thought* —Go to Evans's.

Milburd takes me there. I've often heard of this place, yet

never been there till now.   Much pleased.   Excellent glee-singing.
Milburd, who evidently *does* know London very well, introduces
me to an elderly kindly gentleman, whom he calls Mr. Green,
and whispers to me, "You know Green, don't you?"   I don't.
The kindly gentleman, who is, I fancy, looking for some seat
where he has left his hat, for he is walking about without it,
shakes hands impressively with Milburd "and hopes that all are
well round his (Milburd's) fireside."

This hearty old English greeting Milburd meets, I think, somewhat irreverently by replying, "Thanks, yes.   All well round the
fireside.   Poker a little bent with age, tongs as active as ever,
shovel rather lazy."   Whereat Mr. Green smiles, pats him on the
arm, and takes snuff, deprecating such levity.   Milburd says
"Oh, I must have heard of Green."   *

*Happy Thought.*—Green, of course, aëronaut.

*Happy Thought.*—Ask him all about balloons.

I engage him in conversation.   Has he been up in a balloon
lately?   He smiles, takes snuff, and nods his head as if he knew all
about it, but couldn't answer just now.   I ask him, "if he's not
afraid of going up so high?"   His reply to this is, "that I will
have my joke."   He leaves us.   Milburd explains that he is the
revered proprietor, and tells me a long story concerning the
ancient fame of this great supping place.

We sup most comfortably at the "café end"; as Milburd inartis-
tically puts it, "quite undisturbed by the singing."   He, however,
knows it all by heart; I do not.   Ladies, he informs me, view the
scene from the gallery, veiled and behind gratings, as in St. Peter's.

*Saturday.*—Don't feel well.   Milburd proposes that we shan't
go to Byng's till Monday.

*Happy Thought.*—Run down to Brighton: freshen us up for the
week.   Milburd says, "Yes, by all means; where shall we stay?"
Anywhere.

*Happy Thought.*—The Grand Hotel.

Very well: cold day in train.   Draughts in carriages: shivering.   Colder as we approach Brighton.   Milburd, who is a red-

* "Paddy Green," long since gone to "the Shades."   Green, aëronaut,
also,—or skies.—ED.

faced hearty chap, says, rubbing his hands, "This will freshen you up, my boy—this will make your hair curl." If there is any one thing more than another that sets me against a place it is to be told that "It *will* set me up," or "It'll make my hair curl." I point out that it's beginning to rain. Milburd replies, "Oh, no—sea mist," as if sea mist was healthy : why can't he own it *is* rain? I express myself to the effect that it is raw, to which Milburd returns, being in boisterous animal spirits, "Cook it." I wish I hadn't come with him, he's so unsympathetic. He can't understand what it is for any one to have a pain across his shoulders and a headache. I've explained my symptoms to him several times. I assure him that he is quite wrong in saying that I eat too much, and am getting too fat.

Terminus : damp fly, rattling windows. Brighton looks windy, foggy, damp, drizzly, wretched. Grand Hotel : very grand. An official, in a uniform something between the dress of a railway guard and a musician in a superior itinerant German band, receives us. He is the Head Porter. We are shown into the lofty and spacious hall. We see dinners going on in the Coffee-room. Even Milburd is awed. I have a sort of notion that a gorgeous man in livery will presently request us to walk up and His Grand Royal Highness will receive us.

*Happy Thought.*—Hotel for giants. In corridors seven-leagued boots put out to be brushed.

In the vast galleried hall, Milburd, luggage, and self, guarded by a boy in buttons. Solitary individuals come down-stairs, look at us suspiciously, and go out. Waiters pass and repass us, all suspiciously. Opposite sits an elegant lady in a box, or bar.

*Happy Thought.*—Ask her for rooms.

She has been waiting for this, and is prepared for us. She gives us tickets, numbered, as if we were going to a show. Seems to me suggestive of waxworks.

Milburd says, "We will go up by the lift." A gloomy porter with an embarrassed manner shows us into the lift. It is a dismal place, and after Milburd has tried a joke, which is as much a failure as a squib on a wet pavement, not even making the lift-porter smile, we subside into gloominess.

*Happy Thought.*—Diving-bells: Polytechnic: also, old ascending-room, Colosseum.

(*Note.* During the three days I am at the Hotel, I have either seen the lift-porter starting from the ground floor when I have been going out, or arriving at one of the upper stories, after I have walked up the stairs; I've never caught him descending, nor got him when I wanted him.)

We emerge from the lift, on to the third gallery—helpless. Milburd knows all about it, and finds the chambermaid. Rooms comfortable—very, but with two mysterious draughts which make me sneeze. Milburd orders dinner in the Coffee-room.

*Happy Thought (during the fish course).*—Harvey discovered the circulation of the sauce.

After dinner, into the smoking-room. "Why should a smoking-room, now-a-days, be rendered purposely uncomfortable? Why should it be the only apartment where easy chairs, divans, cheerful paper, are unknown? Why, in a most luxurious hotel, should there be a smoking-room which is cheerless by day, and dingy by night?" Milburd asks me these questions pettishly, and describes the sort of room he would have. Warm and cheery, small tables, lamps, not gas, chess-boards, book-cases well filled, newspapers; writing tables, with supply of writing materials laid on; good fires in winter throughout the day, and let the room have a good view from its windows.

Pouring with rain—and we came here for a change!

*Happy Thought.*—Sunday afternoon: walk on the parade. Wonder how the pleasure-boat-men get a living in the winter. Apparently by talking together in groups, with their hands in their pockets, and smoking pipes without any tobacco.

Everyone looks very bright and blooming, and everyone is making the most of the dry weather, as if they were trying to get the best of a time-bargan with the fresh sea-air. What a nuisance wind is—what a nuisance a hat is.

*Happy Thought.*—My wideawake.

Milburd won't walk with me "while I've got that thing on," he says. I won't give in, so we pass one another, idiotically, on the parade. Think I see the Mackenzies coming—pretty girls: wish I'd got on my hat. They bow and look astonished: walk up the Parade. See Mr. and Mrs. Breemer; they recognise me. Walk down, see the Mackenzies for the second time. Don't know whether to bow again, or not: they smile. I smile: I wonder what we mean? Hope they'll go off the Parade this time. Walk up—see the Breemers coming. How very awkward this is: can't bow again—will look another way. I do, until I come quite up to them, and then, turning suddenly, am flustered. Mr. Breemer nods, and I nod, but don't know whether to take off my hat this time to Mrs. Breemer; I wish these things were settled by law. We pass on. Walk down: the Mackenzies again.

*Happy Thought.*—Turn before they come up.

I do so, won't they think it rude? Can't help it, it's done; and here are the Breemers. I nodded last time, what shall I do this? Wink jocosely? no sense in that, they'll set me down for a buffoon.

*Happy Thought.*—Sit down with my face to the sea.

Wonder whether the Breemers have gone—and the Mackenzies. Look cautiously round. Enjoyment is out of the question, with the Breemers and Mackenzies perpetually meeting one. I feel as if they were saying every time they see me. "Here's Thingummy again, don't take any notice of him," and if you once think yourself shunned you can't enjoy anything. I feel that I'm spoiling the Breemers' and Mackenzies' day at Brighton, and they must feel that they are interfering with my enjoyment.

*Happy Thought.*—The Pariah at Brighton.

Rain settles the question—back to hotel. What shall I do? What can I do? * * * Rain. * * *

*Happy Thought.*—Write letters. Think to whom I haven't written for ages: great opportunity. Write to some relations whom I haven't spoken to for years, and ask how they've been this long time, and why they never write. They'll like the attention. * * *

By the way, Milburd isn't much of a companion. He comes in and says he's been chatting with the Tetheringtons, and couldn't get away. When he's been away for any time he always excuses himself by saying he'd been "chatting." He wishes I wouldn't

wear that old-fashioned wideawake. "The Tetheringtons noticed
it," he tells me; also, that "everyone was remarking it." I ask
him, quietly, "Who's everyone?" and he answers, "Oh, lots of
people." I tell him that I am above that sort of thing, and do
not care for the world. I ask him "If he told them that I was a
friend of his?" He answers that he did, but added, "that I was
slightly cracked." I am annoyed. I shan't go anywhere with
Milburd again. After dinner Milburd goes away to "chat" with
the Tetheringtons again, and I read all the weekly papers through,
including the advertisements.

*Bed-room.*—In the next room on my left to me is a whistling
gentleman. In the room above me is a stamping gentleman; and
somewhere about, perhaps the next room on my right, is a
declaiming gentleman. At night the declaiming gentleman has
a good turn of it, while the stamping gentleman only walks about
a quarter of a mile over my head. The declaiming gentleman is
very impressive for nearly an hour, when he subsides all at once
and utterly, as if in the middle of a speech he had been suddenly
knocked on the head, and put into bed speechless.

The whistling gentleman has the morning to himself. He
wakes himself with a whistle, he whistles himself (operatically) out
of bed. He whistles, spasmodically, amid splashings. He whistles
a waltz while brushing his hair violently: I hear the brushes.
He whistles a polka in gasps, from which I conclude he is pulling
on tight boots. He whistles and jingles things together sounding
like half-crowns and boot-hooks; and faintly whistles himself out
of his room (March from *Norma*, with variations), and down the
passage.

The stamping man has during this stamped himself out of bed.
Judging from the sounds, he must perform all the operations of
his toilet by forced marches. I should say he walks a mile before
breakfast.

The declaiming gentleman is not oratorical in the morning. I
think he is packing: I hear paper rustling, and, after a time,
sounds as of dragging heavy weights about the room. His
struggles with one obstinate portmanteau are awful. He has got
it up against the wall now, and is kicking it. Pause: he is panting
and groaning. A bell: the Boots comes: they are both struggling

with the portmanteau. All is quiet: the door opens. I look out and see the conqueror walking down the passage in triumph, followed by the Boots with the captive portmanteau, bound and strapped, on his shoulder.

By the way, Milburd, returning at about two o'clock in the morning, wakes me up to ask me "if I'm asleep?" and to inform me that "he's sorry he's been away so long, but he's been chatting with the Tetheringtons!"

*Breakfast.*—Milburd not back from his bath. Being late, I am the only person at breakfast in this enormous coffee-room. Waiters in a corner laughing; fancy it is at me. Should like to order them to instant execution. A Chief of the waiters enters, and reviews a line regiment of cold beef, cold mutton, cold chickens, tongue, ham, and cold pork on a side-board. Satisfied with his inspection, he retires. A gentleman comes in to breakfast: looks at me as much as to say, "Confound it, Sir, what do *you* mean by being here?"

I return his look of contempt and scorn. He sits in full view of the sea, and eats his dry toast with a puzzled air as if he was tasting it as a sample, occasionally turning quickly towards the window as if expecting some one to come in by it suddenly.

Milburd, from his bath, with his hair very wet and neatly parted. He complains of my breakfasting without him, and turns up his nose at my chop and egg. He explains his absence by telling me that he was "having a chat with the man at the baths." He's always chatting. I shall *not* come out with Milburd again.

Off to London, and then down to old Johnny Byng's.

## CHAPTER XXIV.

AN INTERVIEW WITH A WATCH DOG—A SURPRISE—VERY COLD
TRAVELLING.

Byng's watch-dog Growler.

MY PRACTICAL joke. . No change. Milburd has to pay the cab; after which he has no change, only a cheque, and I have to pay the railway fares for both. So ends *my* practical joke.

*Happy Thought.* — Sixpence to guard. Hot-water bottle.

Jolly place to go to is Byng's. One needn't (I say) take down dress-clothes; no ladies or dinner parties. You can go down as you are. "As *I* am" means a light-coloured shooting-coat, waistcoat to match, and warm comfortable trousers, rather old, and a trifle shabby perhaps, but as Milburd says, "anything will do for the country in winter."

We reach the station. No flys. We stamp up and down for half an hour warming our feet. It is half-past five, he dines at half-past six. However, no dressing; hot water and dine as we are. Milburd tells me he always dresses for dinner for comfort's sake, and adds, "that it's always safer to bring your evening clothes with you when you're going on a visit." I reply, "Oh, I don't know." No fly. No porter to send. If Milburd will watch the luggage, I, who know the country and where the Inn is, will walk on and get a fly sent down to him.

I do so. Fly is ready. I'll walk on to the house. Another practical joke of mine. Milburd will have to pay the fly. If he has no change the butler will have to do it, and Milburd must settle with him. I know the short cut, and can go in by the yard door.

Brisk walk. Up a lane. See the lights.

Think I hear Milburd's fly quite in the distance. Great fun. I'll be there before him, and then what good trick can we play on him?

Here's the yard-door. Open! no bell needed. It's very dangerous to keep a door like this so unguarded. There ought to be a dog or trap.

*Happy Thought.*—I'll tell Byng he ought to have a dog.

There *is* a dog. An inch more to his chain and he'd have pinned me: how dangerous! I must creep along, keeping close to the wall. He is plunging and barking wildly in front of me: I can just see his form. I hear the fly driving up by the front way: I wish I'd come by that. The dog is still plunging, dashing, and barking.

*Happy Thought.*—To say, "Poor old boy, then—poor old man!"

He is growling, which is more dangerous. I try a tone of the deepest compassion, "Poor old fellow, then; poor old chap!"

He is trying to break his chain: if he breaks his chain I am done. Shall I call for help? It's so absurd to call for help. I am in an angle of the wall, if I move to the door where I came in he can reach me; if I move off along the wall he can reach me. I don't exactly see where he *can't* reach me. "Poor fellow—poor boy!" He is literally furious!

*Happy Thought.*—Climb the wall.

I try climbing the wall: if fall back, he's safe to catch me. Any movement on my part sends him wild: how wonderful it is that they have not been attracted in-doors by his noise.

"Poor old boy!" I hear him shaking his kennel with rage. He will have a convulsion, go mad, and break the chain. If I ever get out of this, I swear I'll never try a short cut to a house again. At last a light. The cook at the door—the kitchen door. "What do I want?" she asks. I reply, "Oh, nothing, I was just walking in the short way, and the old dog doesn't quite know me." The butler luckily appears, he addresses me by name, and orders, with authority, Growler to get down, which Growler does, sulkily.

N

TEA IN THE DRAWING-ROOM AT BYNG'S.—MISS FRIDOLINE SYMPERSON.

I say, as if he was leaving me pleasantly, " Poor old boy!—sharp dog that." It's a bad example to let people see you're at all afraid of an animal. He growls from his kennel, and we enter the house.

Mr. Milburd has arrived, and my luggage. Will I go into the drawing-room? there's tea in the drawing-room, as we don't dine till seven to-day. I take off my wraps with a feeling of being at home. Old Byng comes out to greet me. He says, " I've got a surprise for you." I wish I'd got a surprise for him, it's his birthday. "Many happy returns," I give him heartily. He says, "Such a surprise. I knew you wouldn't come if there were ladies." What does he mean? We walk to the drawing-room. I follow him: I am prepared to have a good laugh at Milburd about paying the fly, and then——

Ladies! six ladies!! all seated round the fire taking tea. Milburd standing on the rug, a young man on a small chair, an elderly gentleman deep in a book. Six ladies!!!

*Unhappy Thought.*—No dress-clothes.

I am introduced, vaguely. I don't hear any one's name, and try to give a different sort of bow to each, which fails. After the introduction, silence. My host goes and talks to elderly lady with worsted.

*Happy Thought.*—Look at photograph-book on table. Quite a refuge for the conversationally destitute is a photograph-book. Think I'll speak to elderly gentleman; what about?

*Happy Thought.*—Ask him how the weather's been here? As he says, "I beg pardon, what?" the door opens, a seventh lady enters—Miss Fridoline Symperson!!!

No evening dress-clothes!

## CHAPTER XXV.

The Dinner Gong.

ELL sounds for dressing. There are, I subsequently discover, bells to prepare us for every meal, and a gong when the meal is ready. The first bell sounding one hour before dinner merely indicates that another bell is coming in half-an-hour's time, which, when it sounds, means that there's one more bell to inform the household that time's up, and then the boom of the gong puts all further chances out of the question, finishing the preparatory process with the decision of an auctioneer's hammer knocking down "gone!"

In Johnny Byng's house everything is done with military precision. The Ladies say to one another, "Well, I suppose we must go up now," for everyone makes a point of not knowing which bell it is—uncertainty on this subject being an invariable excuse for lateness at dinner or luncheon—and I take Johnny Byng aside, and explain to him that as I thought there were no ladies there, I had brought no dress-clothes. He says, "it doesn't matter, p'raps I can rig you out for to-night, and to-morrow you can send up to town."

The rigging-out results in a black velveteen shooting-coat and waistcoat to match. With a black-tie I feel myself in full dress. I always find somebody else's clothes suit me better than my own. Byng has a pair of patent leather boots by him that no one else can wear. *The* very things for me : more comfortable than any I've ever had made for myself.

*Happy Thought.*—Say jokingly to Byng, "I shall keep these boots." He laughs and doesn't say no. Shall let the servant pack 'em up when I go.

Bell. Gong.

*Happy Thought on hearing Gong.*—"Walk up, walk up, just a-going to begin." Say it: not a success as a joke. Milburd tells me afterwards that the ladies thought it rather vulgar. Shan't say it again.

Drawing-room. Ladies all in full grand toilet. I feel inclined to apologise, but getting near Fridoline Symperson (who is superior to mere outward show, and looks lovely with her silky golden hair —it used to be darker—and thin dark eyebrows) I tell her how I abominate evening dress, and what a comfort it is to be in an easy velveteen coat. "I wonder," I add, "why everyone doesn't adopt the fashion." Milburd, who overhears my observation, asks me loudly, "if I ever heard of the monkey who had lost his tail? You know," he continues, seeing he has got an audience,—(*Note*, a man who talks loudly and authoritatively before women can always get an audience, specially in the few minutes before dinner. *Typical Developments.* Chapter on "Superficiality," Book X. Vol. XIV.) "the monkey who lost his own tail told everyone that it was the more comfortable fashion to go without one!"

Miss Fridoline laughs. Everyone is amused. Is there impiety in wishing that the power of brilliant repartee could be obtained by fasting, humiliation, and a short stay in a desert?

*Happy Thought.*—Desert: Leicester Square. I *think* this: how well it would have come out in conversation. I hesitate, as they might think it vulgar.

Byng, who is the courtly host, introduces me to a Miss Pellingle. [I don't catch her name until the following morning.]

*Happy Thought.*—Why should not introductions be managed with visiting cards?

Being introduced to her, I am on the point of asking her if she is engaged for the next dance (my fun), when the gong sounds again, and she says that she supposes it must be for dinner. Butler announces "dinner" to us, having just announced it to himself on the gong in the hall. Byng leads with elderly lady, who crackles, as she moves, with bugles and spangles on a black dress.    The middle-aged gentleman I find belongs to her, and both together are some sort of relations of Johnny Byng's.    All here are, I discover, more or less related to Byng, only as he has no brothers

Dressing for Dinner.    Byng "rigs me out."

or sisters, you have to get at their relationship by tracing marriages and intermarriages in connection with Byng's whole-uncle William and his half-aunt Sarah, which he tries to explain to me late at night.

*Happy Thought.*—I say to him jestingly, "If Dick's uncle was

Tom's son, what relation was," and so forth. He is annoyed. (*Query*, vulgar?)

*Dinner.*—As I pass Byng, he whispers hurriedly, alluding to my partner, "She's been to Nova Scotia. Draw her out." After twice placing a leg of my chair on my partner's dress, and once on that of the lady on my left, we wedge ourselves in. I begin to laugh about these little difficulties, and seeing Miss Pellingle look serious, I find I have been jocose while Byng (behind a lot of flowers where I couldn't see him) was saying grace.

*Happy Thought.*—Exert myself as a conversationalist, and try to draw her out about Nova Scotia. Begin with "So you've been to Nova Scotia?" She replies, "Yes, she has." I feel inclined to ask, "Well, and how are they?" which I know would be stupid. (*Query*, vulgar?) I should like to commence instructing *her* about Nova Scotia. I wish Byng had told me before dressing for dinner: he's got a good library here.

*Happy Thought.*—Draw her out in a general way by asking, "and what sort of a place *is* Nova Scotia?" This I put rather frowningly, as if I'd received contradictory accounts about it which had deterred me from going there.

She answers, "Which part?"

*Happy Thought.*—To shrug my shoulders and reply, "Oh, any part," leaving it to her. She begins something about Halifax, (Halifax I remember, of course, and a song commencing, "A Captain bold in Halifax;" don't mention it, might be vulgar) when we hear a noise as of a band tuning outside the window. Byng explains that, being his birthday, the band from Dishling (Byng's village)——

"*And*," puts in the Butler, with the air of a man who knows what good music is, "the band from Bogley"——

Byng adopts the Butler's amendment, "the bands from Dishling and Bogley come to play during dinner."

Milburd makes a wry face. The united musicians commence (in the dark outside) an overture. We listen. Byng's half-aunt pretends to be interested, and asks, after a few bars, "Dear me, what's that out of?"

I think. We all think.

Except Milburd, who exclaims, "Out of? Why out of tune, I should say." All laugh. Milburd, I suppose, is one of those wags who "set the table in a roar." Pooh ! Vulgar.

Miss Pellingle turns to me and observes, "that was very funny, wasn't it ?"

*Happy Thought.*—To reply, deprecatingly, "yes : funny, but old."

The bands from Bogley and Dishling get through the overture to *William Tell.* Dishling got through it first, I think.

*Happy Thought (which has probably occurred to the leader of the united Dishling and Bogley Bands).*—When there's a difficulty beat the drum.

*Another Happy Thought (which, probably, has also occurred to the leader).*—Ophicleide covers a multitude of sins.

Byng goes out to address them. He likes playing as it were, the "Ould Squire among his Happy Tenantry," or " The Rightful Lord of the Manor welcomed Home." The manor consists of a lawn in front, a garden at the back, and a yard with the dog in it. The united bands being treated to two bottles of wine, offer to play for the rest of the night. Offer declined. Milburd says, "there wouldn't be much *rest* of the night, if they did." Table in a roar again. I smile : or they'd think me envious.

*Happy Thought.*—Funny, but not new.

Ladies retire. Fridoline passing me observes, "You seemed very much interested in Nova Scotia."

She has gone before I can reply. Is it possible that * * Is she * * * I wonder * * because * * * if I only thought that she * * * I should like to know if she meant * * * or was it merely * * * * and yet * * *

*Happy Thought.*—I will.

## CHAPTER XXVI.

REPARTEE PRACTICE—MISS PELLINGLE WITH ROUSSEAU'S DREAM—
FRIDOLINE—AN INTERRUPTION.

Old Mr. Symperson.

OING to the Drawing-room. Old Mr. Symperson, Fridoline's father, has been telling very ancient stories. So has Byng's whole-uncle.

*Happy Thought.* — Laugh at all Old Symperson's stories and jokes. It is difficult to show him that not a word of his is lost upon me, as there are five between us. Byng's whole-uncle, encouraged by this, tells a long story, and looks to me for a laugh. No.

*Happy Thought.*—Smile as if it wasn't bad, but not to be mentioned in the same breath with anything of Old Symperson's.

Milburd (hang him!) interrupts these elderly gentlemen, (he has no reverence, not a bit,) and tells a funny story. Old Symperson is convulsed, and asks Byng, audibly, who Milburd is?

I wish I could make him ask something about *me.*

*Happy Thought.*—Picture him to myself, in his study with his slippers on, giving his consent.

I get close to him in leaving the room. He whispers something to me jocosely, as Byng opens the drawing-room door. I don't hear it.

*Happy Thought.*—Laugh. *Note.*—You can enter a drawing-room easier if you laugh as you walk in.

The whole-uncle enters the room sideways, being engaged in

explaining details of the cocoa-nut trade (I think) to a resigned middle-aged person with a wandering eye. Byng is receiving " many happy returns " from guests who have come in for the evening. Old Mr. Symperson is being spoken to sharply, I imagine from Mrs. Symperson's rigid smile, on the subject of something which " he knows never agrees with him." Milburd is, in a second, with Fridoline.

Miss Pellingle is expecting, no doubt, that I am going to ask her for some trifles from Nova Scotia. I avoid her.

*Happy Thought.*—Look at Byng's birthday presents arranged on the table. Think Fridoline looks at me ? Am I wasting my time ? I think I must be, as Byng comes up and asks me if I am fond of pictures ? I should like to say, " No : hate 'em." What I *do* say is, " Yes : very." I knew the result. Photograph book : seen it before dinner.

Watch Milburd and Fridoline. Try to catch her eye and express a great deal. Catch *his :* and he winks. He is what he calls " having a chat " with Miss Fridoline.

All are conversationally engaged except myself. I hate all the people in the Photograph book. Shut it. Byng is ready at once for me. Am I fond of ferns?

*Happy Thought.*—To say " No ! " boldly.

" You'd like these though, I think," he returns. " Miss Fridoline arranged a book of 'em for me for my birthday." I say " Oh ! " This would have led to conversation, but I *will* be consistent in saying " I don't like ferns." [Note for *Typical Developments,* Chap. 2, Book XIII. Par. 6, " Monosyllabic Pride : false."]

I take a seat near the ottoman where she and Milburd are sit- Difficult to join suddenly in a conversation. Hunting subject. She expects me to say something, I am sure. Feel hot. Feel that my hair and tie want adjustment. Cough as if I were going to sing. Milburd (idiot) says, " He hopes I feel better after that." I smile to show that I consider him a privileged fool. Wonder if my smile *does* convey this idea. Try it in the glass at bed-time.

Will touch him sharply.

*Happy Thought.*—Say pointedly, " How often it happens that a person who is always making jokes, can't take one himself."

He is ready (I admit his readiness) with a repartee. "You ought," he says to me, " to take jokes from anyone very well." I know I do. Miss Fridoline asks why? I think he's going to pay a tribute to my good-nature. Not a bit of it. He says, "He finds it very easy to take jokes from other people : it saves making them for himself."

*Happy Thought.*—*Note for Repartee.*—What I *ought* to have said. " Then, Sir," (Johnsonian style) " I will make a jest at your expense."

[Odd; it is past midnight as I put this down. It strikes me after the candle's out, and just as I am turning on my sleeping side. By the light of the fire I record it. If this conversation ever recurs I shall be prepared.

*Another Happy Thought.*—Wake Milburd, and say it to him now.

Would if I knew his room. Bed again. Think I've thought of something else. Out of bed again. Light. Odd : striking the lucifer has put it (whatever it was) out of my head. Bed again ; strange.

Miss Pellingle is kind enough to play the piano. While she is performing, I can talk to Fridoline.

Miss Pellingle having to pass me on her road to the instrument, I am obliged to rise.

*Happy Thought.*—Say, " You're going to play something ? That's charming."

She drops her fan, and I pick it up. She is already preparing for action at the instrument, when I return the fan. Byng whispers to me, "Thanks, old fellow ! You know all about music : turn over for her, will you ? Clever girl ! Think I've told you she'd been to Nova Scotia, eh ?" And he leaves me at the piano's side. If there was a boat starting for Nova Scotia *now*, I'd willingly pay for her ticket, and Byng should see her off.

*Happy Thought.*—To look helplessly towards Fridoline, as much as to say, "See how I am placed ! I don't want to be here : I wish to be by you." Why did Miss Pellingle leave Nova Scotia ?

She doesn't seem in the least interested.

Miss Pellingle commences "*Rousseau's Dream,*" with variations. Beautiful melody, by itself first, clear and distinct.   Only the slightest possible intimation of the coming variations given by one little note which is not in the original air.

Perhaps arranged for performance in Nova Scotia.

*Happy Thought.*—Turn over.

Miss Pellingle with "Rousseau's Dream."

"No, not yet, thank you."   Too early.

A peculiarly harmonised version of the air announces  the approach of variations.   Two notes at a time instead of one.   The "*Dream,*" still to be distinguished.   Miss Pellingle jerks her eye at me.

*Happy Thought.*—Turn over.

Beg pardon : two pages. Miss Pellingle's right hand now swoops down  on the country occupied  by the left, finds  part of the tune there, and plays it. Left hand makes a revengeful raid into right hand country, bringing *it's* part of the tune up there, and trying to divert the enemy's attention from the bass.

They meet in the middle. Scrimmage. Tune utterly lost.

*Happy Thought.*—Turn over.

Too late. Steam on: hurried nod of thanks. Now again. The right hand, it seems, has left some of the tune in the left hand's country, which the latter finds, and tries to produce. Right hand comes out with bass accompaniment in the treble, and left hand gives in. Both meet for the second time. Scrimmage.

*Happy Thought.*—Between two hands "*Rousseau's Dream*" falls to the ground.

Now the air tries to break out between alternate notes, like a prisoner behind bars. Then we have a variation entirely bass.

*Happy Thought.*—Rousseau snoring.

Then a scampering up, a meeting with the right hand, a scampering down, and a leap off one note into space. Then both in the middle, wobbling ; then down into the bass again.

*Happy Thought.*—Rousseau after a heavy supper.

A plaintive variation.—Rousseau in pain.

General idea of Rousseau vainly trying to catch the air in his own dream.

Light strain : Mazourka time.—Rousseau kicking in his sleep.

Grand finishing up : festival style, as if Rousseau had got out of bed, asked all his friends suddenly to a party, and was dancing in his dressing-gown. I call it, impulsively, by a

*Happy Thought.*—"*Rousseau's Nightmare.*"

All over. Miss Pellingle is sorry to have troubled me : I am sorry she did. Wish she'd go and play it to the Nova Scotians. I leave her abruptly, seeing Milburd has quitted his place and Miss Fridoline is alone. I sit down by her. (*Note.* I *ought* to have spoken first and sat afterwards.)

*Happy Thought.*—Say " I've been trying to speak to you all the evening." (Very hot and chokey.)

She replies, " Indeed ?" I say " Yes." Think I'll say that I wanted to explain my conduct to her : think I won't.

*Happy Thought.*—" Hope you're going to stop here some time ?"

I explain that I don't mean on the ottoman, but in the house. "Oh, then," she says, "*not* on the ottoman." That was rude of me ; accordingly, I explain again. My explanations resemble Miss Pellingle's variations, and, I feel, mystify the subject considerably. I tell her I am so delighted to meet her again. I am going to say that I hope she is delighted at seeing me.

*Happy Thought.*—Better not say it : think it.

Want a general subject for conversation.

*Happy Thought (after a pause).*—Her mother.

Say what a nice old lady her mother is. Said it. I wish I hadn't, it's so absurd to compliment a person on having a mother. Say I didn't know her father before to-night : stupid this. She says, " I hope we shall have the pleasure of seeing you when you visit our part of the world again,"—meaning Plyte Fraser's part of the world.

*Happy Thought.*—Express rapturous hope. Hint that there may be obstacles. "What obstacles ?" Now to begin : allude first to interchange of sympathies, then to friendship, then to——

Byng begs pardon. He wants to speak to me. He and Milburd have got some fun, he says. The evening's dull, and we must do something cheerful at Christmas time. Byng mentions charades, and dressing up.

Milburd suggests "waxworks." Byng asks "how ?" Milburd explains that *I* am to be the waxwork figure, and that *he* will put me in different positions and lecture on me. I am, he says, to be dressed up and treated in fact like a lay-figure.

Before Fridoline ? No.

*Happy Thought.*—Say we'll do this to-morrow night with more preparation.

Byng says we must do *something* now, and, as a preparatory step, we all three leave the room.

# CHAPTER XXVII.

I AM DRESSED UP—REHEARSAL IN THE KITCHEN—PERFORMANCE IN DRAWING-ROOM — FIASCO — FAMILY PRAYERS — ARRANGEMENTS FOR A RIDE.

Masquerading.

YNG takes Milburd and myself aside. "What Christmassy sort of thing," asks Byng, "can we do to amuse them?" Milburd suggests charades. I think we can't get them up. Milburd says, "Get 'em up in a second. Cork a pair of moustachios and flour your face." I admit this is all very well, but we want scenery. Byng doubtful. Milburd pooh-poohs scenery, and says, "there are folding doors in the drawing-room; and chairs and table cloths. Only want a word." We can't think of a word.

*Happy Thought.*—Get a dictionary.

We try A. *Abaft.*—Milburd says that's it.

*Happy Thought.*—I say, on board ship in the back drawing-room. Milburd catches the idea. First syllable: A. Byng asks "how?" So do I. Milburd explains; "A: cockneyism for Hay: some one makes A when the sun shines." Byng interrupts with a question as to how the sun is to be done. Milburd says, "Oh, imagine the sun." *Baft.* Let's see how's *Baft* to be done. Silence. Puzzler.

*Happy Thought.*—Try something else.

Byng says that once when he was in a country-house he dressed up as a Monk, and frightened a lot of people. We laugh. Byng suggests that *that* wouldn't be bad fun. His half-aunt is easily taken in.

*Happy Thought.*—Dress up and frighten his half-aunt.

Byng's got it. He'll get the dress. I enter into the proposition. Prefer talking to Fridoline. Milburd shall disarm suspicion by going back to the drawing-room and saying, that a great friend of Byng's has just arrived from Germany, and that Byng is receiving him. Milburd undertakes this part of the business. Byng says, (to me) "Come along : I'll dress you up." I object. Byng says. "It's like Mummers in the olden time." I never could see the fun of Mummers in the olden time. I suggest that Milburd is better at this sort of thing, and *I'll* go back to the drawing-room and disarm suspicion. Byng is obstinate : he says, "It will spoil everything if I don't dress up." Milburd points out what capital fun it will be. "No one," he says, "will know you." Perhaps not : but where's the fun ?

*Happy Thought.*—Do it another night.

They won't. Do it *now*. Byng appears annoyed : he thought I should enjoy this sort of thing. I say "so I do : no one more," only I can't help imagining that Fridoline will think me an idiot. It is settled. Milburd goes down-stairs. Byng takes me to a lumber-room. I am to represent his friend just arrived from Germany. After rummaging in some boxes and closets, he produces a large cocked hat with feathers, a Hussar's jacket, a pair of cavalier breeches, pink stockings, russet boots, and a monk's cloak with a cowl. He is delighted. Whom am I to represent ?

*Happy Thought (which strikes Byng).* — Represent eccentric friend from Germany. He must be a *very* eccentric friend to come in such a dress. I point out that it can't take any one in : not even his half-aunt. He says it will. His half-aunt must be remarkably weak.

When I've got on the stockings and boots, I protest against the breeches. "Spoil the whole thing if you don't put on the breeches," says Byng. I am dressed. I say, "I can't go down like this." Byng's got it again. What ?

*Happy Thought (second which strikes Byng).*— False nose. Red paint.

Stop ! He hasn't got any red paint.

*Happy Thought.* —What a blessing! A new idea strikes him. Pink tooth-powder will do just as well : and lip salve.

He won't let me look in the glass until he has finished with me. When he's done, I see myself, and protest again. He says "Nonsense : it's capital : he will just see if the road's clear, and then we'll go down-stairs." He leaves me.

*Happy Thought (while alone).* —Undress before he comes back.

*First Reflection* in glass : What an ass I do look. *Second reflection*, What an idiot I was to let them dress me up. *Resolution.* Never do it again. If I had got to act a regular part, with words written, I shouldn't mind ; or even in a charade ; or if everyone was dressed up as well ; or if Milburd or some one else was dressed up ; but this is so stupid. If I don't go on with it, Old Byng will be annoyed, and won't ask me again, and Byng's *is* a very jolly place to stay at. If I'd known that there were people here, and this sort of thing was going to happen, I shouldn't have come. I shouldn't mind it so much if Fridoline were not here. I can't go and sit by her, and talk to her seriously, with a false nose, burnt cork, pink tooth-powder, and red lip-salve on my face. I *won't* go. [Analysing this feeling afterwards, with a view to Chap. 8, Book X., *Typical Developments*, I conclude it to be a phase of False Pride.]

Byng returns : radiant. I follow him, dismally, down the back-stairs. We are not, it appears, going into the drawing-room. Byng opens a door. The kitchen. The cook, two housemaids, and a footman, engaged on some meal. They rise ; uncomfortably. Byng says, "Mrs. Wallett," (addressing the cook) "here's a gentleman from Germany." Whereat the cook and the two house-maids giggle awkwardly. They're not taken in : not a bit. They pretend to be amused, to please Byng. Doesn't Byng see through such toadyism? The footman smiles superciliously, and I feel that none of them will ever respect me again. The butler enters : he is sufficiently condescending to pronounce it very good. Cook evidently feeling it necessary to make some sort of observation, says, "Well, she shouldn't ha' known me ; she shouldn't," which the housemaids echo. They are all bored. Footman patronisingly as if he could have acted the part better himself—[*Happy Though* (which occurs to me in the kitchen). Wish we *had* dressed up the footman.]—observes to his master, "The gentleman doesn't talk, Sir." Impudent fellow: I know he'll be insolent to me, after this, as long as I'm here. Great mistake of Byng's. Byng explains that I (in my character of eccentric friend from Germany) only

"Well, she shouldn't ha' known me; she shouldn't."

speak German; and asks me, *Sprarkenzee Dytch?* which he considers to be the language.

*Happy Thought.*—Yah. Also *Mynheer.*

I *do* wish (behind my false nose and tooth-powder) that I could be funny. I feel that it in this dress I could do something clever

I should have the best of it. As it is I'm a sort of tame monkey led about by Byng. I ought to go out of the kitchen funnily : I don't. Rather sneak out, after Byng. I'm sure the servants hate me : I wish Byng hadn't disturbed them at their meal.

*Happy Thought.*—Say to Byng, in the passage, " I don't think there's much fun to be got out of this." He replies, " Nonsense ; must frighten my aunt."

I would give ten pounds if Fridoline were, at this moment, in the next county. Suppose she should think I'd been drinking !

We are in the drawing-room. Fridoline is singing and playing. Milburd is waiting on her. The elderly people are engaged in conversation, or dozing. The younger are playing the race-game with counters and dice, and some are looking over pictures. Four elders, Mr. and Mrs. Symperson, the half-aunt and whole-uncle, are at whist. " They are enjoying themselves," I say to Byng, " why disturb them ?"

Byng is inexorable.

*Happy Thought.*—Go back and undress before they see me.

Byng introduces me loudly, " Herr Von Downyvassel from Germany." Every one is interrupted : every one is, more or less, obliged to laugh. I see it at once ; I am a bore. Byng takes me up to his half-aunt at whist ; she is not frightened, but only says, " What a dreadful creature !" and the four players laugh once out of compliment to Byng, and go on with their game again. Milburd ought to help me : he won't. He doesn't even take any notice of me. Miss Fridoline merely turns her head and continues her Italian song. Byng having failed in frightening his half-aunt, leaves me, and goes to find some book of pictures for Miss Pellingle. What am I to do ? Dance ? Sing ? I think I hear one of the party engaged at the race-game say, " What stupid nonsense !" I should like to dress *him* up. I'd rub the red powder into him.

Gong sounds. For what ?

The butler enters and whispers the elders, who rise sedately. The guests begin leaving the room gravely : I am following. Milburd asks me if I'm coming as I am. Coming where ? Don't I know ? Family prayers. Byng is very strict, and whenever there's a clergyman in the house, he has Family prayers. The whole-uncle, I discover, is a Reverend. You wouldn't know it to look at him, but you wouldn't know *me*, now, to look at me. In my false nose, dragoon jacket, tooth-powder, and lip-salve, I am a heathen. They want a missionary for *me*. Thinking deeply, what can mere outward adornment matter? The dress is nothing —and yet——

They are at prayers. I am not. An outcast in a Tom-fool's dress. I think I now see why the clergy object to the stage.

*Happy Thought.*—Go to bed.

I resume my own proper dress. It would be cowardice to go to bed. I wait for them to come to the smoking-room. They come in, ladies and all, after prayers, remarkably fresh and cheerful. Conversation general : no allusion to my dressing-up.

Getting near Fridoline I refer to it. She owns she thought it stupid : I tell her, so do I. She hopes it will be a fine day to-morrow. So do I. "Can't we," I suggest, "take a walk?" I want to say "together," thereby intimating that I want no other companions. She replies, "Or a ride," adding enthusiastically, "*Do* ride ; you *do*, of course." "I do," I tell her ; "but regret that I can't get a horse." This presents no difficulty to her. Mr. Byng lends *her* one of his. Byng says, "Yes, Milburd has the chestnut, I ride the bay, and I can get a very good one for you ;" to me, "from Brett's stables in the village." "That," cries Fridoline, "will be delightful ! "

I say to her rapturously, that I look forward to it with pleasure. So I do as far as going with *her* is concerned. But I feel obliged to explain to her that I haven't ridden for some time. She tells me that *she* hasn't ridden for some time, either. This consoles me to a certain degree, but I mean years—she only means months. She tells me, *sotto voce*, that Byng is not a fast goer, so he and Milburd may ride together, and that we'll (she and I) have a good gallop.

*Happy Thought.*—Alone with her ! Galloping through the woods ! Only, after a time, wouldn't she be alone without me ?

*Happy Thought.*—Talk about hunting—stiff countries—fences —brooks. [Thank goodness, no hunting here.]

She is all life and animation, and anxious for to-morrow's ride with me. I'd rather it was a drive than a ride. "She likes," she says, "riding 'cross country." She is sorry that we shall only have roads here.

*Happy Thought.*—Roads! hooray! Twenty to one against falling off on a road.

*Happy Thought.*—Say, "Ah, pity there's no 'cross country." I mean for *her.*

Ladies now retire. Milburd wants to be officious, but she takes her candlestick from *me.* She looks to *me* for a light from the gas. I look at her, and find (when she draws my attention to it) that I am holding the flame about an inch away from the wick. I detain her hand for one second. I just——

*Happy Thought.*—Sympathetic electricity. Write a chapter this evening in *Typical Developments.*

Her last words, "Mind you see about your horse the first thing to-morrow: I should be *so* disappointed if you didn't get it."

I *will* get it. Ride—anywhere—everywhere! For her—and with her! Still I *do* wish it was riding in a carriage.

When I return to the smoking-room, Byng observes that he didn't know I cared about riding.

*Happy Thought.*—To say, "Oh, yes, very much, only don't often get the chance." This will prepare them for seeing me a little awkward, as if I were out of practice.

Do I hunt?

"No," I return carelessly. "Not much. I've given it up for a long time."

*Happy Thought.*—Not to say that I only went out once years ago, and couldn't find the hounds. Gave it up after this.

Milburd gives us anecdotes of his horses: so does Byng. I come away with the general impression about horses derived from their conversation :—

1stly. "If you know something about it, you can buy a horse for next to nothing; one you can ride, drive, and hunt, and be invaluable to you."

2ndly. "That it's cheaper to keep a horse than not."

3rdly. "That I certainly ought to have a horse." So to bed.

## CHAPTER XXVIII.

THE RIDE—I PREPARE TO GO OUT WITH THE DISHLING PACK.

My Hunter.

**M**Y DIARY *and Notes for "Typical Developments."*—Byng's place is curiously situated. Some people say it's in one county, some in another. Three maps have it. So that even Geography fails in this case. Byng himself is uncertain, but has a leaning towards Hampshire, as savouring of the Forest (which is within a hundred miles or so), and of old families. The Telegraphic Guide and the Postal Guide differ as to the locality. Among its disadvantages may be reckoned the fact that you can get to Byng's by five different lines of rail from London, each one presenting some few lesser, some few greater, inconveniences. On one line you go through as far as Stopford, then wait for the half-past ten from Thistleborough, which, being an opposition, makes itself as disagreeable as possible, arriving late, snobbishly, to show its consequence, going beyond its mark, shunting backwards, grunting forwards, coquetting with the platform, frightening the passengers who are taking refreshment, and, in short, behaving generally in a very ill-conditioned manner. On another line to Byng's, you change three times; but you get there, on the whole, quicker than by the Stopford Junction one. By this train you may calculate upon some difficulty with your luggage. On a third you only change once, and then you are taken away in an apparently totally contrary direction to that in which you want to go. This causes anxiety, references to guidebooks, searching questions of guards and porters as to what the name of the next station is (checking them by *Bradshaw*), and as to the time of arrival at one's destination. The fourth has only two trains in the day which stop at Byng's station. If you want to go down to Byng's either very early in the morning or very late at night, you can't do better than go by line No. 4. The fifth is uncertain, slow, safe, and only stops if you give notice previously to the guard—which regulation you discover after you've passed Byng's station. I note all these things, because in *Typical Developments*, Vol. XI., Book XVI., when I come to touch upon Geography and Geology, I shall be then able to offer to the world some theories on the probabilities of iron veins, coal strata, and chalk rock in this part of England. For this part unites in itself the peculiarities of the low marsh of Essex, the gravelly soil of Surrey, the woods of Hampshire, the rich meadows of Kent, the plains of Leicestershire, and the downs of Sussex. And all this I note down, having much leisure, and being very tired, but dreadfully wakeful at night, after a day with the Dishling Harriers. And I note it down for reasons as above stated, and also to account to myself for the varied country through which I have passed,—*Diary.*

*Morning.*—Down to breakfast. Earlier than usual. Half-aunt making tea. Milburd, as I enter, is asking, "How far is it?"

Byng replies, "A mere trot over."

*Happy Thought.*—Fridoline looking as bright as Aurora.

*Happy Thought.*—Don't say it: keep it to myself. Aurora sounds like *a roarer*, and the ladies mightn't like it.

"So soon?" I ask. Don't I know? "No, I don't." "Oh," says Byng, "we've found out that the Dishling pack meets near here this morning, and so we're going to have a run with them."

*Happy Thought.*—Have a run without *me*.

"I suppose he hasn't been able to get a horse for me?" I ask this with a tinge of regret in my voice. If he says he hasn't been able, I shall be sorry; if he says he has—why, I feel I must take my chance.

*Happy Thought.*—Lots of people ride, and never have an accident.

"Hasn't he?" he returns, heartily. His groom (confound him!) has been up and down the village since five o'clock, and has hit upon a very good one—about sixteen one—well up to my weight. "Carry you, in fact," says Milburd, "like a child." "I suppose he's not a hunter, is he?"

*Happy Thought.*—If he's not a hunter, of course I shan't risk him over fences and ditches.

My doubts are set at rest by the groom, who enters at that moment. He informs me that "The old mare was reg'lar hunted by Mr. Parsons, and with you (*me*) on his back, Sir, she'll go over anything a'most." *She'll go,* but will *I?*

Fridoline exclaims, "Oh, how delicious! Shall we have much jumping? It is *such* fun!"

Milburd appears to know the country. "It's all very easy," *he* says. "Into one field, pop out again," (this is *his* description), "into another, over a hedge, little ditch, gallop across the open, little brook (nothing to speak of), sheep-hurdle, and then perhaps we may get a clear burst away on the downs."

"I don't care about downs: there's no jumping there!" says Fridoline.

*Happy Thought.*—Keep on the downs.

I notice, on their rising from the table, that Milburd is in tops and breeches, and that Byng is in breeches and black boots. Both wear spurs.

*Happy Thought.*—I can't hunt as I am.

The whole-uncle (who is *not* going—the coward!) says it won't matter—there's little or no riding required with harriers. He pretends to wish he could join us—old humbug! I wish he could. I should like to see *him* popping out of one field, into another, over a hedge.

Byng has been considering. He *has* got by him an old pair of cords, but no boots.

*Happy Thought.*—Can't hunt without boots. Great nuisance. Better give it up. Don't stop for me.

*A Happy Thought occurs to* Milburd.—Patent leggings, fasten with springs. Antigropelos.

I try them on. They *do* fit me; at least, I imagine so (mean-

ing the hunting breeches), though never having worn hunting
breeches before, I've got a sort of idea that they're not quite the
thing. So very tight in the knee. His leggings are patent antigropelos, which go over my stockings and boots. When I am
dressed I walk down-stairs, or rather, waddle down-stairs, and
can't help remarking that "This is just the sort of dress for

Preparing to go out with the Dishling Pack.

riding in," or, by the way, for sitting in; but walking is out of the
question. [I wonder if they *do* fit.]

Fridoline who looks so bewitching in her habit that I could fall
down on my knees and offer her my hand at once—(My knees! I
don't think they *do* fit; and I question whether this costume
exhibits the symmetry of form so well as the modern style)—
Fridoline says that I look quite military. (She means it as a
compliment, but it isn't; because I want to look sportsmanlike.)
In antigropelos, if like anything, I resemble the Great Napoleon
from the knees. Milburd says I'm not unlike the master of the

ring in a French circus. I can't help feeling that I am something like that, or, as I said before, the Great Napoleon. Milburd remarks I ought to have spurs. I object to spurs. I feel that without spurs I'm tolerably safe; but if there's a question of a spill, spurs will settle it. That's my feeling about spurs. I only say, "Oh don't trouble yourself." Byng is going to fetch them : "I can get on just as well without spurs." The groom says, "she won't want spurs," which awakens me to the fact of the beast being now at the hall-door. A bright chestnut, very tall, broad, and swishing its tail; with a habit of looking back without turning its head (which movement is unnatural), as if to see if anyone is getting up. I ask is this mine? I feel it is. It is. I can't help saying jocosely, as a reminder to others to excuse any shortcomings in horsemanship on my part, "I haven't ridden for ever so long ; I'm afraid I shall be rather stiff." If stiffness is all I've to fear, I don't care. I wish we were coming home instead of starting. "Will I help Fridoline up?" I will ; if only to cut out Milburd and not lose an opportunity. What a difficult thing it is to help a lady on to her horse. After several attempts, I am obliged to give in.

*Happy Thought.*—I must practise this somewhere. Private lesson in a riding-school. I feel I've fallen in her estimation. I feel I'm no longer the bold dragoon to her. I apologise for my feebleness. She says it doesn't matter. Misery! to fail and be feeble before the woman you adore.

# CHAPTER XXIX.

I MOUNT MY GALLANT CHESTNUT—THOUGHTS ON RIDING—ANTI-GROPELOS—THE TROT—THE CANTER—THE GALLOP—HUNTING.

The whole-uncle watching the start.

SO, THIS *is* the horse from Brett's stables in the village, which they talked about last night. I shouldn't have had it, if Mr. Parsons, who always rides it with the Harriers, "hadn't come rather a nasty cropper" at Deepford Mill, and won't be able to go out again for a fortnight. The groom thinks I'm in luck. Hope so. It was off this horse that poor Parsons "came a nasty cropper." Miss Pellingle, on the door-step, says, "What a pretty creature!" and observes that she's always heard chestnuts are so fiery.

I return, "Indeed!" carelessly, as if I possessed Mr. Rarey's secret. The whole-uncle (from a window) suggests that "perhaps you'd rather have a *roast* chestnut." People laugh. Groom laughs. At me.

*Happy Thought.*—"How ill grey hairs become a fool and jester." Shakspeare, I think. What happy thoughts Shakspeare had. So applicable to a stupid old idiot. Keep this to myself.

*Mounting.*—I don't know any work on equestrianism which adequately deals with the difficulty of equalising the length of stirrups. You don't find out that one leg is longer than the other, until you get on horseback for the first time after several years. The right is longer than the left. Having removed that inconvenience, the left is longer than the right. One hole up will do it. "One down?" asks the groom. I mean one down.

*Happy Thought—(just in time).*—No; I mean up.

Groom stands in front of me, as if I was a picture. Placing no further reliance on my own judgment, I ask him, "if it's all right now." He says "Yes," decidedly. From subsequent experience, I believe he makes the answer merely to save himself trouble. Byng, on horseback, curvetting, cries "Come along!" If mine curvettes or caracoles where shall I be? Perhaps the brute caracoled or curvetted at Deepford Mill, when poor Parsons "came" that "nasty cropper."

*Happy Thought.*—Sport in the olden time. Hawking. People generally sat still, in one place, watching a hawk. Not much exercise, perhaps, but safe. Why don't they revive hawking?

Milburd wants to know if I'm going to be all day. Fridoline's horse is restive; the other two are restive. I wish they weren't. Mine wants to be restive: if he goes on suddenly, I go off.

*Happy Thought.*—If I *do* come a nasty cropper like Parsons, I hope I shall do it alone, or before strangers only.

*Happy Thought.*—The mane.

I like being comfortable before I start. Stop one minute. One hole higher up on the right. The whole-uncle, who is watching the start—[old coward! he daren't even come off the door-step, and has asked me once if I won't "take some jumping-powder." He'd be sorry for his fun if I was borne home on a stretcher after a "nasty cropper." I almost wish I was, just to give him a lesson. —I mean if I wasn't hurt.]—says, "Aren't those girths rather loose?" The groom sees it for the first time. He begins tightening them. Horse doesn't like it. "Woo! poor fellow! good old man, I mean good old woman, then." Horse puts back its ears and tries to make himself into a sort of arch. I don't know what happens when a horse puts back its ears.

*Happy Thought.*—Ask Milburd.

He answers "Kicks." Ah! I know what happens if he kicks. That would be the time for the nasty cropper. This expression will hang about my memory. "All right now?" Quite. Still wrong about the stirrups: one dangling, the other lifting my knee up ; but won't say anything more, or Fridoline may think me a nuisance.

Two reins. Groom says, "she goes easy on the snaffle. Pulls a little at first ; but you needn't hold her." I shall, though. Trotting, I am told, is her "great pace." The reins are confused. One ought to be white, the other black, to distinguish them. Forget which fingers you put them in. Mustn't let the groom see this.

*Happy Thought.*—Take 'em up carelessly, anyhow. Watch Byng.

We are walking. My horse very quiet. Footman runs after me. Idiot, to come up abruptly ; enough to frighten any horse. If you're not on your guard, you come off so easily. "Here's a whip." "Oh, thank you." Right hand for whip, and left for reins, like Byng? Or, left hand for whip and right for reins, like Milburd? Or, both in one hand, like Fridoline? Walking gently. As we go along Milburd points out nice little fences, which "Your beast would hop over."—Yes, by herself.

*Happy Thought.*—Like riding. Fresh air exhilarating. Shall buy a horse. *N.B.*—Shall buy a horse which will walk as fast as other horses ; not jog. Irritating to jog. If I check him, he jerks his head, and hops. Fridoline calls him "showy." Wonder if, to a spectator, I'm showy ! Passing by a village grocer's.

*Happy Thought.*—See myself in the window. Not bad ; but hardly "showy." Antigropelos effective.

*Happy Thought.*—If I stay long here, buy a saddle, and stirrups my own length. My weight, when he jogs, is too much on one stirrup.

Fridoline asks, "Isn't this delightful?" I say, "Charming." Milburd talks of riding as a science. He says, "The great thing in leaping is to keep your equilibrium."

*Happy Thought.*—The pummel.

"Shall we trot on?" If we don't push along, Byng says we shall never reach Pounder's Barrow, where the Harriers meet. As it is, we shall probably be too late.

*Happy Thought.*—Plenty of time. Needn't go too fast. Tire the horses.

My left antigropelo has come undone. The spring is weak. I can't get at it. My horse never will go the same pace as the others. The groom said his great pace was trotting. He is trotting, and it *is* a great pace ; not so much for speed, as for height. He trots as if all his joints were loose. His tail appears to be a little loose in the socket, and keeps whisking round and round, judging from the sound. I go up and down, and from side to side.

*Happy Thought.*—Are people ever sea-sick from riding ?

No scientific riding here ! Can't get my equilibrium. Ought to have had a string for my hat. Cram it on. I think, from the horse's habit of looking back sideways, that he's seen the loose antigropelo, and it has frightened him. He breaks into a gallop. It feels as if he was always stumping on one leg. He changes his leg, which unsettles me. He changes his legs every minute. Wish I could change mine for a pair of strong ones in comfortable boots and breeches. Thank heaven, I didn't have spurs ! Hope I shan't drop my whip. This antigropelo will bring me off, sooner or later, I know it will.

End of the lane. The three in front. I wish they'd stop. Mine would stop then. We trot again—suddenly. Painful.

*Happy Thought.*—" Let's look at the view."

Byng cries, "Hang the view !—here's a beautiful bit of turf for a canter." We break (my horse and I) into a canter. He breaks into the canter sooner than I do, as I've not quite finished my trot. I wish it was a military saddle, with bags before and behind. A soldier can't come off. If the antigropelo goes at the other spring, I shall lose it altogether. Horse pulls ; wants to pass them all. Hat getting loose ; antigropelo flapping.

*Happy Thought.*—Squash my hat down anyhow, tight.

The fresh air catches my nose. I feel as if I'd a violent cold. There's no comfort in riding at other people's pace. I wish they'd stop. It's very unkind of them. They might as well. I should stop for them. What a beast this is for pulling ! I can't make him feel.

*Happy Thought.*—If I ride again, have a short coat made, without tails.

Everything about me seems to be flapping in the wind ; like a scarecrow. Fridoline doesn't see me. What an uncomfortable thing a hard note-book is in a tail-coat pocket, when cantering and bumping.

*Happy Thought.*—End of canter. Thank Heavens! he (or she) stops when the others stop.

Fridoline looks round, and laughs. She is in high spirits. In an attempt to wave my whip to her with my right hand, I nearly come that nasty cropper on the left side. Righted myself by the mane quietly. What would a horse be without a mane?

*Happy Thought.*—The hard road. Walk. Fasten my anti-gropelo. Tear it at the top by trying the spring excitedly.

Before talking to her, I settle my hat and tie; also manage my pocket-handkerchief. Feel that I've got a red nose, and don't look as "showy" as I did. On the common we fall in with the Harriers, and men on horseback, in green coats.

Byng knows several people, and introduces them to Miss Fridoline. He doesn't introduce me to any one. We pass through a gate, into a ploughed field. The dogs are scenting, or something. I see a rabbit. If I recollect rightly, one ought to cry out "Holloa!" or "Gone away!" or "Yoicks!" If I do, we shall all be galloping about, and hunting.

*Happy Thought.*—Better not say anything about it. It's the dogs' business.

The dogs find something. Every one begins cantering. Just as I am settling my hat, and putting my handkerchief into my pocket, my horse breaks into a canter. Spring of antigropelo out again. It is a long field, and I see we are all getting towards a hedge. The dogs disappear. Green coat men disappear over the hedge. I suddenly think of poor Parsons and the nasty cropper.

*Happy Thought.*—Stop my horse: violently.

Our heads meet. Hat nearly off. Everybody jumps the hedge. Perhaps my horse won't do it. If I only had spurs, I might take him at it. Some one gets a fall. He's on his own horse. If he falls, I shall. He didn't hurt himself.

*Happy Thought.*—You *can* fall and not hurt yourself. I thought you always broke your neck, or leg.

*Happy Thought.*—Any gap?

None.  Old gentleman, on a heavy grey, says, "No good going after them.  I know the country."  Take his advice.  If I lose the sport, blame him.

*Happy Thought.*—Hares double : therefore (logically) the hare will come back.

*Happy Thought.*—Stop in the field.

Try to fasten antigropelo : tear it more.  Trot round quietly. I'm getting well into my seat now.  Shouldn't mind taking him at the hedge.  Too late, as they'll be back directly.  I explain to old gentleman who knows the country, that "I don't like leaping hired horses, or I should have taken him at that hedge."  Old gentleman thinks I'm quite right.  So do I.  They come back : the hare first.  I see him and cut at him with my whip.  Old gentleman very angry.  I try to laugh it off.  With the dogs I ride through the gate.  Capital fun.  The hare is caught in a ditch by the roadside.  Old gentleman still angry.  I am told afterwards that he's one of the old school of sportsmen, who, I suppose, don't cut at hares with a whip.

*Happy Thought.*—I am in at the death.  Say "Tally ho!" to myself.

*Happy Thought.*—Ask for the brush.  If I get it, present it to Fridoline.

Milburd laughs, and says he supposes I want a hare-brush.

It is a great thing to possess quick perceptive faculties.  I see at once that a hare has no brush, and treat the matter as my own joke.  [Note for *Typical Developments*, Book XVI., " Perception of the Ridiculous."]

After looking about for another hare for half an hour, my blood is not so much up as it was.  We are "Away" again.  The hare makes for the hill.  We are galloping.  I wish I'd had my stirrups put right before I started.  A shirt button has broken, and I feel my collar rucking up ; my tie working round.  I cram my hat on again.  There's something hard projecting out of the saddle, that hurts my knees.  Woa !  He *does* pull.  I think we've leapt something ; a ditch.  If so, I can ride better than I thought.

What pleasure can a horse have in following the hounds at this pace! Woa, woa! My stirrup-straps are flying; my antigropelos on both sides have come undone; my breeches pinch my knees,

Stupid countryman says he's seen a hare about here.

my hat wants cramming on again. In doing this I drop a rein I clutch at it. I feel I am pulling the martingale. Stop for a minute; I am so tired. No one will stop.

*Happy Thought* (*at full gallop*).—" You Gentlemen of England

P

who live at home at ease, how little do you think upon" the dangers of this infernal hunting.

Byng's whole-uncle is at home reading his *Times*. Up a hill at a rush. Down a hill. Wind rushing at me. It makes me gasp like going into a cold bath. Think my shirt-collar has come undone on one side.

*Happy Thought (which flashes across me).—Mazeppa.* "Again he urges on his wild career!" *Mazeppa* was tied on, though : I'm not.

I shall lose the antigropelos. Down a hill. Up a hill slowly. The horse is walking, apparently, right out of his saddle. Will he miss me ?

*Happy Thought.*—I shall come off over his tail.

I have an indistinct idea of horsemen careering all about me. I wish some one would stop my horse. Suddenly we all stop. I cannon against the old gentleman on the grey. Apology. He is very angry ; says, "I might have killed him." Pooh !

*Happy Thought.*—If this is hunting, it isn't so difficult, after all. But what's the pleasure ?

The hounds are scenting again. Stupid countryman says he's seen a hare about here. Delight of everybody. All these big men, horses, and dogs after a timid hare ! Why doesn't the Society for Prevention of Cruelty to Animals interfere ? I thought they always shot hares. The dogs have got their tails up, and are whining. They are unhappy. If they find a hare they give that countryman a shilling.

*Happy Thought.*—Shall write to old Boodels, and tell him I'm going out with the hounds every day. Wish I was at home in an arm-chair. I've not come the "nasty cropper" as yet ; but the day's not over.

# CHAPTER XXX.

I URGE ON MY GALLANT CHESTNUT—A DREADFUL SITUATION—
THE STAGGERS—A HAPPY RELEASE.

Is he going mad?

SK a countryman to fasten my antigropelos. Sixpence. Can he alter my stirrups? He does; not satisfactorily. The hounds make a noise, and before the countryman has finished my stirrups, we are off. Nearly off altogether. I shan't come out again. Up another hill. This is part of the down country. My horse is beginning to get tired. He'll go quieter. Every one passes me. Get on! get up! Tchk! He is panting. Get on! tchk! I feel excited. I should like to be on a long way ahead, in full cry, taking brooks, fences, and ditches Get on! Get along, *will* you? tchk! What an obstinate brute! I think I could take him over that first hedge now. I find my legs kicking him. It has no effect. First tchking, then kicking! I'd give something to be at home. Dropped my rein; in getting it up, dropped my whip. Some people standing about won't see it. Horses and hounds a long way on. I think Milburd or Byng, as I'm his guest, might have stopped for me. Very selfish.

*Happy Thought.*—Get off and pick it up.

If I get off I shall have to get up again. Perhaps he won't stand still. I am all alone; everyone has disappeared, except a few pedestrians who have been watching the sport from the top of this hill. Hate these sort of idle people who only come out to see accidents and laugh at any one if he can't get on. I haven't got the slightest idea as to where I am. What county? How far from Byng's? The horse seems to me to be trembling, probably from excitement. He stretches his head out. What power a horse has in his head, he nearly pulled me off. He shakes himself violently. Very uncomfortable. Perhaps he's rousing himself for another effort. I have seen a "Magic Donkey" (I think) of pasteboard, in the shop windows; when the string is loose the head and tail fall. It occurs to me that my horse is, at this minute, like the Magic Donkey with the string loose.

*Happy Thought.*—Get off.

He *is* quivering in both his front legs. I feel it like a running current of mild electric shocks. Get out my note-book. The beast seems to be giving at the knees. I don't know much about horses, but instinct tells me he's going to lie down. Wonder if he's ever been in a circus?

*Happy Thought.*—Get off at once.

Off. Just in time. He nearly falls. He is shivering and quivering all over. Poor fellow! Woa, my man, woa, then, poo' fellow! I have got hold of his bridle at the bit. His eyes are glaring at me: what the deuce is the matter with the beast?

*Happy Thought.*—Is he going mad !!!!

He pulls his head away from me—he jerks back: he pulls me after him. I try to draw him towards me: he jerks back more and more. His bit's coming out of his mouth. Is he going to rear? or kick? or plunge? or bite me? What *is* the matter with him? Is there such a thing as a lunatic asylum for horses?

*Happy Thought.*—Ask some one to hold him.

Two pedestrians come towards me cautiously, an elderly man in yellow gaiters, and a respectable person in black. Horse snorts wildly, grunts, glares, shivers, jerks himself back: I can't hold on much longer. If he runs away he'll become a wild horse on the downs, and I shall have to pay for him. Hold on. Apparently he's trying to run away backwards.

*Happy Thought.*—Say to man in gaiters, very civilly, "Would you mind holding my horse while I pick up my whip," as if there was nothing the matter. He shakes his head, grins, and keeps at a distance. In *his* opinion, the horse has got the staggers.

The staggers! Good heavens! I ask him, "Do they last long?"

"Long time, generally," he answers. "Will he fall?" I ask. "Most likely," he answers. "Then," I ask him, angrily, "why the deuce he stands there doing nothing? Why doesn't he get a doctor? If he'll hold the beast for a minute, *I'll* run to the village for a doctor."

He says, "There ain't no village nearer than Radsfort, six miles from here." Then I'll run six miles, if he'll only hold my horse. He won't—obstinate fool: then what's he standing look-ing at me for, and doing nothing? He says he's as much right to be on the downs as I have. The horse is getting worse: he nearly falls. Ho! hold up. He holds up convulsively, but shows an inclination to fall on his side and roll down the hill. I haven't got the smallest idea what I should do if he rolled down the hill.

*Happy Thought (which strikes the Person in black).*—Loosen his girths.

*Happy Thought (which strikes me).*—Do it yourself.

He won't—the coward. He says he's afraid he'll kick. Kick! he won't kick, I tell him. I think I should feel the same if I was in his place. I urge him to the work, explaining that I would do it myself, if I wasn't holding his head. He makes short nervous darts at the horse's girths, keeping his eye on his nearer hind leg. I encourage him, and say, "Bravo, capital!" as if he were a bull-fighter. He loosens one girth. Do the other: he won't.

Horse still shivering. Now he is dragging away from me, and trying to get down hill backward, harder than ever. "Staggers" are like hysterics. What do you do to people in hysterics? Cold water, vinegar—hit them on the palms of their hands. Man behind a hedge, about a hundred yards distant, who has been looking on in safety, hallœs out some advice unintelligibly. Why doesn't he come close up? I shout back irritably, "What?" He repeats, evidently advice, but unintelligible. It sounds like,

"If you arshy-booshy-marnsy-goggo (*unintelligible*), you'll soon make him balshybalshy (*unintelligible*), and then you can easily causheycooshey-caushey." Why on earth can't he speak plainly?

I can only return irritably and excitedly shouting to him, "Wha-a-at? What do you say?" He walks off in the opposite direction. I ask who is that man? Nobody knows. I should like to have him taken up and flogged. No change in the horse's symptoms. Where are Byng, Milburd, and the rest? They must have missed me. I think they might have come back. I say, bitterly, "Friendship!" Confound the horse, and the harriers, and everybody. Here, hold up!

Another man comes up. Tall and thin, he stands with the other two, and stares as if it was an exhibition. If there is one thing that makes me angry, it is idiots staring, helplessly. The last idiot who has come up has something to say on the subject. The horse is shaking, gasping; I know he'll fall. If he falls, I've heard cabmen say in London, "sit on his head."

*Prospect.*—Sitting on his head, in the middle of the bleak downs, until somebody comes who knows all about the staggers. If no one comes, sit on his head all night!!!

*Happy Thought (which suddenly occurs to the last comer).*—Cut his tongue.

What good'll that do? "Relieve him," he replies. Then do it. He says he won't undertake the responsibility. He has got a pen-knife, and I may cut the tongue, if I like. Cut his tongue! doesn't the man see I'm holding his head—I can't do everything. He replies by mentioning some vein in the horse's tongue, which if cut instantly cures the staggers. It appears on inquiry that he doesn't know where the vein is. What helpless fools these country people are! I thought country people knew all about horses!—What are they doing on the downs? Nothing. Fools: I hate people who merely lounge about. Will any one of them get a doctor? As I ask this, the horse nearly falls. A ploughboy arrives.

*Happy Thought.*—He shall hold the horse.

I ask him: he grins: what an ass! I command him imperiously to hold the horse. He says, in his dialect, that he can't. "Why not?" I ask, "What on earth can he be doing?" He replies, "Moind'nruks.' "What?" I bellow at him. "Moind'nruks." His reply is interpreted to me by the yellow gaiters—the boy is "minding rooks." The boy grins and shows me an enormous

My horse has the staggers.

horse-pistol with cap on, pointed, under his arm, at me. The idea of trusting such an imbecile with a pistol! "Turn it the other way:" he grins. "'Tain't loaded." He explains that they only give him a cap—no powder. "Never mind, turn it the other way."

*Happy Thought.*—If the long thin man will hold my horse while I go to Radsfort, I will give him half-a-sovereign.  I offer this diffidently, because he is such a respectable-looking person.

Respectable-looking person closes with the offer immediately. Yellow gaiters and man in black propose to show me where the village is : for money.   Is *this* the noble English character that we read of in the villages of our happy land ! !   Mercenary, dastardly, griping, gaping fools and cowards, who've been delighting themselves with my miseries for the last hour, merely to trade upon them at the last.

Long man holds the horse.   The beast just as bad as ever. Don't care now : got rid of him.   Feel that all the responsibility is on the long man.   Wonder what the long man will do if he falls on his side.   It's worth ten shillings to be free.

Miserable work walking.   Beginning to rain.

Man on horseback coming towards me.

*Happy Thought.*—Byng's groom.   I can imagine the delight of a shipwrecked man on a desert island on seeing somebody he knows rowing towards him.   He has come back to look for me. He is on his master's horse, and the ladies and his master are in the pony trap in the road just below.   The ladies !

*Happy Thought.*—Be driven home.   Soft cushions : rugs.

# CHAPTER XXXI.

I AM DRIVEN HOME—THE RETURN—DELICIOUS HALF-HOUR BEFORE
DINNER—DRESSING IN A HURRY—I MAKE LOVE AT DINNER—
AN APPOINTMENT—"BEGINNING OF THE END."

Tubbing in the Middle Ages.

HE ladies in the trap are the half-aunt and old Mrs. Symperson.

*Happy Thought.*—Be very attentive to old Mrs. Symperson. Give her my hand when she gets out. Make her feel she can't do without me as a son-in-law. Perhaps, afterwards, I might have to make her feel that I *can* do without her as a mother-in-law. I don't think so, though : nice old lady, and a little deaf.

Driving home I am very bitter against Brett, who could send out a horse with the staggers.

*Happy Thought.*—The staggers might take something off the expense of hiring.

In the carriage the ladies say he oughtn't to charge me anything : I agree with them, but feel that Brett's opinion will be different. Not sure, if I was Brett, if I shouldn't charge more. I shall, I say, call and blow Brett up severely.

[When I *do* call, two days afterwards, Brett asks me how I liked the mare? I say, "Well enough, if she hadn't got the staggers." He is not surprised, and makes no apology. While receipting my bill, he pauses to observe that "If I'd ha' lest that chestnut it would ha' been a matter of a hundred pounds out of my pocket," as if it would have been a matter of a hundred pounds out of *my* pocket.

*Happy Thought.*—Say, " Would it, indeed," and look at my watch—gives a notion of being pressed for time. Won't discuss this question of a hundred pounds any further. Go.

" Will I hunt with the Croxley to-morrow ? " he wants to know. " He's got just the thing to suit me : I can throw my leg over her and try her now." I haven't time : I should like to hunt with the Croxley immensely. " Nice fencing country, and a brook or two." Very sorry can't—let him know when I'll hunt again. Good morning, Mr. Brett. I'm sure he regrets not having charged me extra for the staggers.]

*In the Pony Trap, driving home.*—The half-aunt expresses her wonder that gentlemen can find pleasure in such a dangerous pastime as hunting. I smile, as much as to convey the idea, " Yes, you're right, but we are such daring dogs." I don't say this, because I *think* Byng knows I didn't go over the first hedge. Mrs. Symperson is of opinion that married men oughtn't to risk their lives. I agree.

*Happy Thought.*—Always agree with Mrs. Symperson.

Say pointedly, " When I am married I shall never hunt again, but settle down comfortably somewhere." At the present moment I can't fancy settling down comfortably anywhere. Don't *say* this : feel it. I *do* feel it.

*Happy Thought.*—To say to her mother that Miss Fridoline seems to enjoy being on horseback. Praise her appearance.

Say she is very like her Mamma. [Byng tells me afterwards that this sounded fulsome. Must take care not to be fulsome.] Mrs. Symperson says, " *she* was very fond of riding when *she* was young." I reply, " that I should think so." By the way, I shouldn't think so if she wasn't Fridoline's Mamma. She is pleased.

Byng, flicking the pony, asks me if I feel pretty fresh. Before the half-aunt and Mrs. Symperson I can't say more than that I am pretty fresh, considering I haven't ridden for years.

"Stiff?" asks Byng. I am surprised at Byng : such a question !

" Loins ?" continues Byng. I am astonished at Byng : before Mrs. Symperson, too ! I reply " No," as if I hadn't any loins.

[Note for " Reticence of Politeness." *Typical Developments*, Vol. XX. Book LI., Par. *m.*]

Driving up to the house. Butler, servants, whole-uncle and Mr. Symperson out to meet us.

*Happy Thought.*—Subject for picture, *Return from the Chase*. Wave my hand to them, as if I'd just come up triumphantly, after flying over five-barred gates and stiff fences. Wish I knew if Byng had or had not seen me in the first field. Painful getting out of the trap. Quite forgot to give my arm to Mrs. Symperson. The whole-uncle asks if we've had good sport? I answer, deprecatingly, " pretty well," to give the old coward who's been in his armchair all day an idea that it's not the sort of sport *I*'ve been accustomed to ; as, indeed, it is *not*.

Mrs. Symperson notices that I walk lame. From a fall ? She is anxious. I say, " No, not from a fall." Fridoline, who has entered the hall, expresses her anxiety too. I almost wish it *had* been a fall. If I say " stiffness" it will flatten the excitement.

*Happy Thought.*—To say " Oh no, nothing at all," and smile. They'll think I've been over a precipice, and am bearing it heroically.

*In my room.*—Warm bath, at Byng's suggestion, before dinner. Looking in the glass ; I am an object. Collar nowhere. Tie anywhere and anyhow.

*Happy Thought.*—Scarf, next time I ride ; with a pin in it.

My face is such a curious colour, a muddy yellow. Wish I'd come up to my room at once, instead of stopping in the hall. How different to when I started. Meditate on this, before the glass ; " So in life, we set out gaily and briskly (as I did on the chestnut), we go on—we go on—odd :—lost the simile." The footman comes in with hot water. He is familiar in consequence of that dressing up as a German friend the other day. He says, " I suppose you ain't much accustomed to riding a-horseback, Sir ?" I should like to put *him* on a wild Arab in a desert : hate familiarity. Tell him to call me in time for dressing. He is now going to sound the *first* gong. That's an hour before dinner.

*Happy Thought.*—Cup of tea. Toast? suggested by footman. Amendment adopted.

How delicious (in bath) is this dreaminess. All dangers of the day past and gone. I feel, triumphantly, that I have seen a hare killed. I should like to hunt every day. At least, I should like to enjoy a bath, tea and toast like this every day.

*Happy Thought.*—When I go up to town again practise leaping in hunting grounds, so much a lesson. Don't believe *Dick Turpin*, on Black Bess, ever cleared a turnpike gate.

*Happy Thought.*—I could clear a turnpike gate—with a ticket. Wish I'd said this in conversation : brilliant : needn't have said anything else for a whole evening. Note it down when I'm out of my bath. Read a book recommended by Fridoline, with *her* name in it. Novel. Read Fridoline's name again. Drowsy. If I don't take care I shall be asleep. * * *

*Happy Thought.*—Dressing-gown : arm-chair. Plenty of time before dinner—delicious drowsiness. * * * Footman enters : I *have* been asleep. Referring to my watch, same time as when I was in my bath : stopped. They've begun dinner.

*Happy Thought.*—Say, " I'll be down directly."

They have sent my evening clothes. Show how different I look to when Fridoline last saw me, in mud and those abominable antigropelos. Ought to be able to dress in ten minutes. Heroes in novels, Walter Scott's, or James's, always do it, with armour too. Tubs unknown to men in armour, unless they took it in breastplates and sponged over a cuirass. Then how about towels afterwards?—interesting subject opened up. Wish I hadn't opened it up now as footman comes in to say, " Fish just on, Sir." Note down the above for *Typical Developments*—chase—armour— towels * * * Wonder if I shall recollect what this means.

Just ready. Bother—no dress boots. Of course, when in a hurry I can only see those infernal antigropelos lying about. My bell is not attended to—and, hang it, no white ties.

*Happy Thought.*—Byng's white ties.

Bell again : wish some one would answer it, I should have been down by now. Just like those servants—don't like to ring again —*must*. Hard : it is a rope-bell. Old-fashioned thing—breaks.

What shall I do now if they don't come? They don't come: I do nothing.

*Happy Thought.*—Stand on the drawers and pull at the wire. After a hard day's riding it isn't easy to climb about. When I am on the drawers the footman comes in. I feel as if I ought to apologise for being so impetuous. Without any explanation I say, "Dress boots: and will he get me one of his master's ties." This last request sounds unprincipled. He returns with my boots. Master hasn't got any: he's wearing his last.

*Happy Thought (which strikes the footman).*—He will lend me one of his, if it will do.

Don't like to refuse. Thanks, yes. He gets it. As folded it is about double the thickness of my waistcoat. Very long. Difficulties. After first attempt the ends stick out straight three inches on each side. Methodist preacher. Try it double: result in appearance, gentleman with mumps. Third attempt, tie it in very broad bow, so as to absorb the length. Result, comic nigger who does the bones. Altogether a sort of entertainment. Tie becoming creased and limp.

*Happy Thought.*—Not in a bow at all. Once round, and hide the ends.

At the last moment it strikes me I want shaving.

*Happy Thought.*—No one will notice it.

General feeling of untidiness somehow; but a strong sense of comfort in no longer wearing breeches and antigropelos.

*Entrance into Dining-room.*—Awkward. Apologise. Byng cuts it short. As I am going to my seat I find I've left my pocket-handkerchief up-stairs. Uncomfortable.

*Dinner.*—Place left for me next to Fridoline.

*Happy Thought.*—Explain why I was late to Fridoline. Opens a conversation.

They are at the Third Course; but have kept soup and fish for me. Wish they hadn't. Can't refuse it.

*Happy Thought (say it in my sporting character).*—Hard work catching up people over a soup and fish course, after giving them up to beef. "There," says Fridoline, "you mustn't try to talk."

I look round at her. (Soup on my shirt front.) Not talk? Not to *her*? Then doesn't she, I ask, wish me to—(wipe it off quickly) —"Now then, don't be shy," cries Milburd to me. I nod and smile at him. Where *are* my repartees? I should like to be a Pasha for just one minute. I'd wave my hand, and the butler and footman should throw a sack over Milburd's head, and then drop him into the Bosphorus. He is *so* rude and thoughtless.

[*Happy Thought (when I am going to bed)*.—I know what I ought to have said to Milburd when he said, " Don't be shy." I ought to have said something about his setting the pattern, or that he shouldn't have all the modesty to himself. This isn't the sharp form in which the repartee should come, but it's the crude idea. Note it in my book, and work it up. Sheridan did it, and was brilliant at repartees.]

After the beef I *do* talk to Fridoline. I don't know exactly what I say. I think once I say I hope her father likes me : I praise her mother. She advises me to make great friends with her mother—I will. I hope that I shall see her after she leaves here—she hopes so too. I hope so again, because, really, I shall be quite lonely—I don't mean lonely—I mean melancholy, without her—I mean, after she's gone. Feeling, perhaps, that I have gone a little too far, I laugh. The laugh spoils the whole effect. She will think I am not in earnest : she'll think I'm a mere flirter.

*Happy Thought*.—To impress this upon her. Ask her, "You think I am not in earnest?"

She asks, " In earnest—about what?" This disconcerts me. I don't like to say, "about loving *you*," because there's a pause in the general conversation, and we two are the only ones talking. The pause began when she asked " About what?" as if everyone was anxious to hear my reply. I laugh again, arrange my fork and knife, and cast a glance round to see if anyone's listening. I catch Mrs. Symperson's eye—for one minute : she looks away instantly.

*Happy Thought*.—Ask Fridoline if her mother won't be angry with her about our talking together so much. (This is nearer the mark, though I put it diffidently.)

Oh, no, her mother is *never* angry with her.

*Happy Thought.*—To say, " Who could be ? "  She replies that her papa can.  Here the subject is at an end, as I can't abuse her father.  Silence between us.  Milburd telling some story making old Symperson laugh ; everyone laughing.  Feel awkward, being out of it, Fridoline will think I'm dull and stupid.  Must

Fridoline in the Conservatory.

go on talking : can't start a subject.  Tell her that I *am* in earnest, once more.  Expatiate on sympathies.  I hope, in a very undertone, to which she inclines to listen, that she will let me talk to her this evening.  I know what I mean, and am uncomfortably and hotly aware that I don't put it so intelligibly as I could wish. She replies, " Of course you may."  " Ah, but I mean I wish you'd let me see more of you, be more with you "——she wishes

I would not be so foolish, there's Mr. Milburd and Papa looking this way. The half-aunt is putting on her gloves, and going to nod to the ladies.

I am going to lose her. As she is preparing to rise she wants to know if I've seen Mr. Byng's conservatory lighted up. I've not—can I see it now? Yes, she'll show it me, but I mustn't stop long over the wine. One look. Byng says something to her as she goes out. I hope *he* hasn't put *me* out of her head.

*Happy Thought.*—No. She half-turns at the door. Half catches *my* eye.

*Happy Thought.*—The Conservatory.

Conversation turns on Free-masonry. Milburd relates stories of masons knowing one another anywhere. Byng tells how a French mason met a Chinese mason in battle, and didn't kill him. The whole-uncle says, he recollects a curious case, but on trying to recall details, fails; but anyhow it is admitted on all hands that to be a mason is a great thing when abroad, or in difficulties, anywhere.

*Happy Thought.*—In difficulties anywhere: then be a mason before I go out hunting again. Wonder if any of those men, who were looking on at my horse in his staggers, were masons. Perhaps they were all making the signs, and I didn't know it. Wish I'd been one. Ask all about it.

Fridoline will expect me. Awkward to leave the table. Getting fidgety. Laugh at old Symperson's stories. He's telling me one now which detains me.

*Happy Thought.*—Left my pocket-handkerchief up-stairs. Go for it.

Promise to return: only my handkerchief.

*Happy Thought.*—Conservatory.

# CHAPTER XXXII.

END OF THE BEGINNING—MATCHED—I HAVE AN INTERVIEW WITH
MY MOTHER—I AM MARRIED.

My Mother is much given to tears.

OETICAL *and Happy Thought.*—"We met, 'twas in a crowd, and I thought she would shun me:" but she didn't.

We are alone: in the Conservatory. I don't know what I am talking about. My slightest sentences are intended by me to be pregnant with tender meaning. She doesn't see it. I say I could stop here (in the Conservatory) for ever. Of course " with you " is to be understood. She answers laughingly that *she* couldn't. "With you." I say it.

(Nuisance, when I want a soft tone, I only get a gruff whisper.) "Had we not better return to the drawing-room?" she suggests. A few minutes more.

*Happy Thought.*—Call the Conservatory a Paradise.

Wish I hadn't, as in calmer moments I reject the simile. " Will you give me that flower?" I don't know its name. She gives it to me.

*Happy Thought.*—Detain her hand.

*Happier Thought.*—She doesn't withdraw it.

*Happy Thought.*—"Fridoline!" I have her permission to call her Fridoline. * * * * * *

Q

Happy Thoughts! Happy Thoughts!! Happy Thoughts!!!

I think I am speaking: she speaks: we speak together. A pause. Oh, for one Happy Thought, now. * * *

"May I?" Her head is turned away from me: slightly. She does not move. "I may?"

*Happy Thought.*—I do.

We really must go back to the drawing-room. She will return first. I will follow presently. "Once more, before we separate?"

*Happy Thought.*—Once more!

She is gone. I am alone, among the geraniums, in the Conservatory.

I can only say, "Dear girl," in confidence to the geraniums. It seems I have nothing else to say. I am stupified. I will go out into the garden. Cold night: refreshing. Smile at the stars. Is it all over at last? Odd: stars beautiful. Everything is lovely.

*Happy Thought.*—Go in and brush my hair.

Enter the drawing-room. Feel as if I was coming in with a secret. Fridoline at the piano. Milburd wants to know rudely enough where the dickens I've been to. I despise him *now*. He is harmless.

*Happy Thought.*—Talk to old Mrs. Symperson.

Fridoline having finished playing, comes to sit down by her Mamma. Old Mr. Symperson is dozing over a book. I should like to kneel down with Fridoline before them at once, pull his book away to wake him up, and say "she is mine!" I am so full of indistinct Happy Thoughts that I find it very difficult to keep up a conversation. She asks me to look over that dear old photograph book again, with her. Milburd wants to join us: she sends him away.

*At night in my room.*—Try to write *Typical Developments.* Can't. Everything's Fridoline. Try to make notes: all Fridoline. Can't get to sleep. Relight my candle. Wonder how asking the parents' consent is done. Must do it. Put out my candle. Fridoline. * * *

*Morning.*—*We* are down before anybody else, and out in the garden.    How easy it is to talk *now*.    We have got onecommon object in view.  *A propos* of " common object," here comes Milburd. Fridoline sends him in-doors for her garden-hat.    Poor Milburd ! As to parents' consent, Fridoline must tell Mamma at once.    No difficulties : they're so fond of her.    I am independent of every one : even my mother.    Should like to introduce Fridoline to my mother. * * * *

*1st Day.*—Old Symperson procrastinates : Mrs. Symperson our friend and ally.

*2nd Day.*—Old Symperson bothered.  Why can't he say " Yes," and have done with it ?

*3rd Day.*—Mrs. Symperson says that her husband is going to cut short their stay at Byng's.    What does this mean ?

*4th Day.*—Byng tells me that Old Symperson has been talking to him about me.    I confide in Byng.    Byng agrees with me. " Why doesn't the old boy " (meaning old Mr. Symperson) " say yes, and have done with it ?"

Byng has great weight with old Mr. Symperson.

*End of the Week.*—Old Mr. Symperson says, " Yes," and *has* done with it.

Mrs. Symperson begins to deprecate any haste.    Mr. and Mrs. Symperson having both said "yes," do not seem to have done with it at all.    Isn't it sudden ?    Do we know our own minds ?

This is infectious.    I find Fridoline asking me, " Are you *certain* you know your own mind ?"    "Certain !" I exclaim.    I can only exclaim, having no words equal to the occasion.

" Will you always love me ?    Never be sorry for " * * *

*Happy Thought.*—Prevent her saying any more for the present.

Being released, she says, " But seriously———"

*Happy Thought.*—Another penalty.

No more doubts.

*Happy Thought.*—Go and buy presents for different people.

Q 2

Write to my mother. Fridoline says I must go and see her. The Sympersons, when I leave, will go home. Then I am to come with my mother, and spend a week or so with them.

*Happy Thought.—Romeo and Juliet.* " To part is such sweet sorrow that "—forget the rest—but think it's something about not going home till morning? Don't care what it is now. Hang *Typical Developments.* Bother note-books.

My mother is a dear old lady. She is much given to tears. She always cries when she sees me ; she always *has* done so, ever since I can recollect, and she invariably cries when I go away. If I talk to her on any subject for more than a quarter of an hour, she is sure to cry. I find her at home, and well. She is delighted to see me, and of course, cries. Where have I been ? What have I been doing ? I tell her that I have been enjoying myself very much lately, and as to health, have never been better. This intelligence sends her off again, and she weeps copiously. When she is calm again, I open the important subject, gradually, so as not to startle her. Had I told her that I had been ordered off to instant execution, she couldn't have been more overcome.

    *      *      *      *      *      *      *

        *      *      *      *      *      *

" God bless you, my dear. I am sure you have chosen well : I hope you will be very happy."

    *      *      *      *      *      *      *

*Happy Thought.*—Solicitor (Seel and Seel, Junior, who is becoming quite a man of business) done with altogether. Everything settled. My mother has taken to Fridoline immensely, and Fridoline to her. Boodels writes to say, he'll be delighted to be best man on the occasion, and has actually postponed the dragging of his pond, which was to have been done on the very day of my wedding.

    *      *      *      *      *      *      *

Mr. and Mrs. Plyte Fraser are coming.

    *      *      *      *      *      *      *

Milburd, it is arranged, is to be very funny at the breakfast. This intelligence makes him very stupid for the next few days.

*Happy Thought.*—Have my hair cut.

*Happy Thought.*—My things *have* come home from the tailor's in time. Also the boots.

*Happy Thought.*—Look over the Marriage Service. Get it up so as to know when to say "I will" and "I do," or whatever it is.

*Happy Thought.*—The ring

It is arranged that we take a tour on the Continent for six weeks. At the end of that time the old folks will join us. Where?

*Happy Thought.*—Paris.

Byng will join us there, too so will Milburd. Boodels would, only about that time he's asked a few friends down to drag the pond, and "He can't," he says, "very well put them off again! Can he?"

       \*       \*       \*    \*    \*    \*

In the summer we shall come back to England. Little place on the Thames, where I tell Fridoline I'll teach her to sniggle for eels, and when she's tired of that, she shall dibble.

*Happy Thought.*—Summer night: under the placid moon: together: in a punt: dibbling.

*Happy Thought.*—Take the cottage before I leave England. We go down, a party of us, and visit the little cottage, next door to the astronomer's, who used to tell me all about Jupiter, and stop the earth's motion. He may stop it altogether, if he likes, now. What do I care?

   \*    \*    \*    \*    \*    \*    \*

Fridoline and I walk in the garden, while the old folks manage the business for us.

   \*    \*    \*    \*    \*    \*    \*

At the end of the garden runs the river higher than usual, it being winter time. There are two strong poles stemming the tide and fixed by a chain to the bank.

Between them is fastened a punt. In it sits a man wrapped up; he is fishing. He turns his left eye towards us; we recog-

Fridoline and I walk in the garden while the old folks manage the business.

nise each other at a glance. I have but one question for him:

"Caught anything?"

Back comes his answer as of old,

"Nothing."

It is half a year since I last saw him in the same place, in the

same punt, with the same rod, and the same answer. I wonder
if *he* is married? Or going to be? No, he'll never catch anybody: or be caught.

Fridoline is charmed with the place. So am I. So are we all.
The day after to-morrow is coming.

*The Day.*—Wake up. Something's going to happen. What?
I know: I'm going to be married. Hope I haven't overslept
myself. Bother breakfast. Hope nothing will drop on my trousers.
Byng and Milburd come in with stupid old jokes about "the
wretched man partook of a hearty meal," "the wretched man
thanked the governor of the gaol for all his kindness," and pretend
to treat me as a condemned criminal. It's an old joke of Fraser's,
and I tell Byng I've heard it done before, as I did,—when the
summons came. Everybody supernaturally cool for half-an-hour.
Everybody suddenly in a hurry, and becoming doubtful as to the
time "by *their* watches."

At last.

The Church. I can hardly see anyone, at least to distinguish
them. If left to myself I should find myself leading a Bridesmaid
to the altar. Everyone appears to be dressed like everyone else.
All gloves and flowers. Gentlemen in difficulties with their hats.
I laugh at something somebody says: I oughtn't to laugh.
Nobody seems to recollect that we are in a church, or rather in
the vestry. The Clergyman, a youngish-looking man, but middle-
aged, dashes himself suddenly into a long surplice, and looks round
defiantly, as much as to say, "Come on, I'm ready for any number
of you." The Clerk says something to him in a whisper, and
he replies also in a whisper. An idea crosses my mind that the
Clerk is starting some objection to the ceremony at the last
moment. It is all right, however. The Clerk takes charge of *me ;*
I surrender myself to him, as also, very mildly, do Byng and
Milburd.

This is the last thing I notice.

The Clergyman is saying something to me at the rails. I
don't know what I am saying to the Clergyman. I brought a
book, but somebody's taken it, or it's in my hat. I am helpless ;
the Clergyman is an autocrat : he tells me what to say, and  say
it ; tells me what to do and I do it, and go on doing it, with
a vague sense of annoyance at seeing Byng's hat on the cushion,

and at feeling that Byng is no sort of help to me in an emergency of this sort.

The ceremony is disturbed by suppressed sobs. It is my mother, in a pew.

Old Mr. Symperson doesn't refuse (as I had some idea he would at the last moment) to give Fridoline away to me, and so I take her "for better for worse, for richer for poorer, till death us do part," and as nobody steps out (I had vaguely expected that something of this sort would happen at the last moment) to stop the proceedings, I and Fridoline are man and wife. Why not "husband and wife?"

*Happy Thought.*—Married.

# MORE HAPPY THOUGHTS.

# CHAPTER I.

IN LONDON --The progress of my book, *Typical Developments*, Vol. I., brings me up to town to find a publisher. Milburd, whom I meet accidentally, says, "A publisher would jump at it." I ask him what publisher? He says, in an off-hand way, "Oh, any publisher," but doesn't volunteer any particular information on the subject. Boodels, I remember, published a volume of poems a year or two since.

*Happy Thought.*—To write to Boodels, and ask what publisher jumped at his poems.

Odd that my wife doesn't enter into my work. We have been married three years. I read her the first chapter of Book I. during the honeymoon. Since that time I have sometimes said, "Now,

I'll read you some more," or have selected some passage that has struck me as peculiarly happy. She has generally been busy. One evening, on my opening the manuscript, she said she didn't want to be bothered. I told her I didn't think it was kind of her. She replied, that rather than I should think her unkind, she'd listen. I returned, "Oh, but don't, if you'd rather not." She said that though she'd rather not, yet she would, to please me. I didn't want to be cruel, so I said, "Never mind." She confesses she'd like to see it when it was in print. Before we married I thought that Fridoline cared for literature. She doesn't : except for novels.

Her mother, Mrs. Symperson, is staying with us at my cottage, in a lovely situation.

*Happy Thought.*—To come up to London to look for a publisher. Also might see the Academy, and the Opera, and dine with some fellows at the Club.

*Happy Thought.*—Not to say anything about this, as of course I don't *know* that I am going to do it : only mention the publisher. They say they shan't be dull without me ; and as I haven't been away for a holiday—I mean away from home—for some time, my wife thinks it will do me good.

*Happy Thought.*—To say it's *not* a holiday—it's business. Going to London, in fact, on business. My mother-in-law suggests that we should all go. *All* means herself principally. I point out that I shall only be away, *probably*, for a day or two. Better to say "*probably*" in case I should stop three weeks. I add that I shall be engaged the whole time, and not be able to attend to them. Fridoline says, "Yes, better wait till we can all go away to Brighton. Baby will want change of air soon."

*Happy Thought.*—To agree at once. Brighton, by all means, for baby, at some time or other. I consider this to be the condition of my getting away now. My own opinion, privately, is that Brighton may wait. Baby is always having a rash, and always wanting, so they say, to go to Brighton.

I leave the cottage (Asphodel Cottage it is called—that is, Friddy *would* call it Asphodel until she thinks of something she'd like better) in the lovely situation, and go up by the 4·40 to town.

*Happy Thought.*—Take my cheque book.

*In the Train.*—It occurs to me that going to an hotel in town is expensive. I'll drive to Bob Willis's, in Conduit Street. Willis asked me whenever I wanted a bed in town to come to him.

*In Conduit Street.*—I jump out and ring. I know Willis well : a good fellow—always glad to see me. Willis is a sort of fellow who'd do anything for you. I foresee how I'll dash past the servant, rush up-stairs, and say, " Willis, old boy, here's a lark : I've come to stay with you." And Willis will jump up, and order the bed, and——The door opens. The maid. " Is Mr. Willis in ? " " Mr. *Who*, Sir ? " the maid asks. " Willis." " No one of that name here," she says, as if she expected me to try another name, as that wouldn't do. I ask her " if she's quite sure ? " On second thoughts, this question was absurd, as of course she'd know who was living in the house. I am perplexed. I say, " Oh, he's not here, eh ? " to myself.

*Happy Thought.*—Perhaps he's next door.

The maid says, " Yes, perhaps next door." She shuts hers, and I go to the next-door bell. I don't know why, but I fancy the cabman doesn't think much of me after this failure. Perhaps his idea is, that it's a dodge of mine for not paying the fare. It's stupid of him if he thinks *that*, because he's got my portmanteau and my hat-box, and my bag with the MS. of *Typical Developments* in it. I've heard of swindlers' portmanteaus filled with stones. He may think mine a swindler's portmanteau, but even then it would be worth more than two-and-sixpence—his fare, at the outside. Besides, there's *Typical Developments*, worth thousands, perhaps : only, not to a cabman.

Next door opens ; I put the question diffidently this time ; in fact, I beg her pardon first, and then request to be informed if " anyone of the name of Willis lives here ? " " Yes, Sir."

Ah, capital ! here we are ! Down come my things. Here, cabman, half-a-crown. He is indignant, and says he's been waiting about more than half-an-hour. I dispute it. He says, " Look here : it was six when you took me at the Station, now it's seven." It might have been six—it *is* seven.

*Happy Thought.*—Always look at your watch when you take a cab. Sixpence makes very little difference : pay him.

" Which floor are Mr. Willis's rooms ? " Second. I rush up. I

bound into the room. "Hallo, old boy——" In another instant
I am begging somebody's pardon (whom I don't know) who is
lying on the sofa half asleep. I explain that I thought Willis was
——He cuts me short courteously. They have a room together.

*Happy Thought.*—Like *Box* and *Cox.*

I don't say this, but think it. Willis may be in by eight, or if
not by eight, not till twelve. Would I like to wait?

*Happy Thought.*—Say I'll come back about nine; and first go
and get some dinner. I add that I think that will be my best
course.

The stranger (Willis's partner—the *Cox* of the firm) politely
agrees with me that this *will* be my best course. He doesn't offer
me any dinner there. I hate inhospitality. I mean if anybody, a
perfect stranger, but still a friend of the partner of my rooms,
came in, I should press him to take something—sherry and a
biscuit. I say, however, that I'll leave my things here (this will
give Willis a hint of what I mean by coming at all), and I will
return when I've dined. The stranger (*Cox*) replies, seriously,
"Very good," and is evidently getting bored by me. I retire.

*Happy Thought.*—At all events I've found out where Willis
lives. Must dine somewhere. Where? At my Club, or somebody else's Club?

*Happy Thought.*—Somebody else's Club.

Turning into Regent Street, I come accidentally upon Wigthorpe. He is delighted to see me. I am to see him. I think
(to myself) that I'll ask him to come and dine with me at my Club.
I think it over while I'm walking with him and he's telling me a
story about what he did last week in Devonshire. He stops suddenly to ask me if I don't think that (whatever it was he was
saying) a capital idea? I reply, "Yes," and put off giving him
my invitation until I see what *he* is going to do. He asks me
what I'm going to do to-night.

*Happy Thought.*—To reply, cautiously, that I've got to go and
see Willis. He says that he's sorry for this, as he should have
liked me to dine with him. I say I can with pleasure. "Or stop,"
he says, suggestively, "suppose I dine with *you?*"

*Happy Thought.*—Too late to order dinner at my Club. Very

inconvenient. Fix it for another day. Say I'll write to him. "Very well, then," he says, "we'll dine together, and you shall have a French dinner." "Capital. Agreed." We walk off together to a French dinner.

The worst of Wigthorpe is, that he's a fellow who never has any change. I make this note the day after our French dinner. I had never met Wigthorpe before in London: always in the country, at somebody else's house, where, of course, one didn't want change.

*Happy Thought.*—One goes down into the country for "change," and gets it. Say this as Sydney Smith's.

He proposes a cab up to the French restaurant. It's somewhere in Soho, and will only be, he says, "a shilling's-worth." A Hansom passes : its driver looking the other way. I don't like to shout in Regent Street, so I hail him with my umbrella. He passes on. Three Hansoms pass on, all looking the other way. One trots up with no one inside. He sees me, but shakes his head, and doesn't stop. Why is this? Wigthorpe says it's because he's going home. I say it's impudence. I say I should like to have taken his number. Wigthorpe wants to know what I should have done with it. I reply, had him up. On consideration I don't know where I should have had him up, or what I should have charged him with. The charge might have been for going home, and not taking me. I stop another. We get in. As Wigthorpe doesn't know the name of the place he is going to, he tells him to drive along Oxford Street, and he'll direct him whenever he has to turn.

Wigthorpe is a fidgety fellow. Odd that I never noticed this before. He keeps popping forward to see where the turning is. He hits up the little trap-door, under the driver's nose, suddenly, and shouts out, "To the right!" then he directs him with his umbrella. Very intricate place, Soho. We are perpetually turning from right to left, and left to right, down little streets. At last we stop at a shabby-looking restaurant. "Now, my boy," says Wigthorpe, heartily, "I'll give you a French dinner." He jumps out, and enters the house. If I pay the cabman now, I can settle with Wigthorpe afterwards. A married man must be careful. When I was a bachelor, a trifle like eighteenpence (it isn't "a shilling's-worth") wouldn't have mattered.

*Happy Thought.*—He says he'll *give* me a French dinner. I

wonder if I'm dining with him, or whether we're dining together ?
Delicate question.

*Happy Thought.*—Better not ask.   Take it for granted that I'm
dining with him.

I follow him in, along a narrow passage.   At the end of the
passage is a perspiring man in a white nightcap, backed by stew-
pans and black pots.   He salutes Wigthorpe, and we pass into the
dining room.

In an off-hand way (just like Wigthorpe, now I know him) he
stops as he is opening the door, to ask me, "Did you pay the cabman ?"   I reply that I did, expecting him to offer his share.   He
answers, "Ah, that's all right, as I hadn't any change."   I think
(to myself) he's evidently *giving* me the dinner, as he has brought
a note out with him, and no small change.   He takes off his hat
to a respectable-looking woman standing behind a counter, and
informs me that it's a French custom.

*Happy Thought.* — Will go to Paris with Wigthorpe.   Will
write and tell my wife.   Better not take her until I've been once
or twice myself, and know the place.   A literary man (engaged on
such a work as *Typical Developments*) must go about and see
varieties of life.   It's business, not pleasure.   My wife and her
mother-in-law (very poorly-read person, Mrs. Symperson) are inclined to call it pleasure.   They never *can* understand what I mean.

Wigthorpe appears to be known here.   He says, "*Garçon !*"
boldly to the waiter, who returns, "*Bienm'sieu !*" and whisks
imaginary crumbs off a table with his napkin.   Wigthorpe reads
several French names to me from the bill of fare, and asks me
what I'd like.     say I'll leave it to him.   "Then," he says, "I'll
give you a regular French dinner, just what you'd get at the
*Dîner de Paris.*"

*Happy Thought.*—Capital preparation for going to Paris.   Come
and dine here often, and speak nothing but French to the waiter.
*Mem.* To do it.

I wish they wouldn't allow smoking while I'm dining.   That's
the worst of foreigners ; all in the same room and at different
stages of dinner.   The room is full of foreigners—Frenchmen, I
suppose—and two or three have evidently brought their wives or
daughters.   They all seem to know one another, and talk across
the tables and to the Woman at the Counter.

*Happy Thought.*—Good name for a novel, *The Woman at the Counter*. *Mem*. in note-book.

The proprietor is a stout Frenchman, who plays with a dog and a cat, and patronises the establishment in his shirt-sleeves, which are very white ; in fact he is so round and white, and so white all round, that his face comes out at the top like a brown plum-pudding. As this is a decidedly happy simile (I am better, I think, at similes than I used to be), I tell it to Wigthorpe, who begs me to "hush," as the proprietor understands English, and hates to be called a plum-pudding. Wigthorpe tells me that most of the foreigners dining here are *émigrés*, who are perpetually plotting something or other. He says that they all stick together like wax. I should say they do, as they all look very hot. [Note this down for Vol. II. of *Typical Developments*, "On *Émigrés*."] I notice that all these distinguished Royalists put their knives in their mouths, recklessly. Wigthorpe asks, "Why not ?" When I tell him that I don't think it's good-breeding, he retorts that I'm narrow-minded.

Most of them have little bits of red riband in their button-holes, and some parti-coloured rosettes about the size of a four-penny piece. Wigthorpe whispers to me that there are lots of secret police always about here. I say, "Indeed !" and can't help looking about to find out a Secret Policeman.

*First Dish*. Mussels in butter. I think I'd rather not. Wigthorpe says, "Absurd ! You don't know how good they are." He adds, that it is *the* dish here. After tasting them, I am sorry to hear it is *the* dish, as I confess I don't like it. Wigthorpe replies, "Perhaps you don't at first—it's an acquired taste." I eat as many as I can, to prove to Wigthorpe that I am not a mere John Bull, and prejudiced, but I can't get beyond half-a-dozen, and those with suspicion. We then have some fish and oil, or rather Oil and fish. Wigthorpe is in raptures. He says it's the best French dinner in London. He pours out a bumper of red wine. I do the same. I suggest to Wigthorpe that perhaps it's a little thin and acid. He won't hear of it, and replies, in-dignantly, "Acid ! Not a bit ! Hang it, it's the wine of the country." He speaks as if we were in France—not within five minutes of Leicester Square. I want some bread, and call out, "Waiter !" Wigthorpe is disgusted. He likes to keep up the illusion about being in Paris. He says, "*Garçon! du pain!*" and puts himself on a par with the *émigrés* and the secret police.

I can't get a spoon for the salt, or the pepper. Wigthorpe laughs. "They never *do* use spoons for salt and pepper," he says, helping himself with the point of his knife. After the fish we have radishes, sardines, and butter. I ask him if we've finished dinner, as I'm still hungry. The waiter brings some *filets de bœuf au cresson*. Wigthorpe is in ecstasies. There is barely enough for one to be divided by two. Wigthorpe is astonished at my appetite. The next thing is the leg of a chicken in a lot of olives. This is also for two. Then there is cheese, then coffee and a cigarette. "For goodness' sake," cries Wigthorpe, "don't take milk with your *café!*" While here he talks all his English in a subdued voice, and his French very loud. "There's a dinner, Sir," says he: "better than you can get at any Club in London; and only two-and-sixpence altogether. Two-and-sixpence each! Very cheap! And threepence for *garçon*—two-and-nine." Wigthorpe feels in his pocket, and confounds it, because he has no change. "I have: what for?" "Ah," he says, "you can't manage a cheque, can you, for twenty?" "No, I can't." "Then," says he, pleasantly, "you square the dinner, and I'll settle with you afterwards." I don't feel I've dined, and say so. Wigthorpe pretends to be perfectly full and satisfied. He adds, "Well, we can sup together somewhere."

*Happy Thought.*—To say I should like it, but am engaged to Willis. Wigthorpe says good-bye, and hopes I'll "come and look him up" in town. I will; and then he can settle with me for the dinner.

Back to Willis's, in Conduit Street. Maid opens door. "Oh, are you the gentleman, Sir, who's going to sleep here, to-night?" I reply that I am. "Ah, then," says the maid, "here's Mr. Rawlinson's latch-eyk." Mr. Rawlinson is, it appears, the sharer of Willis's sitting-room. I ask if he won't want it himself? Maid replies that he left it out a purpose, as he was gone to bed early, and he'd just had a letter from Mr. Willis in the country, who wasn't coming up to town, but had given his bedroom to a friend for the night. Good fellow, Willis. Wonder how he knew I was coming? Or did the maid mean that he had given permission to

Mr. Rawlinson to let a friend have it? Maid says she dare say that was it; only, as Mr. Willis hadn't sent up his own latch-key, Mr. Rawlinson had lent his in case I wanted to stay out late.

*Happy Thought.*—Enjoy myself.

## CHAPTER II.

WHERE TO GO—THE CLUB—BOODELS' LETTER—INDECISION—MILBURD —COUNT DE BOOTJACK—NOTE ON BABY—CONVERSATION ON FARMING—LORD DUNGENESS—IRISH PROPRIETOR.

VERY jolly to have a friend like Willis. A large-hearted generous fellow, who keeps open bed-room for friends. Perhaps he'll let me stay here for a week or so. At nine o'clock in London, with nothing particular to do, it is difficult to decide where to go. The theatres are half over; and then if you haven't got your place, and aren't dressed for the evening, it's uncomfortable. There's Cremorne. But nobody's there until about eleven. Madame Tussaud's is always the same; but I suppose that's shut by this. Besides, I want something more stirring and exciting.

R 2

Wonder if anything is going on at the Egyptian Hall? Might walk there. I go there : it is closed. At St. James's Hall there are the *Christy's*. As I arrive, people are beginning to leave. Policeman at door says it will all be over in ten minutes. No good going in for ten minutes. Three shillings for ten minutes—three into ten—that's threepence-farthing and a fraction over per minute for the Christy's. Won't do. I should like to make a night of it somewhere : but where? I almost wish Wigthorpe had stopped with me. I shouldn't have minded paying his cab to Cremorne, if he would have come. If I went now, I should be in time for everything : perhaps the balloon ; certainly the fireworks.

*Happy Thought.*—Go to my Club, and see if I can get somebody to go with me.

Mine is a quiet Club in a quiet corner. It's very convenient for anyone living in the country, at least so everyone says. But I can't see why it is more convenient than any other when you are once in London. It makes a home for you in town. As I enter I notice a new hall-porter, who notices me, and he evidently inquires my name of another porter. To save trouble, I ask if there are any letters for me. I don't expect any of course. By the way, I do, though—an answer from Boodels about publishers jumping at poems. Porter makes a faint attempt at pretending to remember my name. I help him to it. There *is* a letter from Boodels. Into the smoking-room to read it. I don't want any brandy-and-water, nor a cigar, but I call for them, and take a seat in the smoking-room. As I don't recognise anyone there, I am glad to have Boodels' letter to read. Boodels' letter informs me that *his* printing and publishing was an exceptional affair, as his publisher was a distant connection of his family's by his mother's side, and so they did it more to oblige him than for any other reason ; but he is sure, that if I know any respectable firm, they would be most happy to do it for me. If it is a work of a philosophical and scientific character, why not go (says the letter) to Popgood and Groolly? He incloses Popgood and Groolly's address (cut out of a newspaper) and wishes me luck. "P.S. You mustn't be surprised if you hear of my being married soon. Don't mention it at present. Any day you like to come down and have some fun dragging the pond, do. I shall be delighted to see you."

Oh, Boodels can't be going to be married. Impossible. But why impossible? Why should I be surprised?

*Happy Thought.*—To write him something pretty and neat back in verse. Something he can keep and show to his intended and say, "Wasn't that very thoughtful of him?"

I will. Awkward word to rhyme to—"Boodels." Poodles. Noodles. Toodles. There's a farce called *The Toodles.* Saw it once in a country theatre. *Mr.* and *Mrs. Toodles.* Might say

> "Oh may you, William Augustus Boodels,
>    Be happy as *Mister and Mrs. Toodles!*"

Then Noodles has to be got in :—

> "'Tis true, my dear Boodels,
>    Unmarried are Noodles,
> They pet their small lap-dogs,
>    Canaries and Poodles.
> But you," &c., &c.

*Mem.* To work this up and send it to-morrow. I find that the firm that published Boodels' lucubrations was Winser, Finchin, and Wattlemas. The whole firm couldn't have been distant connections.

*Past Eleven o'Clock.*—No one in the Club I know. If I go to Cremorne by myself, it's dull; and the fireworks will be over. Besides, after all, what are fireworks unless you're in spirits for 'em? A gentleman in evening dress saunters into the Club-room, followed by two others, laughing heartily. They all order "Slings," and as the first turns round, I exclaim, "Hallo, Milburd!" It's quite a pleasure to join in a conversation.

He introduces me to his friends Lord Dungeness and Count de ——. I can't quite catch the name, but it sounds like "Boot-jack;" and Milburd takes the opportunity of whispering to me, immediately afterwards, that he is a distinguished Prussian over here on a secret embassy.

*Happy Thought.*—To say, "No! is he?" and watch him sipping gin-sling.

*Happy Thought.*—Hessian boots.

I put this down in my note-book as a happy thought, because, somehow or other, I can't help associating a Count with Hessian boots. I never met a real one before. Hitherto, I fancy, I had considered it as a stage title—a dashing character in a Hussar uniform, with a comic servant and a small portmanteau. I can't help thinking that (as Wigthorpe said at the French dinner) I *am* narrow-minded on some points. A literary man and a philosopher should be large-hearted. I confess (to myself in my *mem*-book) that I am a little annoyed with myself at finding the mention of a Count only brings up the idea of Hessian boots. Somehow, also, polkas, with brass heels. It shows what early training is : I recollect some picture or another, when I was a boy, of two smiling Hungarians, in red jackets and brass heels dancing a toe-and-heel step to polka time. My nurse used to call them a Count and Countess, and I've never got over it. Must take care how I train my baby with the rashes.

[Our baby always has rashes all over him. There never was such a troublesome baby. When my wife and myself once went to a theatre, we heard a troublesome scoundrel described as a "villain of the deepest dye." By an inspiration I noted down

*Happy Thought.*—Our infant a "baby of the deepest dye."]

The Count de Bootjack does not immediately get up and dance the polka, but sucks his gin-sling rapidly, talking excellent English.

The conversation turns on farming. Ours *is* a country gentleman's club, and therefore, whenever we can, we *do* turn the conversation on farming. Lord Dungeness asks me how things are in my part of the world? I reply (this being safe), that the farmers in my part are complaining. He becomes interested immediately, and inquires "What about?" I have to take time to consider my answer, as I don't know what they are complaining about ; nor, except for the sake of keeping up a conversation, that they are complaining at all. I throw my remark out as a feeler, because *now* is evidently an opportunity for me to learn something about Agriculture. (*Typ. Develop.*, Vol. III., par. 1, letter A, "Agriculture.") Milburd takes the reply out of my mouth, by interrupting with "Pooh! let 'em complain, the English farmer doesn't know how to pull the value off his land." We are all interested now ; ready to pick up intelligence about the English farmer.

Milburd's idea is to "let the soil rest." This appears very sensible, and I can't help expressing myself to that effect : the Count asks me "Why?" I reply that it is evident to reason (not to put it on agricultural grounds), that if you let it rest, it is fresh again.

*Happy Thought.*—Got out of that very well. The explanation doesn't seem to impress them much, as they continue their argument. [I note down what I can of their conversation at odd times, for future use.] Lord Dungeness wants to know "Why let it rest?" "There," he says, "is the ground—there it remains—it doesn't run away."

*Happy Thought*, which I say out loud. "It might in a landslip."

Milburd complains that I *will* come in as a buffoon. I beg his pardon with some asperity, I meant it. The two others, the Count, and Lord Dungeness, agree with me that a landslip *might* make a difference ; but barring landslips, there was your land, you raised your crops, you turned it over, you were always working it, lower soils and top soils, with dressings, and you'd pull off cent. per cent. every year. The Count remarks that that is true, in Turnips alone.

*Happy Thought.*—Cent. per cent. in turnips : go in for turnips. Milburd shakes his head over potatoes this year.

"Except," says Lord Dungeness, "in Jersey—large exports made there now." This diverts the conversation for a time to Jersey. I say *àpropos* of the potatoes, that I've never been to Jersey. Milburd asks me if I'll go with him? We have more gin-sling, and I arrange to go to Jersey with him in a few weeks' time. Shall have to explain this to my wife judiciously.

The Count says that Prussians let the soil work itself ; which seems clever.

"But after three years of top-dressings?" puts in Lord Dungeness.

I feel inclined (Lord Dungeness has pointed this question so strongly) to say, "Yes, what would you do then?" only it occurs to me that in that form, and from *me*, it would sound like a riddle, and Milburd would immediately reply, "Gib it up," like a nigger (*I* know him) which would stop this really interesting and valuable conversation. So I merely listen, and look as farmerish as possible.

An Irish gentleman joins us, a large landed proprietor [Milburd whispers this to me], and then plunges at once, *in medias res*, by observing defiantly that there is no farming like Irish farming. The Prussian Count attends to this closely. Perhaps this is some of the secret information he has come over for. Milburd doubts this statement about Irish farming. The Irish gentleman offers to prove it to him on his fingers, with a cigar.

"Thus, ye'll take so many counties, ye see "—we all say "yes," and nod. "Well," he continues, "ye don't take one crop and there an end, but ye just take one aft'her the other and work 'em on and on, successively, and each one helps the others. Ye take one field with the other "—here he sums up on his left-hand fingers, checking them off as fields, or farmers, or counties (we are none of us, I am sure, quite clear which), "and ye lose nothing 'av the prod'huce. The acres last for ever—it's not like hard cash or paper—and ye get your interest and principal together, increasing the first, and the second too, for the matter of that, in proportion. Ye see how 'tis?" As we all profess to have followed his argument closely, he doesn't continue, but announces himself as being dry, and orders "what you other fellows are drinking there with ice in it." Here are two people I never met before—A Prussian Count and an Irish Landed Proprietor.

*Happy Thought.*—Opportunity for varied information. Ask Irish Proprietor if he's ever been shot at from behind a hedge. He laughs at my credulity. "They *never* do it," he says. I reply that I had thought from the Papers, that——

"The Papers!" he exclaims. "If ye'll believe a word *they* say of Ireland, I give ye up intirely." As I don't want to irritate him, I tell him that I don't believe every word they say, and assure him that I am only asking for information.

"Why, Sir," he says, "my property lies among the worst and wildest parts, and I might walk among 'em any day if I chose, Protestant or Catholic, no matter, without a gun or a dog, or a stick, or any mortal thing, and they'd not touch me."

Interesting conversation this : must get back to Willis's, though.

## CHAPTER III.

CLUB CONVERSATION CONTINUED—A FLAT JOKE—MY FARMING—AN
INVITATION — ANOTHER — PARTY BREAKS UP—PROPOSALS FOR
"LARKS"—IN THE DARK—SNORING — SOMEBODY IN BED —
AWKWARD — SLEEPER AWAKENED — DROWSY STRANGER — A
DIFFICULTY — AN ARGUMENT — GRAINGER — SELFISHNESS —
DETERMINATION—HOTEL—NUMBER THREE HUNDRED, &C.

STILL at the Club. The conversation (kept up,
with animation, by the Count de Bootjack, Milburd, Lord Dungeness and the Irish Proprietor) turns upon Drainage. I can't tear
myself away from Drainage, as this is to me a novel topic. ["D"
for Drainage, *Typical Developments*, Book V.] The Prussian
Count questions (as I understand him, or rather as I *don't* understand him) the utility of Alluvial Deposits. Milburd, who really
seems to know what he's talking about on this subject, observes
that the great point is neither to exhaust the land by over-

manuring and working off three crops for one, nor to under-fertilise it by constant drainage. This (I say, thoughtfully, as I cannot sit there without making some observation) is mere common sense.

Milburd retorts with some sharpness, "Of course it's common sense; but who does it?" to which I can only reply, as he seems annoyed, "Ah, that's it," and take a sip at my gin-sling. A pause. More orders to waiter.

*Happy Thought.*—To say that the Drainage question involves many "slings."

No one seems to notice my having said this except the Prussian Count, who smiles somewhat patronisingly, and says, "Yes, we drain slings," then laughs again. I laugh, out of compliment, not that I see anything funny in what he said, as it was only a sort of explanation of my joke. The Irish Proprietor asks me if I farm at all. I reply, "No, scarcely at all." This reply sounds like a hundred acres or so, nothing to speak of. [It really means five hens that won't lay, two pigs (invalids), a cock that crows in the afternoon only, and a small field let out to somebody else's cow.]

Milburd observes that he's heard I've a very nice place in the country. I tell him I shall be very glad if he'll come and see me there. Feeling that this invitation to only one in the company may be taken as a slight by the others, I add (not knowing their names, and I can't address the Count as De Bootjack) "and any-one who likes to come down." They murmur something about being delighted, and then follows a sort of awkward pause, as if I'd insulted every one of them.

*Happy Thought.*—To break the silence by saying, "I like living in the country."

The Irish Proprietor remarks, that I must come to Ireland if I want to see *country.* "Ye must come over," he says, heartily, "to my shooting-box this side of Connemara, and I'll show you Ireland."

*Happy Thought.*—A real opportunity of seeing life and character: the Fine Old Irish Gentleman; bailiffs shot on the premises: port wine; attached peasantry ready to die for the Masther; old servants saying witty things all over the house: car-drivers; laughter all day; flinging money right and left; Father Tom and whisky-punch in the evening, and no one at all uncomfortable except a hard land-lord and a rent-collector.

I accept with pleasure.

Irish Proprietor wants to know when I'll come, as he shan't be at home for the next four months, but after that will I write to him? I promise.

*Note.*—Jersey with Milburd, Ireland with Mr. Delany.

*Happy Thought.*—Must arrange for my wife to go somewhere with my mother-in-law.

Prussian Count says he must go to bed. I rise too. We say good-bye. He asks me if I'm going anywhere near Brussels this year. I reply, "No. Jersey and Ireland, I shan't go any farther." "Well," he returns, "if you do, look me up." I promise I will.

*Happy Thought.*—Ask him to write down his address so that I may know his name, which of course can't be De Bootjack.

The Count answers that everyone knows him, and that he's always to be heard of either at the Legation or the Embassy; or, if it's after November, and I go on to Turin, "just inquire at the Palace, and they'll tell you my whereabouts, and we'll have a pipe and a chat." I reply, "Oh, yes, of course," as if I was in the habit of calling at Palaces, and having pipes and chats with the Prime Minister.

"He's a greater swell than our Prime Minister when he's at home," says Milburd, to whom I relate my parting words with the Count. I really *must* go and see him, and drop Ireland and Jersey. More character and life in Brussels, Vienna, and Turin. Diplomatic life, too. The Count de (I *must* get his right title, as it would never do to go to the Palace at Turin, and ask for a Prussian Count, describing him as a greater swell than our Prime Minister, with a name like De Bootjack)—The Count would introduce me everywhere.

*Happy Thought.*—Get up my French and Italian.

*Happy Thought.*—Say "good-night," and go to Willis's, in

Conduit Street.    Milburd and Lord Dungeness will walk part of the way.    Milburd is suddenly in wonderful spirits.    It is almost daylight.    Milburd sees a coffee-stand, and stops.    He says, "Wouldn't it be a lark to upset the whole lot, and bolt?"    I laugh—

[*Happy Thought*—like the monks of old, "Ha! ha!"]

—and get him to walk on.    By Burlington Arcade he stops again, and says, "Wouldn't it be a lark to knock up the beadle, and when he came out just say 'How are you this morning?' and run away?"    Lord Dungeness wishes there was a jolly good fire, as we'd all have a ride on the engine.

Milburd observes "he should like to have a row somewhere," and Dungeness proposes St. Giles's or Wapping.    Milburd says to me, "Yes, that's your place (meaning Wapping) for character, if you want to fill up '*Biblical Elephants.*'"    [He *will* still call *Typical Developments* "Biblical Elephants."    That's the worst of Milburd—always overdoes a joke.    I will really get one good unanswerable repartee, to be delivered before a lot of people, and settle him for ever.    One never knows, now, whether Milburd is serious or joking.]    It occurs to Dungeness that he knows what he calls "a crib" where the last comer has to fight the thieves' champion, and "stand liquor" all round.    "It's a sort of den," he adds, "that it's not safe to go into without about five policemen."    But he doesn't mind.

*Happy Thought.*—To say, "Should like to see those places very much, but got to be up to-morrow morning, and must go to bed now.    Very sorry.    Staying with a fellow, so won't do to be too late.    As I open the door, Milburd says, "Don't forget Jersey."    Nod my head : all right.    As much as to intimate that I'm ready for Jersey at any moment.    Can't help thinking what a good fellow Willis is to let me have his room in town, and to write to say I might be expected.

*Happy Thought.*—Simple arrangement, a latch-key.    Feel as if I were getting in burglariously.    Gas out.    Wish I knew where the stairs commenced.    Stupid practice having a bench in the passage.    They might have left out a light—

*Happy Thought (in the dark)*—instead of leaving a light out. [*Mem.* Put this down, and work it up as something of Sheridan's.

People will laugh at it then.] Fallen against the umbrella-stand. Awkward if the Landlady is awoke. She's never seen me before, and I should have to explain who I was and how I got there. Might end in Police. Willis ought to have written to his Landlady about me.

*Happy Thought.*—Stairs at last, and banisters. Willis lives on second floor. Snoring on first floor. Stop to listen. Lots of snoring about. Landlady below, perhaps; maid-servant above; lodgers all round : all snoring. Something awful in these sounds. Not solemn, but ghostly, as if all the snoring people would certainly burst out upon you from the different doors. Simile occurs to me —*Roberto* and the Nuns. That ended in a ballet. Fancy this ending in a ballet—with the Landlady. Daylight streams in through window on second flight. Very pale light : makes *me* feel ghostly, especially about the white waistcoat : a sort of dingy ghost. Up the next stairs quietly. Pass Rawlinson's bed-room. More snoring. Rawlinson snores angrily. The other people down below contentedly; except one, somewhere, who varies it with a heavy sigh. Glad to shut the door on it all, and go to bed.

*Happy Thought (in connection with the ballet and Roberto).*— "Willis's Rooms." Good idea this. Should like to wake up Rawlinson, and tell him what I'd thought of. Won't: don't know him well enough. My portmanteau has been moved into the bed-room evidently. But here's my bag on the sofa : everything in it for the night ready. See these by the pale daylight. Look at myself in the glass. Say, "This won't do: mustn't stop out so late." Hair looks wiry. The bed-room is quite dark, so I must light a candle to go in there, as somehow the stupid idiots at home have put the only thing I really *do* want for the night in my portmanteau, instead of in my bag. Delicious it will be to go to bed, and get up when I like in the morning.

*Happy Thought.*—Bed.

In the bed-room. Hullo ! why, I can't have made a mistake : *there's some one in bed.* Is it some one, or a cat, or—no, *Some One* fast asleep. Willis come back, confound him ! He turns. It isn't Willis. But—I can't make it out : these are the rooms I was in before. Yes. I go gently back and examine. Yes, not a doubt of it. I return still more gently, and examine sleeping stranger by candle-light. Don't know him from Adam. Wonder what he's doing there. Sleeping, of course. He can't be a thief. Thieves don't take all their things off (his boots and clothes are littered all over the place anyhow), and go to bed. Intoxicated lodger, perhaps, mistaken the room. I really don't know what to do. Most awkward situation. Shall I call Rawlinson up to look at him? What shall I say to Rawlinson? Say, "Look here, Rawlinson, sorry to disturb you, but just come and see what I've found in Willis's bed."

I mustn't do it too suddenly, or nervously, or Rawlinson might be frightened into a fit. Recollect hearing once of a man being awoke suddenly, and frightened into a fit. But I think, by the way, that that had something to do with a sham ghost and a turnip. Perhaps, on the whole, I'd better take my things and go away quietly. Where?

*Happy Thought.*—Hotel.

Must unpack my portmanteau, and get my things out first, as I can't lug the horrid thing down-stairs without disturbing the house; in which case I should have to explain to everybody. Perhaps there are eight or ten lodgers, and the Landlady. I still stand surveying him by candle-light, as if there were some chance of his getting up, of his own accord, in his sleep, and going away to a hotel instead of me. I only hope he won't wake. He is waking. I can't move. He is awake. We stare at one another. He says, " Eh! Why? What the——"

*Happy Thought.*—To answer very politely. Say, " Don't disturb yourself. Quite an accident."

*Happy Thought* that will come into my mind. Scene from somebody's opera or oratorio, *The Sleeper Awakened.* Whose? Perhaps a continuation of *Sonnambula.* This all flashes across my mind as he says, lazily, " Accident!" Then starting bolt upright, " Not fire!! Eh?"

As the Stranger comes up suddenly from under the bedclothes, and inquires if it's a fire, I can't help noticing (in the flash of a second) that *his* appearance, about the head I mean, is rather conflagratory than otherwise. His hair is red, long, and rough; his face is red, his moustache and beard are red.

*Happy Thought.*—The Fire King in bed.

I explain that it is *not* a fire, and that, generally, no danger is to be apprehended.

" Then," says he, stupidly, "what's the time?" As if he'd been expecting me at a certain hour, and I had anticipated the appointment.

It doesn't seem to occur to him that he is causing *me* any inconvenience ; and, having once ascertained that there's no fire, he strangely enough appears to take no further interest in me, but lies down again, and, turning away on his side, mutters, " Well,—all right—never mind—don't bother—get out !" He is not a bit afraid ; only, after a short, spasmodic gleam of intelligence, he relapses into the heaviest drowsiness.

This is so annoying that I determine to try if his sense of justice will not bring him out.

*Happy Thought.*—To say, simply, but emphatically, " I beg your pardon : you've got my bed."

He replies, gruffly and drowsily, without stirring, " You be somethinged ! Don't bother."

Now I *do* think that to come home at three in the morning, happily and pleasantly, expecting to turn in and rest, then to find a red-haired stranger, a man whom you never saw in your life before, in your bed, and, on your informing him of his mistake, to be told that you may be " somethinged " (a word worth five shillings in a police-court), and are not to " bother," *is* rather a strong proceeding, to say the least of it.

" Yes," I reply, " but I *must* bother." I am becoming annoyed, and I *will* have him out. Why should *I* pay for a bed at a hotel ? Why shouldn't *he* ? Or, stop——

*Happy Thought.*—If he won't move out, he might pay for my bed at a hotel. By the way, isn't this rather like a street-organ nuisance ? " Give me so much, and I'll go away." Can't help it if it is. It's only fair.

I continue, louder, so as to stop his going to sleep, " You've got my bed."

From under the sheets he murmurs pleasantly, " I'll have your hat !" as if he thought my address to him mere low, vulgar chaff.

As if I should come (I can't help putting this to him pointedly) at three o'clock in the morning merely to indulge in low, vulgar chaff with a stranger! Does he think it likely?

He pretends to have fallen asleep again. Humbug!

I repeat, angrily, "I tell you, Sir, you're in my bed."

He replies, more stupidly than ever, "All right!"

I say, sarcastically, "Well, Sir, as you don't dispute the fact, perhaps you'll kindly turn out."

This *does* rouse him, as he turns round and asks me, in unnecessarily strong language, who the blank I am? what the blank I want? why the blank I come there bothering?

I answer, simply, that Willis lent me his bed.

He retorts, "Well, Willis lent it *me!*"

I did *not* expect this, and am staggered for the moment; so much so that I can only say, very inadequately, "Did he?"

"Yes," continues the Stranger, angrily, "for as long as I like to stop." Evidently implying that he's not going to get up yet.

"But," I remonstrate, "Willis lent it to me *first.*"

"Couldn't," returns Red-Haired Stranger, rudely: "I've just come straight from him. He gave me his latch-key." And, sure enough, on the table lies the fellow to Rawlinson's.

"But I came up this afternoon," I inform him. I feel this is weak as an argument.

To which he replies, "And I came this evening."

"Yes," I reply, admitting the fact, "but I came here first;" wherewith I point to my portmanteau. I don't exactly see why he should take this as corroborative evidence, but it strikes me (as a *Happy Thought* at the moment) that it will quite knock him over; which, however, it doesn't at all.

"Well," says he, clenching the matter, "I came to bed first."

I can't deny this. Don't know what to do. I should like to have the power of producing some crushing argument which should bring him out of bed.

*Happy Thought.*—Fetch Rawlinson.

I look into his room cautiously, and, as it were, breathe his name. I breathe it louder. He is awake, and bolt upright in bed with the suddenness of a toy Jack-in-the-Box. Then he laughs: then he asks me, "Can't you eat 'em?"

I ask, rather astonished, " Eat what ? "

He replies, " Turnips," seriously : from which I gather that he has not yet mastered the fact of my being in his room, and that, despite his sudden liveliness, he is still dreaming. After a few more disjointed words, he laughs and apologises, and adds that, as he's quite awake now, he wants to know what's the matter.

" Ah ! that must be Grainger," he answers, when I tell him of the red man in bed. He says this with an evident conviction that what I've told him is so like Grainger : Grainger down to the ground, in fact. It appears that Willis has been staying with Grainger, and that Grainger has come straight up from Willis, with permission to use his room in town, while Willis uses Grainger's in the country. " I don't see how you can turn him out," observes Rawlinson, thoughtfully, but at the same time settling himself once more under the sheets, as much as to say, " and you can't expect *me* to give up *my* bed."

*Happy Thought.*—To say, " It's rather hard to have to turn out at this time to go to a hotel." I say this piteously, with a view to appealing to his sense of compassion, as I had before to Grainger's sense of justice. Rawlinson, comfortably under the clothes again, agrees with me. " It is," he says, " confoundedly hard." " Such a nuisance," I continue plaintively. " Horrid ! " returns Rawlinson, under the clothes, in a tone which signifies that he really doesn't care twopence about it as long as *he's* left alone.

*Happy Thought.*—The selfishness of bed. *Note.* This is worth an Essay.

I stand there hesitating.

*Happy Thought.*—To suggest " Isn't there a spare bed in the house ? "

Rawlinson answers, decidedly, " No."

I can't help feeling that if he got up and looked, I dare say he'd find one ; or, in fact, that if he interested himself at all in the matter, he might do *something* for me.

It occurs to me at this moment that I have often professed myself able to shake down anywhere, and rough it. I suggest (I can only *suggest*, as I feel that, now, not having any, as it were, legal status in Willis and Rawlinson's rooms, I am there simply on

8

sufferance—a wayfarer—a wanderer, glad of a night's lodging anywhere, anyhow,)—I suggest that the sofa might do.

Rawlinson, half way to fast asleep, replies, "Yes."

*Happy Thought.*—To say that the table-cloth would do for sheets, &c., in the hope that he'll return, "Oh, if you want sheets, here you are," and jump out and give me some out of his cupboard. He does not seem to be particularly struck with the ingenuity of the idea, and again, more feebly than before, replies "Yes."

Hang it, I think he might do *something*. I am angry, I can't help it. I go back to the sitting-room. Broad daylight. I might sit up till Rawlinson, or the red man, rises, and *then* go to bed. The sofa is a hard horse-hair one. Suddenly I become determined. I'll go to a hotel, and then write to Willis, and complain. Complain? of what? Something's too bad of somebody, but who's to blame? I'll have it out to-morrow morning. Go to bedroom to get portmanteau. Red man has locked his door to prevent intrusion. My night things are in the portmanteau. I tell him this through the door. He *won't* hear. I thump. No. I anathematise the servant at home, who didn't pack up my things in my bag as I told her.

*Happy Thought.*—Write down instructions in future. Anathematise Rawlinson, Red Man, Willis, everybody. Descend stairs with bag. Feel reckless; don't care whom I wake now. Landlady, maid, lodgers, anybody. " Confound 'em ! they're all sleeping comfortably, while I——" I bang the bag down in the passage, and open the door. Where's a cab? All gone home. There's one up in Regent Street, crawling. I don't care what noise I make *now*. "Hallo ! Hi ! Cab ! here !" As I put my bag in the cab, it occurs to me that this looks uncommonly like having robbed the plate chest, and coming away with the contents.

"Where to, Sir?" I think. I've only once been to a hotel in town. Morley's. Stop; on second thoughts, Morley's wouldn't like being rung up at this time. A railway hotel is the place where they're accustomed to it.

*Happy Thought.*—Charing Cross, where the Foreign Mail trains come in. Always up and awake there, and suppers, and Boots, and Chambermaids, all alive at night as well as by day.

*Happy Thought.*—Much better, after all, to go to a hotel than to Willis's. Here we are. How sleepy I am. Discharge cab. How sleepy the night porter is. Everything gigantic and gloomy. Large hall, large staircase, large passages, small porter with small chamber-candle. A doubt crosses my mind, and I wish I hadn't discharged the cab. "Can I have a bed here?" "Yes," says the porter, with a sort of reluctance which I attribute to his sleepiness. He then consults a mystic board, and I find I can be accommodated with Number Three Hundred and Seventy Five.

*Happy Thought.*—Go up by the Lift. Rather fun.

Answer : No lift at night. Should like a soda-and-brandy, I say. Not that I want it, but to give him to understand that I am not an outcast, to be placed in Number Three Hundred and Seventy Five, five stories high. No other room ? No.

*Happy Thought.*—"Not got one on the First Floor ?" This also is to give him an idea of my importance. I am *not* a bale of goods, to be shoved up into Number Three Hundred and Seventy Five. I have an idea that rooms on the First Floor are about two guineas a day, and (I fancy) are let out in suites to Ambassadors, or distinguished Foreigners.

*Happy Thought.*—Ambassadors have their rooms for nothing. Paid for by their Government. Wish I could say I was an Ambassador. Milburd would have done it. There is no brandy and soda out. He can give me some, he says, when the bar opens, about three hours hence. Idiot ! Will he bring up my bag ? No ; the house-porter will do that. He communicates with the house-porter through a pipe in a hole. He tells me to go up-stairs as far as I can, and I shall meet the house-porter with my bag.

I go up the grand staircase. As I ascend, I think of pictures of staircases in the *Illustrated London News*, and people going up them. Look down long corridors. All sorts of boots out : keeping guard before the doors. Like a prison on the silent system : the prisoners having put their boots out. On the landing of last staircase I meet the house-porter with my bag. He leads me (gaoler and prisoner—gaoler carrying bag full of stolen property) down one corridor, up another, through a third, up small stairs, into a fourth corridor smaller than the previous ones. We come

s 2

suddenly upon Number Three Hundred and Seventy Five. He has a key ready : the door is opened : bang goes my bag on to a stand. I walk forward towards glass, examine myself leisurely, debate, will give my orders to the Boots, and, take it, generally, very easily, having arrived at a haven of rest.

*Happy Thought.*—A haven where I *wouldn't* be.

*Happy Thought.*—To be called at ten, and have a cup of tea brought. He will be good enough to open my bag, and put out my things. I like a hotel, because you are waited on so beautifully : much better than at home.

Before I can turn (quite leisurely, and with something of a "swagger," just to show him that though I am up in Number Three Hundred and Seventy Five, *I oughtn't to be*)—before I can turn to give my orders, the house-porter has gone, without—confound him !—without undoing a single strap.

*Happy, but very angry Thought.*—To ring, and show him I *will* be attended to. My hand is on the bell. I pause. On second thoughts, I'll pitch into him to-morrow morning. Go to bed now. Let me see—take my note-book to bed, and make *mems* for to-morrow. Royal Academy to-morrow.

*Happy Thought.*—After night's fitful fever he sleeps well. He went away (house-porter did, I mean) without my telling him when I want to be called. Doesn't matter. Call myself, and ring the bell when I awake, to call *him* and pitch into him. Wish I'd got all my regular night things. Know I shall catch cold.

## CHAPTER IV.

THE DREAM—HOTEL BELLS—LETTERS — NOTES — HEROES — HOTEL
PROVERB—TUPPER AND SOLOMON—ACADEMY—SUGGESTIONS—
PLANS.

I WAKE up in the Hotel apparently in the middle of a
dream.

*Happy Thought (on the instant).*—To note it, as it seems a
connected story. My dream. [*Example of Connected Dreams for
Typical Developments,* Vol. IX., Chap. 2, Par. 3, *under 'D," for
Dreams, i.e., Dreams of all Nations.*] I thought Lord Westbury
came up to me, somewhere in a room or a garden, took me aside
and said something to the effect that "his real name was Sarsa-

parilla." I don't think I was surprised at the announcement, or perhaps I hadn't time to express any astonishment, as immediately afterwards I was attempting to creep on all-fours under a kitchen-table which some one (I don't know who it was as I didn't see him) said was a Monastery for Little Boys. Then immediately, I seemed to be in India, about to be executed for insubordination to a General who was crying. I didn't know any of the officers except Boodels, who was explaining to me the principle of the guillotine. I replied to some one (to Boodels, I fancy) that I must write home to ask permission. But for what I don't know, unless I meant permission to be executed. The dream, at this point, became confused, and by the way, on looking over the above notes it doesn't seem so clearly connected as it had at first appeared. I am sure there are some missing links which have escaped my memory. I'll think of them during the day and put them down. My impression about the insubordination in India and the guillotine is so vivid, that I am really quite glad to find myself in the Hotel bed.

*Happy Thought.*—Ring the bell and order cup of tea, to thoroughly wake me. First, to *find* the bell. It's generally, in hotels, near the bed. No it isn't. Or above my head. No.

*Happy Thought.* (*Brilliant in fact.*)—To trace position of bell-handle by following the wires at the top of the room. I should have made a good detective. There *are* no wires. I sit up in bed and then observe that the bell-handles are on either side of the fire-place : as if it was a dining-room. It's absurd to have a bed-room like a dining-room : the architect ought to have known better. By the way, is it the architect's business! Curious how ignorant one is on these really common subjects. I never thought of it before, but now I *do* consider the matter, it appears to *me* that the architect manages the *outside* of the building—its architectural part—and has nothing to do with the inside. Then who does the stairs? and the doors? Carpenters and upholsterers? I wish I had a dictionary here, I'd look out what *façade* means, as I *know* it's the architect's business to attend to *that*. Odd, now I think of it again, I *do* believe I've left out Architecture under A, in *Typical Developments*, Vol. II. However, I shall show the publishers only *Vol. I.*, which is complete up to *Abstractions*. Get up and ring the bell. Get into bed again. Delightful to *think* in

bed. To lie and think : then take note-book and jot something
down. Jot down my arrangements for the day. 1st. *Get up.*
*Wash and dress.* Need hardly put *that* down, but I will. There's
nothing like regularity in details. 2nd. *Have breakfast, &c.* Start
a separate heading. *Letters to write.* By the way they haven't
answered that bell. Out of bed to ring again. Jump in once
more. Quite exercise. Jot on. *Letter to Boodels.* I've got lots
to write, I *know*, but can't think just now to whom. One to Willis
about his bed and the stranger Grainger in it. That's all. No.
One to my wife. Forgot *that*. What can I say ?

*Happy Thought.*—Mustn't say " I'm enjoying myself very much
in London." Will write. " Horrid place, London this time of
year."

[*Happy Thought :* Height of the Season.]

" Wish I was back home in our cottage. But can't : business
with publisher—most important. Kiss baby for me. Love to
Mamma " (I mean Mrs. Symperson, my mother-in-law. *Must* shove
in that). Ring the bell again. That's the third time.

*Happy Thought* ( *for letter to my wife*), to throw in pathetically,
" The longer I stay away the more I am convinced there is no
place like home." This will be a sort of apology for my staying
away ever so long now, perhaps including going to Jersey, and
Prussia to see Count de Bootjack. Looking at the sentence in
two ways, there is one in which it isn't very complimentary.

[*Happy Thought.*—Look at it in the other way. Wife will.
I hope.]

Finish up letter with, " There is no news here." (Where ?
I don't exactly know. Epistolary Conventionalities. Good
title for handy book. Suggest it to publisher. Wonder whether
he'll " jump at it.") Finish with, " I am, dearest Friddy " (short
for Fridoline), " your ever affectionate husband "—— By the
way, why sign my Christian *and* surname to my wife ? (Ring
the bell *again*. That's the *fourth* time. I suppose I am so out
of the way they don't care about me in Number Three Hundred
and Seventy Five. Too bad : because what should I do in case of
fire ? Ah well, p'raps one would hardly want a bell then, except
to ring and order a cab. Say, for instance, " There's a fire here :
so I shan't stay any longer. Get me a cab." Back to bed for the

fourth time. That's eight jumps in and out, and the room crossed eight times: walk before breakfast.) To resume. Why should I sign any name to my wife's letter? Odd I've always done it, but its absurdity never struck me till this moment.

*Happy Thought.*—"*Your ever affectionate Husband.*" Full stop, and a dash to the final "d" of husband. This, as it were, marks an era in letter-writing. I wish they'd answer the bell. Fifth time of jumping out and in and ringing. Pause: no answer. Sixth time. Enter Maid suddenly, "Did you rang, Sir?" Yes, I *did* rang, I answer crossly. Can't help being cross—she's an elderly woman of the very plainest pattern. [*Note for Typical Developments: Physiognomy: Effect on Persons.*] I complain. Rang ten times: exaggeration pardonable. She never heard the bell—it's not *her* landing. "Then *why* did she come?" I feel immediately afterwards that this question is ungrateful. What did I want? Well—I—(my memory is so treacherous. Odd. For the moment I've quite forgotten what I had been ringing six times for?)

*Happy Thought.*—Oh, please take clothes and boots, and brush 'em. "Here they are, Sir, outside." Ah, taken while I was asleep. Oh, (as she is leaving the room) I know: Tea and a bath. She understands me and retires. Note down what else I've got to do to-day. Do the Royal Academy.

*Happy Thought.*—Get up, and go early. It takes me a long time getting up. Wish I could do what heroes in novels do. Their toilet never takes them more than a few minutes. "Ten minutes sufficed him to complete his toilet, and then hurrying down the stairs he met," &c., &c., or "To jump from the rude couch, and to buckle on his armour, was with Sir Reginald the work of a few seconds. When fully accoutred he descended the steps and found Lady Eveline on the terrace," &c., &c. I should like to fill this out ("Come in!" to Boots, with bath) with details. "To jump from the bed, look in the glass, brush his hair, blow his nose, wash his face and hands, tub himself, brush his teeth, put on a clean shirt of mail, get a button sewn on, ask for a clean pocket-handkerchief, and have his armour brushed and polished, was with Sir Reginald the work of fewer seconds than it has taken me to write this."

*Happy Thought.*—After breakfast tell Boots to pack up bag,

bring it down, and I'll call for it in the course of the day. Very Happy Thought, because by this means I don't have to lug it about town. (By the way, where am I going to sleep to-night? At Willis's, if Grainger's gone : call and see.) I don't have to pack it myself, and I fetch it without any ostentation. Without ostentation means that ten to one against this particular Boots being in the Charing Cross Hall, and so I shan't have to tip him. Don't deserve tips for not answering bells. Almost a proverb this— " Who answers no bells, gets no Tips."

*Happy Thought.*—Compose a book of *new* proverbs. Offer *this* to a publisher who'll jump at it. What a lot of things I shall have to offer to the publisher when I go with Vol. I. of *Typical Developments !* Might make a fortune if he only goes on jumping. " New Proverbs " is a first-rate notion. Stop, though—isn't it rather sacrilegious? (That isn't the word I want, but, I mean, isn't it rather treading on Solomon's ground?) Wouldn't do this for anything. By the way, didn't Tupper? That's rather against it. But mine's a totally different notion. " New Proverbs," with the celebrated motto, " Let who will, write their songs, give me the composition of their proverbs," or words to that effect. (*Mem.* Find out *who* said this, and *when :* date, &c.)

Dressed and breakfasted. Now to the Academy.

*At the Royal Academy.*—Early. Very early. No one there. Up the steps into the hall. Not a soul. No one to take the money. Perhaps they've abolished payments. Good that. So gloomy, I'm quite depressed. See a policeman. He reminds me that—of course—how idiotic !—the Royal Academy has gone to Piccadilly, and here I am in the old Trafalgar Square place.

*Happy Thought.*—Take a cab to the New Academy.

Ah, nice new place ! Inscription over the entrance all on one side. Leave my stick, and take a catalogue. Hate a catalogue : why can't they put the names on the pictures, and charge extra for entrance? I know that there used to be a North and a South and an East and a West room in the old place.

*Happy Thought.*—Make a plan for seeing the rooms in order. Go back, and buy a pencil. I'll begin with the North, then to the East, then to the West, and so on.

## CHAPTER V.

AT THE ROYAL ACADEMY—THE CATALOGUE—CRUSH—WORKING OUT
A PLAN—"NO. 214"—MISS MILLAR—A COMPLIMENT—POETRY
—RELATIONS-IN-LAW—A SURPRISE—DISCOMFITURE.

THE Catalogue, on reference to it, is, I find, divided into galleries all numbered.

*Happy Thought.*—Take Number One first, and so on, in order. Where *is* Number One? I find myself opposite 214. I won't look to see what it is, as I want to begin with Number One. This I ascertain by the Catalogue is Gallery No. IV., and the picture is *Landing Herrings.* By C. Taylor. Go into another Gallery. 336. *The Nursling Donkey.* A. Hughes. Oh, *this* is Gallery No. VI. Retrace my steps to another. Let me see : think I've been here before. Have I seen that picture? What I want is Number One. What number is that? Oh, 214. *Landing Herrings* again, of course. To another room. Now then. Old men talking. Can't help stopping before this picture, though I want to go on to Number One. This is 137. *Politicians.* T. Webster, R.A. Capital. But *this* is Gallery No. III. People are crowding in now. Nuisance. Wedged in. Beg pardon. Somebody's elbowing my back. Big lady stops the way. Beg pardon. Thanks. Squeeze by.

*In another Room.*—I hope Number One this time. 429. *Soonabharr.* J. Griffiths, Gallery No. VII. Bother Soonabharr ! Try back again.

Beg pardon several times for toes and elbows. No one begs *my* pardon. Irritating place the Royal Academy, when you can't get a settled place. Where *is* Number One ? Beg pardon, bow, bend, toes, elbows, push, squeeze, and I'm in another room. Hot work.

*Happy Thought.*—Watch old lady in chair. When she goes I will sit down. Getting a seat is quite a game : like Puss in the Corner. She *does* go at last, and, though elbowed, hit, trodden upon, backed upon, and pushed, I've never moved. I sit. Now then to take it coolly. Where am I ? What's that just opposite ? Have I seen it before ? 214. *Landing Herrings.* C. Taylor. Gallery No. IV. That's the third time I've seen the picture.

*Happy Thought.*—To look out in Catalogue for what *is* Number One. Number One is *Topsy, Wasp, Sailor, and Master Turvey, protégés of James Farrer, Esq., of Ingleborough.* A. D. Cooper. Wonder what that means ? He might have called it *Topsy Wopsy & Co.* Funny that. As I am being funny all to myself, I see two ladies whom I know. Miss Millar and her Mamma.

*Happy Thought.*—Offer Mamma a seat, and walk with Miss Millar. Opportunity for artistic conversation. Clever girl, Miss Millar, and pretty. " Do I like pictures ? " Yes I do, I answer, with a reservation of " Some—not all." " Have I been here before ? " I've not. Pause. Say, " It's very warm, though." (Why " though ? " Consider this.) Miss Millar, looking at a picture, wants to know " Whose that is ? " I say, off-hand (one really ought to know an artist's style without referring to the Catalogue), " Millais." I add, " I think." I refer to Catalogue. It isn't. We both say, " Very like him, though."

Miss Millar observes there are some pretty faces on the walls.

*Happy Thought.*—To say, " Not so pretty as those off it." I don't say this at once, because it doesn't appear to me at the moment well arranged as a compliment ; and, as it would sound flat a few minutes afterwards, I don't say it at all. Stupid of me.

Reserve it.   It will come in again for somebody else, or for when Miss Millar gives me another opportunity.

*Portrait of a Lady.*—The opportunity, I think.   Don't I admire that?   "Not so much as ——"   If I say, "As you," it's too coarse, and, in fact, not wrapped up enough.   She asks—"As what?"   I refer to Catalogue, and reply, at a venture, "As Storey's *Sister.*"   Miss Millar wants to know who she is?   I explain—a picture of "*Sister,*" by G. A. Storey.

We are opposite 428.   *Sighing his Soul into his Lady's Face.* Calderon.   We both say, "Beautiful!"   I say, "How delightful to pass a day like that!"   Miss Millar thinks, with a laugh, that it's rather *too* spooney.   (Don't like "spooney" to be used by a girl.)   "Spooney!" I repeat.

*Happy Thought.*—Opportunity for quoting a poetical description out of *Typical Developments*, just to see how it goes.   If it doesn't go with Miss Millar, cut it out, or publisher won't jump.   I say, "See this lovely glade, this sloping bank, the trees drooping o'er the stream, which on its bosom carries these two lovers, who know no more of their future than does the drifting stream on which they float."   She observes, "That is really a poetic description! Do you like rowing?"   Yes, I do, and——

*Happy Thought.*—Wouldn't it be nice to have a pic-nic up the river?   Miss Millar says, "Oh do."   She knows some girls who will go.   I reply I know some men who will be delighted : only she (Miss Millar) must let *me* chaperon her for the day.   (This with an arch look : rather telling, I think.   Couldn't have done it so well before I was married.   Being married, of course there's no harm in it.)   "Oh yes," she replies, "of course."   Wonder if she means what she is saying.   I ask what day? and take out my note-book.   I say, gently, "I shall look forward to ——"   Before I can finish, I am suddenly aware of two girls and a boy (from fourteen downwards), very provincially dressed, rushing at me with beaming faces, and the taller of the girls crying out (the three positively *shout*—the uncouth wretches!) "Oh, Brother Wiggy!" (they *all* say this,) seizes me round the neck, jumps at me, and kisses me.   The lesser one follows.   Same performance. I can't keep them off.   They are my wife's youngest sisters and little brother just from school, whom I used at one time foolishly to encourage. Friddy told them about my song of the little Pig, and they always (as a matter of endearment) call me "Brother Wiggy." I shall write to my wife, or tell her when I get home, that her family must really be kept quiet. I can't stand it. I smile, and look pleased (everyone is turning to observe me except Miss Millar, who pretends to be absorbed in a picture), and say, "Ah, Betty! ah, Polly! how d'ye do? When did you come up?"

*Happy Thought.*—When are you going back again? Give them half-a-crown to go to the refreshment-room, and eat buns and ices. They go. Miss Millar has found her Mamma, and gone into another room. Hang those little Sympersons. Somebody treads on my toes. I will *not* beg *his* pardon. I am *very* angry. Somebody nearly knocks my hat off pointing out a picture to a friend. He doesn't beg my pardon. Rude people come to the Academy. I'll be rude. I'll hit some one in the ribs when I want to change my position. I'll tread on toes, and say nothing about it. Very tall people oughtn't to be allowed in the Academy.

*Happy Thought.*—Walk between tall person and pictures. Must be rude at the Academy, or one will never see any pictures at all—at least, close to.

A hit, really a blow, in my side. I turn savagely. "Confound it, Sir——"

It's that donkey Milburd, who introduces a tall young friend as Mr. Dilbury. "What picture do you particularly want to see?" asks Milburd. I tell him Number One. Dilbury will show me.

"But first," says Dilbury, taking me by the arm, "here's rather a good bit of colour." He is evidently a critic, and walks me up in front of a picture. "There!" says Dilbury.

I refer to Catalogue. Oh, of course——

214. *Landing Herrings*, C. Taylor, for the fifth time. I tell him I know it, and so we pass on.

# CHAPTER VI.

**D**ILBURY takes me to see *Eagles Attacked.* By Sir Edwin
Landseer.   We stand opposite the picture in front of
several people : we are silent.   Dilbury says presently, "Fine
picture that?"   I agree with Dilbury.   Wonder where Sir
Edwin was when he saw it.   I don't see how he could have
imagined it, because, from what one knows of eagles and swans,

it is about the last thing I should have thought of. Perhaps it occurred to him as a *Happy Thought*. But what suggested it? I put it to Dilbury.

"The Serpentine, perhaps," Dilbury thinks, adding afterwards, "and a walk in the Zoo."

Dilbury tells me that that is how subjects suggest themselves to *him*. From which I gather that Dilbury is an artist. I don't like to ask him, "Do you paint?" as he may be some very well known painter.

He says, "I'll show you a little thing I think you'll like." He takes me by the elbow, and evidently knowing the Academy by heart, bumps, shoves, and pushes me at a sharp pace through the crowd. Dilbury has an awkward way of stopping one suddenly in a sharp walk to draw one's attention to something or somebody, that has attracted him—generally, a pretty face.

"I say," says he, after two bumps and a shove have brought us just into the doorway of Gallery No. III., "There's a deuced pretty girl, eh?"

Before I have time to note which girl he means, he is off again with me by the elbow. Bump to the right, shove to the left, over somebody's toes, and through a knot of people into Gallery IV. Stop suddenly. Hey what? "There's a rum old bird," says Dilbury, winking slily, "in Eastern dress, he'd make a first-rate model for my new picture; sacred subject, *Methusaleh Coming of Age in the Olden time.* Wonder if he'd sit?"

*Happy Thought.*—To say, jestingly, "I wish I could," meaning sit down, *now*.

Dilbury is rejoiced. Would I sit to him? He is giving his mind to sacred subjects, and is going to bring out *Balaam and Balak*. Would I give him a sitting, say for Balak? Milburd has promised him one for Balaam, unless I'd like to take Balaam. (As he pronounces this name Baa-lamb, I don't at first catch his meaning.) I promise to think of it. He gives me his address.

*Happy Thought.*—Have my portrait taken. Not as Balaam, as myself. Settle it with Dilbury. He'll paint it this year, and exhibit it next. Milburd, who happens to come upon us at this moment, suggests showing it at a shilling a-head in Bond Street, as a sensation picture.

" I'll be with him," says Milburd, " as Balaam (you've promised me that), and he shall be the ' —— ' "

I know what he's going to say, and move off with Dilbury before he's finished. Milburd *will* talk so loud. He's so vain, too : does it all for applause from strangers. I saw some people laughing about Balaam. Hope the little Sympersons have gone. As we are squeezing through the door, we come upon Mrs. and Miss Millar again. Meeting for the third time, I don't know what to do.

*Happy Thought.*—Safest thing to smile and take off my hat. Miss Millar acknowledges it gravely. Pity people can't be hearty. She might have twinkled up and nodded.

Dilbury points out a picture to me. A large one. "Yours?" I ask.

*Happy Thought.*—To make sure of this before I say anything about it. He nods yes, and looks about to see whether any one is listening. I suppose he expects that if it got about that he was here he'd be seized and carried in procession round the galleries on the shoulders of exulting multitudes. However, there is no one near the picture ("which" he complains "is very badly hung") and consequently no demonstration.

"Good subject, eh?" he asks me. "Yes, very," I answer, wishing I'd asked him first what it was, or had referred to the Catalogue. It is classical, evidently ; that is, judging from the costume, what there is of it. I try to find out quietly in the Catalogue.

Dilbury says, " You see what it is, of course?" Well—I—I—I in fact, don't,—that is, not quite.

" Well," he replies, in a tone implying that I am sure to recognise it when I hear it, "it's *Prometheus Instituting the Lampadephoria.*" To which I say, " Oh, yes, of course. *Prometheus vinctus,*" and look at the number to see how he spells it. I compliment him. Very fine effect of light and shade. In fact, it's *all* light and shade, representing a lot of Corinthians (he says it's in Corinth) running about with red torches. Dilbury points out to me the beauties of the picture. He says it wants a week's study. He informs me that it was taken on the spot, and that his models were " the genuine thing."

*Happy Thought.*—To say, "I could stop and look at this for an age," then take out my watch.

"You can come back again to it," observes Dilbury, seizing my elbow again.

Meet Mrs. and Miss Millar again. Awkward. Don't know whether to bow or smile, or nod, or what this time. I say, as we pass, "Not gone yet?" I don't think she likes it. I didn't say it as I should like to have said it, or as I would have said it, if I had the opportunity over again. I daresay it sounded rude.

Dilbury stops me suddenly with, "Pretty face that, eh?" and looks backs at Miss Millar. Whereupon I rejoin, "Hush! I know them." Dilbury immediately wishes to be introduced. I will, as an Academician, and his picture, too. We go back after them. We struggle towards them : we are all jammed up in a crowd together. I hear something crack. I become aware of treading on somebody's dress. It is Miss Millar's. I beg her pardon. "I hope I——"

*Happy Thought.*—"We met : 'twas in a crowd." Old song.

I say this so as to give a pleasant turn to the apology and the introduction. I don't think Miss Millar is a good-tempered girl. Somebody is nudging me in the back, and somebody else is wedging me in on either side. As she is almost swept away from me by one current, and I from her by another, I say, hurriedly, "Miss Millar, let me introduce my friend, Mr. Dilbury—an Academician." She tries to stop : I turn, and lay hold of some one who ought to be Dilbury, in order to bring him forward. It isn't Dilbury at all, but some one else—a perfect stranger, who is very angry, and wants to kick or hit—I don't know which (but he can't, on account of the crowd), and I am carried on, begging Miss Millar's pardon and his pardon, and remonstrating with a stout, bald-headed man in front, who *will* get in the way.

*Happy Thought.*—Get out of this as quickly as possible.

Getting out again. Lost my Catalogue. Meet Milburd. I ask him what's that picture, alluding to one with a lot of people in scant drapery in an oriental apartment. He replies "Portraits of members of the Garrick Club taking a Turkish bath." It is No. 277. It simply *can't* be. Besides there are ladies present.

T

Milburd pretends to be annoyed, and says, "I needn't believe it unless I like."

Must go to Willis's: see about sleeping to-night, luggage, dinner, and a lot of things.

*Happy Thought.*—Have my hair cut.   Have an ice first.   Leave the Academy.

I look in at Willis's.   Grainger (the stranger) has gone.   Rawlinson says, "if I like to stop here and use Willis's bed, I can."   I will.   Rawlinson wants to know what I'm going to do this evening.

*Happy Thought.*—Don't know——dine with *him*, if he likes.

"He won't do that," he says, "but will meet me anywhere afterwards."   Go to Club.   Ask for letters: two: one from my wife. Keep that until I've opened this envelope with the names of Messrs. Popgood and Groolly, Ludgate, the eminent publishers, stamped on the seal.

Popgood and Groolly have jumped at *Typical Developments:* at least, in answer to a letter of mine, with an introduction from Boodels' second cousin, "they will be glad if I will favour them with an early call."   An early call, say six in the morning.   Popgood and Groolly in bed.   Popgood in one room, Groolly in another, myself in a room between the two, reading aloud Vol. I. of *Typical Developments.*   I say this to a friend in the Club, as I must talk to some one on the subject, being in high spirits.

Must look over the MS. and see it's all in order to-night.   Better read some of it out loud to myself, for practice, or try passages on Rawlinson when he comes in in the evening.

*Happy Thought.*—If I asked Rawlinson to dine with me, he couldn't very well help listening to it afterwards.

Open Friddy's letter.   She says, "Baby's got another rash; her Mamma advises change of air—sea-side.   How long am I going to be away?   Why don't I write?   She is not very well.   Now I am in town I must call on Uncle and Aunt Benson, who have complained to my mother of my neglecting them.   My mother (the letter goes on to say) was down here the other day, and cried about it a good deal.   Her Mamma (my wife's, my mother-in-law, Mrs Symperson) sends her love, and will I call and pay Frisby's bill for her, to save her coming up to town.   Frisby, the Jeweller, in Bond Street."

Write by return ; dash the letter off to show how busy I am :—

DEAR FRIDDY,—

    Full of business just now.  Popgood and Groolly, the great Publishers, are going to buy *Typical Developments*, I'm going to see them to-morrow.  Love to everyone.  Poor Baby !  Will see about Uncle.
Your affectionate Husband, in haste.

P.S.  Going to have my portrait done by Dilbury, A.R.A.

Letter sent.   Send to Messrs. Popgood and Groolly to say I'm coming to-morrow ? or shall I take them by suprise ?

After some consideration I think I'd better take them by sur-prise.   Having nothing to do this afternoon—(I feel as if I had dismissed everything from my mind by having sent that letter to my wife,  saying, " how full of business I am just now.")—I will stroll towards Belgravia and call on Uncle and Aunt Benson.

*Happy Thought.*—Take Rotten Row and the drive on my way.

After the Popgood-and-Groolly letter I feel that I have, as it were, a place in the world.   My mother and Uncle and Aunt Benson have always wanted me to take up a profession ; especially since my marriage.   Friddy agrees with them.   Well, here is a profession.   Literature.   Commence with *Typ. Devel.*, Vol. I.   Say that runs to fifteen editions ; say it's a thousand pounds for each edition, and a thousand for each volume ; there will be at least fifty volumes, that's fifty thousand ; then fifteen times fifty is seven hundred and fifty, that is, seven hundred and fifty thousand pounds.   Say it takes me ten years to complete the work, then that's seventy-five thousand pounds a year.   I stop to make this calculation in my pocket-book.   A sneeze suddenly takes me : I haven't got a cold at all, but it shakes me violently, and I feel that a button has gone somewhere.   The back button to my collar, I think : as I fancy I feel it wriggling up.   I really thought when one was married all these things would have been kept in proper order.

*Happy Thought.*—Might stop somewhere, and ask them to sew on a button.

Where ?  Pastrycook's.   Shall I ?  I look into the window at a jelly, and think how I shall manage it.   I, as it were, rehearse the scene in my mind.   Suppose I enter.   Suppose I say to girl at

T 2

counter, I'll take an ice: strawberry, if you please ; and, oh by the way, (as if I hadn't come in for this at all) have you got such a thing as a button about you which you could kindly sew on for me ? Think I'd better not. It might look odd. Or go into a haberdasher's. Buy gloves : only I don't want gloves, and that'll be four-and-sixpence for having a button sewn on.

I feel the collar is wriggling up, and has got over my waistcoat. I seem to be wrong all over. There's a sort of sympathy in my clothes. On looking down (I'd not noticed it before) I see that one trouser leg is shorter than the other. I mentioned this about the last pair to my tailor. I particularly told him not to make one leg longer than the other. It's his *great* fault. After three days' wear one leg always becomes shorter than the other.

*Happy Thought.*—Can rectify it by standing before a shop window, pretending to look in, unbutton my waistcoat, and adjust braces.

Much the same difficulty about braces as about my stirrups in riding.

Somebody seizes my arm suddenly, and turns me round. I face Boodels, an elderly gentleman and two ladies, very fashionably dressed, to whom, he says, he wants to introduce me.

Horridly annoying ; my shirt collar is up round my neck, my waistcoat is open, and in twisting me round (so thoughtless of Boodels !) the lower part of the brace is broken. Awkward. I can't explain that it's *only* my braces, because that would sound as if it wasn't. Boodels says they've been longing for an introduction. Well, now they've got it. The Elderly Gentleman (I don't catch any of their names) shakes hands with me, (I have to disengage my hand for him,) and says with a smile, " I have heard a great deal of you, Sir. I am told you are a very humorous person."

*Happy Thought.*—To say, " Oh, no, not at all."

What a stupid remark for him to make. I couldn't answer, " Yes, Sir, I am *very* humorous." A gloom falls over the party after this, and we walk silently down Piccadilly. I can't help thinking how disappointed they must be in me as a very humorous person. Then Boodels shouldn't have led them to expect it. I'll have a row with him afterwards.

When I turn to speak to the young lady (rather handsome and tall) my collar turns too, and seems to come up very much on one side. I should like to be brilliant—and humorous—now. The result is that I ask her (round my collar, which I pull down to enable me to speak comfortably) if she is making any stay in town ? which, on the whole, is not particularly brilliant or humorous.

She replies, " No," and leaves the rest to me.

The Elderly Gentleman (her papa, I fancy) on the other side repeats " We've heard of you "—this with almost a chuckle of triumph, as if he'd caught me at last—" We've heard of you as a very humorous person."

I return " Indeed," and we proceed in silence up to Apsley House. They're silent, not liking (as Boodels tells me afterwards) to speak, for fear I should satirically laugh at them, and also to hear some witty remarks from me.

*Happy Thought (by Park Gate).*—Very sorry, must leave ; got to go in the opposite direction. Should like to say something humorous at parting, but can't. Say Good-bye, and *look* as humorous as possible.

## CHAPTER VII.

**W**ILLIS not returned, so use his bed. I awake to the fact that it is the day for Popgood and Groolly, and *Typical Developments.*

Rawlinson is down to breakfast about a quarter of an hour before I am. He always *will* come down a quarter of an hour before I do, and then he begins breakfast without telling me he is there—which is unsociable, as I now know him well enough to tell him. Apparently his object in being first at breakfast is to get hold of the *Times*, which he keeps until five minutes before the boy calls for it (it is only hired) and then asks me if "I'd like to see it," though, he adds, "there's nothing particular in it this morning."

The important question to me now is how shall I appear before Popgood and Groolly? I mean, how dressed? I've never called on a publisher, or a pair of publishers before, and the difficulty (I put it thus to Rawlinson) is, should one be shabbily dressed to give them an idea of poverty (starving author, children in attic, Grub Street, &c., &c., of which one has heard so much) or should I go in the height of fashion, so as to appear independent? Rawlinson doesn't take his eyes off the newspaper but smiles, and replies, " Ah, yes, that's the question."

*Happy Thought.*—To interest him personally, and get his advice by saying, " What would *you* do if you were in my position?"

He looks up from his paper for a second or so, vaguely, and after answering, "that he doesn't precisely know," resumes his perusal.

*Happy Thought.*—To express an opinion, so as to get him to differ from me, and then the subject will have the benefit of a discussion. I say, "I should think one ought to go dressed well, eh?"

Rawlinson (without taking his attention from the *Times*) replies, "Oh, yes, decidedly."

I don't know him sufficiently well to express my annoyance at his selfishness in not going into the matter thoroughly with me. He *is* selfish, very. I took him to dine at my Club with me, in order that on returning to his rooms together he might listen to me reading my MS. aloud, as a sort of rehearsal for Popgood and Groolly, but he picked up two friends on the road, and whispering to me, "You'd like to know those fellows, one plays the piano very well," he brought them in, and they stayed in his and Willis's rooms, singing, playing and smoking, until past three in the morning, and in fact I still heard them roaring with laughter after I had gone to bed.

Rawlinson says this morning, apologetically, that he's sorry those fellows stopped so confoundedly late, as he had missed hearing part of my *Typical Developments*, which he had hoped I would have read to him.

I say, "Oh, it doesn't matter," but I shan't give a friend a dinner at the Club again in order to secure his attention afterwards.

He adds presently and still apologetically, that he should so much have liked to have heard me read some of my best passages to him now, after breakfast, if it hadn't been that he is obliged to go down to the Temple this morning.

As I should really like to try some of it before appearing before Popgood and Groolly, I ask him at what hour he must be at the Temple, as there would be, probably, plenty of time for him to hear *something* of it at all events.

Rawlinson looks at the clock, and says regretfully, "Ah, I'm afraid I must be off immediately," and proceeds at once to look for his umbrella and brush his hat.

*Happy Thought.*—To bring my MS. out of my bag and commence at once on a passage with "What do you think of this?"

Rawlinson has his hat on, and his hand on the door-handle. I read, "*On the various bearings of Philological Ethnography on Typical Development.* The assimilation of characteristic is perhaps, from our present point of view, one of the most interesting studies of the present day." *Mem.* Must cut out the second "present;" tautology would quite knock over Popgood and Groolly.

*Happy Thought.*—Ask Rawlinson to lend me a pencil.

Very sorry he hasn't got one. I say "Just stop a minute, while I erase the word:" he looks at the clock again, and observes, he's afraid he must——

I tell him that listening to this passage won't take a second.

"In Central Africa the present——" very odd, another "present;" scratch it out: only having scratched it out, the next word to it is "present"—can't make it out to all. I pause and consider what I could have meant. I ask Rawlinson to look at the word. What is it? "*Pheasants*, I think," he says, "but I can't stop now : hope to hear good account of your interview with what's-his-name the publisher," and runs out of the room.

*Happy Thought.*—Must really read this through quietly, and see it's all right before going to Popgood and Groolly.

"In Central Africa the Present presents an aspect not remarkably dissimilar from his brother of the American States." I see what I meant : for "Present" read "Peasant," and the next word is a verb.

My eye soon gets accustomed to my own writing, after going carefully over several pages (there are a hundred and fifty-two in this MS.), and I determine upon driving to Popgood and Groolly immediately.

Buy a pencil. Take a cab.

*Happy Thought.*—To appear (in the cab) opening and reading my MS., and correcting with pencil. Anyone passing, who knows me, will point me out as up to my eyes in literary business. I wish I could have a placard on the cab, with "Going to call on Popgood and Groolly, the eminent publishers, with *Typical Developments*, Vol. I." The result of the dressing question is, that I am principally in black, as if I had suddenly gone into half-mourning, or was going to fight a duel with Popgood and Groolly.

*Happy Thought.*—Might buy a pair of spectacles. Looks studious, and adds ten years' worth of respectable age to the character. Perhaps I'd better not ; as if they found me out afterwards, they'd think I'd been making a fool of them.

We drive eastward, and pull up at the entrance of a narrow street which has apparently no outlet. I pay Cabby, and enter under an archway. I feel very nervous, and inclined to be polite to everyone. My MS. seems to me quite in character when in the neighbourhood of Fleet Street, though I couldn't have walked up Regent Street with it on any account. I think (encouragingly to myself) of Dr. Johnson, and Goldsmith, and Mrs. Thrale, and Sir Joshua Reynolds, and then of Smollet and Fielding, and I am saying to myself, "They went to a publisher's for the first time *once ;*" when I find myself opposite a door on which is written

"Popgood and Groolly." I ascertain that this is not the only door with their names on it. There are doors to the right, to the left—

[*Happy Thought* (don't know why it occurs now, but suppose I am nervous)—

> " Doors to the right of me,
>    Doors to the left of me,
>       Rode the Six Hundred ; "

only it wasn't "doors"—it was "cannon " or " foes "]—and on all the doors is " Popgood and Groolly."

There is a great deal of noise from some quarter, as of machinery (not unlike the sounds you encounter on entering the Polytechnic), and I deliberate as to which door I shall enter by. I see, on a wall, a flourishing hand pointing up some stone steps to " Clerks' Office Up-Stairs."

*Happy Thought.*—Go up and see a clerk.

The passages are all deserted. They are divided into, it seems, different rooms ; every room has its ground-glass window. Perhaps numbers of people can see *me*, though I can't see *them.* Perhaps Popgood and Groolly are examining me from somewhere, and seeing what I'm like, and settling how they'll deal with me.

*Happy Thought.* To walk to the end of the passage, and if I don't meet any one, come back again.

I do meet some one, however,—a clerk, bustling. He inquires of me, hastily, " Whom do you want, Sir ?" I reply, " Well—" rather hesitatingly, as if I either didn't wish to commit myself with a subordinate, or hadn't an excuse at hand for being in there at all. (By the way, I never knew publishers had clerks. I had always thought that a publisher was, as it were, a sort of Literary Judge or Critic, who said, " Yes, I'll print your book, and send it to the booksellers." Certainly varied experience enlarges the mind.) " Well," — I continue my reply — " I wan't to see Pop——" I check myself in saying familiarly, Popgood and Groolly, and substitute, " Mr. Popgood or Mr. Groolly." The brisk clerk says, " This way," and I follow him into a small room, with a small clerk in it, who, it appears, doesn't know if

Mr. Popgood or Mr. Groolly is disengaged, but will take in my name.

I fancy they are eyeing my manuscript. I feel that the appearance of the roll of MS. is against me. If I could only have come to see Popgood and Groolly for pleasure, it strikes me I should have been shown in at once. But I can imagine (while I am waiting, having written my name down on a slip of paper) the little clerk hinting to Popgood and Groolly that the visitor has a manuscript with him; in which case Popgood and Groolly, being taken by surprise, and not liking it, won't be at home.

The little clerk returns, and says, "Will I step this way?" I step his way, and, feeling very hot and uncomfortable (much as I did when I was about to propose to Fridoline in the conservatory), I am suddenly ushered into Popgood and Groolly's private office. The boy pauses by the door a minute, apparently curious to see what we'll do to each other, for here sits either Popgood or Groolly, I don't know which, in a chair between a large writing-table and the fender. I think the clerk mentions the gentleman's name, but I can't catch it.

Popgood, or Groolly, rises slightly, bows, and indicates a chair on the opposite side of the hearthrug to where he is sitting.

I bow to him. So far nothing could be more pleasant or charming.

My hat suddenly becomes a nuisance, and I don't know whether to put my hat on the table, and my MS. on the floor, or *vice versâ* —hat on floor—MS. on table.

*Happy Thought.*—To say, " I think you had a letter of introduction to me—I mean, about me—from Mr. Boodels."

It seems so formal to call him Mr. Boodels, that the interview at once assumes the air of a sort of state ceremony.

Popgood, or Groolly, bows again. I wish I knew which it was. He is elderly, and rather clerical in appearance. I should imagine him to be Popgood. I don't like to dash in quickly with " Now I'll read you *Typical Developments*, Vol. I.," though that would be the way to come to business.

*Happy Thought.*—To talk to him about Boodels; to make Boodels *pro tem.* the subject of conversation, to give us, as it were, common ground to start on.

I remark, that (taking it for granted that Popgood, or Groolly, knows Boodels) he is a capital fellow; a great friend of mine; that *he* has (this I say patronisingly) written several little things, and —in fact—oh yes, he is a very good fellow. Popgood, or Groolly, replies that he hasn't the pleasure of Boodels' acquaintance, and that it was a relation of his "from whom we (the firm of P. and G.) received this letter."

*Happy Thought.*—To ask, Did he mention what my Work was?

Popgood, or Groolly (somehow I begin to think it is Groolly), says, "No, he did not. What may be——" he inquires rather sleepily, as if I had failed to interest him up to this point, "What may be the nature of the work?"

*Happy Thought.*—To stop myself from answering hastily, "Well, I don't know," which in my nervousness I was going to do.

I hesitate. I should almost like to ask him "What sort of thing he wants?" Because, really and truly, *Typical Developments* would suit all readers.

I say, "It is rather difficult to explain, as it comprises a vast variety of subjects."

"It's not," says Popgood, or Groolly, "a collection of tales, I mean such as we could bring out, with illustrations, at Christmas?"

I am obliged to say, "No, it's not that," though I wish at the moment I could turn it into that, just to please Popgood and Groolly.

"We should be open for something on this model," says Popgood, or Groolly, producing a thin book with green and yellow binding, and coloured illustrations about *Puss in Boots.* "It went," he adds, "very well last Christmas." It occurs to me that the letter written by Boodels' relative must have given Popgood and Groolly quite a wrong notion of *Typ. Devel.* He seems to have introduced me as an author of *Nursery Books.*

*Happy Thought.*—To say I think *Typical Developments* would illustrate very well.

It appears this is the first time he has heard the title. "A religious work?" he inquires. "Well—no, Mr. Popgood," I am about to say pleasantly, only it occurs to me, as a *Happy Thought*, that if he is Groolly he won't like being called Popgood, so I reply, "Not exactly religious." Feeling that perhaps I have gone too far here, I correct myself with, "But, of course, not atheistical."

Popgood, or Groolly, considers. "We are very busy just now, and our hands are quite full," he says. "Everything is very dull—[*Happy Thought.*—"Except *Typical Developments*." But I don't say it]—and it's a bad time of year for bringing out a book of the—of the—nature you intimate."

I say, to put it clearly and help him along, that it's something after the style of a Dictionary. At this Popgood, or Groolly, appears much relieved, and says, "It's a bad time just now for bringing out Dictionaries, even," he adds, "if they were in our line." It appears, from further conversation, that Popgood and Groolly *did* once bring out a Dictionary, in monthly parts, which nearly proved fatal to them. I explain that, though I said it was after the *style* of a Dictionary, yet it was not *merely* a Dictionary, but if I read him a little of it, he could judge better for himself.

He bows. I take the MS. off the table. It is all curled up, and won't open properly. I tell him I will select any passage at haphazard. He bows again. It is difficult. Something about "Forms in a Primæval Forest" catches my eye. I wonder if *that* is a good specimen to read to him. I've forgotten what it's about.

*Happy Thought.*—To beg his pardon for a minute, just to gain time, and cast my eye over it, to see if I can get at the meaning at once, so as not to give it with wrong emphasis.

I commence, with Popgood's, or Groolly's, eye upon me, "The first forms, or Protoplastic creations, have in themselves such interest to us of the present day, that——" then follows a hard word scratched out, and I have to read on to find out what it ought to be. I can't imagine what this confounded word was.

*Happy Thought.*—To say this is only a mere prelude, and to pass on to a paragraph lower down.

The door (not the one I came in by, but another on the opposite side) opens, and in comes a tall, bluff gentleman with a beard. The clerical person to whom I am reading introduces him.

*Happy Thought.*—Shall now know which is Popgood and which Groolly.

He introduces him as " My Partner." Popgood and Groolly are before me. If I only knew which was which, I could carry on the conversation so much more pleasantly.

*Happy Thought.*—To say " Well, Mr. Groolly," and look at both of them. One of the two *must* acknowledge his name.

No. Both bow.

*Happy Thought.*—Try " Mr. Popgood " next time.

The sitting-down partner (Groolly, I fancy) says to the partner standing up (consequently Popgood), " This gentleman has called about his book on—on——"

*Happy Thought.*—*Typical Developments.*

We all bow to one another like waxworks. Standing-up partner says, " Ha, yes, I was going to ——" and looks about fussily. He evidently thinks that I have been there before, and that he has mislaid my MS. His friend enlightens him with, " He has brought his MS. this morning." Standing-up partner's mind much relieved. I corroborate Sitting-down partner, and we all, more or less, do waxworks again.

A silence. I recommence looking in the manuscript for something to read to them. On glancing over it, rapidly, I don't recognise my own sentences. It would be fatal to everything if I went on reading what I didn't understand. Sure to show it.

*Happy Thought.*—To say. " I think I'll leave this in your hands," pleasantly.

It suddenly occurs to them at this point to introduce each other. It is not quite clear at first which is Groolly and which is Popgood. After a short conversation on general topics I try to name them individually and correctly. I fail. Having exhausted general topics (we all fight shy of *Typical Developments*) I fancy they are getting tired of me, as Popgood says to Groolly (or *vice versâ*) that he must go to somewhere that I don't catch. This awakens Groolly to the fact that it's later than he had imagined.

*Happy Thought.*—Ingratiate myself by taking the hint.

Hand them the MS. Should like to say something witty and remarkable just before leaving the room. If I did, I feel they'd consult together, and say, "Clever man, that; let's read his *Typical Developments*," and so on to publishing.

The nearest thing to the point I can say is, "Well, I'll leave this here, shall I?" placing it on the desk, whence Mr. Groolly (or Popgood) removes it to a pigeon-hole, which looks business-like.

I ask "If I shall call again?" I feel immediately I've said it that it's a mistake. Nothing like taking publishers by surprise. Popgood says, "Oh, we won't trouble you to call; you'll hear from us."

I execute a sort of waxwork mechanical movement again, with my hat in one hand and my umbrella in the other. I say, "Good day, Mr. Popgood," and both return good day at the same time.

*Happy Thought (when I'm outside the house).*—I ought to have said, "Gentlemen, I leave my bantling in your hands, you are excellent nurses, I am sure, and will soon show her how to walk."

I think I've heard this before. Will look it out in Dictionary of Quotations. *Note.* Add a Chapter to *Typ. Devel.*, Book 2, on "Tricks of Memory." By the way, what is a "Bantling?"

I should say, without a dictionary, the youngest chick of a Bantam. If it's not that, it's a foundling put out to nurse. I know the simile comes in happily, somehow. Ought to carry a pocket-dictionary about with me, so as to turn down corners (not of the book, I mean, of the street. *Mem.* To work up this into a joke, somehow, as "Sheridan said," &c.) and look things out while you think of it. It's merely developing my plan of note-books.

To Willis's rooms. Rush up to tell Rawlinson everything about it. He's not there. Pass the evening in dining out, and coming in five times to see if Rawlinson has returned yet. At last he appears.

Sit up with Rawlinson and Milburd chatting. When Rawlinson doesn't go to bed early, he is an excellent hand at sitting up and chatting. He sits up (when he *does* sit up) till three or four in the morning, "expecting," he says, "that it's not unlikely some fellow will drop in." I never yet *have* seen any fellow drop in at that time; so I fancy it's an excuse that Rawlinson makes to himself, so that "sitting up and chatting" may be set down as an act of politeness.

We naturally discuss Popgood and Groolly.

I ask him whether he thinks they'll read it. Rawlinson says,

"Oh, of course," heartily.   Rawlinson always commences with the brightest view possible under any circumstances, and then gradually introduces, as it were, saving clauses.   He continues, "They'll read it : at least their man will.   Publishers keep a man, you know," (I don't know, but I nod, as if Popgood's man was a matter of course,) "who has to read everything and advise upon it."

I observe, "I suppose he'll advise on *Typical Developments.*"

*Happy Thought.*—P'raps he's reading it now, and enjoying it.

I say this.   Milburd says, "P'raps he isn't," which he thinks funny, and I think simply stupid.   Rawlinson doesn't laugh.   *He* sympathises with me in a literary matter, I know.

"I suppose," addressing myself to Rawlinson, "they won't be long before they give me an opinion ?"

"Oh, no time !" replies Rawlinson heartily.

"Quicker, if possible," says Milburd.   (That's the worst of him : he never knows when to stop.   For myself, I enjoy a joke as much as anybody ; but this is out of place now.)

*Happy Thought.*—Not even smile.   Take no notice of him.

Rawlinson says, "Oh yes, they'll soon give an opinion ; that's if they haven't much business.   Of course, it may take a year or so before their man can read it."

*Happy Thought.*—Oh, Rawlinson can't know much about it. He only talks from hearsay.   But then what is hearsay ?

Rawlinson continues.   "Those fellows who are paid to read too !   They're a rum lot."

"Highly educated," I suppose.

They both pooh-pooh the idea.   I don't care about Milburd's pooh-poohing, as he's not in earnest.

"Why," says Rawlinson, who really *does* seem to be up in the subject, "I was staying with a fellow once who did the reading for Shaptur and Werse.   He had piles of print and manuscript : just like yours this morning—[*Happy Thought.*—I say yes, and smile.   Why smile ?]—and he just cut a few pages of one, and dipped into another, and skimmed a third, and threw 'em away like so much trash.   Of course if you *know* him he'll read your MS."

Milburd suggests, "Find out Popgood and Groolly's man, and

ask him to dinner." If it wasn't Milburd who says this, there really might be something in it.

Rawlinson says, "Perhaps they may not even give it to the man. Perhaps not read it at all."

*Happy Thought.* — Really Rawlinson *can't* know anything about it.

"From what I saw of Popgood and Groolly to-day, I should say they were rather inclined towards the book than otherwise."

Rawlinson says heartily as usual, "Oh, most probably. They'll be delighted at your bringing it to them. Only, don't you see, as you're comparatively an unknown man——"

I feel it *is* kind of him to put in "*comparatively*," it softens down obscurity when, as it were, it is only shared in a less degree by Gladstone, Bulwer Lytton, Disraeli, Dickens, and so forth—— "of course you can't expect the same attention as the great names command."

*Happy Thought.* — To take this remark sensibly and calmly and answer, "Oh, of course not."

Wonder (to myself) whether Popgood and Groolly, immediately I was gone, winked at each other, tied up my MS. in a clean sheet of paper, directed it to me, and gave it to a clerk, to be posted in two days' time.

We separate at last, [Milburd finding out at four o'clock A.M. that "it's time to go, by Jove!" as if he'd got to go and meet a bed like a train, and be punctual to the minute. He *does* say such stupid things,] and Milburd, as he goes downstairs, calls out, " Liquor up the fellow who reads, and he'll send to old Popkins and Gruel," [he thinks it so amazingly funny to pretend to mistake names. He will call *Typ. Dev.*, *Biblical Elephants*. Nonsense,] "and say it's the best sixpenn'orth he ever read. Good night."

We retire.

In the morning, as usual, Rawlinson sneaks down to breakfast finishes, and is well in to the *Times* before I have even mastered what o'clock it is. I'm always telling him that this is unsociable. "Then," remonstrates Rawlinson, "why don't you get up in time?"

*Happy Thought.* — Drop the subject, lie in bed and think.

I tell Rawlinson it's much jollier waking in the country than in

U

town. While I dress I expatiate to him on the advantages of rustic residence. Sometimes from the next room he replies, "Ah!" "Yes!" "Oh!" "No!" "Well, perhaps!" and so forth, from which I gather that he is absorbed in the *Times*. It is confoundedly unsociable in the morning. After sitting up late hair looks dried up. They've forgotten to pack up my hair-oil. See Willis's in a bottle labelled *Oil of Merovingia. Balsamic properties*, &c., &c.

*Happy Thought.*—Use it.

Generally find other people's hair-oil better than my own. Other people's collars and shirts always seem made for me. Curious: same with ties. Other people's colours always suit me better than my own. Willis has two or three favourites of mine, which I shall always use when I stop at his rooms. Don't much like the hair-oil, though. It will do, however, for a change.

Come in to breakfast: letters on table. One for me: open it afterwards. Rawlinson observes that there's not a nice smell in the room. Isn't there? (Willis's hair-oil probably—don't say so.) Expatiate again on the sweet fragrance of the country in the morning as compared with London smells on waking.

Breakfast. Open my wife's letter. Say, "There, my boy" (to Rawlinson), "this is perfectly scented with the country." I read it.

My wife writes to say, "Must come home at once: man been here (that is, to our Rural Cottage) about nuisances—dreadful stenches will spread fevers—and it wouldn't do to see her or her Mamma, but the man must see *me*." Also a man for some taxes or other, and dogs; and something about executions in the house, which, my wife finishes, "I do not understand, but *he really did frighten me*, and you oughtn't to stay away so long. Baby's rash has appeared again—the Doctor was here yesterday."

*Happy Thought.*—Say I must go down home on business.

Not a word about fragrance of country. Exceptions prove rules —this seems a very strong exception.

*Happy Thought.*—Shall return again if Willis isn't coming back.

Rawlinson says he isn't just yet, as he's just heard from him that morning, and he's rather seedy. Extract from his letter:

" Please send me down my diarrhœtic mixture (peculiar prescription, made on purpose) which is in my room.    Yours, &c. P.S. By-the-way, the cork went into the proper bottle, so I had my old hair-oil bottle washed and cleaned out, and I put it in that.    You'll know the mixture by its being labelled *Oil of Merovingia.*"

*Happy Thought.*—Say nothing about having used this for hair-oil.

Tell it years hence as a practical joke I played on some one a long time ago.

## CHAPTER VIII.

EXPECTANT—ARRANGEMENTS—DISRAELI'S CURIOSITIES—MR. BUCKLE'S
PORTMANTEAU—NOTES OF STORIES—COMMENCEMENTS—ALPHAS
AND OMEGAS — MEMORY — CAZELL ACCEPTS — THAT FELLOW
JAMES—WRINKLES AND WINKS.

**N**O ANSWER from Popgood and Groolly.
Arrange to go home at once and return.

*Happy Thought.*—Flying visit will enable me to protract my
holiday ; because I can explain that I must return to—

1. Call on Popgood and Groolly.
2. Make arrangements for publishing, if necessary.
3. Sit for my portrait to What's-his-Name.

*Happy Thought.*—Have it engraved as a frontispiece to *Typ. Devel.*, with a little slip in book, "*\*\** Directions to Binder: Portrait to face title-page."

4. Bound to go to Jersey.   Ought to go.
5. Bound to go to Milan.   Ditto.
6. And to go to Austria, and call on Count de Bootjack.

If my wife says I am too much away, that's absurd, when it's business.   Then it's absolutely necessary for my literary work.

*Happy Thought.*—To put down on paper Literary work in order.

Have read somewhere of orderly habits of literary men (Disraeli's *Curiosities*, I think).   Good plan, and divide the week and the days.

First, What work?   *Typical Developments.*   This will probably run to twenty vols.   Notes for these (as did the author of *Civilisation, History of*).   It is said that portmanteaux full of notes were lost.   Good plan that, portmanteau for notes for travelling.

Second, *Book of Repartees*, alphabetically arranged.   These require perpetual refining and polishing.

Third, *Everybody's Country Book.*   This will be capital Shilling volume, with a picture outside (my portrait again, in colours would do—Milburd say, " Better have it *plain* "—and expects me to laugh.   I do, because another fellow's present.   Idiot Milburd), containing a quantity of valuable information on country subjects, when I have collected it.

Fourth, *Humorous Tales and Stories.*   I began to make a large collection of these ; that is, it would have been large only I kept forgetting to carry about the special pocket-book with me, except at first, so that I've only got six down.   It is so difficult to recollect a good story when you come home late at night and write it down.   I've got some commenced in the manuscript, but on looking at them I fancy I must have fallen asleep over them. I have since tried to finish them.

*Happy Thought.*—Might publish a weekly paper of *Commencements and Endings*, as a sort of *Notes and Queries*, and invite the public to correspond and fill up.

Very good idea this. Will try it on friends first: try it everywhere. The plan on paper is this—

*A Commencement.*—" As Brummel was one day coming out of a shop in St. Martin's Court, an urchin who had been eagerly eyeing the Beau, asked him for a penny. The Beau refused, telling the ragged youngster in words less polite than forcible that he would see him at Jericho before he would bestow upon him a stiver. The Urchin——

"Now what did the Urchin say? The public is requested to supply details."

Again. "Soame Jenyns, seeing the Lord Chancellor mount his palfrey at the gate of Westminster Hall, observed to George D'Arcy——

"Now what did Soame Jenyns observe to George D'Arcy?"

"*\*\** Anyone knowing what Soame Jenyns said will kindly forward the same to the Editor of the *Commencements, &c.*"

As an example of *Endings:* "There's a capital Irish story ending with 'Bedad, Dochter, 'tis the same thing entirely.' How does this begin?"

"'His nose,' answered the wit. Erskine smiled at the witticism, but never forgave the satire. How does this commence?"

I would give a trifle to remember one or two things *I've* said also, but I dare say they'll come in in time. A friend of Rawlinson's told me the other day about somebody on a tight-rope, and I made a reply which set everyone roaring with laughter; there were only Rawlinson, Cazell, and self. I couldn't write it down at the time, and two hours after I couldn't recall it.

I ask Rawlinson; he doesn't remember. I ask Cazell, he doesn't. Cazell says he'll think of it, and he's got a capital thing for me for *Typ. Devel.* Will he tell it me when I return? He'll be away. He's going to Busted's, in Hertfordshire, to-morrow.

My Cottage is near the road—will he stop the night, and over a pipe he could tell me all about it? He accepts.

Cazell has his luggage ready, so we start. I complain of luggage. "I'll tell you what you ought to do," says Cazell.

N.B. I subsequently discover that this is Cazell's peculiarity; he is always telling people "what they ought to do." He is great in "dodges," and apparently there is not a single subject he is not well up in. Most useful fellow, Cazell.

As to luggage, he says, "You ought to get one of Spanker and Tickett's bags. Those are the men : only six guineas. Put everything in 'em for a fortnight."

*Happy Thought.*—To say, knowingly, "That depends on what you want." Capital for repartee-book that. Put it down. I should have said it was unanswerable if Cazell (he *is* a sharp fellow, Cazell) hadn't immediately replied, "Yes ; but if you take one of these bags, you won't *want* anything."

*Happy Thought.*—Put Cazell's answer down instead of mine. Better.

"Have you got one ?" I ask.

"No, he has not. He divides things into two lots, one for each week. It is *nearly* as good."

*Happy Thought.*—To say, "Yes, of course," being uninterested. I don't know what he means, and hate uninteresting explanations.

We talk about literature : chiefly *Typical Developments.* I ask his opinion of Popgood and Groolly. He says, "I tell you what you ought to have done : gone to Laxon and Zinskany."

I say if Popgood and Groolly fail, I'll go to Laxon.

*Happy Thought.*—Wish I'd gone to Laxon.

I think Cazell (I put this note down later as an opinion) is calculated to render one dissatisfied.

"Where do you go for your hats ?" asks Cazell.

I tell him. He smiles pityingly, and shakes his head.

"Why not ?" I ask.

He tells me where I ought to go for hats.

It appears that I go to *all* the wrong places for gloves, shoes, boots, coats, shirts—everything. All the people are furnishing me with those things who oughtn't to.

I apologise for them generally, and say, "Well, they suit me very well."

*Happy Thought.*—When Cazell gets out at our Station and sees my boy in livery (as a tiger) and my pony-trap, he won't go on giving advice as if I was nobody at all, and knew nothing about that sort of thing.

*At my Station.*—"Come," I say, heartily, "here's the trap waiting. I shall be glad to get home for dinner."

"My servant here?" I ask the Station Master, with a lord-of-the-manorish air.

Station Master hasn't seen him, and goes off to give some directions to a sub-official. This apparent neglect will not impress Cazell. The trap is not there.

I say, "Confound that fellow James!" (Explain that James is my groom.) The fellow James is four feet high, aged fifteen.

*Happy Thought.*—Better walk.

"Tell you what you ought to do," says Cazell, "you ought to have a communication between the Station and your house, so that you could tell 'em when you come down, and so forth."

I say it would be convenient, but how could it be done?

He says, "Easily; write to the Manager. Represent the case here, and to the London Superintendent, and it's done."

We meet James and the pony-trap. He is doing a full gallop, and, on seeing us, pretends the pony has run away. Young vagabond! Most angry at the present state of his livery, he looks so dirty and disreputable (specially about the gloves, and tie), that I wish I could pass him off as somebody else's boy.

*Happy Thought.*—Blow him up privately behind the stable-door when we get in, and threaten to send him away if he's not better.

He weeps copiously at this, (hope Cazell won't return during this scene: he'll go about telling everyone that I make my groom cry,) but I feel sure that directly my back is turned he makes faces at me. I turn suddenly one day, and find him (I will swear it) executing a sort of war-dance at my back. I charge him with it, and he says, with a look of utter surprise at such an insinuation, "No, he warn't."

I can't say, "Yes, you were," when he says, "No, he warn't." He *must* know whether it was a war-dance, or not, better than I.

As to pony-traps, Cazell tells me "what I ought to do." Go to Lamborn, the fellow who builds for the Prince. This wrinkle (he generally calls his information "wrinkles") he gives with a wink. In fact, when I think of it, Cazell's conversation consists of nods, and winks, and wrinkles.

"You mention my name," says Cazell, "and Lamborn will do it for you at a very moderate price."

I make a note of this. Begin to wish I'd gone to Lamborn originally.

As Cazell hasn't much to say about the pony (I am disappointed with Cazell, as most people coming down observe "What a pretty pony!" Ladies says, "What a pet!" "What a delicious little trap," &c., &c.)—I remark to him that it's a pretty pony, isn't it?

Cazell hesitates. "Yes," he says, dubiously. It appears he doesn't like that sort. He suggests that it is rather touched in the wind. I deny it. Wish he wouldn't say these sort of things before the boy James. "If I want a pony," he says, with a wink and a nod as usual, "he can put me up to a wrinkle. Go to Hodgkins." Here he leans back in the seat, and looks at me as much as to say, "There! there's a chance for you, my boy. 'Tisn't everyone who knows about Hodgkins."

*Happy Thought.*—To pretend (as I get rather tired of Cazell) that I wouldn't go to Hodgkins on any account.

"Then you're wrong," says Cazell. Subject dropped.

We arrive at my gate.

James (the tiger) has been instructed by me to touch his hat on going to the horse's head. He has a salute peculiarly his own : "something between the military and a clown in a ring," says Cazell (rudely, I think. If he sees a fault, he says, it's friendly to mention it).

"You ought to send your boy to Thoroughgood, the trainer. He educates them regularly for noblemen. *I* know him, he'd do it for *me*."

I *should* like to send James to be educated as a tiger.

*Happy Thought.*—To avail myself of Cazell's knowing Thoroughgood.

## CHAPTER IX.

CAZELL.—SHERIDAN MANUFACTURED—CHANGE OF NAME—JOKES—THE
BELL—DOGS—BURGLARS—WHIFFS—IDEA FOR CAZELL—ADAMS—
DR. BALSAM—DOG AND FOWL.

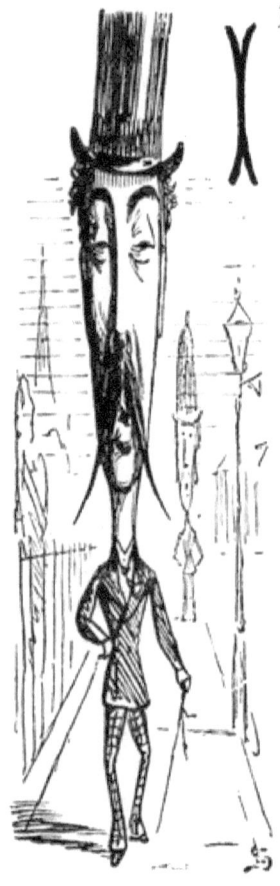

NEVER saw such a fellow as Cazell. I mean, he'd make anyone (who wasn't strong-minded, and able to view things philosophically) discontented with everything around him.

*Happy Thought.*—Never ask anyone to stop at your house suddenly.

When I note down "suddenly," I mean, don't ask a stranger, or a comparative stranger. Cazell is a *positive* stranger. [Note that down on a side page as either for repartee, or for a story from Sheridan. I see how it might be done. Story about a stranger who laid down the law to Sheridan. Some one says to Sheridan, "So rude, too, from a comparative stranger." "Comparative," replied Sherry, " Gad, Sir, he's a *positive* stranger." This will make story No. 6. Good.]

We arrive at Mede Lodge. A little time ago I called it Asphodel Cottage, but, as there are no Asphodels, and it isn't exactly a cottage, I said one day,

*Happy Thought.*—Call it Mede Lodge.

"Why Mede?" says Cazell. "Because," I answer, triumphantly, " it is in the midst of *medes*, or meadows." "Might as well call it Persian," says Cazell.

*Happy Thought.*—To reply, " I knew he'd say that," and pass it over.

Everybody who comes down admires Mede Lodge. It *is* lovely ;

*the* rural thing that I was looking after for years. Everyone, seeing it for the first time—(specially ladies)—is in raptures with it.

I say to Cazell, "Here's Mede Lodge."

"Oh, indeed," says he. "This is the Lodge, eh? Then *where's the house?*"

*Happy Thought.*—To tell him, without a smile, that it's an old joke.

It suddenly occurs to me, "How will my wife like Cazell?" That's another reason why one oughtn't to ask a man down suddenly. Always try your gold in the fire (or some proverb to that effect).

The gate-bell doesn't respond to the tug I give it.

"I tell you what you ought to do," says Cazell, seizing the opportunity. "You ought to have a bell attached to the house——"

"This *is* attached to the house," I return, rather snappishly, I own.

*Happy Thought.*—Host mustn't lose his temper with comparative stranger. But then Comparative Stranger ought not to go on telling me "what I *ought* to do," as if I didn't know.

"Yes," he continues, imperturbably; "but don't you see, if it was attached by means of a metal-plated zinc tube impervious to wet, it would never be out of order, as it is now."

I ring again violently. No one comes. Most disappointing. What I should have liked would have been one servant rushing out to open the gate, another at door (both smiling at my return) to receive luggage, my wife in the hall, beaming, dogs rushing, barking, jumping up and fondling me. Recollect how Sir Walter Scott used to be welcomed by his Deerhounds.

*Happy Thought.*—Buy a deerhound, and teach him to welcome me.

I apologise to Cazell. I say, "I suppose the servants, and all of them" (meaning my wife, and Mrs. Symperson, with perhaps nurse and baby) "are in the garden, and don't hear the bell."

"It's certain they don't hear the bell," says Cazell. "It's dangerous, too, in such a lonely place as this. I tell you what you ought to do; you ought to have dogs about."

I inform him that I *have* dogs about—four dogs, somewhere. I got them because the place was lonely. I purchased a magnificent stable-yard dog that has been chained up ever since we've had him to make him savage, but he won't be vicious at all, and only plays with all the tradesmen and any strangers who may come in. If a burglar came at night I'm convinced the idiotic brute would play with him, and be rather delighted to see him at midnight (when he must feel it very lonely) than otherwise. Now I come to think of it, a burglar would be quite a godsend to the animal as a playmate.

*Happy Thought.*—When the dog first came.—To call him Lion.

He is between a retriever and a Newfoundland, with a placid sheep-like expression of countenance.

*Another Happy Thought.*—To write up, " Beware of the Dog."

If James, the boy-tiger in top-boots, hadn't been a wicked, mischievous young ape, (I was obliged to call him this when I found him inciting Lion to jump over the side of the stye and worry the pigs, which the little fiend considered as fair sport in the absence of rats,) people would have believed in Lion's ferocity. But he told anyone who came up that the dog was as harmless as a kitten. I should never be astonished if we were inundated with tramps and burglars. My dogs *inside* the house *do* bark ; at the slightest noise too. A stranger (Cazell, for instance) would think there were attempts at burglary all night. If they really *did* come, I wonder whether the dogs would be afraid. Perhaps they would.

Cazell is about to tell me where I ought to go for dogs when the maid comes down the garden and opens the gate. Cazell says to me, *sotto voce*, " What a pretty maid you've got."

*Happy Thought.*—To reply " Yes," severely, adding, " and a *very good girl*, too," emphatically.

I don't like Cazell's conduct. *Mem. Certainly* not to ask a fellow down whom you've only met once casually.

" This gentleman sleeps here to-night," I tell my maid.

*Happy Thought.*—Only to-night.

Maid says, " Very well, Sir."

This is as it should be in a country house—no difficulty about receiving a guest, no trouble, old-fashioned English hospitality.

I ask where her mistress is ? She is upstairs with Mrs.

Symperson. Very good; then what does Cazell say to a walk round the place before dinner? Cazell says delighted to view the domain. A whiff of dinner comes down the passage from the kitchen. A nasty whiff.

*Happy Thought.*—Take Cazell out before it gets worse.

I don't know why, but the smell of cabbages boiling conveys the idea of huts, poverty, and living all in one room.

Cazell won't be moved, but stops to sniff.

I say (to take, as it were, the wind out of his sails), "Yes, nasty smell, but the cook *will* do it, though I've told her not to, over and over again."

Cazell says, "My dear fellow, I'll tell you what you ought to do. You ought to get one of Ince's patent door-ventilators. Have it fixed up here," he taps the wall, and begins examining its capabilities, "and you'd be free from it at once."

I say, "Indeed!" and he puts on his hat and accompanies me into the garden.

I never knew such a fellow as Cazell!

He surveys my geraniums and asters with an eye of pity: he looks at my roses, of which my gardener is justly proud, and shakes his head as he observes, "Ah! why don't you have the Double Lancaster? *that's* a Rose." As if *this* wasn't. "You ought to go to Mullins's at Sheffield for them. Mullins is the only man."

We visit my glass-house, where the grapes are. He starts back—he is horrified. What is it? A wasp? A hornet? No. "My *dear* fellow," he says, "you'll *never* do anything with your grapes if you don't move 'em lower down, and syringe them with Sloper's Ingreser Mixture."

*Happy Thought.*—Cazell would be worth anything to tradesmen as an advertiser. Won't suggest it, he might be angry. Host mustn't insult guest.

But I say they (the grapes) are very fine this year.

"Fine? well, so, so," he admits; "but next year you won't have *one*."

*Happy Thought.*—Call the gardener, who will floor Cazell technically, on the spot.

I call loudly, "Adams!" There is no answer. I know by this that Adams has gone to the village.

Directly his work is finished, Adams, every evening, disappears to the village. Being remonstrated with, he says his work's done for the day, and what's he wanted for here when his work's done? For this I had no solution when he first put the difficulty, nor have I now. I think a repartee, quick, cutting, and decisive, would have settled him. ["G" Gardener. Repartee to a Gardener. Never thought of Gardener before. Had only got down Godchild and Gasman. Repartee to a Godchild: Repartee to a Gasman. Rowland Hill and Sydney Smith used to do this sort of thing: also Dean Swift. Swift cuffed his servant Patrick. Wonder where *I* should be if I cuffed Adams?]

Cazell approves of the place generally. He agrees with me, "Nothing like being out of town." But he'll tell me, he says, what I "*ought to do*" with this place. This is given in an interrogative form, and evidently demands the answer.

"What?"

"Why," he returns emphatically, "buy it."

Does he think it worth buying, I ask modestly. No, he doesn't, he says, for the present, but in future it may be valuable. "But," he goes on, "I'll tell you what you want." This is only another form of "what I ought to do," and it's no use answering that you *don't* want whatever it is. "You want to pull down the left wing, construct a new doorway, throw out a bay window, just put a verandah round the dining-room, and there you are."

*Happy Thought.*—To say ironically: Pull down the house in fact.

Cazell replies, "That's it, pull it down, and build two storeys. What's your drainage here?"

*Happy Thought.*—To say, "don't know," because this is a question I hate.

I look upon the country as pure and healthy, and questions of drainage and water-supply annoy me. I say to him, jocularly, "Bless you; we don't know what drainage is here, it's beautifully managed;" I *have* an idea *how* it's managed, but keep it to myself; "and we, none of us, were ever so healthy anywhere as here." I always say this, or my wife would want to go somewhere for the benefit of her health and baby's.

Ring at gate-bell. A gentleman. " Who's that ? "

" That is "—I'm obliged to say—" That is Dr. Balsam."
" Whom has he come to see ? " The maid replies, " Missus and
baby." " Thought you said it was so healthy," observes Cazell.

*Happy Thought.*—Must remember he is the guest, and I am the
host.

Old English hospitality must be observed, or really he is so
irritating I could quarrel with him at once.

Dr. Balsam comes out. Cazell doesn't offer to withdraw, as he
*might* do, on pretence of seeing the plums, or anything, before the
family doctor ; but he walks with Dr. Balsam and myself round
the gardens, while I am being told how my wife is suffering from
a low state of nerves and rheumatic hysteria ; the baby, of course,
from rash.

" Your wife says she's had the Inspector of Nuisances here." I
try to turn the Doctor's question off jocosely before Cazell ; but it
won't do. Dr. Balsam says, " You must have your pigsty cleaned
out, and the drainage is——"

" Ah," cries Cazell, knowingly, " I'd have sworn I smelt something horrid."

" It'll breed fever," says the Doctor.

What fever ! fever ! bad drainage ! pigs cause of illness at Mede
Lodge, in the loveliest part of—— No !

" I tell you what you ought to do," says Cazell : " buy five
tons of Disinfecting Fluid, and ten of Chloride of Amphistartum
Compound, and empty it all about the place. It'll last for two
years."

The Doctor says he's right, and wishes me good-bye.

Inspector of Nuisances to come to-morrow. I see Doctor to
gate.

*Happy Thought* (which I express). —" A little inconvenience
which a few labourers will remove : soon do it. The only
nuisance, after all, in the country."

Man looks over gate with a paper. " For you, Sir," he says.
I open it. A legal document. Summons before the Magistrate
for keeping dogs without a licence. Hang the dogs ! Irate
woman heard at back door. I go round to her. She is holding
up a fowl with its head off. " Well ? " " Well ! " screams irate

elderly peasant, " I ain't going to have this : your nasty (*sob*) dog came into our field (*sob*), and killed (*sob*) my (*sob*) chicken. I wouldn't ha' took five shillin' for it. I wouldn't."

*Happy Thought.*—To say, "Glad to hear it." Offer her sixpence.

Cazell says, " you ought to ask if the fowl was tied up, or not."

I ask the question. This sends her nearly wild. She'll have the law on me. She'll go and fetch a policeman. 'Tisn't because she's poor and hard-worked she's to be insulted, &c., &c. She raves through the stable-yard gate. Lion, instead of attacking her (he oughtn't to have let her pass, the idiotic brute !) pretends to play at something or other with her shawl as she passes his kennel, for which he gets a thump on the head, and retires dismally.

Cazell follows her into the lane to reason with her and tell her what she ought to do.

*Happy Thought.*—Better leave it to mediation and retire.

Go back into house. Screams. Wife in hysterics on sofa. Doctor, man with summons, woman screaming, smells from pigs, baby with rash too much for her, " And," says Mrs. Symperson, ironically, "*I think* you *might* have taken the trouble to come up-stairs and see how we were when you came in."

*Mem.*—Don't bring down a friend suddenly again.

# CHAPTER X.

**A**N INSPECTOR of Nuisances calls upon me while Cazell is at Mede Lodge in the morning.

*Happy Thought.*—Try and get Cazell to take a turn round the garden while the Inspector is here.

Cazell won't. He says that he's never met an Inspector of Nuisances, and wants to see one

The Inspector (I thought he'd have a uniform on, but he hasn't) abruptly observes that he will come to the point at once. I say "by all means." The point turns out to be "drains." He says, without any emotion, he'll have to report me to the Board if I don't attend to it. He is business-like and determined. He goes on, in a loud voice, and with a great deal of emphasis with his right hand, to say that he's been obliged "to bring several people to book who had defied him." Here he compresses his lips and looks at me sternly.

*Happy Thought.*—To reply at once that he's quite right.

x

Hope he doesn't think that I am going to defy him. Defence not defiance.

"In the exercise of your duty," I remark (Cazell tells me afterwards that I oughtn't to have been so patronising to a Government official), "you are quite right."

"Of course," returns the Inspector, firmly, and gives us an anecdote about a man who *would* keep thirty-two pigs, and defied him, the Inspector. "He was a nuisance, Sir," says the Inspector, with grim retrospective delight at his own triumph. "He was a nuisance, Sir, and defied me."

"Says he to me," continues the Inspector, "I've got witnesses to prove they're not a nuisance, says he. Well, I says to him, not going to be defied by him, or any one," he adds, with a glance at me to see how I like that. I nod in appreciation of his sentiments, and he resumes, "*I* haven't any witnesses except myself, and that's enough. We'll try it, says he, at law. Before the Magistrates, I says, for I was bound to prosecute him. And prosecute him I did, as he defied me. And," says the Inspector, warming with the recital, "the Magistrates wouldn't hear him at all, but when I put it to them, they said the case was clear, and those pigs had to be cleared out, they had, every one on 'em. He defied *me*, Sir, and it cost him, Sir, a 'underd pound it did, if it cost 'im a penny, it did. But I wasn't to be beat, I told him, and if he went on a defying me I'd fight him I would, I said, and so I did, and won. Government protects me, you see it does, that's where it is ; and it ain't no use, as I says to him, your defying *me*, I says."

He is so excited that I am afraid he'll do something violent in my case. He's a sort of walking Inquisitor, and Government takes his word against anybody's in a matter of (for instance) pigs.

*Happy Thought.*—To applaud him and say pleasantly, that I hope it won't come to that (meaning the hundred pounds) with me.

He hopes not, too ; as though this was a subject not to be treated lightly.

*Happy Thought.*—To appear interested, and ask if the man keeps pigs now.

"Yes, he do still," says the Inspector, somewhat mournfully (Cazell says afterwards that I oughtn't to have asked this, as I evidently touched on a sore point), "and I ain't done with him yet. He wanted to 'ave me hup for perjury, he did," the Inspector goes on. As he drops an " h," and puts one in occasionally, I suppose there is no examination for Inspectors (he'd called himself *H*inspector) of nuisances. " There was a trial at Westminster it was, about these very pigs," he continues, proudly ; " it was before Baron Bramwell "—(he calls the Judge Brammle)—" yes—and when the Baron 'ears it, he says to the Jury, says he, Look 'ere, says he,"—here the Inspector gives us what he takes to be an exact and correct report of Baron Bramwell's summing up, supposing Cazell to be the Jury, and myself the plaintiff with the pigs. Cazell smiles, and so do I, as if delighted with the whole thing as an entertainment—" There ain't no case against the Hinspector in this ; not a bit, says the Judge. The pigs was a right down nuisance, says he, they was, and the hofficer—that was me the Baron meant—the hofficer was right in having the law on him. And so you see," he adds, coming somewhat abruptly, but artistically, to the finish, " that's how it was."

We reply, at least I do, speaking for self and Cazell, that I do see clearly. The Inspector adds the moral, that I must see about *my* pigs at once, and, of course it is understood, that I don't defy him.

*Happy Thought.*—Ask him to have a glass of sherry.

As he " doesn't know but what he *will* just have a glass," I order in the bottle, and he helps himself and pledges us. We then resume business on, as it were, a more friendly footing, though (by frequent reference to the celebrated pig case) he gives me to understand that he is, personally, a favourite with the Government, and, generally speaking, not a man to be trifled with, or, of course, defied. In the matter of pigs and drains he is adamant.

*Happy Thought.*—To say (Cazell tells me afterwards that this is servile, and I ought *not* to be bullied) that I'll do whatever he likes.

" Well then," says he, " make a job of it." Cazell goes with us round the garden and into the piggeries, where he pretends to be disgusted, and makes the case out worse than the Inspector does himself. It's unkind of Cazell to do this, and I tell him so subsequently. Cazell now (before the Inspector) tells me " what I

ought to do." " You ought," says he, "to take up all the old
pipes, lay down new ones, turn on the water in a fresh place, open
a new ditch, move the piggeries, and put a wall right down the
side, and have bell-traps."

I pooh-pooh this. The Inspector is serious and agrees with
Cazell. In fact, he says, that's the only way to (what he calls)
"make a job of it."

It appears (on my pleading ignorance of anybody who can do all
this in the neighbourhood) that a friend of *his* can make a job of it.

*Happy Thought.*—To say By all means let your friend come.

If the job isn't made, the Inspector says, with regret (on account
I think of the friendly feeling evoked by the sherry) that he *must*
proceed against me.

Alternative, Inspector's friend to make a job of it, say twenty
pounds, or Law Proceedings, Counsel, Judge, Jury, Magistrates,
writ, summons, police, Westminster Hall, and Government backing
up the Inspector, and, dead against me, say, two hundred pounds.
Affair settled. Inspector departs. Friend (he undertakes to say,
for curiously enough he's going to meet him quite accidentally to-
night, when he'll tell him) will come and make a job of it in the
morning.

When he's gone, Cazell tells my wife what I *ought* to have done.
He says I've been imposed upon ; that I'm weak and have allowed
the Inspector to bully me. Fridoline says, "Yes, that she heard
us, and *knew* that I'd be *talked* into anything by that horrid man."
Mrs. Symperson (who doesn't understand the case at all, no more
does my wife) gives it as her opinion that I oughtn't to have
listened to him for a moment. Both agree with Cazell. Row. All
through Cazell, too.

*Happy Thought.*—To say jocularly, but ironically, " What I
ought to do is to have ten thousand a year, pull the house down
and make a mansion."

The presence of a stranger (Cazell) prevents recriminations. On
the whole it's not bad to have a stranger present when there's a
chance of a family quarrel. He can agree with the wife-party
when they're all together, and with the husband-party in the
smoking-room afterwards. Have done it myself : and therefore

can understand Cazell's being a humbug. What I object to is his telling my wife that while all these alterations are being made she ought to go to Brighton, or the Isle of Wight, or some other expensive place.

*Next Morning.*—Inspector's friend at work early : with bricklayer's hods, pickaxes, spades, bricks, mortar, and things enough to build a house instead of a pigsty.

Inspector's friend hopes I'll "'scuse *him* mentioning it, but that there tool-house isn't safe quite—not as *he* should like to see it on a gentleman's place." Wonderful what a regard Inspector's jobbing friend has for my respectability. Cazell says, No, ought to have that down. Dangerous. I say, Well have it down. Inspector's friend wants to know if I'd mind stepping this way. I step this way. He stops before the coach-house.

"'Scuse me," says he, "for mentioning it, but this coach-house ain't in a proper state ; you see this here pipe," &c. : he shows me a pipe which does something or other, I don't understand what, but something poisonous, or dangerous, or both : at all events it's "not the sort of pipe as he," the Inspector's friend, "would like to see on 'a *gentleman's*' (meaning my) place." Cazell says I ought to have it up, and adds (literally playing into the Inspector's friend's hands), "You might have the hen-house done now—it'll be a nuisance in time, you'll see." We inspect the hen-house. Inspector's friend shakes his head gravely. "It's not the sort of hen-house he'd like to see," &c. He points out that the house will be infected with fl**s if the chickens live where they now are. "Chickens are full of fl**s," he says. Curious fact in Natural History. Inspector's friend has come "to make a job of it," and a nice job he's making. We now discover (through Inspector's friend) that we have been living in the midst of danger without knowing it. "Why, Sir," says Inspector's friend, who suddenly ascertains that soapsuds are poured out on the ground near the kitchen-window, "there ain't no poison like soapsuds : it's worse than drainage and pigs."

*Happy Thought.* — Then leave the drainage and pigs, and merely give up throwing soapsuds.

Inspector's friend and Cazell smile. Cazell says, "No, go in for making a thoroughly good job of it." Inspector's friend says he means to : judging from the bricks and mortar and men (three more have just come in with wheel-barrows and ladders) it looks like it.

At breakfast I happen to complain of rheumatics. Cazell almost jumps from his chair, and shouts (before the ladies, too!), "Rheumatics! *I'll* tell you what you ought to do for rheumatics. Go abroad. Take baths. Drink waters." Wife says, "Yes, by all means." Mrs. Symperson says she did it years ago, and it cured *her.* I answer, "Did it, indeed?" but don't express joy.

*Happy Thought.*—Go abroad. Vienna : and call, as I promised, on the Count de Bootjack.

Cazell says I ought to go by Antwerp to Aix. He knows a fellow going : Chilvern—Tom Chilvern. Odd : old schoolfellow of mine. Cazell is going to see a friend in Hertfordshire, for a day or so, but will give me Chilvern's address in town. Cazell says, "You ought to go and consult a doctor about your rheumatism." He oughtn't to say this. It makes one nervous when you're not really nervous. Wife begs me to consult a doctor. She is nervous about me : thinks I must have caught something from the pigs or the chickens. Cazell has told her (he *is* an ass in some things and ought not to frighten women) that babies can catch measles from fowls, and chicken-pox too. She is frightened, sends for the Doctor and examines the baby three times an hour. New rash discovered. Doctor says, "Best thing to go to Brighton, and Mrs. Symperson can take care of both." Wife in delicate state ; Doctor says to me, Better go away for change. I smile. He smiles. We both smile. We nod. We understand one another, only what do we mean exactly? He says good-bye, and hopes to hear we're all soon better, taking it for granted that I'm going abroad.

*Happy Thought.*—Go on the Continent while Inspector's friend builds pigsties, and generally speaking "makes a job of it," which at present looks uncommonly like making a mess of it. If I'm away he can't have any authority for doing anything more than precisely what he has got to do.

*Happy Thought (No. 2 on the same subject).*—Quiet place to write *Typical Developments,* and correct proofs of first volume for Popgood and Groolly.

Cazell leaves. I promise him, as I really *am* bad with rheumatics, to go and see Dr. Pilzen in London. Wife says she wants a considerable cheque before she goes away. Argument on economy. Mrs. Symperson points out what I *should* have spent if it hadn't been for her and Fridoline's admirable arrangement.

I see some sort of a repartee (might come under heading *M. Mother-in-Law. Repartee to a Mother-in-Law*), but can't quite put it into form. The *sense* is " what I would have spent without them." Feel this would be cruel. Draw cheque. Affecting parting. Arrangement as to correspondence : I am to write from abroad to Friddy ; Friddy to me abroad from Brighton.

London again. At Willis's rooms. Letter from Popgood and Groolly with MS. Know the MS. by sight at once : it is *Typical Developments* returned. Civil note :—

" Messrs. Popgood and Groolly present their compliments, and thank the author of the enclosed work for favouring them with a perusal of it ; but as they understand from him that it is to reach twenty volumes *at least* before it is finished, they are unable to pronounce an opinion on its merits in its present condition. If the author will kindly allow them to look over it when it has attained a more perfected form, and is near its completion, they will esteem it a favour, and will give the work their immediate and most careful attention. Sincerely wishing the work in hand a successful issue,

" They beg to subscribe themselves, Sir,

" Yours faithfully,

" POPGOOD AND GROOLLY."

" P.S. We enclose the list of our latest publications, and also of those works which can now be obtained from our stock *at something less than half-price.*—P. & G."

*Happy Thought.*—They've read it. Evidently they've read it, because they want to see it again when it's in a more advanced state. Can't find fault with their answer. Sensible, when you come to think of it. Will write, saying that I agree with them : will get on with the work as quickly as possible, and let them see it. Will take it abroad, and work at it.

Next thing is to go about the rheumatics at Pilzen. Meet Milburd in the Club. He exclaims, "Well, old Gropgood and Poolly, how are you?" I check him by replying that, seriously, Popgood and Groolly entertain the idea of publishing *Typical Developments*. He replies, that the idea of publishing *Typical Developments* will probably entertain Popgood and Groolly. "Old joke," I say. "Who said it wasn't?" he retorts, and roars with laughter.

I wish I hadn't told him about my rheumatics (as I did immediately after the Popgood conversation), as he directly begins to imitate the *Pantaloon*—tottering about on his stick (and *this* in the Club hall), and then he says, as *Clown*, "Poor old man!" in a quavering voice. Then he changes to a boisterous manner, and says, "*You* got the rheumatics! Walker!" and slaps me on the back. I tell him (being annoyed, I can't help speaking to him with asperity) that if *he* had the rheumatics as *I* have, *he* wouldn't laugh. Upon which he winks, and replies, "Yes, but I haven't, you see—that's where it is;" and pokes me in the ribs, and says, "Tchk!" and, in fact, so plays the Tom-fool that the Hall-porter disappears behind his desk, and I hear him suppressing a burst of laughter. "Well," says Milburd, "you're looking awfully well: never saw you better."

He is most irritating. I return, that it's very good of him to say that I'm looking well, but I know I'm *not*.

*Happy Thought.*—Try and make him sympathise with me.

I shake my head, and say, sadly—at the moment I am so impressive that I can almost fancy myself at my last gasp—(picture of the sad event in the Club hall—porters kneeling—butler coming, terrified, down-stairs—members explaining to one another —commissionnaire just come in from a message, weeping, and rubbing his eyes with his only arm—Milburd, suddenly struck with remorse, vows never again to be unsympathetic with a sick man, &c., &c.—really good subject for picture : lights and shades of our hall, marble columns, &c., might be as perfect as the late Mr. Roberts's Cathedral interiors)—I shake my head, and say, sadly, "Yes, I am going to see Pilzen to-morrow, and he will," more sadly, and with intensity, "order me off abroad, somewhere."

Milburd says, "Hooray! Then I will go with you, my pretty maid: I mean, I dare say I'll join you. Bravo!" And he slaps me again on the back. N.B. Give up talking rheumatics with Milburd.

Doctor's to-morrow, and next day with Chilvern to Antwerp. Note from wife to say what a tremendous job Inspector's friend is making of it. Wonder what he's doing?

## CHAPTER XI.

HAPPY THOUGHT. —On my way to the doctor's call on my Uncle and Aunt, whom I was going to see just before I left town last time, but didn't.

Don't know *why* I didn't. Very odd, but it's always been the same as regards my Uncle and Aunt ever since I can recollect. I used to be taken to their house by my nurse. Perhaps the fact of being *taken* there has remained in my inner consciousness ever since. *Mem. for Typical Developments*, Vol. IV., *Early Compulsion, damaging effects of.* By the way, must hurry on with *Typ. Devel.*, Vol. I., for Popgood and Groolly. I remember the street, but forget the number. I don't know why I hit upon thirty-seven, but I do, and am right. (Stop to make this note in the hall. *Mem. for Typ. Dev., Tendrils of Memory, seize on*—leave blank here for word to be selected in calmer moments—*in early youth, and so on*, &c. *I* shall understand this when I wish to develop the note into——).

I find that the butler has held the drawing-room door open for more than a minute, while I am making this note, coming up-stairs (not easy), in my Pocket-book. My Aunt says, "Shut the door, Mussels," sharply. Mussels, the butler, retires.

*Happy Thought.*—Mussels rhymes to Brussels, and I am going to Aix.

If my Aunt or Uncle had any sense of humour, I'd say this as a pleasant commencement. (*Note. Typ. Devel., On Commence-ments.*)

My Aunt having stood up to receive me, in the draught which Mussels had made by keeping the door open—(funny name, Mussels)—is cross, and coughs behind her hand.

*Happy Thought.*—To say cheerfully, and smiling lightly, "How d'ye do, Aunt?" ignoring the draught. It appears she doesn't do particularly well, nor my Uncle either.

*Happy Thought.*—Suit your manners to your company : drop smiling and look serious. My Uncle is sitting in an arm-chair, very feeble, and occasionally groaning. My Aunt describes her own symptoms with painful and touching accuracy, but has no pity for *him*. She says impatiently, "Oh dear, your Uncle groans and coddles himself up if his little finger aches. I tell him to go out for a good walk, and take healthy exercise." On examining him reproachfully, as much as to say, "Why *don't* you take my Aunt's advice?" he appears as if he might possibly venture as far as the centre pattern of the carpet and back again. Think my Aunt a little hard on my Uncle. Better not say so. Merely observe gravely, "I am sorry to see you so unwell " (to my Aunt, as if I didn't care how my Uncle was, dismissing him in fact as a shammer.)

[*Query.* Isn't this "time serving," and oughtn't I to be above it?]

My Aunt gives me a list of her complaints; I appear to be listening with great interest, like a doctor. If Cazell was here, he'd tell her "what she ought to do." While she is talking I can't help remembering that I have always heard what expectations I have from my Aunt. Friends have joked me about it. Many have said they envy me. Everyone seems to know what a lucky dog I am going to be except myself. She continues her list of maladies, she shakes her head mournfully, says she's getting an old woman now.

*Happy Thought.*—Say politely, " Oh no."

Feel that she must see through this. If she sets me down as a humbug, it will ruin my chance. Yet I can't sit, as it were, gloating over my victim like a Vampire. Feel inclined to say solemnly, " Well, Aunt, we must all come to an end" (substituting this expression for "die" which had first occurred to me) "sooner or later." Should have been obliged to say this, if she hadn't turned the conversation to my wife and baby.

*Happy Thought.*—To answer, "They're longing to come and call on you, but have been so unwell."

Partly truth—partly fiction. They have been unwell, but I *never can* get Fridoline to call on my Aunt. She says, "It's such a horrible idea to go and see, not how people are getting on, but *getting off*, when they're going to leave you money." The discussion has never ended pleasantly. I can't help feeling that my wife is honest, but impolitic; so I put it to her reasonably, and she retorts that I want her to be a hypocrite. It is *so* difficult to explain to a woman the difference between policy and hypocrisy. She won't go, so *I* have to call. I own to feeling (as I have said) like a Vampire myself. Perhaps it's as well as it is.

*Happy Thought.*—One Vampire's enough in a family.

Interview over, glad of it. My uncle, who has not joined in the conversation, except by groaning at intervals, mutters, "Good-bye, won't see me again." I really could cry if it wasn't for my Aunt, who, having rung for Mussels to open the door, is now saying good-bye to me, and remarking quite cheerfully, "Your Uncle is very well, only if he *will* make stupid mistakes" (with such a look at the poor old gentleman, who groans) "he can't expect to be well. Good-bye."

On inquiry, I ascertain from Mussels that the "stupid mistake" my Uncle had made was in drinking his lotion and rubbing in his mixture. As my Aunt said, of course he couldn't expect to be well.

*Happy Thought.*—Good-bye, Mr. Mussels.

Always be polite to the Butler. Recollect Mussels years ago when I used to look at picture-books in the pantry; at least, I think I do, or another butler, just like him. Mr. Mussels asks civilly after my wife and family. I return thanks (to Mussels) for them, and add playfully that "the family" has the rash.

*Happy Thought.*—Return compliment, "Mrs. Mussels quite well?"

Wish I hadn't. Mussels has been a widower for five years. Don't know what to say to this. Not the place for a repartee : opportunity for consolation. The only consolation I can think of at the moment is, "Well, never mind," with the addition of what I wanted to have said up-stairs about "We must all be buried sooner or later." Pause on the top step, fumble with umbrella, feel that on the whole nothing can be said except "Dear me!" and walk into the street abstractedly. Door shut. I (as it were) breathe again. Re-action. Walk cheerfully to the Doctor's.

Wonder what his opinion will be. Shall tell him that friends (really Cazell) have advised me to go abroad for the benefit of my health.

*Happy Thought.*—Nothing the matter with me except, perhaps, a little rheumatism. However, just as well to see a doctor.

"Prevention better than cure," sensible saying that, and I shall be able to finish off several volumes of *Typ. Devel.* at Aix (a very quiet place, I am told), and astonish Popgood and Groolly.

*Happy Thought.*—Before I go to Doctor's, wrap up the fee carefully in a piece of paper, and put it in a pocket by itself. Watch in one pocket; fee in the other. Then you can get at it at once, and give it with a sort of grace.

*At the Doctor's.*—Door is opened immediately by a most respectable gentleman (it isn't the Doctor of course) who shows me at once into a room, and somehow manages to show somebody else out at the front door at the same time. And yet he doesn't seem to move. Odd and spectral.

*In the Waiting-room.*—Several people waiting, like waxworks at Madame Tussaud's, only they are sitting instead of standing. Some look up, with one movement of the head, at me on my entrance, and then with what they call in machinery "a reverse action," look down again. (*Query.* Do they call it "Reverse action!" *Note.*) There are three doors to the room: one by which I entered; from one of the other two the Doctor will appear, or we shall go to him. Which?

*Happy Thought.*—Sit as near the middle as possible, by table.

Door on my right opens. Doctor looks in, says nothing, takes away an elderly lady. Wonder what's the matter with her? Open a volume of *Punch,* commence looking at the pictures vaguely. Door opens again. Can't be my turn? No. Doctor takes off a middle-aged man with his arm in a sling. Wonder what's the matter with *him?* Rather expect to hear cries and screams in the distance: everything mysteriously quiet. We are fetched, one after another, like victims for the guillotine. (I make notes while I am sitting here. *Note.*—Was it for the guillotine where the victims sat all in a room and were called out one after the other? or was it something in Japan? Look it up when I get home.) Open another volume of *Punch.* Doctor wants somebody else.

*Happy Thought.*—*My* turn.

No. Old lady and her companion (evidently a companion) have been waiting there nearly an hour.

*Happy Thought.*—To try and catch the Doctor's eye next time he looks in.

Throw into *my* eye an expression which will say to him, "Never mind these people, let *me* come; *I'm* worth your trouble. Can't waste time like *they* can, being engaged on a great work, *Typical Developments.*"

Doctor looks in again. Arranged my eye: not quickly enough, as I didn't catch his. A gentleman and a little boy disappear into the sanctum. I open another volume of *Punch.* During the morning I read five volumes of *Punch,* and for an hour and a half I am perpetually attempting to catch the Doctor's eye.

Doctor looks in for the twentieth time (I count them, and also keep on looking at my watch, with a sort of idea that if the people see me doing this they'll say to themselves, "He's a man of business, got appointments, wants to be off; let him go first.")

*Happy Thought.*—Feel if my fee is all right in waistcoat pocket.

It is. Arrange a little drama with myself as to *how* I'll give the fee. Let the Doctor see it, then, when he's not looking, place it on the mantel-place; sort of conjuring trick. When I'm gone he'll say, "Where's he put the fee?" Joy on discovering it. End of drama, and enter another patient.

*Happy Thought.*—Twenty-first appearance of Doctor's head at door. Jump up—*at* him.

I hear a rustle behind me of several people, and a murmur Tall lady in black is by my side, in a second, protesting. I give in. Tall lady retires with Doctor. Feel I've done something rude. Never mind, show I'm not to be trifled with. I take a seat, defiantly now, near the door.

*Happy Thought.*—Next turn *must* be mine.

*Twenty-second* appearance of Doctor's head. My turn? Doctor speaks this time; most politely, "my turn *next*," he says; "this gentleman" (indicating a short stout man with a florid face and a carpet-bag in his hand) "has, I think, the *pas*." I bow, *not* to the carpet-bag invalid, but to the Doctor.

Twenty-third appearance of Doctor, and disappearance of Myself. Interview. Yes, decidedly go abroad. Take baths and waters, and get the incipient gout out of me. I am quite right (Doctor says)—prevention *is* better than cure. He won't give me a prescription, but an introduction to a Doctor at the watering-place, which he dashes off there and then.

*Happy Thought.*—Pick up some medical notes for physiological portion of *Typ. Devel.*

Commence a discussion with him on Homœopathic theories as applied in Allopathic practice. Would it not, I say, in some cases be allowable? He replies, "Undoubtedly," and seals up the letter. (He evidently feels he has no ordinary patient to deal with. I can presently introduce *Typical Developments* to him: he'll be interested.)

*Happy Thought.*—To draw him out.

The science of medicine, I observe, is in a state of change. The old practice I suppose (I add) requires readaptation to the increasing knowledge of the present day.

Doctor replies, courteously, "Just so," and opens the door. Most annoying, the fee has got out of the paper—or, where the deuce has it gone? Awkward to be fumbling for fees, while the Doctor holds the door open. Can't say anything funny, or scientific. I have got the sum in half a sovereign and silver in my trousers pocket, but that's mixed up with coppers and keys; and I have got studs in my other pocket to be mended.

[*Happy Thought.*—Everything in separate pockets : have always intended to tell the tailor this.]—I must have lost the fee.

*Happy Thought.*—No! feel it just over my hip bone.

Hole in pocket; slipped through and got round into lining. Tear, recklessly, the pocket lining, and catch the fee. Might make some jocund remark about " Fee-nominal."

Doctor smiles courteously, but appears pre-occupied. I can't do the trick I had arranged about placing the fee on the mantel-piece, as he is looking. On the table, or in his hand?

*Happy Thought.*—On the table.

Am just about to do it, when it strikes me, being in white paper, it looks too staring.

*Happy Thought.*—Pass it into my other hand (by a sort of leger-demain) and when saying good-bye, press it on him, secretly, as much as to say, "Don't tell anybody."

Do it. Good-bye, and leave.

*As I walk along the street.*—Wish I *hadn't* done it in this manner : bad taste. I should like to have done it in a less underhand way. For instance, to have said, jovially, " Here! what's this!" holding up fee. " There, take that, you rascal," playfully, as Mr. Pickwick did to Job Trotter, and adding, " I'm very much obliged for your advice. Bless you, good-bye, my boy," and so go out whistling.

*Happy Thought.*—To my Handbook of Repartees will add Con-versations and Interviews.

Odd, just as I've thought of this, I find myself in front of a Bookseller's shop. In the window is a red-book, *Manual of Con-versations in French, English, German, and Italian.*

*Happy Thought.*—Buy it. Most useful. And can work up my own from it when travelling.

Full of the idea. When I am full of an idea, I should like to dash it off in the street. If we lived in a literary age, and in a literary town, there might be writing-desks, with pens and ink chained to them (as they did with the Bibles in the Parish Churches), at the corner of the streets. Enter. Pay a halfpenny. Write down idea, stop and develop it if you like ; then go on again. If another idea strikes you on the same walk, another halfpenny will, as it were, register it there and then.

Go to Willis's. Pack up. Say good-bye to Rawlinson. Milburd has just been there. A card. "If you'll dine with me and Chilvern *chez* club, Cazell and another fellow coming, we'll all go together to Antwerp by boat to-morrow."

*Happy Thought.*—Will dine with Milburd.

## CHAPTER XII.

WHEN I go in, Milburd's guests are waiting for their host. Cazell is there, and three other men in evening dress. Cazell knows one of them, but doesn't introduce me to him. We evidently, more or less, consider one another as intruders.

*Happy Thought.*—To say it's been a nice day.

Some one (elderly gentleman with yellow grey whiskers) says he doesn't think so, "but perhaps," he adds, sarcastically, "you like rain." Forgot it had been raining. Should like (only he's my senior) to inform him that my observation was only thrown out to give the conversation a start. Pause. Cazell who *might* talk to two of us, doesn't. The third is a gentleman with tight waist, long legs, and a glass in his eye. He manages to pass the time, apparently, by stretching out his legs as far as he can away from him, smoothing them down with both hands, and regarding them critically through his eye-glass. We are all drawn towards him. His smoothing his legs has evidently a mesmeric effect upon us, and we all, at least so it seems to me, begin to take a silent but intense interest in his legs. If we were left there two hours, he would probably become mesmerically mechanical in his movement, and we should all be fixed staring at him in our chairs, unable to move, with mesmerised legs. (*Note.* Not to forget Mesmerism, under M., in *Typ. Devel.*, Vol. VI.) Another old gentleman is shown in by the waiter. He is portly and enters genially, with his hand out ready to grasp Milburd's. I can't help pitying him when he *doesn't* see Milburd.

*Happy Thought.*—Respect age—rise. Old fashion and good.

The old gentleman seizes me by the hand. So glad to see me again. "Capital," he says, "not met for an age." I answer that I am delighted to meet him. Wonder to myself where I've seen him before : puzzle, give it up.

"Well," he says, "all well at home?" I answer, "Only pretty well." He is sorry to hear it.

*Happy Thought.*—To ask him if *he's* all well at home.

"Yes," he says he is, "though Milly isn't," he adds, "quite so well as she might be." I reply, "Indeed," thoughtfully, for as I don't know how well Milly might be if she tried, nor who Milly is, I fancy that there must be a mistake. Still if I *ought* to know him, to tell him that I haven't an idea who he is, would be rude—specially from a young man to his senior. Man with eye-glass, in meantime, has lowered himself in easy chair, and is stretching out, complacently, farther than ever. (*Note.* Silent Gymnastics.) He is still criticising his legs favourably, and varying his movements by pulling up his wristbands, which are very wide, long, and come up to his knuckles.

Old gentleman suddenly puts his hand in his pocket and says to me, "Oh, that reminds me, you didn't hear from Martin, did you?" A dilemma for me. Of course I don't know *his* Martin. Shall I say, simply to make a conversation, "Yes or No?"

*Happy Thought.*—Say the truth. "No."

"Ha!" he exclaims, "then I must settle with *you.* How much am I in your debt?" This is awkward. It's difficult at this moment to tell him that I never saw him before in all my life, but I am certain of it. If I had any doubt of it, his recollecting a debt to me would put it beyond question, as I shouldn't have lent him anything.

"Well?" he asks, pausing with his purse in his hand.

*Happy Thought.*—Tell the truth again.

I commence, "The fact is——"

Milburd enters. He oughtn't to leave his guests. "Ha! Commodore!" he says to the old gentleman, "I'm glad to see you're acquainted."

I explain at once that we're not; and he, putting on his spectacles, for the first time (without which the aged mariner is it appears as blind as a bat) discovers that he has taken me for Milburd.

*Happy Thought.*—Aged mariner. Wish I could recollect a quotation. Ought to have something about an albatross at my fingers' ends.

After this, Introductions : myself to Commodore Brumsby, Chilvern to me, we are to be travelling companions, Milburd says; whereupon Chilvern and myself both smile vaguely at each other, as if such a notion was too preposterous or absurd. After all, if smiling means nothing (when done in this way), it's better than frowning. [N.B. Make a note in pocket-book to effect that under A might come important article on Amenities.] After this, myself to Captain Dyngwell, who has risen, and on being introduced screws up his glass into one eye, his forehead down on to his glass, and his mouth up on one side, as if undecided whether to scowl, or receive me pleasantly. He murmurs something to himself (for me to take up if I like) about something's being "doosid funny," and tries to pull himself out of his coat by tugging at his wristbands. Standing on the rug and stretching the right hand out with a jerk, he catches the elderly gentleman with sandy grey whiskers just behind the ear. Milburd, with admirable presence of mind, introduces them at once.

"Sir Peter Groganal, Captain Dyngwell." They bow politely, and the Captain is understood to apologise, but as he is struck by something's being "doosid funny," the conversation with him, beyond this point, doesn't progress. It appears, subsequently, that the circumstance of Commodore Brumsby's having mistaken me for Milburd, has struck the Captain as "doosid funny;" in fact, so utterly and out of all comparison droll has this appeared to the light-hearted soldier, that he is perpetually recurring to the circumstance throughout the evening.

"Sir Peter Groganal," whispers Milburd to me, "is a great chemist : you'll like him : you must draw him out." I say " I will," but I don't quite see my way to drawing out a great chemist.

*Happy Thought.—Manuals for the Dressing-table.*—Drawing-out Questions for various professors. A. How to draw out an Artist, &c., say, generally, "Are you hard at work now?" (then he'll tell you, how hard ; what at ; why ; what next ; what he thinks of other Artists ; what other Artists think of him, &c., &c. ; of ancient art ; of old masters, &c.). B. How to draw out a Bishop. "Your Lordship must be very much overworked?" No? "Well, it's not large pay?" This raises interesting subjects, "Bishops' Income, Church Property, Establishment, Simony, Lay-impropriation, &c. C. Chemist. How to draw out Chemist? *Question.* "Now should *you* say,"—put this as if *you* wouldn't or he won't be interested ; great secret this, interest your man, "Should *you* say that Carbolic acid gas acting on the," &c., &c. Of course, it is necessary in scientific questions, in order to obtain information, to master up to a certain point the *rudiments.* Thus you must be sure of its being "Carbolic" not "Carbonic ;" acid gas, not "acid *in* gas ;" also, as to whether it "does act on the," &c., &c. —whatever it may be, just to start it, because there'd be an end to all conversation if A or B or C replied, "No, Sir, such a case couldn't possibly happen ; a *child* wouldn't ask so foolish a question as *yours.*" Only, of course, if he *did* say this he'd be a bear, and people would get tired of asking him out. I am so convinced of the utility of this Manual that before I go to bed to-night I make notes for its commencement. I'm afraid I'm getting too many irons in my literary fire.

Milburd really has mixed us well. There's a military man Captain Dyngwell, there's Chilvern an architect, then Commodore Brumsby, R.N., a great traveller, Sir Peter Groganal a tremendous chemist, Cazell who will tell everyone "what he ought to do," and I hope get well set down, Milburd for funniments seasoned by the courtesies of a host, and myself, as a representative, to a certain extent, of Literature.

*Happy Thought.*—To ask Milburd in a whisper, as we go in to dinner, "What *is* a Commodore?" Milburd returns, also in a whisper, "Don't know."

We all sit down: Captain Dyngwell, stretching out both his wristbands over the table as if he were imparting a fashionable sort of blessing to the knives, forks, glasses and napkins. Will I face Milburd? With pleasure, if he wishes it; but won't——? "No, no," says Commodore Brumsby, "Young 'uns do the work." Sir Peter says, gravely, "Yes, Sir, you can experimentalise." We are arranged. Milburd at the head: myself, his *vis-à-vis;* on my right the Commodore, on my left the Chemist. Captain and Chilvern *vis-à-vis* one another, and there we are. Excellent number, eight. Cazell is on Milburd's right, and there's an empty place for a man who ought to have been there but isn't. None of us care one dump whether he comes or not. No one knows him: he's a barrister, "very rising man," says Milburd, whereat one or two of us observe, "Indeed? is he?" and go on with our soup.

# CHAPTER XIII.

ON DINNER COMPANY—START OF CONVERSATION—CAPTAIN DYNGWELL
—THE MOZAMBIQUE—IGNORANCE—ANCIENT MARINER—ABSTRACT
RIGHT—TWO THINGS AT ONCE—DINNER ARGUMENT.

**M**ILBURD manages to mix his company well for a dinner.
Thinking over it next day when on board the packet for
Antwerp, how much better it is when you give a dinner, to have
one Chemist (for example), one Cavalry Officer, one Architect, one
General Conversationalist (almost a profession in itself), one Barrister, one Commodore, one Literary, and one Funny (but not *too*
funny) man,—I say, how *much* better it is to give a dinner of this
sort, than of all Architects, all Chemists, or all Commodores, or
all Funny men as the case may be.

Sir Peter Groganal the Chemist remarks as a starting point,
that it's excellent soup. This sets every one off. I don't know

why. Captain Dyngwell pulls up his shirt-sleeves sharply, nearly knocking over the water-bottle in front of him, and says, "Yes, hang it, they don't give *him* that soup at the Rag." Catching my eye, he suppresses a laugh, and murmurs, "Doosid ridiculous." I ask him across the table "What is?" He answers by leaning a little back, winking his disengaged eye, jerking his head in the Commodore's direction, and saying, not too *loud*, "Mistaking you for——" Another jerk, and a wink towards Milburd. Whenever the Captain alludes to this ludicrous incident henceforth, this is the method he adopts. He then chuckles, pulls up his wristband, drops his eye-glass, searches for it with the other eye, replaces it, looks defiantly round, ready either to smile or scowl, and suddenly dives down at his plate of whatever-it-is at the moment.

Sir Peter Groganal the Chemist takes us, *via* soup, into various questions of adulteration. At this point Cazell tells us what we ought to do, and Chilvern the Architect takes that opportunity of recounting an instance in point when he did what he ought to have done, but without effect ; the anecdote being introduced for the sake of letting us know that he had once tenders and contracts (or sent in tenders and received contracts, or whatever it was), with Messrs. Ferry, Rust, and Co., the great iron-merchants. This brings out the Commodore, who, remembers having seen their name somewhere, when he was in the *Mozambique*, which in turn brings *me* out.

*Happy Thought.*—Ask him about the *Mozambique.*

What I should really like to do at this moment is, to request him to draw a map showing me exactly *where* the *Mozambique* is situated ; and, while he's about it, *what* the *Mozambique really* is.

I thought up to this moment it was an island ; now as he begins talking, I fancy it must be a Bay or a Gulf.

Really when one considers these every-day matters (afterwards and in cold blood,—that is over an atlas quietly in my own room, before I go to bed), it is astonishing how little one knows about them. Milburd, who as host ought not to say anything rude, hearing our conversation, asks me, as if it were a riddle—

"What's the *Mozambique* ?  Do you give it up?"

I nod and laugh, as if, of course, it was too absurd *not* to know what the *Mozambique* is. I feel that Milburd sees through me, and am a little uncomfortable, as he doesn't mind what he says.

*Happy Thought.*—Perhaps Milburd doesn't know any more about it than I do.

*Happy Thought.*—Discover what the *Mozambique* is (whether a Gulf, or a Bay, or an Island) from the Commodore's conversation.

Wish I hadn't devoted myself to the Commodore. He doesn't tell me anything particularly distinctive about *Mozambique ;* but his story commences with something about " headwinds on a forecassel and furling sails after soundings." The mention of "porpoises" seems to put me, as it were, at home again ; but from these he gets into reefs, shoals, deep waters, watches, yardarms, and going aloft, and evidently hasn't got a quarter through his story whatever it is.

*Happy Thought.*—He holds me, the guest, like the Ancient Mariner. Should like to ask him about albatrosses. He wouldn't see the joke, or perhaps, know the allusion. Besides it would prolong his story. I listen respectfully. The worst of it is, that in the meantime a controversy has got up between Sir Peter Groganal, Chilvern, and Slingsby the Barrister (who has just come in, apologised for being late, and plunged into dinner and conversation as if he'd been there the whole time), which really *does* interest me. It is on the Existence of Abstract Right.

They are playing at a sort of dummy whist with this controversy ; that is, Slingsby and Chilvern are on one side, and Sir Peter on the other. I hear every word they say, and am deeply interested. Should like to cut in and make a fourth, but can't, because I am bound to listen to the Commodore, who is still beating about *Mozambique* in headwinds. He is telling me something about the maladministration of naval affairs by the Admiralty, illustrating it with an argument just as Slingsby is asserting confidently that there is no such thing as Abstract Right.

*Happy Thought.*—To say to the Commodore, " Yes, it wants reform," and turn at once, without giving him an opportunity of dragging me into his nautical conversation again, to Slingsby, asserting the existence of Abstract Right. (1 *Vol. Typ. Develop.*)

The Commodore won't give me a chance ; I am waiting for even a semicolon in his conversation ; but he continues, " Now I'll just give you a case in point, and you'll say "—then off he goes into something about a Lieutenant who had been twenty years in the service, and had never got away from Malta, or something to that

effect ; while in the meantime I hear Slingsby laying down most
outrageous laws with regard to his proposition, which I consider
false in itself.

*Happy Thought.*—While the Commodore is in the middle of
some Admiralty grievance to turn a little aside towards Slingsby,
smile, and shake my head, as much as to say, " No, that won't do,
you know ; " look round at the Commodore immediately afterwards,
and say, blandly, " Yes, of course it was very hard," *à propos* of
his story, showing that I *can* listen to two things at once. Milburd
takes off the Commodore's attention for a second, and I join in
with Sir Peter the Chemist, against Slingsby and Chilvern.

I like a thorough philosophical discussion. We all get very warm
over it. Chilvern objects to the introduction of theology, and Sir
Peter says " Quite so." Slingsby denies, for the fourth time in my
hearing, the existence of Abstract Right, and at it we go again.

I say, " There *must* be, in the nature of things "—here Milburd
recommends some of that pudding, to which I help myself, talking
all the time (for in an argument at dinner, if you once stop talking
even to take pudding, some one will take your turn away from you.
People are so selfish, and want to have it all to themselves.) I say,
" There *must* be, in the nature of things, an Abstract Right."

" Why ? " asks Slingsby the Barrister.

" Why ? " I retort, " *Why !*—Why, if "—I don't quite see what
I am going to say ; but by talking steadily and cautiously, you're
safe to come upon something worth saying, at last : besides, this is
the true method of induction, or " leading *into* " a subject—" *Why,*
if Abstract Right," this with great emphasis, " did not exist," pro-
nouncing each syllable distinctly (to gain time), " then there would
be no Certain Criterion "—(N.B. Talk slowly, and you'll always be
able to get good words.)—" no Certain Criterion by which to
judge "—here sauce is handed for the pudding—" by which to
judge the actions "—here a liqueur is handed round—" the actions
of mankind."

" Take a savage," says Slingsby.

" Take a glass of Chartreuse," says Milburd, from his end of the
table. We dismiss Milburd with a nod and a smile, and go back
to work again at Abstract Right. Somehow we all get very warm
over the subject. Slingsby puts arguments forward which sound
unanswerable ; but which, I am sure, if I could put them down on

paper and go into them, are simply preposterously absurd. Yet, at the moment, I can't confute him.

*Happy Thought.*—To ask him if he's read *Tomlinson on Abstract Right?* No, he has not. "Ah," I say, much relieved, "then when you've read *that* we'll talk. You'll find *all* your arguments answered and confuted there over and over again." I must get Tomlinson's book myself: I looked into it once, at a friend's house.

At this point there is a pause.

"Well, Captain," says Milburd, chaffingly (that's the worst of him, never serious!) leaning over to Captain Dyngwell, who has been silently attentive to the wine all the while, "what's *your* opinion on the subject?"

The Captain smiles, and replies, "Eh? Oh, it looks uncommonly like a universal tittup."

I never was so much taken aback. "A what? A universal *what?*" asks Sir Peter.

"Tittup," says the Captain.

"I never heard that word before," says the Analytical Chemist, seriously.

"No?" returns the Captain, carelessly. From this moment the Captain is an object of attraction. It appears that he has quite a vocabulary of his own. The interest I have in him is beyond this, as he has just come from Aix, and is going back again there for the benefit of his health. Will he, I ask, tell me what sort of a place it is?

"Well," he says, "it's not much of a place for a tittup. There are one or two jolly old cockalorums there, and, when the season's on, you can go on the scoop in the way of a music-caper, or a hop, and you can get rid of the stuff there as well as anywhere."

*Happy Thought.*—To note these words down. To take him aside afterwards and ask him for an exact explanation of "tittup," "cockalorum," "scoop," "music-caper," and "stuff." "Stuff," I discover, he applies equally to money or liquor of any sort. He passes the stuff at table, he "makes no end of stuff," or "loses no end of stuff" (the latter, generally, from his own account), on the Derby.

He tells me that he is going back to Aix, to be the "perfect cure," and "do the regular tittup in Double Dutch," from which I gather, when I know him better, that he is returning for the benefit of his health, and to the study of the German language.

He kindly tells me he can give me "the correct card for hotels, put me up to all the little games, and do the trick without any kidd, no deception, no spring or false bottom, my noble sportsman." I laugh at this, whereupon he adds (he has not spared the wine), "That's your tip, old Buck ; you just screw on to this light-hearted soldier," meaning himself, "and you'll turn out right end uppermost, A one copper plate." Here he drinks off a bumper, and chuckles at "Old Cockalorum," meaning Commodore Brumsby, "having mistaken you for Milburd." This is what he says, "he can't get over."

He adds presently, "I say, you were nearly having a universal tittup just now."

He alludes to our getting warm in our discussion about Abstract Right, and simply means that we should have quarrelled if we'd continued.

We go into the smoking-room ; and as Chilvern and I are going by boat to-morrow, we leave early. When the party breaks up, everyone wishes he was going with everyone else abroad next day ; and everyone hopes in default of that to meet everyone else, heartily and pleasantly, but vaguely, somewhere else at some time or other. So the evening finishes. To-morrow, away from England.

*Happy Thought.*—Write to Friddy before I start. Ask her to send newspapers out to me.

## CHAPTER XIV.

VOYAGING—THE BARON OSY—ADMIRAL—FOREBODINGS—ADVICES—
DIFFICULTIES—ADMIRAL'S BREVITY—GETTING OUT INTO THE
OPEN—MORE FOREBODINGS—TITTUPING.

HERE we are on board the *Baron Osy*, for Antwerp—
Chilvern, Captain Dyngwell, Cazell, and self.

Lovely day, with occasional clouds.

*Happy Thought.*—Secure a berth.   Each cabin holds two.
Chilvern takes top berth ; I take the bottom one.

I say, "Let's go up-stairs." Cazell corrects me.   He says,
indignantly, "You *ought* to say, up the companion."   He talks to
the Captain—I mean the Captain of the *Baron Osy*.

*Happy Thought.*—Make friends with the Captain.   To distinguish him in my note-book from Captain Dyngwell, put him

down as Captain Osy, or say Admiral Osy. Chilvern thinks this a good idea, and improves upon it, *he* says by proposing to call him to his face " Baron " Osy. I protest, as I don't want to quarrel with the Admiral of the vessel at starting, or even afterwards. He might make the passage uncomfortable to us. He might tell the man at the wheel to steer *into* waves, instead of *over* them, and take every opportunity of splashing us. So I go up and talk to him. He is a foreigner. Odd! a foreigner in command of a British ship. Besides, I thought that *no* foreigners were sailors. Always thought, up to this moment, that that's why Nelson won all his victories—because foreigners were so ill at sea. (*Note* down this now as narrow-minded. Travel expands the ideas.)

Admiral Osy, in answer to my question, answers that, " He not think anybody ill to-day." " Anybody " means, in my question, myself. Cazell is rather anxious about it's being rough outside. The Admiral doesn't know anything about it outside. His opinion generally is that the sea will be like a river to-day, and that we shall do the whole trip in seven hours less than the usual time.

Cazell immediately assumes a knowledge of nautical affairs (my only wonder is that he doesn't *at once* tell the Admiral " what he *ought* to do "), and informs me confidentially, " that we ought to have a splendid passage."

I say, " Ah, it's all very well here," in the river.

Captain Dyngwell, after looking at the clouds through his eyeglass, gives it as his opinion, " That there'll be no end of a tittup outside." I am inclined to agree with him about the " tittup " in this instance, only I feel it won't be confined to " *outside*." Cazell says, " You oughtn't to talk about it."

Perhaps we oughtn't, but we all do, and at once begin comparing experiences as to being unwell.

*Happy Thought.*—Not to boast about being what Captain Dyngwell says *he* is—" Quite the sailor," but observe, modestly, that, " I don't exactly know ; sometimes I'm all right, sometimes I'm all wrong." Inwardly I sincerely hope I shall be all right ; my belief is that I shall be all wrong.

Cazell says, " Lor' bless you, you can't be ill here ; why the sea'll be like glass ; there won't be any tossing."

Chilvern observes, " Yes, that *that's* what he hates—the tossing."

Cazell tells him, " It's not the tossing *you* mean, you ought to say the ' rolling.' The ' roll ' of the vessel makes you unwell."

Chilvern replies, that he dares say it is. Conversation then turns on preventives. Chilvern inclines towards filling yourself with porter and chops. Captain Dyngwell says, " A good stiff glass of brandy's the correct tittup " (everything's a tittup to-day, with him), and he adds, " go in for being quite the drunkard."

None of us think this a good preventive. Cazell says, authoritatively, " You ought to stay on deck *all* the voyage ; or if you think there's a chance of your being ill, then, while you feel *well*, go *at once* to your cabin and lie down."

*Happy Thought.*—Go at once to my cabin.

They all say, " Pooh !—no use until you get out to sea ;" and it appears we shall be seven or eight hours before we're out of the Thames.

Captain Dyngwell says, " The doose we shall ! Why, I thought we got into the briny at Greenwich." Greenwich is *his* farthest point on the Thames.

*Happy Thought.*—Dyngwell's England is bounded by Greenwich and Whitebait.

Say this. Expect roars of laughter. No roars. Cazell takes me aside afterwards and tells me, " You oughtn't to have said that. You don't know him well enough to joke him, and he's a tetchy fellow."

*Happy Thought.*—Lovely day !

We glide along like—like—anything. (Am *not* good at similes.) " Swans " won't do, as we're not going like swans. " Like a nautilus," I propose, in conversation. Captain Dyngwell thinks I might as well say, " like an omnibus." They all laugh. *I* don't. Serve him out. If he had laughed at mine, I would have at his. Chilvern says, " going along like winking," which seems to suit, and we drop the subject.

I make another attempt at raising the tone of conversation by saying, " See how the clouds fleet above us ! it makes one feel " ——Dyngwell cuts in, " There's nothing makes you feel so mops-and-brooms as doing that."

How strange it is ! Here are four fellows met together under conditions for inspiring poetical feelings, and not one of them can think of any simile but " winking," and the other says, that looking up to heaven, while you're sailing, makes you feel all " mops-and-brooms."

*Happy Thought.*—Come down to their level.

Talk of horse-racing, for instance, then bring out newspapers and get seats. Very difficult to sit comfortably on deck : manage it at last on a camp-stool. Chilvern and Dyngwell have both been seized with a strong thirst, apparently from the moment they came on board. Dyngwell is always " doing a little tittup in the way of a moistener," and Chilvern is joining him in what he calls " a modest B and S," brandy and soda-water. I never heard fellows suddenly become so slangy. I feel a loose sort of style coming over me too ; sort of feeling that makes you turn down your collar and dance a hornpipe. Quite understand why a sailor is a roving, rolling, careless sort of dog. Odd, on board I feel inclined to swear, purposelessly, but in keeping with nauticality.

*Happy Thought.*—Dinner.

We are all (at least I am, and I think the others are) surprised to find we *can* take dinner on board. We are all in good spirits. Admiral Osy at the head of the table, that is, in the chair, doing terrific feats with his knife, mouth, and the gravy. Makes one think of the African sword-swallower. Should like to be yachting. What a jovial life a sailor's must be, at least if it's all like this.

*Happy Thought.*—Still in the river.

I say to the Admiral Osy, " I suppose that the sea between here and Antwerp is nothing more than the river, after all." I am anxious to hear his answer. His answer is, " Nasty passage, very, sometimes ; not much pitch to-night ; bad if wind gets round." Don't like the sound of this : will draw him out. I say to him, " I suppose he's seen a deal of nasty weather." I put this in what appears to me a nautical style. The Admiral Osy nods his head, and walks away. Chilvern says to me that he's not rude, only I oughtn't to bother him. Admiral Osy is never without a long clay pipe in his mouth. Chilvern, who is very fond of pipes, says he must get one of them.

"Get 'em—scores," says the Admiral, whose English is disjointed.

"German?" asks Chilvern.  "Dutch," replies the Admiral.

"Dear?" asks Chilvern.  "Cheap," returns the Admiral.

"You're a German, I s'pose?" observes Chilvern, knowingly.

"No; Dutch," answers the Admiral Osy, and stumps away.

*Happy Thought.*—Seen a Dutchman.

From this moment I feel a great interest in the Admiral, a Dutchman.  I say to Cazell, "Doesn't it remind you of Vanderdecken, the Flying Dutchman, and Washington Irving's tales?" Cazell, who is reading a paper, says, "No it doesn't."

The Captain, who has been looking through a small pockettelescope, gives his opinion that "it won't be long before we're in for a bit of a tittup."  He means that the clouds are gathering, and that out at sea it looks rough.

Wonder if the Admiral puts on a cocked-hat when he's out at sea.  Chilvern says, "Better ask him."

*Happy Thought.*—Better not.

*Happy Thought.*—Have a cup of tea.

In cabin, not quite so steady as it was; or perhaps it's fancy, because I've been *told* that we're coming near the sea.  Don't like the cabin now; shall go on deck.  Things seem to have changed on deck, it looks duller.  Evening coming on.

"Aren't we pitching a little?" I ask Cazell, as if merely out of curiosity, and not as taking any personal interest in the movements of the vessel myself.

Cazell says, with a doubtful air, "Yes, I think we're beginning."

## CHAPTER XV.

STILL NAUTICAL—NAUTICAL NOT STILL—BORN A SAILOR—AT SEA—
TURNS—UNCERTAINTY—HOME THOUGHTS — LURCHES — CONUN-
DRUM — OTHER THOUGHTS — PUNS — LE MOMENT — FEARFUL
STRUGGLES—PROSPECTS OF PEACE.

T HE Admiral comes abaft (or astern ; I mean he comes
towards us, and we're about the middle of the ship),
smoking, always smoking. Somehow I didn't notice the smell of
his tobacco before : it begins to be unpleasant ; so does Chilvern's
pipe ; so does Captain Dyngwell's cigar.

"Won't I 'baccy ?" Dyngwell inquires. "No, thank you, I
won't baccy ! " Feel that to baccy just now would be as it were

the turning point (or the turning-up point) in my existence. " If you want to keep well," I say to myself, " be cautious." Cazell says, " I tell you what *you* ought to take—a good glass of stout." No, I don't want stout, specially just after tea : I feel in fact that stout would—but, no matter—no, thank you, I'd better stay on deck.

Night is coming on. We are no longer in the river. Chilvern says, " If it's no worse than this he doesn't mind." I like to hear a fellow cheering up.

*Happy Thought.*—No worse than this, I shall be all right.

Admiral, at the end of his pipe, tells us that the wind's getting round. " Bad ?" asks Chilvern.

Admiral nods and walks abaft, or afore, or somewhere out of sight.

I don't like to turn in. Horrid expression just now " Turning in." Odd, how even an expression seems distasteful to me just now. The Captain has a large overcoat and a rug. He intends to " weather it, and do the regular Tar," he says. I ask him, "If he is ever——?" I don't like to say the word. He doesn't mind it, and takes it out of my mouth. (Bah ! horrid expression again !) " No," he replies, " Never. Stand anything," and he lights another cigar. He politely asks me, "if I mind his baccying?" Of course I politely rejoin that I don't. In reality I feel (despairingly) that it makes no difference to me *now*. I am sure my fate is sealed. Only a question of time.

I miss Cazell. I wish he wouldn't go away. He has gone to be ——no, I won't think of it. Perhaps he hasn't.

*Thoughts (whilst leaning against paddle-box so as to keep in middle of vessel as much as possible. Vessel lurching horribly).* Is travelling worth this? Aren't there many places in England one hasn't seen? Why should I go abroad?

Wish they'd make a tunnel under the sea—or a bridge over it. Never mind expense. Anyone would subscribe handsomely who'd ever been abroad, and had to cross the sea again. Horrid. So helpless too. Recollect suddenly that Cazell told me, before *he* disappeared, that you oughtn't to keep your eyes fixed on one spot. I won't. I feel that I can hardly take them off a lump of something. No ; it's a man lying in a rug with his head on a

camp-stool.   Captain Dyngwell is walking up and down deck,
with his hands in his great-coat pockets, and a cigar in his mouth.
He lurches from side to side occasionally, but still he walks, and
appears to enjoy it.   I can only stick with my back to the paddle-
box.   Chilvern too.   Chilvern volunteers the statement that he
doesn't feel ill, Do I? he asks.   I don't know, I am uncertain.
Perhaps after all—that is—*if I don't talk much or move, I may be
all right.*   Feel that everything is uncertain.   Wish I was at
home : would give a sum of money to be sitting with Friddy.

*Scarcely Happy Thought.*—Remember having heard of somebody
being Home-sick.   (Ugh !—why do I—) I never was *that* * *
but * * *

A lurch.   My camp-stool nearly fell.   A wave has broken over
us from somewhere.   Helpless.   Can't do anything.   Let waves
break over us.   Let the water trickle down to my feet.   Very cold.
Captain comes up unsteadily, but quite well and smoking.   He
has been having hot brandy-and-water with the Admiral.   He asks
us, briskly, " How we're getting on?   Quite the gay Sailor, eh ?"
he inquires jovially of me.   I try to smile, I would smile (to be
something of the gay sailor, and show my spirit to the last), but I
feel that the slightest relaxation of face, or alteration of position,
would be fatal.   Chilvern and myself are against the paddle-box,
with nothing to hold on by, and a strong inclination to fall face
downwards on the deck at every lurch, or roll, or whatever the
horrid action of the ship is called.   *Thought (vaguely).*—There's a
dog called a Lurcher.   When well might make conundrum :
" When is a ship——or——when is a dog * * * * * * *

The vessel now takes a very peculiar motion, and I feel myself,
as it were, following all the very peculiar motions of the vessel in
detail, as if by some internal (and infernal) machinery.   She goes
down with a rush, quivering : so do I : that is, I don't move from
where I am, but the machinery does it.   It seems as if I'd
swallowed the engines.   The vessel slides or glides, and then comes
up with a sort of scooping motion : exactly the same with me.
" On the Scoop "—think of Dyngwell, who seems perfectly happy.

I wonder to myself how Chilvern feels.   I turn my head
slightly to look at him, and notice that he is staring before him
in a blank, helpless manner.   The machinery gives a surging
groan every time we dive down as if we were going right under

the sea, and I feel as if I was being lowered into my boots; we come up again with a rush, and a noise between a shriek and a groan from the machinery. I feel myself entirely dependent on the machinery.

The Captain comes up (he is pacing the deck to keep himself warm) and observes that "We've got a deuced fine passage;" and adds, that "He shouldn't think there'd be a soul ill to-night."—I can't answer him: there's only a glimmer of hope in his speech. My thoughts become gloomy, anything but happy. Except one

*Happy Thought.*—The mind can abstract itself so as to be insensible to pain. Therefore, if I can only think of something else, I shan't be unwell; or rather, as I feel unwell *now*, I shan't be worse, but probably better.

I have tried thinking of conundrums. Perhaps they're too frivolous for this state. Try something else. Think of stars. See only one. Wonder what it is. Think of the ancient sailors who, without compass or ——. *Tremendous lurch.* I struggle against interior machinery, and again try to think of the stars. Wave breaks over vessel. Some one says "That's a nasty one." Perhaps it is. I am past expressing an opinion. If anyone was to point a pistol at me I couldn't run away. Try to recall passages of Shakespeare; to think of my next chapter of *Typical Develop-ments;* to recollect what Sir Peter Groganal's argument on Abstract Right was; to think of—— *Lurch. Wave.* All machinery (internal) in motion. No more stars. Shall I leave paddle-box, *Now, or stop a little longer?* * * * suspense * * * I think I'll move * * * I make for the opposite paddle-box * * striking out with my legs at the deck, and waiting for *it* to come up to me * * jerk to the right * * just miss cannoning against Captain, who is pacing up and down (still with a cigar), and dexterously gets out of my way.

*Happy Thought (flash across me even at this supreme moment).—Decks-terously * * wretched * *

I am looking down into the dark waters—at the white foam * * * * if the bulwarks were suddenly to give way! * * * * Can I help it? * * * * * * * * Lurch * * roll * * stagger * * grapple with bulwarks * * silent anguish.

Can anything on the Continent be worth this!!!!! Cathedrals

—Churches—pictures—pleasures of Paris—*can't* be worth *this*
* * * And * * Oh! *I've got to come back again ! ! !* Stagger to
staircase * * Companion, I mean.

"Quite the jovial Tar, eh?" asks the Captain, who is lighting
another filthy, beastly cigar.

"Yes," I answer, in somebody else's voice, not mine, and feeling
that, if I could see my face, I should never recognise the once
joyous author of *Typical Developments.*

Go down-stairs ; horribly awkward stairs. Why couldn't they
be made straight down instead of curling round? specially in a
steamboat * * * * when * * * one so * * * particularly
* * * wants to go straight * * * *

To my Cabin.—Will undress and regularly get into bed.

*Happy Thought.*—Give myself the idea of being quite at home.

Haven't fastened door : it bangs against me, I against it, then it
bangs back again, when I bang against chair, then against side,
then my head against upper berth, then nearly into lower berth,
then over portmanteau, then clutch on desperately by side of
lower berth, and try to recover myself. Tear my things off; try
to hang them up neatly. Dash at a hook. The hook comes to
me and I fall back against berth. Everything seems to be going
topsy-turvy. Collapse, like a punch-doll, without any middle
joints, into lower berth. On the whole rather astonished to find
myself there.

Shut my eyes ! * * * * Open them again very quickly.
Awful sensation. I am wide awake, and painfully conscious of the
oil-lamp, and of the want of air. Out of berth again, to open the
door—same performance as before. Put chair adroitly between
open door and wall : chance of air now. Stagger—bump—pause
for breath. Stagger again : fighting with everything, berth,
washstand, door, chairs, which all, apparently, keep coming at me.
I notice the name of Scott Russell in the washing-stand basin
* * * I hold on * * * I wonder * * * Did Scott Russell make
the washstand * * * or the ship * * * if so * * * why didn't
he * * * Lurch—bang * * * * * * Into berth again, backwards, anyhow, exhausted. This is what Dyngwell calls a "Tittup
outside." * * * * * * Ah * * * * * * Shall I have to get up
again? * * * * * * * If not * * * * I think I can * * * * * *
Less Lurching * * * *

# CHAPTER XVI.

IMPROVEMENT—STILL ON BOARD—CAZELL—THE PILOT—MORNING—
WASH AND BRUSH UP—PLAN—ANTWERP—ARCHITECTURE—
A CICERONE—THE LIGHTS—CHILVERN'S CHANGE—HIS COSTUME
—QUITE THE TOURIST.

AM better.

Sleep, gentle sleep, or an imitation of it, with people walking about, shouting, shutting off steam, going backwards and going forwards, and apparently getting (thank heaven!) into still water.

Cazell looks in once, and looks out again very quickly. He merely puts his head in at the door with the view, I believe, to tell me "What I ought to do" under the circumstances, but he thinks better of it. Chilvern comes down—he says he is very jolly *now*. I won't attend to him.

I'm afraid he's coming to occupy the other berth above me. Dreadful! He'll drag my things about, and tumble over my boots.

*Happy Thought.*—Pretend to be asleep.

*Ruse* successful. He looks in, says, "Hallo! asleep? eh? The pilot's come on board," and then he disappears. He re-appears at intervals after this, to inform me (if awake) that, 1st, the pilot *hasn't* come on board; 2ndly, that the pilot *won't* come on board; 3rdly, that the pilot *can't* come on board (we are pitching awfully, and horrors are returning); 4thly, that if this pilot doesn't come on board, we must get a pilot who *will;* 5thly, that they can't get a pilot at all; 6thly, that the pilot *has* come on board. Altogether, I wish the pilot was——but it doesn't matter now.

*Morning.*—Recognise feeble portrait of myself in the looking-glass. Recognise several other feeble portraits of yesterday's originals at breakfast.

Captain Dyngwell comes out of a cabin, "Fit," he says, "as a fiddle."

Cazell re-appears. He has not been seen since nine o'clock last night, when he told somebody "what he *ought* to do," and then vanished down the companion.

He looks as if he'd been to a ball for three nights together, and was going to bed.

Captain Dyngwell says that Cazell "looks as if he'd been on the scoop," which strikes me, somehow, as expressive, though not capable of exact definition. "Slang," some one says, "is the language of the future;" if so, Captain Dyngwell is a sort of gay Wagner.

All more or less represent the Great Unwashed. Chilvern, who is five feet two, represents the Small Unwashed.

N.B. No amount of basining (Scott Russell & Co.) *can* be satisfactory on board. Look forward to bath at hotel. Wish I hadn't put my comb and brush and clean pocket-handkerchief in some (apparently) secret part of my portmanteau.

*Happy Thought.*—To have a bag, specially for this sort of thing, with compartments, so that whatever you want at the moment comes out first.

It appears there have been some difficulties with the pilot, and so we are some hours late. This accounts for Chilvern's several visits to me during the night. He was much interested in the pilot, he says; if he hadn't been, he adds, he should have been unwell, or rather, worse than he actually was.

*Happy Thought.*—Shore. Antwerp.

Captain Dyngwell says, "Here's Antwerp," pointing it out to us, which is unnecessary, as there is no other place near at hand.

I say, "Thank you, I know it." Consequent coolness between Captain and self. Custom-House officers. Chalked baggage. Crush. I assure a passenger who is digging into me with an umbrella, a bag, and an Alpine stick, that "there is no hurry." Man in front, whom I am pushing, tells me the same thing. We all struggle and push. Difficult to carry two rugs, umbrella, stick, and coat, to struggle and kick, and at the same time to get one's ticket out of one's waistcoat pocket. Do it though, somehow, desperately. Suppose I should lose it at the last moment?

*Happy Thought.*—Carry it in my teeth : like Newfoundland dog with a stick.

Collector takes it. Ceremony over. Cross the plank. Dangerous. Take breath, and look about.

Captain and Cazell get off first. Chilvern and self follow. Hôtel de St. Antoine. AT ANTWERP.

*Happy Thought.*—Foreign Town.

Our party of four is split up into, so to speak, three sub-parties. First Sub-party is Captain Dyngwell, who doesn't particularly care about seeing anything, and when I say, " Why, my *dear* Sir, look at the Churches !" he merely answers, " Oh, blow the churches !" evidently not the spirit in which to come to Antwerp. He is entirely, as he expresses it, "for a tittup at the theatre, and then some sort of Bal Mabille," here he winks knowingly behind his eyeglass, "and go in for a regular rumti-iddity." Whereupon he calls out "Waiter !" imperiously, with an aside to us that "he'll bustle 'em a bit," and on the appearance of the waiter, the captain orders a " B and S," just as if he were in his London club, and confounds the fellow's ignorance when his command is not exactly understood.

Second Sub-party is myself and Chilvern. Bond of sympathy between us is that he really *does* want to see the town. Being an architect, he will enjoy (I know he will, and I tell him so) the queer old buildings, the Cathedral, the other Churches, and the pictures. Don't know why, being an architect, he should enjoy pictures ; but it seems natural when you think of it for the first time. Years ago I've been to Antwerp. Chilvern observes, " You'll be able to show me everything." He adds, " that he likes going about with a fellow who really can show him everything, and who has an artistic appreciation of queer buildings, old houses, fine churches, and pictures."

Dyngwell says, " If you've seen one, you've seen all." We agree, when talking Dyngwell over, that the Captain isn't troubled with brains. [*Analytical Physiological note for Typ. Devel.* Isn't this a form of mental pride ? Isn't it also flattery ? It means that Chilvern has a great quantity of brains—so great as to be troubled by them—and that I have also. It's as much as if I said to Chilvern, "I say, you're a clever fellow, because if I don't you won't say *I'm* a clever fellow." Wonder what Chilvern says of me to Dyngwell. In speaking of Chilvern to Dyngwell, I say with truth, that "Chilvern's clever in his own line," meaning architecture; this is after we've seen the pictures and the town.

*Happy Thought.*—Chilvern *can't* say that of me—nobody can, in fact—because I haven't got a particular line.]

Third Sub-party. Cazell. By himself. He says he has been a great deal on the Continent, and will insist upon telling every one what he *ought* to do. Besides, he pretends to know the language. He also orders, with an air of superior knowledge, dishes and drinks, which he says are peculiar to the place. He talks German and French. That is, he talks German, but I don't think much of his French. We fall out, in fact, on this subject. He professes to speak it like a native. I own I don't do that; but I say I have a thorough knowledge of it, and can read it easily. Chilvern takes my view of the question. I like Chilvern. A very good fellow, and really clever as an architect; only I *do* wish he had come abroad with more money than two sovereigns in English money. Will I lend him some? Yes. But why can't he ask Dyngwell or Cazell? I don't exactly put this to him in so many words, but he intimates that he can't go to *them* for it, as he has "rather quarrelled with *them* by siding with *me*?"

*Happy Thought.*—To tell him he must write home for money at once. See him do it, and post the letter myself.

He is bound to me now. He will fight for my opinions as a sort of mercenary.

*Happy Thought.*—To secure a companion, I promise to pay for him everywhere, but I won't lend him any ready money. I point out to him that I am going to show him the town, and that our tastes assimilate. If he had the money in his pocket, perhaps our tastes wouldn't assimilate.

Cazell tells us we ought to go and see the Cathedral (it isn't a Cathedral, I say,—dispute), and the Church of St. Jacques and St. Paul, also the Museum of Pictures.

I reply that I will take Chilvern to see the great Church, then the Museum, &c., in fact, choosing my own arrangement.

The head waiter asks me, "Will I have a guide?"

I am indignant. As indignant as if I'd lived in Antwerp all my life. Hate guides. Explain to Chilvern that it's no use having a guide, one can find one's way so easily about Antwerp.

Chilvern replies, "yes;" then suddenly, "I say, let's go and have some lunch."

I inform him that abroad there is no such thing as lunch, it's *déjeûner à la fourchette.* "All right," he replies, "let's go and have anything that's something to eat."

I notice, for the first time, that Chilvern, in Antwerp, is peculiarly and offensively English. He seems to have learnt slang, or a slangy manner from Dyngwell.

He is dressed in a suit of what *he* calls "dittos" and a wide-awake hat.

*Happy Thought.*—To stop him *before* we get out of the hotel, and say, "You can't go out like that."

"Why not?" asks Chilvern.

"Well, my dear fellow,"—I put it to him reasonably,—"you wouldn't do it in a town in England."

"Wouldn't I!" he exclaims, and cocks his wide-awake on one side.

I request him as a favour, to get his hat, and put on a black coat.

"Haven't got a hat or a black coat," he returns.

"Quite the tourist," observes Dyngwell, with his feet on a small table in the courtyard of the hotel smoking a cigar. *He*, at all events, is well dressed. He *is* sensible on that point. I hold him up as a model to Chilvern.

I hesitate about going out with Chilvern. Chilvern says, "It's all ridiculous humbug." I reply, "That it isn't." He returns, "That it *is.*" I observe, "That he ought to consider other people's feelings." He rejoins, "That I ought to consider *his.*" I tell him "I do." He answers flatly "You don't!"

*Happy Thought.*—Say I won't lend him any money.

*Happy Thought.*—No, not say it, let him *think* it. See by his face that he *is* thinking it. Row ends. We go out. To *déjeûner* somewhere.

## CHAPTER XVII.

ANTWERP — CHILVERN'S FUN — SNOBBISM—EATING—DRINKING—THE
CRESSES—*CHILVERN LE POLISSON*—THE CARTE—THE LANGUAGE
—*THE DEJEUNER PROGRESSES*—SALAD—*MONEY.*

WE find a *café* in an open sort of square.

I call for the *carte.* Chilvern makes some joke about *cart* and *horse,* something about eating horse cutlets.

*Happy Thought.* — Stop his English, by telling him that it's dangerous to talk it when every one understands, though they don't speak it.

Waiter attends. "*Que désirez-vous?*" I ask Chilvern, in an off-hand manner.

*Happy Thought.*—*Garçon* thinks I'm a Frenchman. [On considering this question at night quietly, Chilvern says, "That the feeling is snobbish." "Snobbish!" I retort. "Yes," he replies, "A fellow's a snob who wishes to be considered anything better or worse than he really is."

Wish I'd never lent him any money. *This is a note at the end of the day.* Ever since he's become bound to me he's been disagreeable.]

Chilvern says, laughing, as if it was the greatest joke in the world, "Ask the cove if he's got some roast beef and plum puddang." ["Plum-pud*dang*" is *his* notion of fun in French.]

I *hate* this sort of thing. I tell Chilvern so afterwards. Hate calling a waiter "a cove," and ask for plum-pudding in the middle of the day. He wouldn't do it if he was in England. He replies, "Yes, he would, if he liked." Hate a man who's provoking.

*Happy Thought.*—Not express disgust publicly before waiters in *café*, but smile as if I was tolerating a *drôle*.

*Happy Thought.*—Call Chilvern in French a *polisson*. *Garçon* smiles.

Chilvern replies, "*Wee*, let's have some of that," thinking I'd spoken of fish.

The waiter here asks me a long question in rapid French. Haven't an idea what he means.

*Happy Thought.*—Won't tell Chilvern that I don't understand him. Consider for a few seconds, then reply, in French, "Yes, but make haste." *Garçon* says something, and hurries off. Wonder what the dickens I've agreed to? Wonder what this will result in. Chilvern asks me, "What did the waiter say?"

*Happy Thought.*—To answer, "Oh, only something about what we are going to have." Chilvern presses to know what we *are* going to have.

*Happy Thought.*—To say, slily, "*You'll see.*" So shall I, for at this minute I haven't a notion what I've ordered, by saying, "Yes; but make haste" to the waiter.

*Happy Thought.*—I shall find out soon, though; and then If I don't like it, won't do it again. Just coming from England, one's out of practice at these things.

While Chilvern and myself are waiting for our *déjeûner*, I begin to feel the rolling of the vessel again. I remark this as "very curious" to Chilvern. "Curious," perhaps, I think to myself, is hardly the word. Chilvern observes (also carelessly) that he is experiencing the same sensation. We look at one another—we know what we mean. Begin to fear we shan't enjoy lunch. Wonder what I've ordered by saying "*oui*" to the *garçon*. Here he comes. *Voilà.*

Three little dishes,—sardines, butter, and radishes.

*Happy Thought.—Hors-d'œuvres.*

Chilvern asks which are *hors-d'œuvres.* I explain to him. He at once commences with a sardine and bread-and-butter. I tell him, to encourage him in foreign manners, that that's quite the correct thing to do, and eat some myself, also a radish.

*Garçon* appears with a fish of some sort done up in oil, with mushrooms, (I think,) truffles (I fancy,) and mussels (I am not quite sure about these, but, as it's not oyster season, they must be mussels). "What wine?"

"Well," says Chilvern, "I should say——"

I know he's going to ask for beer, and stop him with *Happy Thought (before Chilvern can answer).—Vin ordinaire.*

Explain to Chilvern that this is the correct thing. Chilvern, who is much pleased with the first course, says, "capital idea of yours," to me, "ordering fish. What is it?"

*Happy Thought.—Sole Hollandaise.* This is as good a title as any other,—better.

Odd, by the way, this fish coming, as I didn't recognise the word *poisson* when the waiter asked me rapidly that question about what I'd have, or how I'd have it.

*Happy Thought.*—Another time will call for the *carte*, and point out each dish that I want—no mistake then.

Waiter appears with the wine.

Chilvern says, "I wish you'd ask for a pepper-box and salt-spoon."

I frown at him. I tell him that it's a Continental custom *not* to have salt-spoons (I don't see any), but to take it out of the salt-cellar with your knife.

"Horrid custom!" says Chilvern.

This is what I don't like in Chilvern abroad; he is insular. Because *we* have pepper-casters, therefore all the world must. [*For psychological analysis,—a note in pocket-book.* Is it by force of antagonism that I suddenly become pre-eminently foreign, and peculiarly un-English, when with such a mind as Chilvern's?

Good article for *Typ. Devel.* Heading, *Ant.* Word, *Antagonism.* Division, M. *Mental.*] I help myself with my knife to salt, and with my fingers to pepper.

*Garçon* adds watercresses to the *hors-d'œuvres.* "Bravo!" I exclaim. "*J'aime beaucoup le cresson!*"

"Watercresses, by Jingo!" shouts Chilvern. He begs my pardon for his excitement, but says he really thought that 'cresses were peculiarly English. I beg him not to shout. Some young men (French or Belgian) are breakfasting at another table, and turn round to stare at him.

I say, "*Vous êtes un Anglais pour rire.*"

*Happy Thought.*—To ignore my own nationality, and pretend to be a foreigner (of some sort—don't know exactly what), taking an Englishman out for a holiday.

*Happy Thought (when I say L'Anglais pour rire).*—Seen this somewhere in a French picture. Don't wonder at the idea, if the French take their notions of *us* from men who behave like Chilvern. Wish I'd come alone.

*Happy Thought.*—To suggest to Chilvern that, if he holds his tongue, they won't know what he is.

Chilvern replies, "You be blowed!" If it wasn't mean, I'd tell him that I wouldn't lend him any more money. Everything is "odd," and "rum," and "queer," in Chilvern's eyes. He has got into a habit (from being with the Captain, I think) of calling every one a "cove." He observes, "What rum coves those are!" meaning at the other table. I tell him, deprecatingly, that *I* see nothing "rum" about them. I reproach him with being insular. He replies, "Oh! insular be blowed."

Waiter brings cutlets. Admirable. It seems then I ordered cutlets—fish and cutlets. He then adds salad. He asks me a question. I am taken by surprise.

*Happy Thought.*—Oui.

Result of the answer is that he takes the salad away.

"What's he done that for?" asks Chilvern.

I am obliged to own that I don't know, "but fancy," I add, "that he misunderstood me."

*Happy Thought.*—To add, by way of explanation to Chilvern,

that it's the custom. Chilvern won't be satisfied. Waiter brings salad back again : he took it away to mix it.

*Happy Thought.*—Now then coffee and cigar. This, I explain to Chilvern, is the real delight of *déjeûnering* abroad in any *café*— you can always smoke immediately.

" *Du café, garçon* " (in an off-hand manner).

" *Deux ?* "

" You'll take some?" I ask Chilvern, to show him that I *can* hold a conversation with the waiter.

" Yes, I'll have caffy," replies Chilvern.

" *Oui, deux tasses,*" I translate.

We begin to lounge luxuriously. Suddenly motion of vessel returns. Horrid. I hope * * *

Coffee arrives. Chilvern produces cigars, and I ask the waiter for fire.

" *C'est défendu de fumer ici si tôt,*" he informs us apologetically.

I can't believe it. Being unable to argue the point satisfactorily with him, I can only explain to Chilvern that this is not France, but Belgium. Chilvern says, then let's pay and go. As much as to say, "Let's go to France, and not stay in Belgium." Both dissatisfied.

*Garçon.*—" *L'addition.*"

It turns out that we have had the only two dishes that were not on the *carte du jour*, and that the waiter had asked me, " Would I leave it to him to order?" and it was to this I had answered "*Oui.*" Horridly dear : thought everything (especially *vin ordinaire*) was so cheap abroad. Eight francs a-piece. I explain to Chilvern that this is very different to France. Chilvern (who hasn't had to pay) returns, uninterestedly, "Is it?"

*Happy Thought.*—Put down in pocket-book everything I pay for Chilvern, or he may say I didn't. Shall astonish him by-and-bye. He doesn't know what he's spending ; and therefore doesn't seem to care. Also keep the bill. We walk out. Wish Chilvern hadn't brought his umbrella. Suit of dittos, coloured wideawake, and umbrella. "Quite," as Captain Dyngwell remarked before, "the tourist." The people will think he's a Cook's excursionist, or some sort of "there and back for seven shillings," or "a Happy Day at Antwerp for half-a-crown."

## CHAPTER XVIII.

CHILVERN stops at every shop.

*Happy Thought.*—To walk on and leave him.

When I do this I hear behind me (this in the open street, too),
"Hi, old boy! hi! look here! Here's a rum thing."

In Antwerp there is a statue—an object of religious devotion
—at the corner of nearly every street. People going past, I
notice, generally touch their hats. Chilvern stops opposite one
larger than the rest : a light is burning before it.

"Hi! hallo! look here!" he cries. "Ain't this a rum go?
This is a queer sort of dodge for lighting the streets."

A A

*Happy Thought.*—To take his arm. I explain (I am always explaining to Chilvern) the meaning of these figures. I beg him not to expose himself (and *me*) to ridicule. I point out that already his umbrella and costume have attracted the little dirty boys. His appearance *does* rather remind one of "the swell" in a pantomime: dressed in enormously loud check "dittos." Thank goodness he hasn't got a white shiny hat turned up with green. They (the dirty boys) are really following us, and laughing at us—I mean at *him ;* but, unfortunately, we are together.

*Happy Thought.*—Turn down a street.

Boys still following : joined by other boys. Chilvern getting angry, turns suddenly on them with his umbrella. Yells, scrimmage, shouts. Quite the swell in the pantomime losing his temper with clown and crowd, at the end of a scene.

It occurs to me, as a stranger here, what must be the feelings of that unhappy Chinaman whom one sees in London, perpetually walking about in the costume of his country, pursued by little ill-bred, dirty, vagabond boys. We are in precisely the same position, all through Chilvern's confounded "dittos" and umbrella. There really isn't another man dressed like him in Antwerp.

*Happy Thought.*—See the door of a church open. Enter. Refuge from persecuting boys.

*Happy Thought.*—Sanctuary in the olden time. Boys peep in after us, but a verger, or some sort of official person in seedy black, darts out at them from a recess, and hits the ringleader over the head with a bunch of keys. Delighted. *We* are. Rout of boys.

*Happy Thought.*—If we stay long enough in here, boys will get tired of waiting outside. Luckily, it is, we discover, the Church of St. Jacques. The seedy black man locks the door, and commences at once to take us round the church and explain. He is the regular guide.

Of all things I hate it is what Chilvern does at this minute.

He winks at me, and puts his hand in a side-pocket, where there is something bulky, which hitherto I had thought was a large cigar-case. No. Out comes—a big red book.

*Murray's Guide to Belgium.*

Suit of dittos, coloured wide-awake, umbrella, and *Murray's Guide-book !* And I was hoping that we shouldn't be taken for English ! If the boys see this when he comes out, it will be worse than——

*Happy Thought.*—To borrow it of him, and leave it, when he's not looking, in one of the side-chapels. Do it. Wonder what devotional Belgian will think of this book when she finds it on going to Mass to-morrow. Murray's Guide to Mass.

*Happy Thought.*—Leave Antwerp to-morrow, and go on to Aix. Not so much " leave *Antwerp*" as leave Chilvern.

He is a nuisance. Respectably dressed, I shouldn't mind him. If he had his own money with him, I could get rid of him. But in his, as it were, celebrated character of a British Excursionist in a suit of " dittos," and entirely dependent upon *me* for money, Chilvern *is* a nuisance.

*Happy Thought.*—Like the Monster in *Frankenstein.* I'm *Frankenstein :* Monster in " dittos " with umbrella.

He has contracted a habit of staring about him, stopping at corners and before shop-windows.

*Happy Thought (while he's in front of a picture-shop window).*— Go on some way ahead, as if I was not connected with him. He'd be sure to find his way to the hotel again. If he didn't, though ? He can't be robbed, as he has no money, and has only got a steel watch guard with a bunch of keys at the end of it.

" Hi ! Hi ! Hi !" Chilvern shouting. " Here ! Look here, I say. Here's such a rum cove at the corner of the street !"

The " rum cove " turns out to be a monk of some order or another. I suppress the strong desire to regard him curiously, and only say, as a lesson to Chilvern, " Oh, of course that's nothing here. *Do* come on."

*Happy Thought.*—Take his arm, and walk him along briskly

Chilvern can't get over the monk. " Why," he says to me, " he had regular sandals." I am silent. A few seconds afterwards, he continues, suddenly, " Why, he was shaved all over his head !" His next idea on the subject is that " he'd make his fortune at Covent Garden in the season, at so much a night, for the *Huguenots* or *Favorita.*"

Why can't Chilvern see that he offends the prejudices of the people by talking out loud like this, and staring at a monk? *I* don't stare at a monk. I should like to, but I don't.

We go to the Museum—where the picture-gallery is. Woman at gate wants to know if I'll have a catalogue. Chilvern says, "Oh, yes, do have a catalogue!" and takes one off the counter. This costs me three francs. He shouldn't take it and open it, and read in it, before it's paid for. He replies, that it's all the same to him, as it's in French, and he can't make it out. Shall certainly go on to Aix to-morrow, and leave Chilvern.

*In the Gallery.*—Full of Old Masters. Students at easels making copies in oils. I like enjoying pictures by myself. Get away from Chilvern. He is at one end of the room, I in the middle. I am admiring a masterpiece by some Flemish artist, date 1406. What queer attitudes people fell into then!

While I am making this note, I hear Chilvern shouting—positively shouting—"Hi! Look here, I say!" to me. Everybody turns round, and stares. The whole place is disturbed.

*Happy Thought.*—Ignore him.

He won't be ignored. He comes towards me, calling all the way, "I say, *do* look here! Come along. Here's such a rum go!" I return, quietly, "I wish, Chilvern, you would not insult the prejudices of foreigners, like this. It really does *not* do. You wouldn't shout like this in the Royal Academy." "No," says Chilvern, knowingly, "but this *isn't* the Academy." I tell him that his answer is not clever, and is *not* a repartee. He drops the subject, and continues in a tone a little more subdued, "But I say, *do* come and see this." I ask him what it is. He is bursting with the discovery of an artistic curiosity, and leads the way quickly up the room, stopping at last in front of a picture. Everyone is watching him. The students are eyeing him with interest. I walk up slowly, staying on my way before a picture of a St. Francis. Most of the subjects are religious.

Chilvern thinks I am not coming, so he shouts out again, "Look here! do come, here it is! Look! Here's an old cove praying like anything, and two other coves kissing behind a door."

He thinks I'll laugh at this. I tell him I am annoyed. Referring sternly to the Catalogue I found the picture he alludes to is

*St. Bonaventura in an ecstasy, a Pope and a Cardinal standing in the antechamber.*

I tell Chilvern once for all that I really will *not* go about with him, if he behaves like this. He has a rude unpleasant habit of leaning over the students' shoulders while they are at work, and examining their paintings as if he understood them critically. I remonstrate with him.

"Lor bless you," he replies, "they rather like it ; they think I'm going to buy."

A small bandy-legged amateur is hard at work before an *Adoration of the Magi*, by Rubens. His manipulation is most creditable. Judging from a distance I should say this earnest student will make a good copy, and will advance in his art. Chilvern looks over his shoulder—quite bends over him. I think the little man rather resents this as he shakes his head sharply, and a slip of the brush is the result. Instead of begging his pardon and taking off his hat politely, Chilvern observes to him with a wink, "Hallo, Rubens Junior, you're making a nice muck o' this, *you* are." Disgusting ! The student doesn't understand English, and says so, in French.

*Happy Thought.*—Leave the Gallery while Chilvern isn't looking. If he picks me up I'll take him back to the hotel, and leave hi there.

Lost my way. Thought I recollected the streets : ask at a shop. Will they have the goodness to show me the route to the Hôtel de St. Antoine ? They understand the question in French, or they catch the name. A little woman bustles out into the street, catches me by the elbow, and gives me directions in rapid Flemish —at least, I suppose it's Flemish ; if not, it's German. Perhaps German *and* Flemish. I thank her politely.

*Happy Thought.*—Say *Merci beaucoup*, and take off my hat. She appears dissatisfied with her own instructions, and recommences more volubly and more emphatically than before. I'm to do something "rechts," then "links."

*Happy Thought.*—Watch her arms and hands. During the instructions she makes herself into sign-posts. Deduction from watching : *Rechts* is Right : *Links* is left.

I again say, *Merci beaucoup*, salute her more profoundly than before, and she retires to the door of her shop.

As I haven't understood her in the least, what is the best thing to do ?

*Happy Thought.*—Walk straight on.   I look back : she is watching my movements.   I bow again, to encourage her in the idea that I have clearly comprehended everything she has been telling me.

Looking back again, I find the delay has just upset my plans. Here is Chilvern running after me, waving his umbrella and shouting, "Hi ! here ! stop !   I say, stop !"

*Happy Thought.*—Better stop, as he's attracting attention, and I might be taken for a thief, or the boys might come out again. Hang Chilvern.   I let him come up with me.   "To-morrow," I tell him decidedly, " I go on to Aix, and leave you."

## CHAPTER XIX.

ACCOUNTS—MEMS — DIFFERENCES — CHARACTER — ROUND SUM—AC-
QUAINTANCES—VOW—SIGNED—ROW—WAKING MOMENTS—DODGE.

**HAPPY THOUGHT** (*before
I go away from Antwerp*).—
Find out *exactly* how we (that
is, Chilvern and I) stand.

This is a polite way of putting
the question, "How much does
Chilvern owe me?" Chilvern
himself says that's just what he
wants to know. Have I kept an
account? "Yes, I have," I am
able to answer, "to a certain extent,
and we can leave the rest to
memory." Chilvern says *his*
memory's a very good one: so, I
return, is mine.

I know I put down most of what
I paid for Chilvern in my pocket-
book, yet, on looking carefully
through it, I can only find one
entry—"Chilvern, *Soap*, 1fr. 50c."

[This discussion takes place in
our bed-room on my last evening
in Antwerp. Dyngwell and Cazell
have, I believe, quarrelled, and are
enjoying themselves separately.]

Chilvern remembers the soap. "Odd!" he says. "Now I
come to think of it, I can't call to mind anything else."

I search the pocket-book again. I *know* I entered his account
somewhere, and headed it in large letters, "Chilvern."

*Happy Thought* (*while I am looking in note-book*).—His share of
the *déjeûner à la fourchette*.

Chilvern admits this. "How much?" "Seven francs" (at a
guess). Chilvern thinks it was six; because he says "Don't I

recollect asking him whether it was fifty or a hundred centimes that went to a franc."

No, I *don't* recollect this. I shouldn't have asked such a question. "Well," says Chilvern, "I know you asked me something about centimes, because you didn't want to change another franc, and wished to use the coppers in your pocket."

[*Note here for Typical Developments.*—My mind is so constituted to believe in others, that if a man positively asserts something, and continuously goes on asserting it, I give in : against my better judgment, I give in.]

How a man's character comes out in travelling ! Chilvern is obstinate. Chilvern is ungrateful. Chilvern is niggardly. Again, what I did *not* expect, Chilvern repudiates, and condescends to mere details. I am at least three pounds twelve shillings and sixpence out of pocket by him, and he says "he doesn't see how I make that out." I answer that "*I* don't go into details, but put it down as a round sum, which may be a little more one way or the other."

He says he doesn't see what there is beyond "soap" and "breakfast." I tell him, "Lots of little things, that mount up."

*Happy Thought.*—To say, playfully, "I'll draw it out as a bill." If this wasn't said playfully, I feel it might be unpleasant.

|  | Fr. | c. |
|---|---|---|
| Porters from boat and hotel . . . | 2 | 0 |
| For several things on board boat . . | 5 | 0 |
| Breakfast, 7.0 ; Cigars, 3.0 . | 10 | 0 |
| Catalogue at Museum . . . . | 3 | 0 |
| Tips to men for showing churches, &c. (at least) . | 7 | 0 |
| Soap, 1.50 ; Matches, 0.25 . . . . . | 1 | 75 |
| Total . . | 28 | 75 |

These are all I can recollect. Then there's the hotel bill. Chilvern admits it will be all right, if I lend him three pounds more to take him back again. I say, "Won't Cazell do that?" He returns, that he'd rather not ask Cazell.

*Happy Thought.*—Say, "We'll see about it to-morrow." Will pretend to forget it, and get off by the train when he's out of the way.

To bed.

*Happy Thought.*—Tell Chilvern to go and see the Cathedral to-morrow morning at 11·30. Give him a franc to do it with. My train starts at 12·15; and directly he has gone I can be off. Leave him to Cazell.

*In bed (with note-book).*—Can't sleep, whether it's the foreign atmosphere or whether it isn't I don't know. I ought to be tired, but I am not.

*Happy Thought.* -Take note-book and jot.

Jot down memoranda. Perhaps while I'm jotting mems. for future. I may recollect what I've spent on Chilvern. Shan't travel with Chilvern again unless he has money, and hasn't a suit of dittos. Also, he *must* be less insular and narrow.

*A propos* of " narrow," *note* for my own improvement ; *mems.*, Books to read while I'm away ; French—Balzac (what works?—find 'em out and select two or three), Victor Hugo's *l'Homme qui Rit*. Also some standard works, say Molière's plays. While I'm taking baths at Aix, might devote my time to learning German, and reading Goethe's *Faust* in the original. List of books also to read when I return Froude's twelve volumes. *Must* read this : every one who reads anything talks about this.

Met an elderly gentleman and his sister, who were well up in it, to-day, in the hotel drawing-room.

*Happy Thought (in reply to any question about Froude).*—No ; I've not been right through it yet. The next question will be, probably, " Of course you've read his third volume?" To which the reply (if you haven't) must be, thoughtfully, " Let me see,—the third volume, -what is that about?—I forget at this moment ——" Then rely upon your interrogator, who, ten to one, is a humbug after all. *Note.*—People read History by short cuts now-a-days, in Reviews.

*Happy Thought.*—Will make the acquaintance of a German philosopher, and ask him what he thinks of the idea of *Typical Developments.* Get him to translate it. Should like very much to get into a set of German philosophers. Must learn German. I'm sure my leading ideas are thoroughly German—deep and profound : only while one is with such men as Dyngwell, Boodels, Milburd, Chilvern, and so forth, one fritters away one's deeper feelings. I'm waiting my time.

As I finish this note, and am about to blow out the candle, I record this, as a sort of vow or resolution, in writing.

(Chilvern's room is next to mine. I never heard such *fearful* snoring: "fearful" is the word.)

*Resolution.*—I have two months or so before me. Got to get rid of rheumatic gout (if any in me, which must be discovered) at Aix. While there will study German, and go in for German philosophy. Will avoid all frivolity, and take this opportunity of working at *Typical Developments*, Vol. I., in order to have it out with Popgood and Groolly at the beginning of the year. This I vow. Signed (in bed).

If there is anything I detest, it is a fellow snoring when you want to go to sleep yourself. I call to him. More snoring. I will call till I wake him. Call. Snore. Call. Louder snore—apparently derisive. Call. Snore: irritating to the last degree. Call again. Shout. Thumping at wall: man next door begs (in American-English) I won't do that. I reply that it's a fellow snoring. Call to Chilvern again. Louder. American next door shouts out that he'll complain to the hotel manager. I tell him that I really must stop a friend of mine's snoring. The door between Chilvern's room and mine is open, that's why I hear him so plainly. Why should I get out and shut it? "Hi! Chilvern, wake up!" American, next room, thumping, wants to know if I mean to insult him and his wife?

No, I don't. Confound Chilvern! These Americans think nothing of revolvers, and in a foreign country he'd be applauded for calling me out. Chilvern suddenly grunts, gasps, and, apparently, wakes himself up with a start. He asks, "What is it?" vaguely, and adds, that "he's just been dreaming of frogs." I tell him to shut his door. He won't get out of bed. No more will I. He says, "Shut it yourself, if you don't like it." I tell him it's *his* door. He says, "It's yours as much as mine." Row. He suddenly changes his tone (it occurs to him, probably, that I may not lend him his three pounds, or may go off without paying his share of the bill), and, getting out of bed, shuts the door.

Never catch me with Chilvern again. Shall certainly send him to the Cathedral to-morrow, and leave while he's there.

## CHAPTER XX.

ADIEU !—ANVERS !—TICKETS—CHILVERN FINISHED—*CHANGE-T-ON?*—
THE BUFFET—STOPPAGE—COCKALORUMS—AIX LA CHAPELLE
—BAGGAGE—FLY—L'HÔTEL—PICK UP NAMES—OBSERVATIONS—
RECEPTION—POPULARITY—LANGUAGE—NOVELTIES—CHAMBER-
MAID—RESTAURANTS—RETURN—MISTAKE.

A T THE Railway Station, Antwerp, *en route for Aix.*—
Rather a crowd at the ticket place, and I come in at the
tail. My ear not having been accustomed to rapidly-spoken
French (by-the-way, I wonder how a Frenchman ever masters the
names of our stations as called out by the porters?) I am unable
to grasp the exact sum demanded of me for my ticket.

*Happy Thought.*—Put down a Napoleon, and see what change
comes out of it.

Clerk doesn't take it, but says something more rapidly in French.

*Happy Thought.*—Say *bien*, and put down another Napoleon.

I am not able to count the change, owing to being pushed away by an excited person behind, and led off, at once, by an intelligent porter to get my luggage weighed, for which I have to pay almost as much as for myself.

I suddenly come upon Dyngwell in a smoking carriage. We are the only two—the Captain and myself—out of our original party, going to Aix. He informs me that Chilvern received some money this morning from London. End of Chilvern. Still he's got to settle up with *me*.

I make a point of asking the guard at every station, whether we change here. Nothing like being certain. Dyngwell wants to know how long we wait at Liège. I advise him (knowing his peculiar French) to ask the Guard. The result is that the Captain addresses him thus : " Hi, Old Cockalorum, do we stop the waggon here, eh ? " Cockalorum returns some answer, and Dyngwell asks me what he said. I interpret it as, " We hardly stop here five minutes." The result is, in point of fact, that we don't go on again for nearly half an hour. After ten minutes Dyngwell decides upon going to "the buffet." He immediately asks for bitter beer loudly, and gets it at once. I can't make up my mind whether it's more Continental to take coffee and a cigarette, or *vin ordinaire* and some roast chicken. I have decided upon the former, and am trying to attract a *garçon*, when Dyngwell says, "time's up : the bulgine's on again." *Bulgine* with him means "Engine ;" but I somehow fancy that he imagines it to be French. I remark that everyone (with the exception of such Cockalorums as the Guard, who rather stands on the dignity of his uniform, I imagine) understands the Captain's English, while they don't seem to get on very well with *my* French. Dyngwell notices this too.

*Happy Thought.*—To explain it to him thus, that these are Belgians, and don't speak like *les vrais Parisiens*. (When in Paris I can look forward to saying that Belgium and Germany have spoilt my accent—satisfactory.)

We cross the frontier, and suddenly hear nothing but German.

Very strange this at first. Dyngwell thinks it would be a rum sort of a start if one went from Kent to Sussex (from Tunbridge Wells to Brighton, for instance) and didn't understand the language at Three Bridges Station. Dyngwell, I note, has more in him than meets the eye.

Aix at last. When you get there it is called Aachen. Dyngwell explains this happily; he says a Frenchman expects to find *Londres*, and it turns out to be *London*.

*Examination of Baggage.*— Questions in German: answer in dumb show, like a pantomime. We have too much luggage for one trap, so Captain goes on alone. He calls his coachman a Cockalorum, and the man touches his hat. I feel somehow desolate: wish I hadn't come. Everything looks dreary. I think of Fridoline, and the baby with the rash, and my mother-in-law at Brighton. Wish I'd gone with them. But as I *have* come all this way to find out whether I've got latent rheumatic gout anywhere about me or not, I am determined to go through the ordeal, whatever it may be. I am put into a fly—such a machine! Three miles an hour, and an unwashed coachman in a glazed hat. Destination. *L'Hôtel du Grand Monarque.* Sounds well.

*First Observation in Note-Book.*—*Strasse* means *street*. *Mem.* Will learn German while here. We descend the broad *Theater-Strasse.*

*Happy Thought.*—Then there's a *Theater* here.

We pass a large hotel—we pass a colonnade. More hotels —plenty of people about: nearly all, apparently, English.

*Second Observation.*—That at the first glance Aix has a highly respectable appearance, but not gay.

The Hotel at last: courtyard as usual—very fine place. Like a courtyard. I descend: a bell rings—sort of alarm of visitors. More bells. Two porters, an under-waiter, a head-waiter (evidently, though more like an English Curate in an open waistcoat), and in the distance on the stairs two chambermaids come out to receive me. Foresee donations to all these when I leave.

*Note.* Continental Chambermaids always so neat. Dressed exactly to suit their position. No snobbishness.

*Happy Thought.*—Commence in French (French carries you everywhere) *Je désire une chambre au seconde, et*——

*Immediate Reply of the Low-waistcoated-Curate.*—"Yes, Sir, if you'll step up this way, I will show you." Very annoying. If you want to speak another language than your own, merely for practice, they won't let you.

The Head-Waiter insists upon my taking rooms on the first instead of the second floor, as the season is just ending, and it will be all the same. He leaves me, and enter the Chambermaid. She smiles (sweetly), and addresses me in her own native tongue —German. She is asking me, I imagine, from her thumping the bed and then putting a question, whether I am going to bed now. Good gracious, it's only five o'clock.

*Happy Thought.*—*Nein.*

This I fancy sounds rough, so I soften it off with *Merci.* She is now putting another question, this time with a jug in her hand. Evidently, will I have some water. I distinguish the word *wasser.*

*Happy Thought.*—*Yah*—adding with a smile "*s'il vous plait.*" Another question from her. *Wasser* again, but this time she mentions *Hice-Wasser.* Iced-Water? *Nein,* on no account, *merci,* thank you. But I should like some—some—(I want to say warm water for my hands). Why isn't there one universal language, say, English?

*Happiest Thought.*—To say Warm Wasser. She is intelligent [and sweet-looking though not young], p'raps she's heard Englishmen try this before, for she replies, laughing good-naturedly (as if I had said something not quite proper, but which she would look over as only attributable to my ignorance of the language) "*Varm-vasser.*"

*Happy Thought.*—"*Oui,* I mean yes, *Yah, Varm-vasser.*" She leaves me.

*Note.*—It's a great thing to have the command of a language. Within half an hour of my arrival I have mastered three words. *Strasse* is street, *Wasser* is water, *Warm* (I think, but am not sure) is warm; and I establish one rule, that "w" is pronounced like "v."

I recollect, when travelling a long time ago, that *Yahzo* (spelt

"*Ja! so!*") means a good deal. Try it presently, and watch the result.

After unpacking, examine the Hôtel. Very nice. Everything looks worthy of the *Grand Monarque*, to whom this Hôtel is dedicated. Go out and examine the town. Although I've never been here in my life, I seem to have seen it all before, somewhere. Excellent shops: large restaurant. No out-of-door seats and tables. Those who are not English are in uniform, at least so it seems at first. Men in uniform are wheeling barrows, men in uniform are driving carts, men in uniform and spectacles are saluting superior uniforms with epaulettes, and also spectacles. To the English eye the town appears to be garrisoned by our postmen. Becoming accustomed to them, you gradually pick out the officers, most of whom are, apparently, short-sighted and use the pince-nez. Everybody is smoking, except the ladies, of course. The toilettes here are not remarkable.

In the Theater-Strasse an enormous building is guarded by a very small sentry. Think the building is a bank, or a post-office. He (the small sentry) carries a big gun in a slouching way, and occasionally stops to look at nothing in particular, with one hand in his pocket. Servant maids walk about like the Parisian grisettes in clean-looking caps, generally carrying a basket, and an umbrella. [*Mem. again.* Continental servant-maids *are* servant-maids. No mistaking them for anything else. No aping superiors. How much better than red ribands, green gloves, yellow parasols, and extravagant Jupes.] Umbrellas are popular. I meet a large sprinkling of the clerical element in chimney-pot hats with narrow brims. The Don Basilio type is not here. Sisters of Charity (also with baskets and umbrellas) in plenty, all looking particularly cheerful and happy. In the window of a bookseller's shop I see a Manual of Conversation in Four Languages.

*Happy Thought.*—Buy it.

With this purchase I return to the Grand Monarque. The Head-Waiter, who is politeness itself, begs me to inscribe my name in a book. I suppose Dyngwell has been telling him about my writing *Typical Developments*, and bringing out a work with Pongood and Groolly. I say I will give him my autograph with pleasure.

It is in the List of Visitors.

I write it down. Head-Waiter smiles, "Ah," he says, "I know it well." I am flattered. "Indeed?" I return, thinking of Dyngwell. It's rather nice of Dyngwell if he *has* done this; I really did not imagine he had such an appreciation of literature. "Yes," the Head-Waiter continues, with his peculiar accent, "I remember him well in London, in 'Olborn. Name well known. I am glad to see you here, Sir."

I don't live in Holborn, and I never had any association with the place. Is it possible that my intention of publishing has got about, and that even this waiter——No, it can't be. He goes on to explain. I find that he has mistaken the spelling, and has confounded me (confound *him!*) with a Large Cheap Tailor's Establishment. Annoying, but lucky I discover it in time.

## CHAPTER XXI.

THE WAITER—PANTOMIMIC—CONCERT—EARLY HOURS—PROBABILITIES
—GERMAN DIALOGUES—KALT—ZIMMER—COUNTERPANE—PRAC-
TICE—BAD.

**D**INE with Dyngwell at the large Restaurant.

*In my Room.*—Ring bell. Tall German waiter answers.
He has a way of understanding you before you speak—antici-
patory style, provoking.

He enters with "You ring?" I reply that I did. He returns, "I thought so. You want some tea, some eggs, some coffee—what?" No. I *was* going to have ordered tea, but I won't now, just to show him that this is not the sort of thing to try with *me*. That I'm not one of his ordinary travelling Englishmen. I order, consequently, some sherry and seltzer. "Sherry and seltzer," he repeats, "anyting else? No? No meat, no bread, no butter, nutting? No?"

This sort of thing makes one very angry : It's a liberty. I answer sternly, "No, nothing else."

*Happy Thought.*—"Yes, a biscuit." I order this, because he hasn't suggested biscuits. He replies, "Sherry, seltzer, biscuits, nutting else? No? I bring you dem," and disappears. I say "disappears," because he is round the corner of the door and out on the landing before I know he has gone. A pantomimic German.

Open my desk and commence reviewing my papers. Waiter back again. "Sherry, seltzer, biscuits, all you want? No?" I say, almost savagely (for it is just as if I was being worried into ordering something else, or hadn't ordered enough), "Open the bottle."

He echoes me again. "Open? yes." He performs this quickly and jerkily. "Zo. Put him in?"

*Happy Thought.*—To nod instead of replying, by way of checking him.

"Anyting else?" he immediately asks. "No? nutting else? no." He has vanished, before I recollect. But I *do* want to ask him something. "Here, *Garçon !*"

*Happy Thought.*—*Kellner*, not *Garçon.* "Kellner !"

He is back again from the bottom of two flights of stairs, in less than five seconds. "You call, yes? You want someting? No?"

'Yes ; I want to know if there is anything going on here to-night?" He shrugs his shoulders, and smiles vaguely.

"Is there?" I repeat.

"Yes, going on? Yes," he answers. His "Yes" is very pro-longed ; a thoughtful affirmative.

"What is it?'

" Yes. Going on for day ? " Then, after a moment's consideration, he decides upon telling the truth, which takes this form, " I
not know what you say."

*Happy Thought.*—To put it thus, slowly, " Is-there-a-Concert,
any Music, or is the Theatre open ? "

" Oh ! " a light breaks in upon him, " A Concert? No, no Concert. De Tayarter is for tree days open. Not dis night. De
Band in de Elisa-garten in morgen play."

*Happy Thought.*—Very nice. Stroll there about eleven to-
morrow. Rank and fashion.

Ask the exact time of performance.

" Seven hour," he answers.

" Plays for seven hours ! " I exclaim.

" No ! " he laughs, and shakes his head as correcting his own
mistake. " Seven o'clock " (this very distinctly) ; " de Band play
all morgens from seven to eight."

What ! ! ! Get up at six-thirty A.M. to go to a Concert at
seven.

" Do many people go to this concert at seven ? " I can't help
inquiring.

" All people here," he replies. I am staggered. What time is
the Theatre then, I wonder. P'raps at 4 A.M.

Suppers at ten in the morning. Fierce dissipation at midday.
That'll do. No, I don't want anything more.

*Decision at present.*—Not to go to the Concert in the Elisa-garten
at seven to-morrow morning. Examine conversation-book in four
languages, in order to address the Chambermaid to-morrow
morning on the subject of wasser, boots, clothes, and bath.

The Chambermaid, I find (to begin with ), is a *Zimmermädchen*
This is satisfactory.

*Happy Thought.*—To arrange (before I go to sleep to-night) a
conversation with the Zimmermädchen. I think *Guten morgen* is
good morning. Can't find it. *Guten morgen, Zimmermädchen,* will
do very nicely to begin with.

*Happy Thought.*—Must also master the coinage. They took
francs to-day in payment for my conversation-book. One thing
at a time. Zimmermädchen at first. How travelling does
enlarge our views. I little thought two weeks ago that I should

be calling anyone a Zimmermädchen, and understanding what I meant by it. Also, mustn't forget what I came for ; *i.e.*, to call on the Doctor, to whom I have an introduction, and ask him if I have got rheumatic gout latent anywhere. If so, where, and what's to be done for it.

It is very cold at night.

*Happy Thought.*—To ask the Zimmermädchen in the morning for a counterpane and more blankets. Look out "counterpane" and "blankets," before I go to sleep, in dictionary, so as to remember them in the morning.

Can't find "counterpane." *Das Betttuch* is blanket.

*Happy Thought.*—Look out "coverlet" instead of "counterpane." Got it—*Oberdecke.* "Zimmermädchen," I will say, "*Ich wünsche eine Oberdecke und zwei Betttuchs.*"

Sleep on it—I mean sleep on the phrase.

Wake in the morning : rehearse the speech to myself two or three times. Add to it. *Bringen Sie mir*—["Bring me," nothing more simple : and it's wonderful how sleeping in a foreign town brings the language out of you in the morning, like the sulphur waters do to the gout]—*Bringen Sie mir heiss Wasser.*" "*Heiss*," is "hot," and yesterday I thought by the sound it meant just the contrary.

Am I ready to converse with Zimmermädchen ? Yes. Ring the bell. Rehearse again to myself quietly. Let me see, I've forgotten what "blankets" was. Shan't have time to look it out before she comes, and it looks so absurd to read to her from a book.

Enter the Zimmermädchen. She wishes me, in her own native tongue (I'll astonish her presently), "Good morning." I feel a little nervous—why should I be nervous? It's nonsense to be nervous. By the way I want a bath, and I've forgotten to look it out. She *has* brought some *heiss Wasser*, so the words I know best I have not got to say.

*Happy Thought.*—Begin the conversation by alluding to the *heiss Wasser.* Try to assume a careless easy tone, as if talking German had been the amusement of my leisure hours for years. Odd, I feel that I don't pronounce the words nearly so well as at my rehearsals.

"*Sie haben heiss Wasser,*" I say it boldly. She is as much

astonished as Balaam was, I should imagine. It must come upon her like a voice from the bed itself.

She laughs and replies, "*heiss Wasser, ja.*" Success: now for number two.

"Oh, Zimmermädchen, I want"—failure. She stares—perhaps it strikes her that I'm a great linguist, and know so many languages that I'm mixing them up—perhaps it doesn't—" I mean *Ich wünsche eine Oberdecke.*"

"*Nix varm genouf?*" she asks; at least, so it sounds, and I understand it perfectly. Very like English, "Not warm enough?"

"*Nein,*" I return in, this time, admirably grammatical German.

Now all I want her to say is, "Yes, I'll bring your oberdecke," and while she's gone I'll look out "tepid bath" in the dictionary. But she commences a series of questions, or remarks, or both, founded evidently upon the mistaken impression, which my starting so fluently in her own native tongue had given her, that I talk and understand German.

*Happy Thought.*—Stick to "*Yah, eine Oberdecke.*"

She laughs (what at? I don't know) and goes away. Now then. *Bad* is bath; tepid is . . . tepid is . . . not down—what a dictionary! It will be worth while studying German here for the sake of my fellow-countrymen who want dictionaries. Tepid is not in the conversation-book. *Kalt* is cold, but I don't want a cold bath. "*If you please*" isn't in the conversation-book. Yet they seem a polite people. Perhaps it wasn't a polite person who compiled this book.

*Happy Thought.*—*Ein Bad mit kalt und heiss Wasser. Kalt und heiss* together must be tepid.

Re-enter Zimmermädchen, with such a coverlet! A bed in it-self—a sort of balloon stuffed with feathers, which she plumps down on the bed. I can't explain that it is not at all the sort of thing I mean, because I don't know the German for the phrase, and I can't keep her waiting in the room while I find out the words in the dictionary. She says something about "*Das ist gut, so.*" And I reply (not to hurt her feelings) "*Yah, das ist goot.*" (*Yah* should be spelt, I find, "Ja"—odd.)

"*Varm?*" says she.

"Very varm," I reply weakly, giving up my German and running into bad English.

Then comes the "*Ein Bad*" request.  She *does* understand me, and brings it.

Rise and go to breakfast with Dyngwell.

*Impressions of German language at first.*—Not unlike broad Scotch if talked by a nigger.  "Yah, yah," just like the Christy minstrels, is always coming in.

## CHAPTER XXII.

DOCTOR'S VISIT—INVALID'S BREAKFAST—DYNGWELL'S ADVICE—SYSTEM
—PROFESSOR WANTED—INVALIDS AT DINNER—TABLE D'HÔTE—
—MIXTURE—THE TIMES — DECEPTIONS — DIFFICULTIES — NOTE
FOR POPGOOD—MY TUMBLER AND I.

THE Doctor comes while we are at breakfast, and takes me by surprise. There are eggs, tongue, grilled chicken-cum-mush-rooms on the table; also, coffee, tea, and preserve. I am munching buttered toast, and generally speaking haven't been so thoroughly well or less like an invalid in the whole course of my life.

Waiter says, " This is the Herr," pointing to me, and introduces us.

Doctor Caspar begs I won't derange myself (in excellent English), and will call again. I suppose he means call again when I've done the buttered toast, and am more like an invalid.

*Mem.*—It's odd that whenever a doctor calls upon me, as a patient, suddenly, I generally happen to be looking remarkably well, and all the symptoms that made me send for him (when, of course, he couldn't come) have vanished. My idea of a doctor's visit is, that he should find one moaning, groaning, and looking wretchedly pale: also, " unable to touch a morsel," not, as Caspar finds me, eating breakfast enough for two, and enjoying it.

*Happy Thought.*—Apologise for being in such good health. Captain Dyngwell and Dr. Caspar, I perceive, know one another. They talk about what has happened in Dyngwell's absence. It appears that nothing has happened in his absence (which they expatiate upon to a considerable extent), whereupon he puts his glass in his eye, and asks after several "Cockalorums." [Dr. Caspar and the Captain both use glasses; the first invariably, the second occasionally.] The Cockalorums generally seem to be doing very well, judging from the Doctor's statistics, who is quite *au fait* at Dyngwell's peculiar English.

"This Cove," says Dyngwell, when the conversation has come to a standstill, inclining his head sideways towards me, "has got the regular rumti-iddities, papsylals, and pande-noodles all in one. Reg'lar bad case—quite the invalid—give him something to rub in."

With which piece of medical advice he nods to both of us, and lounges out of the room, observing that we shall meet at the *table d'hôte.*

Alone with the Doctor, and the remains of the breakfast. Short conversation. Serious moment. Feel that Frivolity has gone out with Dyngwell. Doctor examines me through his eye-glass, which seems a sort of operation in itself. Decision soon arrived at; namely, that probably I've got rheumatic gout somewhere about me, and that if I don't know what's the matter with me now, I soon shall. "The waters," Dr. Caspar explains, "will bring it out, whatever it is."

The summing up appears to me to be, "if you've come all the way to Aachen without having something the matter, we'll soon knock up a disease for you, and you'll be as bad as anyone here in no time."

Doctor says I must begin the system to-morrow.

*System.*—Rise at 6·30. Take the waters at the Elisa Fountain. Take a short walk : take this *with* the Concert in the garden. Take another glass : take some more Concert. Return to hotel— light breakfast—emphatically, *light* breakfast. I again apologise for to-day's excess in breakfast, and lay it on Dyngwell.

*System continued.*—An hour and a half after breakfast take a bath : stop in, twenty-five minutes. Return to hotel. Keep warm till dinner-time at 1·30, when serve myself up at *table d'hôte*, hot.

Understand it all. Write it down. Determine to do it. Wonder what will be the result. Wonder what *will* be the matter with me when I've gone through a course of the system.

*Happy Thought.*—If I don't like it, shall go home.

Caspar being gone, I am *not* a man again. Remember suddenly lots of things I ought to have asked him.

Make *Mems* to ask him when we meet again. May I take champagne ? or sherry ? or both. If not, which, or what ? How about vegetables ? How about tea and coffee ? Will sugar hurt me ? Will milk make any difference ? Where am I to get the waters ? Where *is* the Elisa Garden ? Who gives the waters ? Must one be a subscriber to get the waters ? If so—How much ? If much—Can't I get the waters somewhere else ? What am I to do in the bath ? What am I to say when I go there ? In what language am I to ask for a bath ? Will they know what I want ?

*Happy Thought.*—Ask Dyngwell. When I ask him a few of these questions, adding that I am going through the course, he observes, interrogatively, " What, my light-hearted invalid, coming out as the perfect cure, eh ? "

Must ask about learning German. Get a German professor. Quite common, I suppose, a German professor.

*Happy Thought.*—If they're swimming-baths, I could learn German while swimming about with a professor in the water. Dyngwell, to whom I mention this as an idea, remarks that, as for swimming, of course it depends how much water I want for that, as the bath is only about six feet by four. Still, it *is* a good idea.

*Happy Thought.*—The Doctor, who also dines at the *table d'hôte*, will stop me if he sees me eating or drinking anything wrong. Can take everything till stopped. Several English there—all invalids : also invalids of various nations. Dr. Caspar points them out to me, so does Dyngwell. Dyngwell tells me that the Cockalorum opposite me was quite a cripple when he came, but now, he says, " he's no end of a hand at skittles." He nudges me

(Dyngwell is quite conversational here) to remark the "rum coon next me on my left." I do so. He is a cheerful-looking elderly gentleman in spectacles. Captain informs me that "he's a Prussian Attorney in very good practice, which would be better if he wasn't for four months in the year in a lunatic asylum. The waters," Dyngwell adds, "are bringing it out of him," (bringing what out of him ?—lunacy ?) "but he's not all right yet : in fact he's liable to be taken worse at any moment."

*Happy Thought.*—Shall change my seat to-morrow.

Dining is different in Prussia to anywhere else, I believe. We start with soup and fish, as in England ; after this I lose myself. Better appear as if I was accustomed to this style of living.

*Happy Thought.*—Take a little of everything. When I dine here again shall know more about it. Besides, if I'm wrong, Doctor will stop me.

Result of this determination is, that having got clear of the soup and fish, I find myself taking beef and jam (I think), chicken and cutlets, salad and stewed pears, some sort of game very bitter, and pudding and cheese on the same plate. "The whole to conclude," as the play-bills say, "with the laughable farce of walnuts." Then coffee and cigars. The Doctor doesn't stop me.

I can't help remarking *sotto voce* to Dyngwell, that it's a queer sort of dinner. "You mean," says he, "it's a queer sort of mixture you've made of it." He explains that though the waiters hand round these dishes quickly and together, yet it's only that everyone may make a choice of what he likes. Dyngwell says, "Never mind ; waiters will put it into you ; waters will take it out of you." The waters, according to Dyngwell, will take everything out of you.

After dinner we all become conversational, inclining towards argument. The Skittler is introduced to me ; the lunatic attorney retires (thank goodness) ; a tall Englishman (who hasn't dined there) saunters in and joins our end of the table. The theme of his conversation is that he can dine somewhere in the town on a rumpsteak, eggs, and beer for a shilling. Nobody denies it ; and, apparently, nobody envies him. An American moves his coffee-cup up to us, and wants to know who's seen the paper to-day. No one has, and a lull takes place in the conversation.

*Happy Thought.*—We get the English papers here.

*Note.*—When the *Times* arrives is uncertain: but it does come very early in the morning. Much dishonesty is practised to get it at once. The porter is entreated, the waiters are sent all over the hotel with indignant messages from one person to another about "keeping it so long." Dyngwell has craftily told the porter at the door, that, at whatever hour of the morning the *Times* arrives, he is to come and wake him up to read it. Consequently Dyngwell is awoke, to have first look at it: which operation, I ascertain, he performs, *first*, by being angry at having been roused; *secondly*, by getting half awake, and saying, "Hey, what? the Cockalorum with the thingummy:" *thirdly*, by a delay of two or three minutes, to discover "where his infernal eyeglass has got to," which he finds somewhere over his shoulder, with one string entangled in his whiskers; *fourthly*, to "shake himself together;" *fifthly*, to select one attitude for reading in bed less uncomfortable than another: and, *lastly*, to unfold the *Times*, confounding it because it isn't cut, and asking, vaguely, "why don't they cut it, hang 'em?" He just dashes through it. I observe, while craftily waiting in my dressing-gown to take it to my own room, (and, perhaps, *Happy Thought*, hide it, which I admit is wrong,—but if I don't, and once go out, there'll be no more chance of seeing it for to-day) to him,—"Surely you can't get much out of the *Times* that way?" he replies that he only wants to see if they say anything about *him* in it. It appears that they don't on any morning; which causes the Captain to use a vast amount of strong language about the old Cockalorums at the Horse Guards, through whom, it seems, he has got some transactions about selling out, or purchasing in, or exchanging. I don't exactly understand what he is so irate about, but, from his explanation, I conceive that Commissions are not to be had for purchasing; or his isn't a good one for selling; or that no one will exchange with him; or that the fellow who said he would, wouldn't; or some other military difficulty.

*Happy Thought.*—Get Dyngwell to explain the army system to me. Include it under A, *Typ. Devel.*, B. I., Vol. I. *Published by*

Popgood and Groolly, *with Addenda to the Thirteenth Edition.*
Dedicated to—to—whom ? Must think of that. Something to
think of while I'm at Aix.

*Happy Thought.*—Put *Times* in my room. Go and take my first
waters at Elisa Fountain. Porter at door tells me I must take
my own tumbler. Porter at door, wonderful linguist, in a sort of
uniform. Speaks every language : shouldn't be astonished if a
Chinaman were to arrive, and the Porter were to tackle him in
his own native tongue at once. I take my tumbler, and, feeling a
little odd with it, put it in my great-coat pocket.

## CHAPTER XXIII.

DRINK THE FIRST—ELISA—MISS ELISA—A SMELL—OTHER DRINKERS
—IDEA OF LANGUAGE—SPIRIT—OBSERVATIONS—DYNGWELL ON
PRUSSIAN NAVY—POLYTECHNIC MEMORY—COSMOPOLITANISM—
SULPHUR—COMING OUT—STRONG—APPROPRIATE MUSIC—INVEN-
TION OF TERMS—MARVELS.

ENTER under a colonnade in front of a small garden. This
is the Elisa Garden. There is something peculiarly Heathen-
Templish about the pillars, about the steps down to the
mysterious spring which comes out of a lion's mouth in marble

hot and hot, about the maiden of the waters, and also about the water-seekers with their glass mugs of various colours and dice-box shaped tumblers, that the idea crosses my mind (I have no one to tell it to, so it only crosses my mind, and then, I suppose, re-crosses it) that we are engaged in some Pagan rite, and that the Undine—[*Happy Thought* that, "Undine." Who was Undine? Let me see : German legend, Undine and the Water-Spout ; or the lion. No. Think of this as I descend the steps slowly]—the Undine of the fountain is the High Priestess.

*Happy Thought.*—Elisa's fountain, and this is Miss Elisa.

We are in a curious atmosphere under these Pagan columns. This is the smell of the mineral springs. It might (the smell, I mean) be produced, I imagine, artificially by stirring up a slightly stale egg with a lucifer match until it boiled. In ten minutes' time one ceases to notice it ; though, at first, I think of writing indignantly to the Board of Works at Aachen, and complaining of defective drainage. I left my Cottage near a Wood on account of drainage, so it's natural to be annoyed at being followed by a smell. The cure, on this supposition, is homœopathic. Here I am to take my first draught. I feel a little nervous.

*Happy Thought.*—Stand aloof to see what the other people do. Look about.

Having descended the steps, I find myself, with two or three dozen others, invalids of all nations—[*Happy Thought.*—Good subject this for a Cartoon in the House of Lords, "Invalids of all Nations"],—as at the hotel, in a sort of large area, with railings at the top, over which lounging spectators look down upon us and make remarks, just as the people do to the bears in their pit at the Zoological Gardens when they give them buns, only they don't give us buns. Shouldn't mind a bun, by the way, only Dr. Caspar says, nothing before, or with, the waters ; nothing, in fact, until breakfast, and then, if possible, less.

German, English, and French is being spoken freely ; English, I think, predominating. There are three languages that puzzle me ; I subsequently find they are Russian, Dutch, and Greek. The Dutch I always thought was a rolling sort of tongue, so to speak ; but, on reflection, I fancy this idea was mainly founded upon the remembrance of having heard "Oh, that a Dutchman's draught should be," by a bass singer, late at night, years ago. (*Mem.* for *Typical Developments. Early Impressions. Technical Education. Children. Dutchmen.*)

Miss Elisa stands behind a semicircular counter, and is rapid, sure, and business-like in all her movements. I put forward my hand to her with my tumbler in it. She looks at me for a second or so. Not to see what I want, but because (I found this out afterwards on being accustomed to the scene) I am new to her. She is very pretty; I should like to say in good German to her, "Gretchen, my pretty one, wilt Thou me some of the so tepid and so limpid Stream that rushes from the Lion's Mouth give?" I am sure I understand thoroughly the German spirit, if I only knew the language.

*Happy Thought.*—Say " *Wasser*" as sweetly as possible, because I don't yet know what German for " if you please " is, and *Wasser* alone, that is, *Wasser* neat—[*Happy Thought.*— *Wasser* neat. Good. Full of *Happy Thoughts* this morning: effect of air and early rising] —sounds rude and abrupt; and, worse than all, sounds so *insular.*

*Happy Thought.*—Talking of insular, when I get in with some Germans, students and professors, for instance, I must ask 'em how they like being without a Navy. Curious, a nation without any admirals, or jolly tars; but then, after all, they've got their mineral waters.

Dyngwell says, " You're thinking of the Swiss Cockalorums. They've got no navy. The Gay Prooshians have no end of ships." I ask " Where?" He puts his glass in his eye, and replies, carelessly, " Oh, all over the shop. Adoo ! " and saunters off.

Elisa catches the water in my tumbler, jerks it out, catches some more, and hands it to me, smiling. Wish I knew what "thank you " is.

*Happy Thought.*—Say " *Danky.*" It sounds like good German, and I shouldn't be much surprised to hear that it is. On second thoughts, yes, I *should* be surprised. How difficult it must be to *invent* a language. This leads to deep thought, and will occupy me while I stand and sip the Mineral *Wasser.* I begin sipping thoughtfully, as if I were tasting to see if I would have a case sent in in the course of the morning. It's warm : it's not exactly nasty; it's not precisely nice.

*Happy Thought.*—Epicures say that, to make a perfect salad, you ought first to *soupçonner* the bowl with a shalot. Mineral *Wasser* to the taste is as if you'd cleaned out the tumbler with lucifer matches of the old blue-tip school. It's what I should expect that water at the Polytechnic to be like after it has been flavoured by an experimental blowing up of the *Royal George* under water by the Diving Professor, or some other scientific gentleman connected with the establishment. (I don't know whether this goes on now; it used to. But that's the idea.)

*Happy Thought.*—Got half through tumbler. Nothing happened to me *as yet.* Nothing's happened to any one that I can see. All chattering in little knots and groups and côteries. Regardless of their doom, the little victims drink.

*Happy Thought.*—Finished tumbler, all but a quarter of an inch depth of water at the bottom. Don't know what to do with it. Wonder why I've an objection to the last drop? Instinct, somehow.

*Happy Thought.*—Go and hear the band.

I see everyone leaving a quarter of an inch, or so, of water in their tumblers, and then turning it out into two little receptacles, like the lower part of umbrella stands, placed at the corner of the stairs. Do this also. Just as if I'd been doing it all my life.

*Happy Thought.*—That's where I feel myself beyond Dyngwell or Cazell or Chilvern and Milburd, and so forth. I am, I feel, cosmopolitan. In a second, by just turning this tumbler topsyturvy, I feel myself, as it were, free of the place. A walk in the garden, hear the band, another tumbler (this sounds like dissipation and the bottle, but it isn't—it's only high, airy, breezy spirits before breakfast, and sulphur mixed), and I shall be naturalised.

Somehow I feel, having finished my glass, that I am *de trop* here; for everyone is talking to everyone else—quite a family party. All know one another, and are perpetually nodding and bowing, and smiling and smirking, and inquiring after healths, and "what you did last night after we left," and "whether you're going to So-and-so to-day," and so forth. I feel that I am isolated. Wish Fridoline was here. Should like to have her here—to talk to. (*Mem.* Isn't this selfish? Is the real use of a wife only to be

talked to when you don't know anybody else ? *Note for psychological inquiry.* Plenty of time for psychological inquiries, if I
don't know anyone here except Dyngwell.) I feel, besides this
sense of isolation, a desire to speak to somebody—to throw myself
into their arms, and unbosom my pent-up emotions. I haven't an
idea, on reflection, what my pent-up emotions are like, or what I
should say if anyone—for instance, that little Frenchman (who's
taken three tumblers to my one in the same time)—stepped forward
and said, " *Me voici!* unbosom yourself ! " I don't think I should,
know what to do. I should set him down, speaking rationally, as
mad. Stop ! I pull up. This burning desire for conversation, this
hysterical yearning, of course, I see, it *is the effect of the sulphur.
Sulphur.* I must tone myself down again.

*Happy Thought.*—Bow to Miss Elisa (who seems to notice it as
an impertinence ; sulphur again—I suppose there was a lurking
something in my eye), and ascend steps. Stroll into the garden.
People walking up and down rather fast. I walk up and down,
round and round. There's only one path, and you do it in different ways. There *are* two others, I discover afterwards, but they
are short and retired. It is very exhilarating : it isn't Cremorne ;
it isn't Vauxhall ; it isn't Mabille ; it isn't Hyde Park ; it isn't the
seaside ; it evidently isn't Tivoli (where I've never been) ; but it's—

*Happy Thought*—it's exactly what *the inclosure in Leicester
Square might be made into,* with mineral waters coming out of a
pump under a statue.

*Mem.*—Recommend this to the Board of Works. My statue,
equestrian, as a benefactor.

I feel inclined to suggest supper somewhere, and regret stopping
up so late. I also have a sort of notion that later in the day the
thousand additional lamps will be hung up. (Sulphur again.)
There is a pond with two sorts of fish, red, and not red. Sulphur
water, I suppose, and sulphur has taken the colour out of some
of the weaker ones, or those that have been in the longest. Good
band. Pretty faces. There is a Dutch young lady (I hear some
one say she is Dutch) to whom I should like to talk—only because
she *is* Dutch. Is this incipient libertinism, or only sulphur ? Or
is the former the effect, the latter the cause?

*Happy Thought.*—Don Juan ended, operatically, in sulphur.

c c

Good. "*Orphée aux Enfers*" Quadrilles just played. Appropriate. Will go down during the *ent'racte* (it is a quarter to eight A.M.), and take another sulphur. Descend. Fewer people there. I want another tumbler, please. More difficult to ask when there's not a crowd, as what you say can be heard. Approach Elisa. She *is* very pretty. (Sulphur.)

*Happy Thought.*—Say "*Mair wasser.*" Scotch is an excellent substitute for German. After all, it isn't so much *the language itself*, but the spirit of it, which is the great thing to catch.

*Note.*—That idea of the difficulty of inventing a language is worth enlarging upon. Suppose one had to do it. What should I have called a cup? I don't think anything would have suggested "cup" to me, unless it was done suddenly by a *happy thought*. Or *e.g.*, hat, or handkerchief, or neck, or *head*. "Head" seems really difficult. Who would have thought, without having a name for it ready to hand, of calling a head a "head?"

A man couldn't have called his own head a head; but another man—a friend, for instance—must have done it. Perhaps he did it offensively at first, and meant it as an insult; and then gradually it settled down into an every-day name. Odd occupation, when you come to think of it, for two people, sitting down, and having nothing else to do, saying to each other, "Now what shall we call *this?*"—a hand, for instance—like a game of forfeits. Then, after some deliberation, friend says,

*Happy Thought.*—Call it *hand*.

*Happy Thought.*—People who call a spade a spade. I never thought of it before, but he must have been a very clever fellow who *did* first call a spade a spade. He might have called it a bonnet, and he wouldn't have been wrong then; that is, if bonnets weren't made before spades.

\*\*\* I review this at night in my note-book, and set it down to sulphur acting suddenly on the system. Dyngwell said "the waters would bring it out of me, whatever it was." Something's coming out. But what is it? I can't help being nervous. Shall tell Caspar to-morrow, and write down my symptoms.

# CHAPTER XXIV.

THE BATHS—THALERS—DESCENT—BATH-MAN—CELLS—SUGGESTIVE—
CONVERSATION — TROUBLE — BOOK — DIRTY AND THIRTY —
SOLVITUR.

**F**IRST *Visit to the Baths.*— I choose the nearest baths not the Kaiserbad, which is the largest and grandest, and where the baths form part of the hotel.

Am received by a courteous elderly lady and her daughter, who look as if I was the *last* person they had expected to see.

*Happy Thought.*—Say what I've come for. A few baths. Will I take them all at once, which is cheaper, or not? I don't quite understand: possibly because I am talking French (in English), and they are speaking the same language (in German). Becoming intelligible to one another, I ascertain that their question is one of tickets. I take a lot, recklessly, paying I don't know quite how much, in thalers. Elderly lady smiles encouragingly on me, and asks me if I will descend the steps? If they lead to the baths, yes. They do. Elderly lady sounds a bell. I descend, and pass through the glass folding-doors into a passage with whitewashed walls and ceiling, and a row of small doors on either side.

*First Impression.*—Prison on the Silent System.

A small, fresh-faced man, in a chronic state of mild perspiration, looking, in his white jacket and apron, something like a superior French cook without a cap, appears before me, and says—

"Good morning, sare."

*Happy Thought.*—Bath-man speaks English : in case the bath shouldn't agree with me, useful.    "Which bard?" he asks, laconically, and allows me to look in at the doors of several cells. No prisoners in just now.    Attendant shakes his head.    "Late for bard (*bath*)," he says.    "Twenty, dirty, men season."    From which I readily gather, that in the season, which is now almost past (there are three days more of it) the baths are full.

Finding that I don't make up my mind on the subject, he settles it for me peremptorily, and showing me into a cell, observes, " Nice bard," and shakes his head solemnly, as much as to say, "You couldn't get a better than this, if you tried ever so much."    The compartment I am in, is a small undressing-room of the very plainest description : either a cell, as struck me at first, in a prison, or in the monastery of a very ascetic order.

*Happy Thought.*—The Bathing Monks.    Never were any, I fancy.    Good idea.    Might suggest it to ecclesiastical authorities.

The bath is where the sitting-room would be if these were lodgings with apartments *en suite*.

At first sight there appears to be a sort of scum on the water, which suggests my remark to the attendant.    "Dirty!"

He smiles.    "Goot," he replies.    "Dirty ; goot," and dips a large thermometer into the bath.

This doesn't satisfy me as to its cleanliness.    On the wall is a notice, informing the visitor that he has a right to insist upon seeing the bath prepared in his presence, by order of the Committee.

I draw the attendant's attention to this, and then pointing to the bath, I shake my head, and say emphatically, and with an air of disgust, "Dirty!"

*Happy Thought.*—Wish Mr. Payne, the pantomimist, were here. Wonder how he'd explain my meaning to the attendant.

The man nods in reply, "Ja so ; dirty, hot," which is not a cheering view.    I've seen "Third Class" written up over the doors of Baths and Washhouses in London.    It strikes me that mine will be something of this sort unless I can explain that I *do* insist upon its being prepared in my presence.

*Happy Thought.*—My Conversation-Book is in my pocket. Difficult to find the correct place at once, so as to exactly suit the occasion.

Open quickly and come upon—

| The Chandler | . | . | . | . | *Der Lichtzieher.* |
| The Chimney-Sweeper | . | | . | . | *Der Kaminfeger.* |

No ; that won't do. Still it will be useful to know where to find the Chandler and Chimney-Sweeper when I *do* want them another time.

*Happy Thought.*—Mark the place. Look at Index for " Bath," " Dirty," and " Clean."

is the Index at the end or beginning ?

Look at the end. No. Only " Models for Notes." " Note on not finding a person at home." " Note of invitation." " Note of apology."

*Happy Thought.*—Mark these. Useful another time. Index in beginning. Under what heading ? Don't know. Begin at the beginning. Bother : it's not alphabetical, and it occupies four pages of small print.

The attendant is busy preparing my bath.

I run my eye and finger quickly down the first page of " Contents."

*Happy Thought.*—It ought to be dis-contents. (N.B. Work this up ; do for something of Sheridan's or Sydney Smith's ; more like Smith.)

" *Fractions, Army, Ammunition.*" Hang ammunition ! " *Time, Man.*" I pause here. *Man.*

*Happy Thought.*—Look out *Man.* Perhaps find " Bath-man " under that heading. No ; on reflection, it's " *dirty* " and " *clean* " that I want. Go on again with Index : " *Reptiles, Insects, Maladies, Kitchen, Cellar, Servants, Mountains, Rivers, Agricultural Implements.*" Hang these things ! Where are Adjectives, good strong Adjectives ? " *Affirmative Phrases, Negative Phrases.*" This is nearer, *warm*, as children say in hide-and-seek. " *Ecclesiastical Dignities.*" Cold again. " *Music.*" Absolutely chilly.

"*Field Sports.*"   Oh, bother!   Ha!   "*Imperative Phrases.*"
Warmer.   "*With a Woollen Draper.*"   Lost it once more.   "*A
Lady at her Toilet.*"   *Toilet* may be of some use to me now.
"*The Master before getting up.*"

*Happy Thought.*—Look out *Imperative Phrases.   Lady at Toilet,*
and *Before getting up.*   Combine some words for present use.

The attendant has finished.   The bath is steaming.   "Nice
bard," he says.   "Nice ; hot ; dirty."   Here he points to 30°
Réaumur on the thermometer.

*Happy Thought.*—I understand him at last.   He thought I
wanted the bath at *thirty*, what *he* calls *dirty.*

No : Dr. Caspar particularly said 27°, and, from what I've heard,
you can't do better than follow Dr. Caspar's advice implicitly.

*Happy Thought.*—Point to that number on Thermometer.   Hit
myself on the chest, frown, say, "No, no, *Nein, Nein, Ich wünsch*
(I *mean* I want) twenty-seven.   Doctor order."

"Not dirty?" he asks, in astonishment.

"*Nein, Nein,*" I reply, we are beginning to understand one
another beautifully.   "I said dirty, not *Thirty* "—pause to let
him digest this.   He is intelligent.   He smiles.   "Ah !" he says,
and pulls a huge wooden plug out of the bath, I suppose to alter
the temperature.

*Happy Thought.*—While he is busy, look out *The Master before
getting up.*   Here it is—" Peter, what o'clock is it ?"   " Will you
shave ?"   No.   Ah, here, " You must give me my cotton stockings
with my boots and my kerseymere trousers"—pretty dress !
" Give me my boots, as the streets must be dirty."   *Dirty*—here
we are.   [N.B. German manners and customs deduced from Conversation-Book ; *ex. gr.* if the weather hadn't been dirty, he'd have
gone out *without* his boots.]   " Dirty " is *Schmuzig.*

*Happy Thought.*—" *Das Wasser in dem Bad is Schmuzig.*"

He is indignant.   To prove his assertion of its cleanliness he
takes a handful and drinks it.   *Solvitur bibendo.*   I am satisfied.

The bath is ready—and so am I.   A voice, resounding beneath
the small dome, whence daylight comes in, calls out something.

" *Kommen,*" replies the attendant and leaves me to my bath.   I
am to stop in half an hour, and forty minutes if I can do so.   Now
to commence.

# CHAPTER XXV.

A DIP BY DAYLIGHT — THOUGHTS — WHAT TO DO — A SINGER —
ASSISTANCE—DER HERR—EIN LIED—DER ANDERE MANN—
BOX AND COX—A THEORY—THE INDEX—SULPHUR.

WHAT can you do in a bath? How slowly the time goes! Forty minutes in 26° Réaumur. You can't read with comfort. You can't talk, unless to yourself, which is, I believe, the sure forerunner of madness. If you have some one in the next bath, you can talk to him, if you're acquainted; but even then your conversation is heard by everybody else. No, it's the sulphur silent system and water. But one can't positively lose forty minutes of the day. What can one do in a bath?

*Happy Thought.*—Think.

This reminds me of the celebrated Parrot. Besides you can think just as well out of the bath; better. Might learn German in my bath. *Might,* and also mightn't.

The Bath is a good place for "wondering." You can wonder what good it will do you? Wonder what's the matter with you? Wonder who's in the next bath? Wonder what the time is? Wonder, if you had a fit, whether you'd be able to seize the bell in time? Wonder if it isn't all humbug? Wonder if it is?

Wonder if the Bath-man flew at you with a knife and attacked you, what chance you'd have? Wonder if you might sleep in the bath? Wonder what possible pleasure the Romans found in always bathing? &c., &c., &c.

The Bath-man suddenly looks in. "Time," he says, as if I were going in for another round at a prize-fight. I look at my watch: no, I don't think so. "*Nein.*" I add, with courage, "*Fünf Minuten mair,*" I *mean* five minutes more: *mair* being, of course, Scotch.

He understands me. I am sure there is nothing like dashing boldly into a language.

The gentleman either in the bath next me, or a few doors off, doesn't find any difficulty in amusing himself in the bath. I never heard such a row as he makes. He sings snatches of songs, chiefly Operatic, and *never* correct, in a stentorian voice. Wish I could silence him. I *now* have something to do in my bath; to silence this dreadful noise.

The question is, hasn't a man a right to do what he likes in his own bath? Yes. If *I* may think, *he* may sing; but, on the other hand—— [I always like to put the *other* side of the question fairly to myself: by the way, I generally see the other side better than my own] he may not sing to the obvious prevention of my thinking. My thinking doesn't interfere with anybody; his singing does. Stop, though; if *I* interfere now, the result of my thinking is evidently that I *do* interfere with his singing. This assumes quite a casuistical appearance. He is beginning an air from *Norma* that I know by heart. When I say singing, I mean roaring. He gets to the seventh bar, and then pauses, evidently in doubt.

*Happy Thought.*—To finish it for him.

I do so, with diffidence, and not so loudly as he has been giving it. Pause. This will evidently lead to a struggle, unless he has caved in at the first shot from my battery—I should say, bath-cry. I am allowed to think in peace for about a minute. Then he breaks out again. I believe he has been collecting a *répertoire* during the silence. "*Voici le sabre, le sabre, le sabre!*" &c. He gets into difficulties at the high part—about the fourteenth bar, I should say.

*Happy Thought.*—His weakness is my opportunity. I come in at the finish, whistling this time. Without waiting, he begins, " *Ah, que j'aime les Militaires !* "

*Happy Thought.*—Puzzle him. Sing the quick movement in *Italiano in Algeria,* slightly adapted by myself, on the spur of the moment, to the occasion.

He now sings *Largo al factotum* hoarsely, but not merrily ; for I detect a certain ferocity in his voice. I must be careful ; because, if he is a Prussian officer, he will call me out when he meets me outside.

*Happy Thought.*—Can say what the Clown does when he's caught by a shopkeeper, " Please, Sir, twasn't me."

Bath-man appears with towels.

" *Fünf Minuten,*" says he. I should rather say it was ; twenty-five minutes, more likely. " Towel : nice varm," he continues, and having dried me carefully in one, he wraps me in another, and leaves me.

Classic dress this. Think of Socrates. The Singing Man has holloaed for the bath-attendant, and is evidently preparing to leave.

*Happy Thought.*—Ring for Bath-man, and (after consulting Conversation-Book and combining my question) ask him who the singing bather is. Can't find " singing " in Conversation-Book. I find " a song :" *i.e., ein Lied. Der Herr* is " the gentleman."

*Happy Thought.*—Recollect having seen in playbills the part of So-and-So, Mr. Blank (*with* a song). That's the idea. The Bath-man enters. " You ring ?"

" *Yah. Wer ist der Herr mit ein Lied ?* "

Triumph ! only I wish he wouldn't answer me in German. However, I make out that he doesn't know. He merely speaks of him as " *Der andere Mann ;* " that is, with a concession to my language, "the other man." There are two men, then, in the bath ; one is myself, and the other is *Der andere Mann.*

*Fifth Bath Day.*—*Der andere Mann* is in the bath every day. I *hear* him. I never see him. He comes in either just before me, or just after me, and leaves in the same relative proportion of time.

*Happy Thought.*—The Bathing *Box and Cox.* Similar in situation, except that we never meet anywhere. I discover that this is one consequence of the Season being terminated. *Der andere Mann* and myself are the only two remaining to bathe in the New Baths. Other bathers go to the Kaiserbad, or to other springs; for there are sulphur springs everywhere in, out of, and round and about Aix.

*Sunday.*—Visit the Cathedral in the morning. It is crammed full, as, by the way, are all the Churches, apparently at any hour, in Aachen. I am here struck by a most

*Tremendous Happy Thought.*—A new idea for Popgood and Groolly. It is a *Theory of Origination.* It comes to me all at once. It will astonish Colenso, upset Descartes, scatter Darwinian theories, and perhaps create an entire revolution in philosophy and science.

*Happy Thought.*—Perhaps become a Heresiarch. New sect: *Happy Thinkers,* not Free-Thinkers. Be condemned by the Pope, be collated (or something, whatever it is) by the Archbishop of Canterbury, denounced by the Chief Imaum, held up to execration by Dr. Adler and the principal Rabbis, pronounced contumacious by the Alexandrine Patriarch, and be anathematised as dangerous by the Grand Lama of Thibet; and, finally, the Book placed on the Index by the Roman Congregation.

*Happy Thought.*—Splendid advertisement: in large type. New Book, just published, on the Index. Might get *Typical Developments* on the Index; and then, if both could be excluded from Mudie's Circulating Library, its fortune and mine, and Popgood and Groolly's, would be made.

*Happy Thought.*—Write to them, or telegraph at once. Shall give up my baths, and run over to England. Tell Doctor Caspar so. He says, "No; on no account. We must get it out of you." I tell him I feel that it *is* coming out of me: apparently in the shape of a new heresy, but I don't add this.

Capital fellow Caspar. Speaks English so well. Dyngwell observes, "I wish I had as many sovereigns as Caspar speaks English," which is vague, but expresses Dyngwell's intense admiration of the Doctor's culture.

## CHAPTER XXVI.

CATHEDRAL. — AACHEN — HIGH MASS — THE HERETICAL THEORY —
TELEGRAM — DYNGWELL'S PRESCRIPTION — KAGELSPIEL — LETTER
— THE VAPOUR — DER ANDERE MANN.

I VISIT the cathedral again, and I am confirmed in my first impression. My theory (the heretical theory mentioned before) is, that *Man is made in moulds ; not of* mould, but *in* moulds.

Now I arrive at this, thus :—

On going into the Cathedral, High Mass is just commencing. I struggle into a good place. We are all standing, and seats are an impossibility. Duchesses and draymen elbowing one another, but this by the way ; only I *do* approve of this religious equality, and think it worth noticing.

Before mass, all the canons, choristers, deans, and precentors walk into the body of the church, and commence versicles and responses. What they are I do not know, nor can I attend to the service, for, to my utter amazement, I find that, from the chief dean or head canon, or whatever he is, to the smallest man chorister (not boy), *all are thoroughly well known to me.* Yes, I recognise every one of their faces. They are as familiar to me as possible. Yet I have never been to Aachen before. Never. I have never been inside this Cathedral prior to this occasion. No. But I know every one of the ecclesiastics here by sight.

I find myself staring at one in particular. He is short and sharp-looking, with a large mouth. He catches my eye : he can't help it ; nor can I help keeping mine fixed on him. We are mesmerising each other. I feel that he is chanting his verses mechanically, and, as it were, addressing them chiefly to me. I wonder whether he is too much mesmerised to move with the procession when it gets in motion again. *But who is he?* Who are they? I have known only one foreign priest in my life, and he was a Frenchman, and not a bit like any of these. It breaks upon me, on my second visit, all at once. They are well-known theatrical faces, some familiar to me from childhood, and indelibly engraved on my memory, and others known to me in later years.

This small mesmerised priest (a minor canon he is), in a short surplice and a tippet, is Mr. Dominick Murray—neither more nor less. The Chief Dean is Mr. Paul Bedford,* in a cope, assisted by Mr. Buckstone of the Haymarket, and Mr. Rogers of the same company, who hold two candles for him to read small print by. Mr. Barry Sullivan, in a collar with lace, is scowling at his breviary; and Mr. Honey, with his hair cut, is chanting, hard at it, from the lowest note in his register. The others are all well known to me, only I can't remember their names, except, by the way, Mr. Horace Wigan, who stands out from the rest, because he has lost his place in a large book he is carrying, and has got into difficulties with his spectacles.

Hence my theory of Moulds. I find Mr. Dominick Murray (let us say, for example, as he was my chief attraction : he *did* sing so energetically, and knew his part without a book!) in Germany as a Minor Canon, in England as an excellent comedian. The same with Mr. Buckstone, Wigan, &c. Well, why not in India find the same type of man among the Brahmins?—that is *another lot out of the same mould.*

\*\*\* Dr. Caspar has just called in late at night, and finding me at my notes (above) on my new theory, has ordered me not to write any more for a day or two, and to go to bed at once. Caspar is an excellent fellow, and really takes a personal friendly interest in a patient. He is much struck with my theory of "moulds," and says he will callin and talk it over in the morning. In the meantime (that is, between this and breakfast) I am to go in for a hotter bath up to 28° Réaumur, be very careful in

---

* I regret to say, the *late* Mr. Paul Bedford. And, alas, this applies to all the other names, except Dominick Murray.

diet, rely upon *Friedrichshallerbitterwasser*, and not write a line about this new theory till he gives me permission. Should like to telegraph to my wife and tell her. Have sent to Popgood and Groolly a telegram to this effect :—

"*New theory. Moulds. Upset everything. Great Idea. Write again. Will you publish ?*"

Dr. Caspar insists on seeing me into bed. He says "the sulphur is doing its work well." Something is coming out of me. What?

Dyngwell looks in. "Well, old Cockalorum, got the papsylalls, after all, eh? Doctor given you something golopshus. Rub it in." This is his general idea of a prescription. "Good night."

Dr. Caspar prescribes douche and vapour baths. It'll be all out of me, whatever it is, in another week or so. I ask him if I may employ my leisure in writing *Typical Developments* and the *Theory of Origination*, for Popgood and Groolly.

He says, "No, decidedly not." That instead I must devote myself to *kagelspiel*. *Kagelspiel* is skittles. I remember that Dr. Whately used to relax his mind by swinging on the chains of the post in front of the archiepiscopal palace. Caspar is right. He is, I find, invariably right ; being a thoroughly scientific doctor, without a grain of humbug. Baths in the morning, dinner midday, *kagelspiel* in the afternoon ; tea in the evening, and attendance at a concert or any musical meeting.

Plenty of music in Aix. I have now been here long enough to observe that my first impressions were remarkably superficial.

I note down that for recovery of health, and generally for getting anything out of you, there is no better place, I should imagine, than Aachen.

*Happy Thought.*—To write to Milburd and forestall him in the joke which I know he will make when I return about leaving my Aches (Aix) behind me.

*Second Happy Thought on Same Subject.*—Set the idea to music, "*The Girl I left Behind Me,*" i.e., "*The Aches I left Behind Me.*" Say to Milburd in my letter,—

> "If a girl you see who asks for me,
>   And doesn't know where to find me ;
> You may say that I've gone across the sea,
>   And left my *Aix* behind me."

Copy this into three letters to other people, including one to Friddy. The other people don't know Milburd, so it will be all right.

*The Vapour Bath.*—Shown into a bed-room at the *Neubad*, whitewashed walls and window near the ceiling. *Idea.* Prisoner's dormitory, still on the Silent System. Bath-man presently returns looking warmer than usual, and says something that sounds like *Der Damp Shift is fertish*, which I am right in taking to mean that the Vapour Bath is ready. I follow him, in what I may term, delicately, my popular character of *Unfallen Adam*, across a paved passage, cell-doors on either side (from which I imagine people suddenly looking out and saying "Hallo!" as Milburd would, if he were here) to a small jam-closet without any shelves, but with a skylight above.

In this closet is the case of, as it were, a small quaint old-fashioned piano, only without the works and key-board. This is the Vapour Bath. The Bath-man opens it: I see at once that I am to step in. I step in. I see that I am to sit down over where the steam is coming up. I do, nervously. The Bath-man then boxes me in by closing the front, and putting up a sort of slanting shutter, which only leaves my head out of a hole at the top, like some sort of Chinese punishment of which I remember a picture. I fancy the Bath-man rather enjoys this, as his only chance of a practical joke. Hope he won't think it fun, or do something stupid. He hangs my watch on a nail opposite me and says, "fifteen minuten in der bad."

*Happy Thought.*—"*Nein. Fünf.*"

He won't hear of such a thing. I don't like being left alone. He smiles and nods, "Nice varm?" he asks, and shuts the door on me. It is *varm*, but it is *not* nice. How horribly slow the time passes. Yes, it *is* like a Chinese punishment. I try to distract my mind. Let me see what can I think about? Odd, I can't think of anything except the time and the bath. Yes, one thing, "Can anyone see through this skylight?" No—ground glass. Suddenly I become aware of myriads of little insects, on the wall, near my watch. Ants. They are nowhere else.—They are very busy. Suppose they were to forsake the wall, and run all over my face and hair? I can't do anything. What is Ant in German? I will complain when Bath-man re-appears.

He does re-appear on the instant—that is his head re-appears smilingly, and asks "Nice varm?" I reply "*Ja.*" He adds, "Time, no?" and retires.

I have forgotten the Ants. Who was it, Bruce or Wallace who became King of Scotland by watching a spider? Galileo made a scientific discovery about the pendulum while watching a church-lamp during a stupid sermon. These Ants might lead me to turn my attention to natural history, if I stay here long enough.

Odd : the Vapour Bath doesn't seem to be taking anything out of me. I thought it would be something fearful, and that I should yell, half suffocated and parboiled, for help.

Bath-man's head again, "Nice varm? Time, no?" and dis-appears.

At the expiration of a quarter of an hour, he enters with a warm linen mantle. He unpacks the box (I could have travelled from here to London in this case, labelled "with care," and "this side uppermost") and I come out, like a character in a pantomime, when a watch-box or something is struck by harlequin's wand and out steps a boy dressed like Napoleon (only I'm dressed like Nobody and *in* nothing), and am immediately clothed in the warm garment.

Then I follow Bath-man back to bed-room.

Here I am tumbled into a hot bed at once. Bath-man savagely tucks me up. "Nice varm?" he asks again. "*Heiss*," I reply. "*So ist goot*," he answers. He surveys me in bed. I am helpless. "*Der andere Mann*," he informs me, "take dampf bad to-day."

He says this in an encouraging tone, as much as to impress upon me that in all matters connected with the baths I can't do better than follow the example of *Der andere Mann*.

## CHAPTER XXVII.

DER ANDERE MANN—COMPARISONS—DISGUST—END OF VAPOUR—THE
FAILURE — THE DOUCHE — HAMLET'S GHOST — PROCEDURE —
DOUCHING CONVERSATION—BON MOT—NIAGARA.

I FEEL that I *ought* to be dreadfully, unbearably hot, but I'm not. There seems, as I lie on my back, bound down by sheets under a huge feather bed or two, to be a sort of infernal jingle of a rhyme in my head.

I ought to be hot,
But I'm not, I'm not.
I will if I can,
Like Der andere Mann.

Who *is* this Andere Mann? I've never seen him. Perhaps he is in the next cell to me. Wish I could sleep. Should like to, but mustn't; at least Caspar says it's bad to do so. Must stay in for forty minutes. Impossible to read, even if one had a book. Why don't they invent some plan of fixing up a book before you? Wish Friddy were here: she'd read to me. Devoted wife, reading to vapour-bathed husband. I am *not* very warm. Wonder if it's doing me good? or harm?

Bath-man looks in. He takes a towel, and wipes my forehead: apparently without any satisfactory result, as he is more disgusted with me than ever.

"*Nein,*" he says, "*nix varm.*"   Then in a tone of expostulation, "*Der andere Mann much varm: sweat,—der andere Mann.*"

I am getting angry : I feel it.  I am annoyed.  What do I care about Der andere Mann's state of heat ?  I wish I knew the German for "comparisons are odious," I'd say it.  All I do is to restrain my impatience, and merely say, "Oh, very odd.  Twenty minutes," by which I mean that in that time I will leave this bed, whatever happens, "much varm" or not.  Begin to think I've had enough of it.

*Ten Minutes after the above.*—Interval of thinking of nothing, except trying to recollect poetry, and failing.  Bath-man enters. He is puzzled by my comparative frigidity.

"*Der andere Mann,*" he begins again, "*much varm : sweat, der andere Mann, much sweat.*"   This in a loud tone, and as if at a loss to find terms to make me comprehend the admirable conduct of this infernal Andere Mann ; "but," he goes on, more in sorrow than in anger at my utter failure, "*you,* nix varm, nix sweat ; nutting," and he consequently comes with towels rather before his time, having decided upon giving me up as a bad job.  He shakes his head dejectedly, as he goes through the mere formality of wrapping me up, and rubbing me down, to preserve me from sudden chill, and soon leaves me as unworthy of further attention, probably to report my extraordinary conduct to the Andere Mann. and to praise him in fulsome language for his exemplary bearing in and out of the vapour bath.

"Try again another day," I say to Bath-man as I leave.  But he has no reply for me : he is dejected.  There are only two men, who, now the season is over, come to these baths.  One is myself, and the other is Der andere Mann, and the first is, in the Bathman's opinion, beneath contempt as a "Dampf-shifter."

English party here, small by degrees, and beautifully less ; which quotation also applies to the gouts, and rheumatisms, and other ills the flesh is heir to, under Dr. Caspar's treatment and application of sulphur waters.

System in my case undergoes a change.  Besides the vapour bath, where after several ineffectual attempts I never can come up to the temperature of Der andere Mann, I am now *douched.*

*The Douche.*—The Doucheman, I mean the man who gives you

the douche, appears dressed in a sort of nightgown and nightcap. I get out of his way at first, under the impression that he is an elderly lady, who has mistaken her compartment in the bath. He beckons me, I hesitate under the above-mentioned impression, naturally. He smiles, and beckons me again.

*Happy Thought.*—Not unlike *Hamlet's Father's Ghost.* " His custom always of an afternoon."

*Another Happy Thought in the same line.*—" Lead on, I follow." He *does* lead on, and I *do* follow. To a cell with bath, similar to the others, only with a large water-pipe in it, coming down the back wall, above where your head would be if you sat under it.

We are both silent. He shuts the door. There is something unpleasantly mysterious in these movements. Feel that I must be on the defensive. (Nervous system a little out of order, or else why be afraid of a Doucheman, who, I know, will not do me any harm? Shall refer this to Caspar, who will feel my pulse, which of itself is an operation that disturbs me considerably until the Doctor speaks, when I invariably feel relieved, whatever he says.) Doucheman suddenly takes off his bathing-gown and appears something like an acrobat who is going to support another acrobat on a pole. I am the other acrobat. Wish I knew the German for "acrobat." He speaks French, so I try "Acrobar." I say, "We are two Acrobars," pleasantly. He nods (he is now standing in the bath, doing something with the mouth of the pipe), smiles, and turns the water on to himself, just to see how *he* likes it before he tries it on *me*.

He is satisfied with the waterworks, and again imitates the *Ghost* in "*Hamlet.*" I descend the steps. "Speak! I'll go no farther."

He speaks; "*plus bas,*" he says, whereupon, after thinking for a few seconds what he means, I take up my position one step lower. I can imagine a very nervous man being thoroughly frightened by the next proceeding, which is to take you, quite unawares, by the leg. Somehow it's the last thing any one would think of. It seems to me that the Doucheman has no settled plan, but that after considering the patients for a few minutes, he is suddenly seized by a—

*Happy Thought.*—"Take him by the left leg" (*vide* poem about the infidel Longlegs) and pummel his foot.

The noise of the water rushing through the pipe on to my leg prevents conversation (it is Niagara in miniature), otherwise I should like to talk to him about the art of douching, and what is *his* idea of the particular benefit to the subject. In a moment's pause, that is, before he gets hold of my other leg, I collect myself for a question in French, "Why do you do this?" It sounds piteous, I fancy, as if I had added, "I never did anything unkind to you!"

He answers that it is "*pour faire rouler le sang,*" and begins kneading my instep.

*Happy Thought.*—A kneaded friend is a friend indeed, or, a friend who kneads is a friend indeed.

Think it out, and put it down to Sydney Smith.

Douche on my hands, arms, chest, everywhere.

*Happy Thought.*—All round my hat. Happier thought, on expanding my chest to the full force of the water, "All round my heart." Niagara on my back. Squirt, rush, whizz, sky-rockets of water at me. I am catching it heavily over the shoulders.

*Happy Thought.*—Should like to turn round suddenly, and see if the Doucheman is laughing. I daresay it's very good fun for *him.* Sort of perpetual practical joke. Capital employment for Milburd if he ever wants a situation.

In twenty minutes it is all over.

*Happy Thought.*—Write a description of it all in some cheap form. Call it "Twenty minutes with a Doucheman." Telegraph the idea to Popgood and Groolly. They haven't replied to my other telegram.

Fresh sulphur water is turned on up to 30° Réaumur, and I sit calmly meditating on the stirring events of the last half hour in the tranquillity of the ordinary bath, the Doucheman having resumed his nightgown and wished me *bon jour.*

*Happy Thought.*—"Oh that a Doucheman's draught should be," &c. Sing it myself. Stop on remembering that if Der andere

Mann is in the building, this will encourage him to begin his operatic selections.

*Back in my Room at Hotel.*—Never felt so well. Premonitory symptoms of gout have come out and gone. Caspar right. Telegraph to Popgood and Groolly. Say, "Premonitory symptoms gone. How about theory — origination? Will you? Wire back."

# CHAPTER XXVIII.

TABLE D'HÔTE — OUR PARTY — CONVERSATION — CLASSICS — NAVAL TOPICS—CUTTING IN—FOURTH WEEK—LETTER FROM HOME—OUR PROFESSOR—COCKALORUMS—DYNGWELL—A CLUB—GERMAN EXERCISES—GERMAN LETTER—RESTORATION.

OUR *table-d'hôte* party is very select. At the head of the table sits distinguished guest ; sort of oldest inhabitant. He knows Madame the proprietress of the Hotel, a lively and agreeable French lady of commanding figure, and with, I should say, an eye to business. Near her are her son (who is, of course, a soldier, and sits at his desk in his bureau, attending to the Hotel accounts, dressed in full uniform) and daughter, and there is no pleasanter party at the table than this most united family.

*Happy Thought.*—Sit with them, and practise my French. Mention this to Dyngwell, who replies, "Nobody axed you, sir, she said," which is true.

*Our* end of the table is the inquisitive and critical department.

We are always asking " Who that is?" meaning some new arrival, and, generally have, amongst us, an Eye for Beauty.

Beauty, however, seldom having an Eye for us in return.

Dr. Caspar takes the chair at our end, and we are very sociable and cheery.

There are two gentlemen in a state of progressive convalescence who compare notes as to health across the table. A nervous person who eats preserved peas with a knife, and has a jerky way like an automaton-diner, with his fork and a bit of bread when eating fish. There are two naval gentlemen, one a Commander and the other a Lieutenant. The Commander has been all over the world, and has a great story about a Mongoose. No one has heard the end of it, as he generally forgets a date or somebody's name essential to the *dénouement* of the Mongoose. Always thought, till now, that a Mongoose was humbug, like the Phœnix. The Lieutenant contradicts the Commander on most naval matters, but has never seen a Mongoose. There is a charming old gentleman who has translated Æschylus and Euripides into English verse ; he has been complimented by the greatest scholars of the day, and his publishers have just sent him in his bill for printing, and a letter to know what the deuce they shall do with the first thousand. We talk together about Greek poets.

*Happy Thought.*—Take up Greek again. Read Homer. Old gentleman quotes passages. Of course I remember, he says to me, the passage in the *Iliad*, commencing "*Dinamenos potty,*" &c. Of course I don't.

*Happy Thought.*—To encourage him, say as if cogitating, " Yes," dubiously, " I fancy I recollect the gist of the passage." "Ah ! " he replies, "and what would *you* make of the epithet there : an epithet used only once, as I believe, in that sense by Homer, or any later Greek poet?" I can make nothing of it, and leave it to him. What does *he* make of it? "*That,*" he returns, "has always been *his* difficulty." Don't like to ask what epithet he means.

*Happy Thought.*—To quote carelessly "*Poluphoisboio Thalasses,*" and say with enthusiasm, "Ah, *there's* an epithet ! How grand and full is the Greek language ! " Luckily at this moment the Commander asks me if I've heard what he was telling the Doctor about the Mongoose, and the waiter hands the sauer-kraut (excellent dish ! !) to the translator of Æschylus.

When we sit late and have Champagne, as is the case on Sundays or on the departure of a friend or a birthday, we all get into philosophical discussion, all except the Commander and the Lieutenant, who nearly come to high words (invariably) on points of seamanship, as to whether it *is* better or not, in a storm, to rig the boom taffrail, or pay out the gaff. The Commander appeals to our common sense, in behalf of the boom taffrail, and the Lieutenant observes scornfully, that "Any one who knows how to sail a vessel would immediately pay out the gaff."

*Happy Thought.*—To say conciliatingly, "Well, I suppose it doesn't much matter."

They retort, "Oh, doesn't it !" and explain. More Champagne. The Commander afterwards takes me aside and depreciates the Lieutenant's theories in confidence. The Lieutenant takes Dyngwell apart, and says he should be very sorry to be sailing under his (the Commander's) orders. Dyngwell observes, "That both the nautical Cockalorums have been going on the scoop, and are slightly moppy." By which we understand him to mean, that the two naval officers have had as much as is bad for them.

*Happy Thought.*—A naval officer half-seas over. (Think this out, and put it down to Sydney Smith.)

*First Day of Fourth Week at Aix.*—I am quite well. Three more douches, two vapours, and four ordinary baths will settle the question.

*Happy Thought.*—Present Dr. Caspar with a testimonial; say the first volume of *Typical Developments*, when it appears, with plates. "Anatomy" (under A) will interest him.

Letter from Friddy. I *must* come back, she says——

*Happy Thought.*—Nice to be written to affectionately.

I turn over the page : she continues, "—*or send a cheque.*" It appears I have stayed away longer than she expected. The baby is less rashy than he was. Regret that I must go home before I've got on with my German.

*A German Lesson.*—My Professor of languages is the most

amiable, patient, and persevering gentleman.   He is much tried
by Captain Dyngwell, to whom he has been for some time giving
lessons.    Dyngwell invariably salutes him—he is Doctor-of-Law or
some degree or other, and a man with whom anyone of a philo-
sophic turn would at once commence discussing German meta-
physics or deep and interesting psychological questions,—but
Dyngwell invariably salutes him with a slap on the back, a hearty
slap on the back, or with a pretended lunge of his walking-stick
into the professor's fifth rib, making him wince but smile, and
addressing him as " Hullo ! old Cockalorum !    *Sprechen-Sie
Deutsch ?*"

At first I ascertain the Professor went home and looked out
"Cockalorum " in the dictionary—he is a great man for roots and
derivations, and knows Beaumont and Fletcher, Massinger,
Shakspeare, and most old standard authors by heart.    Not finding
Cockalorum in any known glossary, he gets near it as a probable
genitive plural of Cock-a-leekie, and humbly sets this down to his
ignorance of Scotch dialects.    Later on, he determines, after a
night's deep thought, that it is a compounded form of *Custos
Rotulorum,* and announces this as an interesting philological discovery to Dyngwell, who receives the information with his glass in
his eye and the remark, that it's " Whatever you please, my little
dear, only blow your nose and don't breathe upon the glasses." To
which he gives an air of authority, very confusing to the Professor,
by adding, " hem ! Shakspeare," which causes the good Herr
another sleepless night in his library.

*Happy Thought.*—Explain Dyngwell to him.

We have an interesting discussion on ancient and modern slang.
To assist me in reading German, the Professor kindly takes me to
his Club ; an excellent social club with a reading-room full of
newspapers, German, French, and English.

I take up the something *Zeitung,* and am helpless.   End by
reading the *Times.*

Commence German lesson.   Read and translate out of German
into English, and back again.   The principal characters in the
exercise are the shoemaker and the tailor, and, of course, my father
and my mother.   Dyngwell is satisfied with this sort of thing, and
copies out reams of examples.

*Happy Thought.*—Make my own examples and gradually compile a new exercise-book. My Professor is pleased with the idea as original. I make selections on paper, modelling them on Ahn's *La Langue Allemande.*

*Examples for the Use of Students* (might include these in *Typ. Devel.*)—The shoemaker is sad. The father of the shoemaker is fat. The wife of the gardener has given an umbrella to the shoemaker. The mother of the carpenter was often in my garden. Will you fight the gardener? No, Henry will fight the gardener, because the shoemaker is ill (*krank*). Here is Ferdinand! Have you washed your boots? Yes, my mother, I have also washed the boots of the gardener.

*For more Advanced Students.*—At what hour do you sup? I sup at nine o'clock with the wife of the shoemaker. Have you seen my brother? No: but I have written to my uncle and my aunt. Will you eat some ham? No: I will not eat some ham. The lion is ill. The shoemaker laughs at the gardener's aunt (*i.e.*, the aunt of the gardener). Your cousin was looking for his hat while the merchant was dancing. The hound is not so fat as the cat (*als die Katze*).

I dance better than you, but you do your exercises better than I. Your father was playing in the garden with your uncle when the lion came. The industrious schoolboy is loved by everybody. My neighbour has sold his chickens to the lion. The coachman is eating plums and apples, and we have wine and beer. Give me some soup, some wine, some beer, some sugar, some vegetables, and some ink, and do not call me till four in the morning. The tailor is here, so is the shoemaker, but the lion has eaten the gardener.

*Happy Thought.*—(Finishing sentence to the exercise.) The big lion has eaten the tailor, the shoemaker, the gardener, their aunts and uncles, the brothers and neighbours, and also the ink, the sugar, the tea, the cream, the ham, the plums, and the boots.

*Happy Thought.*—To astonish Friddy with a letter in German. Write home and say, "*Meine liebe Frau,* I am not *krank* now, but very much *besser ;* in fact, quite well. *Hast du mein cheque-buch gefunden ? Ich habe mein bad genommen. Ich habe mein cheque-buch nicht. Bist du krank ?* "

Capital exercise the above.

Dr. Caspar compliments me on being thinner.   I feel pleased.

Note that generally every one is pleased at being thinner.

Go and get weighed at Miss Helenthaler's tobacconist shop. Every one gets weighed here.   Wonderful how Miss Catherine, who keeps the shop, speaks English perfectly without ever having been in England.   Wonder if I should ever speak German without going to Germany, or even *with* going to Germany.

*Note.*—A writer in the *Daily Telegraph*, whose article I see here, describes two gardens as existing at Aix.   One, he says called after the faithless spouse of Menelaus.   There is no such place. There is the Elisa Garden, and there is Miss *Helenthaler* (*i.e.*, Miss Catherine), who is much amused at being called a garden.

*Happy Thought.*—Write to *Daily T.* and correct mistake.

*Happy Thought.*—Leave it alone.

I shall be sorry to leave.   The longer one stays in Aachen, the more you learn of the people, the pleasanter it is.

But Popgood and Groolly call ; or rather, as they haven't answered my telegrams, I really must go and see what's the matter.

*Happy Thought.*—Return home by Paris.   Ask Friddy to meet me there with her mother.   On thinking this out (nothing like thinking a thing out), decide that it's better (*besser*) *not* to ask her and her mother.   Shall like a few days' holiday in Paris.

*Happy Thought.*—Celebrate my convalescence by a dinner given to the Professor, Caspar, and Dyngwell.

## CHAPTER XXIX.

MUSIC—DYNGWELL'S NOTION—ECONOMY—THE PARTY—THE CONCERT
—HERR SOMEBODY—FIDDLING—THE SHIPBOY—CONCERT OVER
—SUPPER—BILLIARDS—MONGOOSE—COMMANDER'S STORY.

A IX is musical, as musical as Manchester, and much in the
same way too. Two excellent bands here; and once a
visit from Herr Something-or-other on the fiddle of world-
wide reputation, the Commander informs me, though he's the las
man whom I should suspect of knowing anything about it.

*Happy Thought.*—Has sailed round the world, and met Herr Something with his fiddle everywhere.

Dyngwell won't join our party to the Concert. He says, if the Cockalorum would give us a "right-fol-iddity, or a chant with a coal-box to it" (he means chorus when he says "coal-box," and the Professor makes a mental note of it, in order to look out this particular use of the word coal-box in the Dictionary) "he would come;" but as there is no chance of his taste in this direction being gratified, he stays in his room and runs through his German exercises.

*Happy Thought.*—*Beer* is the same in both languages. Bavarian Beer excellent. So also the lightest wines; *e.g.* Zeltinger.

*Happy Thought.*—Take home a cask of the former and a case of the latter. I point out to Dyngwell what a saving this will be, and how necessary it is, as the father of a family (one with rashes) to be economical. He sticks his glass in his eye, and exclaims, "Bravo! quite the drunkard!" which was not, on the whole, exactly the encomium I had expected from him.

*At the Concert.*—Our party consists of the amiable and learned translator of .Eschylus; the jovial, good-natured Yorkshire Squire (who has got well of severe gout, in a week, in consequence of rubbing in his draught, and drinking his lotion by mistake); the Lieutenant, who has come to the Concert in the hopes of there being a "hop" afterwards, which appears to be his one great aim in going to any evening entertainment of any kind; the High Church Anglican clergyman, whose resemblance to a Catholic Priest would be perfect, if there was only the slightest chance of his being mistaken for anything else but an English Protestant Minister; and Dr. Caspar, who knows every one and everything in the place, and is welcome everywhere, and can go anywhere now that Aix is deserted by strangers, and he has time for shaking hands without feeling pulses. Our nervous compatriot does not appear anywhere except at *table d'hôte*, having probably jerked himself into bed at an early hour, and shaken himself into a sound sleep.

*Happy Thought.*—Perhaps I shall discover who *Der Andere Mann* is.

First overture of Concert over. Room crowded. Elegant

toilettes ; pretty Saxon faces ; Prussian officers, in uniform of course. Commander has been listening in rapt attention to the music. We all listen to a part-song critically.

*Happy Thought.*—To beat time with my head and hand, in order to show that the English *are* a musical nation. Commander does the same. I ask him which he prefers, Rossini, Auber, or Wagner. He hesitates. He asks thoughtfully, "Let me see, what was Rossini's great work?"

*Happy Thought.*—(By way of reply, while I think what Rossini *has* written,) "His *great* work ! Why he's written so many."

The Commander says, "He's alive still, isn't he ?" I own I am taken by surprise, never having considered the question of his being alive : having, in fact, generally ranked him among the "Old Masters," and got him back somewhere near Shakspeare's time.

*Happy Thought.*—To laugh slily and say, "I suppose so." If he isn't, and was in Shakspeare's time, I can say I thought he (The Commander) was joking. *Mem.* Read up Musical History : odd, I've quite forgotten it : under "C" (Composers) and "M" (Music) in *Typ. Devel. Part III.* Concert continues.

*Herr Somebody on the violin.*—Great applause on his appearance. He has long hair, turn-down collar, and a pale face, at least so it seems from this distance. Strange, now I come to think of it, that all great violinists, whom I have ever seen, are always the same, and I always see them from the far end of a room. He plays a melody slowly, with which he appears pleased : so do we. Commander thinks "he must be wonderfully strong in the chin to hold the instrument while his left hand is jumping up and down it." People look round at Commander and say "Sssh !" repro vingly. Herr Somebody takes three decided scrapes at the strings, and then as it were scrambles about the violin wildly. Three more scrapes ; more scrambling ; tune nowhere — one, two, three (fiercely) ; twiddley-twiddley-twiddly-iddley (wildly). Down below like a double-bass, making a sensitive person, like myself, experi ence a feeling not unlike that caused by the steamboat when it dives in between two waves on a rough passage ; then up again, notes running one after the other like mice in a wall, and his four fingers and thumb chasing them nearly to the bridge and not catching them. Back again in among the screws, up the handle, on to the bridge, hand still trying to seize on something, his eyes watching the performance intently, and chin fixed. An occasional shifting his head a little on one side, just for a second, as if he was ticklish, but liked the sensation. Then a plaintive bit, which seems to make him stand on tip toes, and causes me almost to rise out of my seat. Then short note, still plaintive, which brings him down on his heels again. As I watch him he seems to become all violin and arms. Sudden appearance of a little tune, immediately knocked on the head by the bow. Up and down the chromatic scale, in and out the flats and sharps. Herr Somebody loses his way in a labyrinth; more mystification; at last he's out of the maze; pause, flourish of bow, grand triumphal movement (no tune to speak of, but no mistaking the time), chords crisp, and chords loose. Running up and down the chords; violin swaying as if (so to speak) he'd tumble off it every minute. We hold our breath in suspense. I almost feel inclined to say, "Oh, do stop, Sir! take care! for goodness sake! take care!"

*Happy Thought.*—A sort of Musical Blondin. On consideration this *is* a sensational performance.

Flourish, scuttle, scuttle, scuttle, up and down wildly, chords hard, fast, and marked up the scale full pelt, *whack!* whacker!! WHACKEST!!! and the exhausted performer is bowing his acknowledgments. A sigh of relief from everyone, audibly, as if we congratulated ourselves, and him, on getting through such a dangerous performance without an accident. He is encored; but only reappears and bows. He will not tempt Providence again. Everyone says Admirable! Charming! Wonderful! "almost equal to Joachim," cries Dr. Caspar, enthusiastically.

*Happy Thought.*—"Yes, almost."

Caspar is gone, before I can add that I've never heard Joachim. I turn to the Commander to ask him what *he*, as a musical man, thinks of it. The Commander is fast asleep.

*Happy Thought.*—To quote to him when he wakes, "The Rugged Shipboy"—only I forget the rest; but the idea is that the Shipboy sleeps tranquilly through all dangers and tempests on the top of a mast. I have always wondered what he held on by? Will wake the Commander, and ask him to illustrate this passage in Shakspeare. Commander wakes. On being remonstrated with for his drowsiness, he admits confidentially to me, as a thing not to go any further, "that it's not much good his being here, as he doesn't know one tune from another."

After Concert, which is over early (another excellent thing in the Aix arrangements, everything is over early), we adjourn to a *café*, where we each partake of a Wiener Schnitzel, some Sauerkraut, and a tankard of such beer as won't interfere with your waking in the morning. The Commander commences (with the cigars) his usual story about the Mongoose. The Lieutenant begs his pardon for a minute, and seeing a table in the ante-room vacant, proposes billiards as a wind-up. Billiards, by all means.

We rise, and go to the billiard-room. The Commander is, I see, a little disappointed. At this moment, Dyngwell happens to stroll in with his professorial friend, who joins us in much the same spirit that Dr. Johnson did Beauclerk and the others, when they got him out of bed for a frolic. It appears they've been to supper (one of Dyngwell's ingenious methods of doing a German exercise) at *Klöppel's* or Kruppel's (I think that's what they call it), and thought, that he (Dyngwell), and Old Cockalorum (the Professor), would find us here. Dyngwell opportunely salutes the Commander with "Hallo, old Mongoose!" which puts an extinguisher on all chance of hearing the story from the naval officer to-night. He has been trying to tell it for weeks. He proposes to walk home with the Professor. Has probably hit upon the *Happy Thought* of "Tell *him* the Mongoose story." Professor says he shall be delighted, only he must speak to a friend first. He does so; to some one at the other end of the room, and is not seen again, except for a second by me, when I catch sight of his hat, which there is no mistaking, as he is making a quiet exit by the front door.

Commander takes a seat between two Germans, with whom he enters affably into such a conversation as his command of the language permits; *i.e.* at the rate of two words in five minutes, with an occasional *ja* or *nein*. Then he goes to sleep again. Then he wakes up. Then he disappears.

# CHAPTER XXX.

LEAVING — THE SCOOP — FOREIGNERS — MORE EXERCISES — GERMAN
VERBS — DYNGWELL'S EXERCISE — HYMN — TO PARIS — POETRY —
ARRANGEMENTS.

IN FIVE days I leave this. Sorry; for a pleasanter time
I've seldom spent, and shall regret leaving Dr. Caspar and
our Professor, but must get back. Dyngwell thinks, he says,

of running with me to the "gay and festive village,"— he means Paris,—"and going on the scoop for a short burst of it." I represent to him, gravely, that I can't go on the scoop; to which his answer is, "Never mind, Cockalorum, we'll bustle 'em somehow."

Dyngwell asks me to come and have a chat in his room. We fall into German and French. I propose talking in both languages as a capital plan for foreigners. He says, "Who's a foreigner?" I reply, "*We* are," which seems to astonish him. He had thought that Englishmen never could be foreigners.

*Happy Thought.*—Suggest that he was thinking of Rule Britannia and chorus. "Never, never, never, never, never, shall be" foreigners.

I say, for practice, will he talk German to me? He won't. For practice, will I talk French to him? I will. He doesn't understand a word I say. He says he catches one now and then. We read French to each other. Getting tired of this, he draws my attention to his exercises, and professes to be getting "Quite the German."

*Happy Thought.*—To *test* him and his system. Represent the conventionality of his exercises. Get one of mine (intended for my forthcoming "Method of learning German, French and English simultaneously," if Popgood and Groolly will have it. Wish they'd answer telegrams) and try him.

*For Beginners.*—I am fat (*gross*). You are poor. We are fat and poor. Am I fat or poor? Are you ill or fat? He is old and little. Is he little or old? I am rich (*reich*) and fatigued. Are you little (*klein*), and fat (*gross*), and rich and ill (*krank*)?

*Next Exercise.*—I am not tall. They are short and idle. Is the father good and fat? The mother is happy and tall. The father and the mother are small and polite. My aunt is with the shoemaker, but my uncle is in the garden. The wife of the doctor (*des Arztes*) is in the fat carpenter's garden.

I have seen the tailor's uncle's boots (*i.e.*, I have the boots of the uncle of the tailor seen).

This is what Dyngwell says is *his* difficulty; viz., that the verb is (so to speak) round the corner; or comes, as it were, at the end of the book.

*Happy Thought.*—There are more things in heaven and earth, Dyngwell, than are dreamt of in your philosophy.

Dyngwell puts before me *his* idea of our exercise.

*Dyngwell's German Exercise.*—Will the Cockalorum liquor? The old Cockalorum is moppy. Rub it in. The tailor was bustled a bit by the wife of the Cockalorum. The old cove went on the scoop. The venerable Cockalorum ain't in good form. The shoemaker is a Hass. The carpenter's grandmother was quite the drunkard. The gardener has the papsylals in his great toe. Act on the square, boys, and be quite the c'rrect card, your vashup. The carpenter retires to his virtuous downy. My Aunt and my Uncle. The noble swell was all there. Well, my Lord and Marquis, how was you to-morrow? Hallo! says the Dook. Quite the tittup, says the Duchess. The Cockalorum was on. I'll have your German Exercise!

"Now," says Dyngwell, "get that into real up and down German, and you'll be quite the scholar."

*Sunday.*—In the Jesuits' Church. Expect, from seeing the crowd, that I am going to see something peculiarly grand. Edge myself as near as possible to the front row of people all standing. A German hymn which I don't understand.

*Happy Thought.*—Never offend prejudices. Look devotional, and hum as much of the tune as I can catch.

No ceremonial, but a sermon. After the first twenty minutes look round to see if there's any chance of getting out quietly. None. Wedged in. Think of saying *Ich bin sehr Krank*, and getting them to let me pass. Say this to my next neighbour. He shakes his head : either he won't believe me, or doesn't understand. Try it once more and give it up. Sermon lasts one hour at least.

*Happy Thought (for any one who doesn't understand the language, and is uncertain what service he is going to hear).*—Get close to the door.

*Day of Departure.*—Early in the morning get weighed at Miss Caroline s. Find I'm considerably less.

*Happy Thought.*—Thinner.

Say good-bye to everybody. Dyngwell will accompany me to Paris. Everybody in hotel suddenly seems to find an opportunity for coming into my room. Waiters, chamber-maids, porters, boots and people whom I've never seen before. I call in to see the Bath-man and the Doucheman. They receive their gratuity sorrowfully, being puzzled at the non-success of the vapour-bath in my case as compared with that of Der andere Mann.

The Commander appears at the hotel door. He is also coming to Paris. "Capital fun, we three," he says. He promises that he'll tell us the story of the Mongoose in the train.

Madame Dremel lends me a triumphal car in the shape of a magnificent carriage and pair, and coachman in livery (looking, on the whole, something like a foreign ambassador's equipage in Hyde Park), and Dr. Caspar is determined to see the last of me, for the present. I add this because I really hope to return, whether there's anything the matter with me or not. It's a long journey to Paris ; ten hours.

*Happy Thought.*—Take light wine, chicken sandwiches, and French literature to prepare for the gay capital. Get Dyngwell to talk French all the way there. Good practice.

*Happy Thought.*—Ask Dyngwell and Commander to get light wine and sandwiches, *also.*

Dr. Caspar's interest secures us a carriage to ourselves—not to be disturbed on any account.

*Happy Thought.*—As invalids.

Before going, take the names and addresses of every one I leave behind. Will write to them ; must see them ; will all meet again, jovially—somewhere. We all mean what we say.

" Here's old Cockalorum ! " shouts Dyngwell, catching sight of our good-humoured, kind-hearted Professor's hat. I ask him to watch for the first volume of my *Typ. Develop.* He says, " He will do so, with the greatest possible interest."

*Happy Thought.*—Paid the bill.

*Happy Thought.*—Less than I'd expected. *Grand Monarque* excellent and moderate.

In making this note I feel as if I was doing it for a Guide-Book. Winter is beginning. Can't help looking forward, away from the German stoves, to the wood fires of France and the roaring logs and coal of England. Good-bye, sulphur waters ! Farewell, Miss Elisa !

*Impromptu in my Pocket-book :—*

> Fairest of all Aachen's daughters,
> Thou who gave'st me sulphur waters,
> See, I go to winter quarters ;
>     Medical adviser
> Says I may, so fare thee well,
> What I feel I cannot tell,
> No, nor in thy language spell,
>     Pretty Miss Elisa.

Dyngwell says " Elisa " is pronounced " Elesa."   Oh, is it ? very
well.

*Happy Thought.*—Think of rhymes and settle Dyngwell.   Lesa
—Please,   Sir—teaser—greaser—tea,   Sir—she,   Sir—we, Sir—
Pisa, &c.

*To  my  Friend* * * * *

> " Youthful friend, say, have you quaffed
> At her hands the sulphur draught ? "
>     " *Whose* hands, if you please, Sir ? "
> Then I answer, " She the nymph
> Of the boiling sulphur lymph,
>     Lovely Miss Elisa."

What's a " Lymph ? " says Dyngwell.

*Happy Thought.*—To say, " My dear fellow, I suppose you've
never  read any poetry ? "   Dr. Caspar draws our attention to the
Station.   (If Dyngwell's going to be unpleasant on the journey, I
shall travel in another compartment with the Commander.)

Once more, adieu.   No, not adieu, rather *au plaisir !*   Tickets.
Luggage.

*Happy Thought.*—Booked through, and change nowhere ; so
whatever they say to us in German, French, or Dutch, we don't
stir.

Where is the Commander ?

Train in motion.   Farewell.   *Au revoir.*   Hands to hats.   The
last hand, the last hat (the Professor's tall crown), I can just see ;
and also sudden appearance of the Commander, too late.   He had
stopped behind to tell the Professor the Mongoose story (I hear

afterwards), and was obliged to leave in the middle. Aix, farewell!

*Happy Thought.*—To be prepared for everyone, beginning with Milburd in London coming up and saying, "Well; left all your *Aches* behind?" on my telling him that I've just come from *Aix.* But have already settled *him* in that letter: that is, if he got it.

*Happy Thought.*—Shall simply observe I've been staying at Aachen, which will lead to the learned explanation that Aachen is the same as *Aix.*

Telegraph to Fridoline from Paris. "Home, sweet Home! Wherever I wander, there's no place like Home!"—that is, of course, when the drains are not up, and the Inspector of Nuisances is not bothering about the grounds. *Viâ* Paris to England.

## CHAPTER XXXI.

RETURN — POETIC—REALISATION — ALTERATIONS — MR. FRESHLIE —
WORKS—EXPLANATIONS—WINKS—LOGIC.

RETURN home. Imagine what it will be. Wife, child in arms, retainers, dogs, all ready to meet me. Picture —Return of the Wanderer.

*Reality.* — Nobody here. Wonder what's the matter.

*Happy Thought.* — Ring bell. No rushing in and saying, "Behold me!" On the contrary, am kept waiting at the gate, and have to ring twice. Gardener appears suspiciously. Then a dog barking. Then I am recognised; but only as if I'd just been round the corner for five minutes, and had come back again. "Mistress is up in town; will be down in the evening —to dinner, p'raps; if not, to-morrow." See the cook.

"There ain't no dinner ordered, Sir." Oh, hang it—here is a welcome to the Weary Traveller! Instant arrangements made for dinner. Look over the house.

*Happy Thought.*—Scotland stands where it did.—*Shakspeare.*

Look over the garden: go all round it. Well, how about the drains? "Oh, the Inspector of Nuisances friend's men have been working here, Sir," says Gardener, with an air of doubt as to the result. "Well?" I inquire. "Well, Sir," he replies, "I don't see as they've done much good—if you just come round here." I come round, and am nearly knocked over by an infernal odour which the Inspector of Nuisances had inspected before I left, and turned over to his friend to obviate with pipes and bell-traps, and gutters, and ditches, and sinks, and a disestablishment of pig-styes.

*Happy Thought.*—What rhymes to "sinks?"

*Happy (but angry) Thought.* — Send for Mr. Freshlie, *i.e.,* Inspector's friend; builder, &c.: "&c." means everything. There's nothing that Mr. Freshlie, I find on inquiry, does not profess to do. When once I get him on to my estate (three acres and a shrubbery of uncertain tenure) I find from his account that something wants doing in every direction, and that it all comes in his line of business. Locks, blinds, chimneys, carpentry, drains, wire-work, gravel paths, stones, cement, pond cleaning, hedging, ditching, tanks, pumps, in fact, he makes no difficulty about anything at all.

He is a lively, burly, impressive, honest-mannered man, who floors me with technicalities in the presence of my gardener (who pretends he understands all about it as well as Mr. Freshlie, and follows him silently, addressing him with an occasional nod of corroboration) and, when he answers, in person, my message in the morning, is for taking up the paths and opening the brick-work, and, knocking *this* down, and putting *that* up in another place by way of a preliminary inquiry into the state of the case.

*Happy Thought.*—To say, "But your new drains which you *were* to have put in before I left for Aachen"—(Aachen has no effect upon him whatever)—"when I was so ill"—(he is perfectly undisturbed)—"they" (the drains) "were to have obviated"—("obviated" doesn't take him aback one bit)—"the nuisance. Weren't they?" I put this to him in a question which he *must* answer honestly in the affirmative.

He is ready with his reply. "Just so, Sir,"—(Gardener puts his arms akimbo, and watches the case for the defence)—"only you'll see at once, Sir, where the mischief is." He appeals to my keen perception in drainage questions. But I won't be flattered, and am not to be put off the scent, &c.

*Happy Thought.*—Wish I *could* be put off the scent

# COLLECTED UNIFORM ILLUSTRATED

EDITION OF

# F. C. BURNAND'S

# WRITINGS.

*VOLUMES NOW READY:*

# VERY MUCH ABROAD.

# RATHER AT SEA.

# QUITE AT HOME.

# HAPPY THOUGHTS.

"Mr. Burnand's Writings are well worth collecting. He has produced a very large body of comic writing of a high order of merit, and the amount of it that is first-rate is considerable. There is a perpetual gaiety and airiness about his work which makes it always pleasant to dip into, and few humorists have the power of making their readers laugh so agreeably, so innocently, so often, and so much."--*Athenaeum.*

Price 5s. each, Large Crown 8vo, gilt top.

BRADBURY, AGNEW, & CO. Ld., 8, 9, 10, BOUVERIE STREET, E.C.